Limerick City and County Library

3 0027 **00852491** 7

Chasing Rainbows

D1386442

WITHDRAWN FROM STOCK

WITHDRAWN FROM STOCK

Chasing Rainbows

NUALA WOULFE

POOLBEG

This novel is entirely a work of fiction. The names,
characters and incidents portrayed in it are the work of the
author's imagination. Any resemblance to actual persons,
living or dead, events or localities is entirely coincidental.

Published 2009
by Poolbeg Press Ltd
123 Grange Hill, Baldoyle
Dublin 13, Ireland
E-mail: poolbeg@poolbeg.com
www.poolbeg.com

© Nuala Woulfe 2009

Copyright for typesetting, layout, design
© Poolbeg Press Ltd

The moral right of the author has been asserted.

1 3 5 7 9 10 8 6 4 2

A catalogue record for this book is available from the British Library.

ISBN 978 1 84223 414-3

All rights reserved. No part of this publication may be reproduced or
transmitted in any form or by any means, electronic or mechanical, including
photography, recording, or any information storage or retrieval system, without
permission in writing from the publisher. The book is sold subject to the
condition that it shall not, by way of trade or otherwise, be lent, resold or
otherwise circulated without the publisher's prior consent in any form of
binding or cover other than that in which it is published and without a similar
condition, including this condition, being imposed on the subsequent
purchaser.

LIMERICK CITY AND COUNTY LIBRARY

00252491

Typeset by Poolbeg Press in Sabon 11/15
Printed by Litografia Rosés, S.A, Spain

www.poolbeg.com

About the author

Nuala Woulfe is a thirty-something mum of three, who lives in County Tipperary with her husband and children. Nuala always saw herself as something of a social anthropologist and was naturally "interested in people", spending her twenties working as a journalist and researcher and studying "people" subjects in university, such as psychology, sociology and politics. Unfortunately, in Nuala's current world of small people none of this education is of much use – especially in the area of getting children to sleep through the night. When not writing, salsa dancing, swimming or suffering from sleep deprivation, Nuala tends to fantasise about her future amazing life. Current fantasises include looking like Catherine Zeta Jones, doing the tango in Buenos Aires (while looking like Catherine Zeta Jones), and chaining Jamie Oliver to the kitchen sink for a week (for culinary purposes only).

Acknowledgements

To all at Poolbeg, thank you – especially Paula for being so normal and nice and so open to all my suggestions, and Niamh for always being friendly and helpful. Many thanks to Gaye, for your keen eyes and quirky sense of humour. Editing was a bit like going to the dentist, but you held my hand and made all the filling, polishing and extracting almost pleasurable. I look forward to working with you again. To all the wonderful women of Tipperary, thank you for your good humour, support and encouragement in writing this book. Thank you to everybody else who helped out with *Chasing Rainbows* – you know who you are and I know where you live.

For my family

1

It was not the first Monday morning that Ali Hughes had given some thought to deliberately falling down the metal stairs that led to her place of work. Not that she was thinking of throwing herself from the top – Jesus, that would be mad altogether – but perhaps she could manage a little skid as she approached the last few steps, a skilful wobble, and then it might be a sprained ankle, a bad back and some decent compensation from the dull little company that she worked for.

It could all be made to seem quite plausible really. After all, it was September in Dublin and the city-centre trees were shedding their foliage, leaving a greasy sludge of rot behind to tempt the accident-prone. Her brain went into an excited state of overdrive as she thought about the possibilities. Crikey, she might even meet a nice doctor in casualty and be married before she turned the dreaded thirty!

Of course she didn't need sympathy to get a date; she wasn't that desperate. Ali was pretty enough, with shoulder-length dark-brown hair flecked with the odd strand of auburn, and with slate-blue eyes that many a gobshite had described as 'expressive'. No, it was just that bringing home a doctor would be the ultimate coup in making her mother tongue-tied for a week, particularly if he was some tall chap who'd significantly overshadow Ali's five-foot-five-inch frame.

The last step was approaching rapidly. It was now or never: to wobble or not to wobble? But even deliberately staging an accident on those steel steps could only be painful. Besides, she doubted whether the small firm she worked for actually had the money to pay her any decent compensation – they would say they didn't, that's for sure. The scabby bastards might even contest the case, she thought as she reached the basement of the Georgian building and the office.

Looming in front of her was the big heavy door that she desperately tried to forget about all weekend, every weekend, the door that once shut would have her in its grasp for another eight hours – eight valuable and wasted hours of her life. And she was late again, and even though the Irish transport system was conveniently unpredictable her excuses were beginning to shift from the somewhat ridiculous to the downright outrageous.

This time she reckoned she would have to own up to having overslept, not that that was the truth either: she had lain awake in bed for half an hour listening to the news programme *Morning Ireland*, letting her head take flight with one dream after another.

As she went to place her key in the lock, she noticed that the door was slightly ajar and that Maggie was inside the main office, rooting around in a pile of papers on her desk.

Maggie O'Shea looked up and smiled in her bemused manner at her old college acquaintance and Ali was struck for the thousandth time by the natural beauty of her friend who even without make-up could look stunning with her exotic "Black Irish" looks. Maggie's curly black hair framed her heart-shaped face and her eyes were big and dark with long dark lashes stroking her tanned cheeks. Even now at the end of summer Maggie was a dusky brown while Ali struggled to hold on to her freckly tan.

"Is he in?" Ali asked, hoping that Simon (or "Little Bastard" as she called him) had got caught in a traffic jam or that he had an early meeting with a client and hadn't yet graced the staff with his divine presence.

"He's been and gone, girl. Little Bastard noticed you were running late but he had to leave to meet some woman who runs a food business. Was so excited about it he didn't even have time for his Power Juice Special this morning!"

"Maybe I need to get power-juiced. My motivation is up me arse these days, Mags, and Little Bastard is chalking up every little thing he can against me so he can tell it all to the Big Boss the first chance he gets."

Maggie put down the book she was holding and lifted a paper cup to her lips, inhaling the exotic aroma of morning coffee. "I think you're exaggerating just a bit. Sure, what do you care? The *Real Boss* couldn't care less what you're doing, He's seldom here anyway."

It was true that the owner and chief executive of O'Grady Marketing was a man as elusive as Charlie from *Charlie's Angels*. Joe O'Grady, aka Charlie, was one of those invisible business magnates who was so busy making easy money that his marketing company was practically a hobby. Mostly Joe left the day-to-day running of the place to his second-in-command, his captain, his little general in the making, Simon Webb.

"I think I need a fix of coffee," said Ali. "Where's Luce?" she added, noticing that the receptionist's desk was unoccupied.

"Upstairs: photocopying something for a mail-shot."

"And Lucky Pam's still on holiday getting her arse roasted in the sun," quipped Ali as she exited the basement door before she was hardly five minutes inside it.

* * *

It was a lovely day, one of those September mornings that has some heat of sunshine in it and the throngs of people hurrying through the streets of Dublin still had their summer clothes on, with maybe just a light jacket or a cardigan slung over their shoulders.

Watching them scurrying around like ants, Ali wondered what their lives were like and if they were happy with their lot.

In the shop around the corner Ali continued her musings as she waited for her coffee, inventing careers for the toned young guy in front of her, the self-assured young girls in tight skirts and heels and the thirty-five-plus brigade of women who looked tired around the eyes and jaw-lines despite the bit of slap on their faces.

The queue was moving slowly. It seemed to Ali that the entire city was gathered in the one coffee shop, all needing their Monday morning fix of caffeine to inspire some motivation into their hunched shoulders and shuffling feet. Motivation: it was getting harder and harder to drag herself out of bed these days and into the drippy shower of her one-bedroom apartment on Dublin's south-east coast. It didn't even matter what day of the working week it was. Ali found she was now leaving just enough time to shower, dress and brush her teeth before getting the train into the city. Breakfast had become a luxury that she was prepared to take on the hoof.

The woman at the counter took her order for a latte and Ali heard the machine swish into life as the milky froth was added to the large paper cup. The price was ferocious. Sometimes it was enough to make Ali think of unscrewing the cap of the coffee jar in the office kitchen but deep down she knew she'd just continue with the daily extortion. It was ludicrous, she knew it, but buying coffee she could barely afford sort of made her feel dangerous as if she was living on the edge and, considering the state of her bank balance, maybe she was.

Holding a paper napkin around her steaming coffee, Ali popped into the shop next door and bought a packet of luxury cookies for the office, trying to ignore the horrifically expensive price label and the grams of fat per bickie.

Back at the office, with the coffee already firing up her veins, she plonked the goodies a little too firmly on the communal desk that served as the general junk station and watched as they worked their usual magic.

"Oh, you're a pet!" squealed Lucy as her eyes landed on the

unopened packet. "These are *so* yummy! Do you mind if I have two with a cuppa?"

Ali smiled. Lucy, the receptionist, was a tonic. She was twenty-two with a wasp-like waist, huge boobs and slim but curvy hips and her crowning glory was undoubtedly her curly waist-length honey-blonde hair. Young and arrogant enough not to give a damn about anything, Lucy would flash a look of contempt at Simon which just dared him to fire her, every time he issued her with some petty administrative demand. When you're young jobs are just ten a penny as long as you can party and have fun. Ali sighed; she wasn't so old herself. These days your late twenties was practically babyhood, or so she'd been told. Plonking herself at her desk, she listened as her computer cranked into life. Poor fecker sounded like it too could do with a cup of coffee just to get it going.

The thump of feet was heard on the steps outside and they all saw him as his highly polished shoes then trouser legs appeared silhouetted in the giant basement Georgian window that let in the only natural light to the office. It was Simon. Suddenly everyone shut up and pretended they were busy. He was struggling with a large box which seemed to be sapping the strength out of his five-foot-six featherweight frame, but nobody was rushing to help him down the steps.

"Well, girls, start of the week again, what?" he said as he finally made it through the door, panting with the exertion.

He was greeted by a collective low mumbling, which could have been an acknowledgement or a form of mass indigestion.

"Well, Lucy, how's the head this Monday? On the pull again this weekend, were we? Like the top, is it new?"

Fluffing his white-blond hair with his hand in an attempt to look sexy, Simon fixed his cold, dark eyes on the lovely Lucy. For some strange reason Simon thought he was God's gift to women. Well into his thirties, Little Bastard still lived at home with a maiden aunt. "We're like John Lennon and Aunt Mimi," he would joke. "But John Lennon was good-looking," Ali would say when they'd gossip and roll their eyes in the adjoining employee kitchen – or even better – the loos. "And talented," Lucy would add.

So as usual Lucy shot Simon one of her most contemptuous looks but Little Bastard either didn't notice or he really did have skin as thick as rhinoceros hide.

"Well, if anyone is under the weather from a bit of weekend overindulgence with the demon drink, I have the *perfect* cure right here. Rashers, sausages and pudding from the Perfect Pig company whose account I have just *personally* landed! Should save you girls a few pence during the week – you can all take some home with you when I work out how many we should each get."

He looked like he was waiting for a round of applause to acknowledge his double whammy, landing an account with a meat company and getting a few rashers thrown in by way of a bonus. He had probably asked for them and all, such was the way with Simon. The office remained resolutely silent. For a split second he looked annoyed and then he recovered himself.

"Put the kettle on and make us a cup of tea, will you, Maggie, and bring us in one or two of these as well." He gestured at Ali's biscuits which had cost her an arm and a leg.

He would never buy anything more expensive than Marietta, thought Ali as she marvelled yet again at the arrogance of the little fecker, ordering his staff around like minions.

"Right, will I put everyone's name in the pot so?" asked Maggie to a chorus of assents and she disappeared into the nearby kitchen.

Simon was nearly out of the main office when he uttered a very deliberate aside. "Oh, by the way, Ali, I'd like to see you in my office for a chat and bring in that proposal you are working on for Sunshine Travel, the one you gave me a copy of on Friday. You can bring the tea with you."

How generous, maybe he would even let her bring in some of her own biscuits too. It took a few minutes to root out the file, a few minutes more than necessary, and then she followed him in reluctantly, trying desperately to disguise any signs of unease. *For God's sake, you're twenty-eight – you're not some school kid about to get a talking-to from the headmaster!*

Sitting down at the breakfast table which he'd recently installed in his spacious office for "friendly" brainstorming sessions with staff, she tried to hide as much of herself as possible behind her opened work file, knowing that no matter where she sat or how she tried to screen herself he would have a bull's-eye view of her famous bazookas. Annoyed, she crossed her arms in front of her chest as extra armour and waited for him to begin.

"As you know, Joe is mad to land this account and Sunshine Travel is desperate to capitalise on the youth market. Now, about this proposal, Ali, I've got some suggestions as to how you could *radically* improve it."

Simon leaned his forearms on the small table and pushed his upper body closer to Ali in an effort to show her the pieces of typed paper he had corrected.

"For example, see here where you say O'Grady would be assessing the average *income* of student youth – I would prefer if you would use the phrase '*spending power*' instead. Now down here where you recommend targeting the youth sector through beer-mat advertising in pubs, I've deleted *pubs* and put in *bars*."

Amazed, Ali watched as he continued to circle and delete and add words to her copy in luminous green marker until page after page was a mass of huge, untidy squiggles.

After an extensive monologue Simon smiled his fish-like smile and handed her back the sad piece of work, adding condescendingly that she could resubmit it for another once-over before the final deadline.

"Simon, while I appreciate your comments," – Ali didn't – "do you not think a lot of these suggested changes are superficial?"

Leaning back in his chair, Simon placed a hand to his chin as if he was thinking over what she was saying, while in reality she knew he was not. He clicked his ball-point-pen repeatedly in irritation and Ali felt her chest tighten as she closed her folder on the shameful mess of green circles and slashes.

"Don't forget the deadline is Friday." He smiled coldly, then turned his attention to his diary in a gesture which signalled that the meeting was now definitely over.

Fuming, Ali got up and left.

Something had to change. She knew that as she headed out the door that evening and fought her way onto one of the commuter trains.

* * *

Back home, her answering machine was flashing red and, switching it on, she heard her best friend Karen cackle out their familiar greeting, "Seen any good willies lately?"

Ali sighed. Good willies had been in short supply ever since she had given that annoying policeman, Detective Garda Dave O'Connor, the bullet. He would have got her out of this black mood, he would have wrestled with her until she screamed, let her bang a few cushions and pretend it was Simon's head, kissed her and told her to cheer up. Struggling hard, she tried to remember why exactly they had broken up. For the life of her she couldn't remember.

2

At quarter to five in the afternoon Lucy packed her trendy designer bag, signalling the end of yet another interminable day at O'Grady's. Madame wasn't meant to knock off early but she had to make her dance class on time and the thing about Lucy was that she always had her priorities straight in her own mind. The office minx was only a week in the job when she sussed that the management could not survive without her and, since they could not afford to pay her what she obviously was worth, she had to extract payment by other means. Yes, Lucy danced but she made sure she only danced to the beat of her own drum.

"Ladies, could you all please e-mail today's work of fiction – otherwise known as your timesheets – to me?" she roared. "For customer billing purposes, time spent picking noses, farting, scratching arses and sighing all to be labelled under research."

Ali looked at her output for the morning and afternoon and was embarrassed at how little she had achieved.

Meanwhile Maggie was pushing back her chair and heading for the toilets where she would change into her tracksuit and trainers, ready to hit the corner gym. It seemed a bit unfair to sabotage her plans – Ali knew how much her colleague wanted to drop a dress size by Christmas – but she needed her advice and it just wouldn't wait.

"Fancy a pint, Mags?"

"It's only *Tuesday* for Christ's sake!"

"Oh, you're getting old, Mags, girl! I remember a time when you didn't care *what* time of day it was, never mind what *day* it was. If someone mentioned pints you'd be there. Besides, I have a problem that needs a bit of cute-country-girl input."

"I have *no* idea what you mean by that remark!" Maggie said laughing, but she did.

In reality Ali knew Maggie inside out just as Maggie had figured Ali out from almost their first acquaintance. Savvy Maggie was always the one with sense in their group, the one who could scull pints, give the impression of being drunk but wake up bright-eyed and able to go to lectures the next day. Maggie could do her wild woman impression, going off backpacking with the rest of them, but Maggie would be the one who would have the job to come home to and a job which would enhance her career prospects to boot.

"Now look it, Ali, cute country girl or no, I have to go to the gym and work off this lard on my backside and belly or I will be fit only for a tent by Christmas and not anything that resembles a sexy black frock."

"Ah, come on, Maggie baby, a couple of nice creamy pints and you won't be feeling fat at all, only voluptuous and sexy. Do you think men really want to go to bed with a bag of bones anyway? They're all little boys at heart and want some nice big boobs and bellies to bury their noses in!"

"For feck sake, if you ruin my good intentions today you could set me off course for the entire week!"

"Oh come on, just two pints! I'm paying. I'll even go to that dingy old man's pub you like so much, the one that smells of pee and disinfectant all year round." Ali put on her most pathetic pleading voice and sad eyes. "Please come, I need you, please!"

"You're the devil himself, do you know that?"

"Please!"

"Oh stop it – you're worse than a child! I'll go, okay, but it's just for two, right? And you better really need my help or I'll wring that neck of yours for having added a few more fat cells to my midriff!"

"God, I love it when you're angry, Maggie. An angry *and* voluptuous woman! You'll have half the pub chasing your skirt before we're hardly in the door."

"Fat chance that being any use to me if it's an old man's pub we're going to! Lead me into temptation then, girl. Come on, get your coat and bag and let's get out of here."

The snug little pub around the corner didn't really smell that horrible – it was quite charming really with worn table-tops and chairs, and yellowed newspaper cuttings framed on the walls. It was a genuine old pub too and not one of those huge imitation "auld world pubs" that had sprung up all over the city in recent years. The virgin pints of Guinness were nearly too gorgeous to disturb.

Maggie relaxed back into the tattered leather bench. Putting her hands to her face, she began rubbing the tension out of her eye-sockets and brows.

"Well, girl, where's the fire? What's so urgent that you have to drag me from my precious gym?"

Ali pulled a mauled newspaper cutting from her bag and placed it on the table under Maggie's nose. The print nearly went translucent as the paper soaked up a bit of spilt stout and Maggie raised an eyebrow and laughed when she read it.

"Oh Christ, not another course, Ali!"

"Well, thanks for the encouragement, and no, this is not just *another* course. This will be a *special* course, a life-changing course. And there are still places available – didn't I just happen to see the ad in the Sunday newspaper that I only got round to reading yesterday? Do you know what this is, Mags?"

"Madness!"

"Destiny."

"Same old Ali – always chasing rainbows. When will you realise, girl, that life isn't meant to be exciting *all the time*?"

"But you've got to dream, Maggie – you've got to have dreams!"

"Okay, let me get this straight. You've thought about becoming a psychologist, a teacher, a meteorologist, an actress –"

"Don't forget sculptress."

"A sculptress – but now you *definitely* want to be a journalist."

"Definitely, and as you know I'm definitely so over my present prison sentence of writing, researching and marketing everything from dog food to breath mints. Got itchy feet, Mags, I want to move on."

"And you're doing this course to set you up. Great. So, Ali, would you mind telling me why exactly I'm here and not drowning in sweat in the gym?"

"Strategy, sweetie. How do I make it happen when I'm broke and how do I dupe management into giving me the time off for two evenings a week when our contracts say we *must* be available for work outside office hours for *unpaid* overtime?"

Maggie made a face. The unpaid overtime was a sore point with all the staff of O'Grady's.

"Well, have you got any solutions for me?" asked Ali.

Maggie's brow furrowed as she went into her trance-like state where she tapped into her old-crone consciousness, became the Big Brained Buddha, the human pinball machine which was going to deliver Ali all the answers to her problems.

"Well?"

"Hold on, hold on – I'm working on it."

"Now, don't forget, if I sign up for this course I need to be certain that I can get the time off, but then I can't exactly admit I'm doing a course in journalism in case they rightly suss that I'm planning to scarper."

Savvy Maggie was taking it all in. Her finger and thumb stroked her upper lip as she pondered Ali's dilemma. She took another mouthful of porter and placed the glass down.

"Maggie, come on, tell me how I'm gonna swing this thing in the next week!"

"Christ, you're cutting it a bit fine, but then you were always a fly-by-the-seat-of-your-pants kind of nutter. All right, I'll think of something, I promise."

"You'd better, Maggie, I'm relying on you."

"I won't let you down but somehow, Ali, I think whatever we come up with you might have to tell a few white lies, maybe even do a bit of grovelling, eat a bit of humble pie, that sort of thing – and it might involve grovelling in front of Simon too."

"Oh Jaysus, Maggie – if I had to do that I'd be prostituting myself!"

Maggie reached for Ali's hand, patted it a few times and smiled her wry country-girl smile. "There are times, Ali girl, when we all have to wear a short skirt and show off our ankles."

* * *

All week Ali was in a fluster as she mused over Maggie's words of advice about eating humble pie and learning how to grovel a bit more if she wanted to get on in life. True, sucking up to Simon could pay dividends in the long run but the thought of being even slightly sweet to the little reptile set her teeth on edge.

In any event she hadn't had time to think about her future career plans. The travel agency rewrite had taken longer than she had expected with several late nights and muscle fatigue a nasty reality. Tiredness was sapping her enthusiasm for any new career, but so too were the August sales which had totally maxed out her credit card. Ali sighed. "Excess fat" had already been trimmed when she got rid of her beloved bashed-up car and then her private health insurance.

Late on Thursday evening she was finally able to slip her revised proposal on Sunshine Travel into Simon's in-tray and even though he could still insist she make changes he was unlikely to do so since the submission deadline was the next day. He had made his power felt, she reasoned, and was unlikely to muck things up at the last minute. But the bastard did.

Sensing Ali's frustration at being told to make more changes to her proposal on the Friday, both Maggie and Lucy hardly dared say two words to her all day.

"Jaysus, you look like shite," commented Lucy at last as she prepared to leave the office by backing up the day's work on computer.

A ferocious glare from Ali was enough to quieten her normally brazen colleague who quickly slipped out the door and left for her dance class.

"Do you want me to wait with you for the courier?" asked Maggie in her softest voice as she hovered around the door. "We could go for a quick drink afterwards."

Ali shook her head and smiled a half smile at her friend. "No thanks, Mags. The spirit is willing and all that but to be honest if I went for one I'd probably only fall asleep."

"Well, take care of yourself this weekend, Ali. You could do with some pampering, girl."

* * *

The courier disappeared out of sight, zooming into the city with the precious travel proposal, and Ali felt she could breathe again. The train home was nearly empty; no doubt every city-centre worker had decided to go for at least one drink to celebrate the end of the week.

Too knackered to cook for herself, Ali ordered a gorgeous and fat-saturated takeaway from her local Indian and gorged herself on naan bread, onion bhajis and chicken tikka masala. Relaxing in a bubble bath with scented candles, she closed her eyes and felt the tension ease from her limbs but still she could feel the irritation growing in her brain. Why was her life so bland? She'd spent three years in university getting a degree in Arts. It had to be Arts really – Arts was full of people like her who hadn't a clue what way their lives were going to go but who were nevertheless certain that they would one day be successful and happy. After a few short months of backpacking in America, there was the Master's and then a year

14

travelling Australia doing various odd jobs, followed by the year doing substitute teacher work at various schools around the county, followed by her current stint which was turning into a stretch at O'Grady's. Life was once full of fizz but now everything was fizzling out.

Curled up on the couch in her jammies and her duvet, Ali flicked through the channels on her TV set until her eyes dazzled. As she sipped some neat Cointreau, she realised just how cold it was in her apartment but she was too tired to light a real fire and she was relying on her pathetic electric heater to keep her warm. A small smile curled round her lips when she thought of what Lucy would think of her freezing cold pad, totally lacking in bling or any cool appliances. Ali didn't care. When you turned the corner of her gaff you saw the sea and Ali would sacrifice bling any day of the week for a view of the sea.

Gradually the fumes from her drink made her feel warmish, light-headed and strangely optimistic. Maybe if she had a decent career together she could afford a better apartment, maybe she might even be able to buy her own place. It really was time to move on with her life and grow up. Even her apartment, although ridiculously cheap for the area, was stuck in a 1970's student time-warp. African batiks and ornaments brightened up the magnolia-painted walls and a huge red striped throw brought a bit of glam to the worn-out brown sofa but she knew she couldn't stay here forever.

Turning the light down low Ali let the mute TV illuminate the room as she picked up the phone and dialled her parents' house.

He was alone. She could tell that nearly immediately as her mother's shrill inquiry of "Who is it?" was absent from the background noise.

"Hello, Dad, what you doing? Mum away?"

"Oh, you know your mother, playing bridge with the girls. I'm just here watching a documentary – the boring life of an old fogey – didn't think *you'd* be home though, sweetheart, on a Friday night."

"Hard week at work, Dad, too tired to do much. To be honest I was just ringing to ask if I could come to dinner on Sunday."

"Alison, you *know* no daughter of mine has to *ask* if she can come to dinner. It's an open house. I'd *love* to see you, darling."

"Thanks, Dad."

Feelings of guilt consumed her as she switched off the television and scrambled into her cold bed. Ali Hughes was twenty-eight but she wasn't yet an adult. It was embarrassing to even think about it, but she was going to have to tap her dad for a "long loan" to finance yet another one of her life-changing career plans. When the cash was tight and the credit card melting, a girl could always count on her daddy to have a heart – she hoped.

3

On Saturday afternoon, when Ali had finally pulled out of the snooze of the living dead, she noticed that the flashing light was on again on her answering machine and the familiar voice was asking more mischievously than ever, "Seen any good willies? Will ya *ever* give me a call!"

With a groan Ali pulled the duvet over her head and tried to ignore the day but she was restless at the same time and itching for some trouble. An hour later the phone screamed and she knew who it was before she even answered.

"Me again, meet me tonight, nine o'clock!" Karen ordered.

"Ah, I don't know. I'm really knackered, Karen, and I've had a *really* shit week."

"You're turning me *down*? I hardly ever get off at the weekend and you're turning me *down*?"

"It's not that I'm turning you down, it's just with you there's no such thing as a quiet night and I'm meant to be at my parents' tomorrow for a *very* important life-changing dinner."

"Me arse important, Ali. I'm not having any of it. Meet me at nine and look tarty."

* * *

Tall and willowy, Nurse Karen Maguire was well into propping up the bar when Ali walked through the door. A childhood friend of Ali's, Karen with her black witchlike hair had always had the personality of a cat on a hot plate. Even as a child she'd been restless, her mad jittery coal-black eyes seeking out fun and now, an alleged adult, she got to inflict her crazy personality on the unfortunate public in casualty at one of the city's busiest hospitals.

Now out of her hospital uniform and dressed in a short tight red skirt, spiky heels and a killer top, Karen's painted face was breaking into smiles as she said something, no doubt filthy, to two guys who were nudging past her to get in an order. On a night out Karen was never alone: like most nurses she travelled in packs and tonight her companions were on the surface a busty blonde and a fair-haired angel. Yes, on the surface butter wouldn't melt but Ali *knew* that, underneath, this lot were volatile stuff. No, as always when it came to Karen, it wasn't likely to be a quiet night, Ali thought as she crossed the room to meet her.

"Howya, Karen, see you've gone for the understated look again tonight," quipped Ali as she took in the divine appearance of her slappered-up friend.

"Feck off, Ali, you're just jealous because *I'm* the daughter your mother always wanted. I'm sure she might even have said so once." Karen flicked her shoulder-length hair in a contemptuous manner and eyed up a fit guy across the room.

"Yes, I know, and if I saw as much death and devastation as *you* do every day *I'd* be a die-hard slapper too who'd be living in the fast lane."

"That's it completely, Ali Hughes. I'm having my fun before I die or at least before I have to use a commode. Speaking of fun, any news in the willie department?"

"You daft bitch, you know the answer to that one. What about yourself?"

"Do you mean in my professional capacity as a nurse or are you delving into my private life again?" asked Karen with an arch of the eyebrow.

Ali laughed. The sexual innuendo was a running joke since adolescence. "I meant, have you had to cut the underpants off any young hunks in casualty recently?"

"Oh no, we were a bit low on motorcycle crashes the last few days. Besides, you should know that in my professional capacity I don't actually *notice* willies, Ali." Karen was using her snootiest nurse voice. "They're just another part of the body when I'm at work. At play now, that's another matter. See that short, flabby fella over there with the big feet, hands and nose? Although he mightn't look it, I'd be willing to bet any money that *he* has a big one. That's what *my* years of research would indicate!" And she laughed as she poured some more Bacardi Breezer down her throat.

It didn't take long for Ali, the three nurses, some latecomers (consisting of two radiographers and a phlebotomist) to become the rowdiest revellers in the pub. By eleven o'clock the gang had practically commandeered a party of Scots who were over in Dublin for a mate's stag and dressed to thrill in their kilts and knee-high socks.

"What are you then?" asked Ali as she gazed at the tartan colours of a fair-haired youth.

"A McDonald!" he shouted back proudly.

"Prove it. Show us your quarter pounder!" goaded Karen, at which the young Scot lifted his kilt and obliged the girls with a bird's-eye view of a full frontal.

Thrilled at being flashed, Karen's two blonde friends nearly fell off their bar stools with laughter and Ali thought she'd have to be resuscitated from the delicious shock.

"Christ, now that *is* a big one!" gasped Karen as she gulped back the rest of her drink in one go.

It was shaping up to be one of those nights, which was then accelerated by just one more round of tequila shots.

* * *

The entire left side of Ali's body ached when she awoke on Sunday morning and her head was spinning. Moving her head just a fraction, she groaned and felt suddenly sick. The blankets covering her were not enough to block out the early-morning cold and the rays of sunshine peeping through the room hurt her eyes. No doubt about it, it was Karen's house and Karen's uncomfortable brown couch with the banjaxed springs that she was lying on.

Looking down, Ali saw herself dressed in an unfamiliar faded black *Metallica* T-shirt that barely covered her arse and, pulling back the crumpled blankets, she found the reason why her knees were stinging – they were skinned. Feeling dirty all over right down to her gums, she hauled her battered body off the couch and dragged it up the stairs, hoping that Karen's famously drippy shower and cold bathroom would stir some life into her alcohol-polluted veins.

The bathroom door was barely within her sights when she felt her stomach spasm and she knew she had only seconds to find the toilet bowl. The old familiar tears she felt every time she became physically ill began to pool behind her eyes and she longed for her father's familiar hand on her childhood forehead, telling her that everything would soon be all right. Torrents of foul liquid gushed out until there was just empty retching and Ali realised the contents of her stomach were ejected and there was nothing left but bile and a horrible taste in her mouth.

Her heart prayed to die there on the bathroom floor but her hands and knees attempted to crawl away to find somewhere a bit softer to expire. It was while looking down that she noticed a pair of pink fluffy slippers appearing in the bedroom doorway and as she raised her head slowly and painfully upwards she became aware of Karen standing there, belting her silky red dressing-gown.

"Well, at least you're alive," Karen said in a tone somewhere between relief and motherly disapproval.

Ali made a face of pain and held her hands to her temples in an attempt to alert her friend to the fact that she wasn't in the mood for any talk, particularly a lecture, but Karen either didn't see or else couldn't resist a mock rant.

"Do you have *any* idea of what happened last night?" she asked with a smirk on her face. "Christ, you look like shite. I suppose I had better see if I can find any drugs to revive you."

Lying on the bed, getting the spins, Ali searched her brain for any remembrance of the night before.

"Do you remember the pub?" asked Karen.

"Bits."

"You were so drunk you told every man who would listen that you were a private investigator and demanded to know any juicy secrets they might have. You can *imagine* the amount of dirty talk *that* started off."

"Wasn't it sort of a dirty night anyhow?" asked Ali, somewhat confused.

"I suppose it was," grinned Karen as she handed her friend two Paracetamol and some Dioralyte from her supplies, which she kept in a massive carpetbag under her bed.

"Jaysus, I reckon one of these days, Karen, you'll be arrested by the drugs squad," said Ali as she knocked back the Paracetamol with some water her friend had put by her bedside.

"Oh, don't mention the police to *me* – it was *you* who was nearly arrested last night."

In embarrassing detail Karen filled her friend in on the previous night, when she had fallen in love with a short-legged, hairy-backed gorilla from Scotland, otherwise known as the groom, and was on the way home with him before being rescued by her friends, and how at the close of the evening she had even managed to throw up in a bucket of sawdust.

"If that wasn't bad enough, there wasn't a bloody taxi left in town and we'd hardly walked out from the city centre when you decided you needed to pee and were going to go right there in the street."

"You're making this up, Karen!"

"I am not. If you don't believe me you can ring the guards – they stopped the squad car to talk to you. Do you realise peeing in the street is an *offence*, you daft cow? If it wasn't for the fact that your

21

ex, Dave, was in the car at the time you could have been waking up in the cop shop this morning – his words, not mine."

Ali could feel herself breaking into a sickly sweat as Karen insisted on prattling on about her obnoxious behaviour, how Ali had sat in the unmarked car and asked Dave did he want to see her g-string and hold-ups, which were around her ankles at the time and which had two holes in the knees where she had fallen.

"Thank *God* he was an old flame. He threw you in the back of the car and gave us a lift home, although he told me if anyone official stopped us I was to pretend we were being lifted for soliciting. Then we dragged you through the door and he helped me undress you and stick you on the couch."

"Did you *have* to let him undress me?" shrieked Ali, thinking how pleasurable Dave would have found the whole humiliating experience.

"Well, it was either him or the other fella in the car. I needed someone to help me. Do you know how heavy a comatose drunk is? Anyhow what do you care, it's not as if he's never seen you starkers before and if you have to be undressed down to your knickers and bra it might as well be by a dark-haired, dark-eyed, well-built young buck like Garda Dave O'Connor."

Karen lit a fag, inhaled and exhaled deeply and Ali felt she was turning ten shades of green as the clouds of tobacco swirled around her head.

"I take it you wouldn't like some grilled sausages and rashers – tea?" said Karen. But then, realising that Ali wanted to crawl into bed and die, the "nursey" element of Karen just about came to the surface. "Listen, you can stay in my bed for the day if you want – I'm going into town. I'll see if I can hunt down some fizzy orange. Oh, did I tell you Dave's going to ring you when he gets off nights?"

Despite the pain, Ali suddenly sat bolt upright in the bed. "I hope you told him I've moved!"

"But that would be a lie. Can't lie to a guard, especially when he says he'll need to drop round your charge sheet."

The door slammed shut.

4

After several blood transfusions of fizzy orange, Ali began to come alive somewhere in the late afternoon. When she finally felt there was some blood flow to her legs she went and scrutinised her complexion in the bathroom mirror and had the age-old make-up debate with herself.

Skin devoid of slap would be frowned upon by her mother who would scold her for not making the most of herself. On the other hand, if she went for the *au naturel* look, her father might feel a bit sorry for her because she was looking so haggard and throw a few quid her way. In the end she decided not to wear any foundation or eye concealer and settled for a lick of mascara and a smear of lipstick. That way her mother could only half give out, but her underlying crappy complexion and shadowy eyes and consequently her miserable life would still be obvious for all to see and empathise with.

Her father was in the kitchen when she arrived at the four-bed semi-d in one of Dublin's respectable suburbs. Ali saw him before he spotted her and she was filled with affection for the earth-mother father she beheld. He was sticking a fat chicken in the oven, complete with rosemary potatoes and a side dish of Parmesan parsnips for roasting.

Liam had retired from his civil service job two years ago and, now in his sixties, had enthusiastically thrown himself into becoming a fully-fledged domestic goddess. In his two years of retirement he had sifted through the collection of his wife's unused cookery books, had learned how to make culinary masterpieces and had even devised his own secret mouth-watering recipes. When he wasn't cooking or baking he was glued to cookery programmes on the telly and had a self-confessed crush on that original British culinary sexpot, Delia Smith, although in recent years Nigella was also floating his boat more than a little.

Casually, Ali poured a glass of red wine from the bottle her father had opened and winced as she inhaled its fruity bouquet "Where's Mum?" she asked as she bravely tried a mouthful and felt the sting of alcohol hit her abused and wretched body. She already knew what the answer would be.

"Poor Mammy's in bed – the arthritis has been very bad the last few days," said her father as he began to stir together the dry ingredients for a chocolate pudding. "She hasn't even been well enough to go for her gym session and swim this morning."

Alison sucked her bottom lip in under her front teeth and said nothing. It had always been the same. Even when she was a child her mother seemed to survive until just about the weekend when her arthritis would suddenly flare up and then her dad would cook herself and her sister Ruth something edible – something very basic in those days, maybe chops with vegetables and potatoes.

Her father used to bath her and her sister when they were tots too and brush their hair and their shoes while her mother went to bed and slept away her terrible torments. Miraculously, however, she always seemed to recover enough to go shopping for clothes during the sales or to play a few rounds of golf on ladies' day with her pals. Ali's childhood memories of her mother were completely coloured by her mother's affliction; either she was feeling terrible and in bed with the arthritis or feeling much recovered and off enjoying herself.

"Oh, by the way, your sister is coming to lunch as well," said her father as he broke a few eggs and expertly whipped the yokes into a silky mixture to be added to the dry chocolate-pudding mix. "She's bringing Damien – Conor is going off with his daddy to an antiques fair in Kildare."

Brilliant, bloody brilliant – Mammy and Ruth, Ali thought. Two life coaches determined to get her life in order before she hit thirty. "That's nice," she said. "Haven't seen her in ages."

An upstairs toilet flushed and Ali heard flurried activity coming from the vicinity of her mother's bedroom. The resurrection had begun. It wouldn't be long now before Julie would be down in the kitchen, looking fabulous but in pain. When she was in form you'd definitely notice her presence in a room – it would be like a tornado had swept out of nowhere and was suddenly hovering right in your face.

"Alison, lovely to see you, darling!"

Ali's perfectly made-up mother kissed her dramatically on the cheek, flashing a bit of bosom and a pretty camisole in the process.

God, Ali thought, she really was getting better and better looking. Dyed, styled hair, painted nails, a waft of perfume, a well-cut trouser suit and expensive heels made her pass for much younger than her actual fifty-two years of age. Her mother looked like she could play the older but dangerous vamp in some TV miniseries.

"You're looking well, Mum. You really must be a vampire to be looking this good at your age. Either that or you've gone the plastic route and are keeping quiet about it," Ali said, more than a touch sarcastically.

"Now, darling, you know I'd never consider going under the knife, but a woman should always make the most of what she's got," said Julie as she playfully but deliberately scooped the hair back from her daughter's face and tut-tutted. "You know, Ali – a short-styled cut would be *much* more flattering."

"Mum, a short cut would make my face look fat. Besides, all the *young* women are wearing their hair like mine."

"Really, I don't know how women your age expect to *meet* men, let alone marry them, if they don't look after their appearance. Men need to be wooed!" The last bit was spoken softly into Ali's ear. Then she raised her voice to a screech. "A waft of perfume, a touch of lipstick, isn't that right, Liam?" When her husband didn't respond she turned back to Ali. "By the way, darling, that lipstick you're wearing is much too garish on its own."

Bristling with anger Ali turned to top up her wine-glass, thinking that now she was shot of her car she could afford to be a bit overindulgent with her alcohol consumption. Not that she was drinking for pleasure, more for medicinal reasons she thought as she tried to knock back some "hair of the dog" and immediately wanted to gag.

Thankfully a diversion from her mother's attentions was soon to arrive as her elder sister barged through the front door with her youngest in tow. Not surprisingly, Ruth was screaming some instruction or reprimand to her three-year-old. The poor inoffensive kid always looked like he was about to have a nervous breakdown.

"For Christ's sake, Damien, did you *have* to walk into the first puddle you came across when you got out of the car? Your new trousers are *completely* ruined!"

"Oh Ruth, will you leave the child alone!" said Julie. "Little boys aren't supposed to be all squeaky clean. Where's my little man, where's my little man?" She held her arms wide open to the three-year-old whose face suddenly lit up. He threw himself into her arms and they bear-hugged each other tight. "Oh my, you're getting to be so big and strong. Do you want to come and play football with your granny in the garden while Granddad's doing dinner? Come on – let's see if we can't find a ball."

Ruth lit up a cigarette in the living room as her fashion-savvy mother, who loved hauling on and off outfits, went off to change in order to take Damien outside for a kick-about. Catching her mother glaring at the fag on her return attired in snazzy sports pants and trainers, she made the age-old familiar gesture that she would open the window to let fresh air in and the fumes out.

Ruth's brows were knitted together with tension and Ali noticed that these days her sister was letting her bushy hair go wild and wasn't tidying up her roots. There probably wasn't a lot of time for personal maintenance, not when you factored in the daily work commute, the drop-offs to school, the pick-up from childcare and whatever else married people with kids did. Still, Ruth was looking a lot older than her thirty-two years.

"*Amazing*, isn't it?" Ruth snorted. "When do you ever remember her tearing around the garden after us when we were little?"

"Maybe she would have preferred to have had sons instead of daughters."

"She wouldn't if she bloody had them! Boys are *much* harder than girls!"

"Apparently the arthritis is very bad today and all," said Ali.

Ruth made a face. "Poor Mammy – isn't she lucky she doesn't have to work *and* suffer her arthritis as well?"

Then she launched on a rant about hardworking teachers and the good-for-nothing youth of the country. Every so often Ali mumbled some sort of grunt back at her but mainly concentrated her efforts on staring out the window at her mother and nephew. Damien had just slipped in a pile of mud – Ruth would be furious.

"Christ almighty, if the public only knew what the next generation of adults was really like! The little bastards don't want to be in school anyway – they all want to be WAGs and celebs and you can't reason with the parents at all. They think the faults lie purely with the teachers or that their children have every sort of learning disorder going. Oh no, parents can't handle the simple truth that their offspring might be just lazy or plain thick. This teaching game, I tell you, it's going to be the death of me!" Ruth sucked hard on her cigarette and flicked some ash into a nearby ashtray. Her hand shook as she took a mouthful of wine.

"Oh, you're just in bad form because school has started again and you've got used to your three-month break," said Ali. "Relax, you'll be on your midterm before you know it and from there it's just a short stop to Christmas."

"Christmas, that'll be more bloody money to worry about! Money, that's the problem. We're totally broke. The car will need to be traded in soon, and we've just paid for the extension. In fact, to tell you the God's honest truth, Gerry and I have something of a cash-flow problem at the moment." Ruth wriggled in her seat, looking uncomfortable, as she checked through the half-open door to see if her father was still busy in the kitchen. "Hey, Ali, do you think if I asked Dad for some money, a loan, do you suppose he'd lend me a grand or two? I'd be paying it back within a year, maybe even eight months. You're his favourite – what do you think? Do you think he'd be open to lending us some cash just to get us over a tight period?"

Ali felt she had been run over by a two-ton truck. This bombshell was just typical of her older, bossy sister. Ever since they were children Ruth was always making sure that her slice of the cake was bigger than Ali's, that Ali's Christmas toys were not any better than hers, that unfair "mistakes" be rectified on the spot. Now when Ali needed to ask for a loan so that she could change *her* life, Ruth who had everything – two cars, a house of her own, a reliable husband whom she didn't deserve and a stable job – was planning to ask her parents for money just because she had a temporary "cash flow" problem.

"No, you can't, it's not fair!" Ali blurted out.

"Oh, for God's sake, why not? It's just a loan. They're obviously not short of a penny or two what with weekends away down the country and city breaks in Europe. If I opened up *Hello* magazine next week and saw the two of them in it I wouldn't be surprised. Besides I've never asked them for a bean – not like you, always penniless and bumming around. Thank God, you *finally* seem to be turning into an adult with the ability to commit to a job. Anyhow, I don't care what you think – I'm going to ask Daddy about it as soon as we get a moment alone after dinner."

Totally flabbergasted, Ali didn't get a chance to open her mouth to protest further as her father announced that dinner was ready just as her mother and nephew burst through the back door breathless and laughing.

Right, so she'd just have to corner her father first before Ruth could muscle in. After all, she was her dad's favourite; that much was true. If she could just get him alone after dinner, maybe she could charm him into giving her some cash. The thoughts were racing through her head as her father hoisted the Sunday chicken out of the oven and plonked it on the kitchen table.

"Ah the bird, the bird! One juicy chicken ready for carving and devouring!" he said with a chuckle.

The aroma of crispy garlic skin, real herb-and-onion bread stuffing combined with rosemary potatoes filled the kitchen and Ali knew that if she'd been on form it would be mouth-watering, but the thought of knocking back a Sunday lunch was almost horrific – maybe she'd just try the potatoes and some gravy – she was craving salt badly.

Their mother opened another bottle of red wine and made contented purring sounds as the liquid swirled around her tongue and hit the back of her throat. Ever since she'd done the wine-tasting course at the local wine store, Julie had become an expert on the old vino and wasn't shy about sharing her new-found knowledge with anyone who would listen.

"Fabulous bouquet this one, don't you think? Ruth, don't forget you're driving." She kept an eye on the amount of wine her eldest daughter was pouring into the glass.

"I won't be leaving for *hours* yet. It will have well worked itself out of my system by then," said Ruth tetchily.

"Good job I'm not driving so," Ali smirked as, out of badness, she filled her glass to the brim under her mother's frosty stare – not that she was thinking of drinking it – her wretched body was definitely making a stand.

Then a large helping of potatoes was heaped onto Ali's plate by her caring father and the family wholeheartedly threw themselves into a carbohydrate splurge, while Ali pushed her food around the plate and hoped that nobody would notice.

Watching her father bask in the praises of his family and

enjoying every mouthful of his own delicious food, Ali became more relaxed and more and more confident that her dad would lend *her* and *not* Ruth some cash.

Before the last plate was cleared Liam quickly hopped up from the table and, like a perfect host, left to prepare some freshly brewed coffee and check on his chocolate pudding. He was clearly pleased at the "oohs" and "aahs" of pleasure that had come from his family as they enjoyed his sumptuous dinner.

Meanwhile their mother was looking somewhat flushed in the face as she continued her inroads into the wine and raved about the medicinal benefits of her favourite tipple.

Ali prayed that her stomach would hold out as she gazed at the monstrously chocolatey pudding that was placed in the centre of the table.

"Isn't your father just the most amazing cook?" gushed Julie. "I would have loved to have entered him into that Master Chef contest on the BBC."

Liam had the grace to blush just a bit and wave his hand as if such talk was all nonsense, but deep down he would probably have jumped at the chance to show the world what he could rustle up in the kitchen.

"No, you *truly* are a treasure," said Julie and in a rare display of affection she placed her hand on his and patted it gently.

He shot her a shy smile and a look of gratitude and then Ali noticed the small nod Julie made in his direction.

He seemed to hesitate and then he said, "Well, it's lovely to see our two daughters here today and to be sitting down, having a meal, all of us together just like old times. In fact, I was *glad* you rang on Friday, Ali, and asked to come to dinner, not that you had to ask of course as I said, but we were meaning to get you girls together in the next while anyway." There was an awkward silence as he paused and fidgeted with a spoon. "Well, your mother and I, you see, we're not getting any younger the pair of us and your mammy's arthritis is getting worse all the time. We've in the main got our health of course but time is precious and you can't put off till tomorrow what you would be better off doing today . . ."

"What your father is trying to say," said Julie, "is that we've decided to unlock the hidden equity in our home."

"*What?*" said an incredulous Ruth, spilling some cold coffee into her saucer.

"We've had the mortgage paid off for years and the house has increased massively in value due to the explosion in property prices," her mother went on. "Why, even if prices were to collapse completely and Daddy and I were *both* to require nursing care in the future and we had to sell the house, we'd still have some left over. So we thought we'd use that extra cash now."

"I'm sorry, I don't think I quite follow you," lied Ruth in one of her haughtiest tones.

"Your mother and I have decided to go to one of those institutions where they give you money now on the basis that when you die they get their money back through the sale of the house," said her father. "Effectively it's a loan, but we won't have to worry about paying it back and we can enjoy our last few years and have a few little treats. We just thought we'd tell you girls because realistically there might not be much of a house to leave to you both when we're both pushing up daisies so to speak."

This was greeted with a stony silence, which their mother finally broke. "You're both grown up and doing all right. Ruth has her own home, herself and Gerry are both working, and Ali has a good career going now . . ."

This only succeeded in making things worse. Ruth's face was like thunder and Ali was sure that, although she had herself under control, the heat of her outrage was escaping through her ears and turning them a bright pink.

"The truth is, the cost of living isn't getting any lower – every year things increase," said Liam. "Mammy's gym membership for example and with Mammy not being well, who knows when she might become permanently immobile and we might be pushing her around in a wheelchair. She, I mean *we*, both want to see a bit of the world, have a bit of fun before we're two decrepit old fogies."

"Isn't this a bit sudden, even a bit reckless?" asked Ruth. "You might get a lot of money now but don't those institutions rip you off in the end?"

"I'm sure Daddy has looked into all that, Ruth," her mother answered coldly.

"Well, I still think that –"

"Oh for *God's* sake, Ruth," said Ali, "it's *their* house – they can do what they want with it!"

She knew her older sister was thinking that her parents were being massively selfish and self-indulgent and this was one of the rare occasions when she was inclined to agree with her, but Ali wasn't going to burst into tears, wasn't going to tell them how strapped for cash she was nearly on a weekly basis, wasn't going to tell them that she wasn't doing that well, that she didn't have a pension or any savings for a future home or that she hated her job so much that she sometimes felt she was on the verge of a nervous breakdown.

This was all Mum's doing, of course. With Mum it was all bling and looking good. Mum was the one who wanted to have the high-maintenance lifestyle. Dad, by himself, would never think of doing something like this. Well, there could be no asking for money now for any course. They were effectively telling both their daughters that they were cutting the apron strings, that they wanted to kick up their heels before they fossilised, that their days of parenting were over.

In an attempt to be tender, Julie lowered her voice and tried to offer some consolation and in the process irritated the bejaysus out of Ali. "I know, Alison darling, you don't have your own pad yet but I'm sure with all those qualifications you can demand a good salary and things will improve when you find a man and get married, and you have someone to help contribute to a mortgage. I'm sure it won't be long now before you'll be bringing home a nice doctor or an architect for me to meet. How *are* things anyway on the man front, darling?"

There and then Ali would have loved to let rip, but she kept herself under control.

"Not seeing anyone in particular, Mum. Still having my fun, you know." What a generalisation that was! The truth was she hadn't been seeing "anyone in particular" for more than two months, not since she broke up with that funny but irritating Dave O'Connor.

With raw determination Ali smiled weakly in her mother's direction but in reality she was staring right through Julie, right through the kitchen window and on to the back garden, to their neighbour's yard beyond and on into the distance where the trees were merging with the skyline.

Her life was a mess. God, this bombshell her parents had dropped on her was going to require a bit of serious thought. It isn't every day you find out over dinner that you've been effectively disinherited.

5

Lunacy reigned at the start of the week as Ali rang her bank and cockily asked to speak to the woman who dealt with loan approval. The bank official rang back later that afternoon to explain to Ali that her credit rating wasn't too healthy at the moment and, what with her current salary, the bank couldn't really consider extending her existing loan.

Ali knew it was hopeless but she rang one or two other banks in a vain attempt to get some easy cash out of them instead. Her delirium was short-lived. "Easy" money had just got hard. One bank official asked Ali how long she had been in her job and would she not be able to negotiate a pay rise or look for a new job to generate extra cash. Ali felt quite cross with her and told her that she wasn't a particularly valued employee and since she wasn't exactly being headhunted every day of the week she needed to get a bank loan to change her career. At least the condescending cow had been somewhat polite – the other loan-approval woman in the rival bank was downright rude and almost irritated that a candidate as pathetic as Ali had wasted her time by asking for a single penny.

One quiet afternoon towards the end of the week, Maggie, seeing her despondent face, came over to her cubicle. "How's the cash drive going? And have you spoken to himself yet about the time off?"

Ali slowly shook her head, massaged her temples and drummed her pen off her desk in an irritated rhythm.

"Synchronicity, Ali."

"Uhm – what?"

"You know – synchronicity. Sometimes everything falls in place easily and sometimes no matter how hard you try you meet nothing but obstacles at every turn. Maybe you'll just have to wait till next year until you've saved up enough money. How long more do you have, anyway, before you have to sign up for the course?"

"Four days."

"Well, don't beat yourself up if you don't get there this time." Maggie leant forward and whispered mischievously in her workmate's ear. "I know this won't exactly take away your problems now, girl, but would you like a nice cup of tea anyway?"

Ali couldn't help but laugh. "Oh sure, go on – you're a terrible woman to be tempting me with tea, Maggie girl. Make it nice and milky and just put in one sugar. I'm on a diet. Well, I'm thinking of going on a diet."

"Not at the rate you're scoffing chocolate, you're not, Ali Hughes."

Ali kneaded the tyre around her waist and eyed up the half-demolished giant bar of raisin and nut chocolate that sat beside her computer. No doubt about it, she was getting fat and puffy and she couldn't even blame water retention, it was the wrong time of the month. Now that she thought about it, that meant she couldn't blame her massive chocolate binge on PMT either. Fat cells can't lie – she was just a pig. A big, fat, stupid, financially challenged pig who hadn't had the sense to become an architect herself even though she would have been bright enough to study that at college.

Imagine if she had been an architect! Her mother would never again be able to ask her when she was bringing home an architect or a doctor for dinner because Ali would be able to say she was a highly qualified professional in her own right, a woman who was financially secure and who didn't need a man to prop up her life.

Her tea arrived. It wasn't sweet enough so she ate more chocolate and looked up at the huge basement window that dominated the room.

The September weather had changed. Outside the brown and russet leaves were being tossed around by a bad-tempered wind. The air felt damp and the office room, which was always too hot in summer, was beginning to regain its draughty, stuffy and smelly character now that the hot days had turned to autumn chill.

It was already gone five when Simon stuck his head around the door and asked her to pop in and see him for ten minutes before she left. Ali fumed. If she stayed she'd miss her usual train home and she would have to try and fight her way on to the later one. She was already ravenous too, but when Simon asked you to stay late for a chat after work it was never really a request that you could turn down.

Maggie filed past in sweatshirt and pants, on the way to the gym that was going to hammer her body into film-star proportions by Christmas.

"Asked to stay back?"

Ali rolled her eyes in acknowledgment.

"Now, girl, see what he wants first before you shoot your mouth off. You might even try being a small bit nice to him for a change. It could disarm him."

"Don't think I have your natural tact, Mags."

"Well, take care. See you tomorrow, girl."

"Bye, Maggie."

Irritated, she walked into Simon's office with her coat on and clutching her handbag so that he could be in no doubt that in her mind at least this wasn't going to be a long meeting.

He made her sit at the breakfast table for a minute or two without speaking as, keeping his head down, he read some terribly important-looking document at a snail's pace.

He looked up at last. "Won't keep you long – just wanted to let you know that Sunshine Travel is not going with us for their expansion plans into the youth market."

"Oh, that's a pity. Did they say why?"

"Apparently they thought the other submissions were more creative and of a higher calibre. Joe will be disappointed of course. It would have been a good account to land with plenty of potential for future spin-off."

Pretending to be distracted by his documents he cast his eyes down again and then, when she least expected it, he looked up and gave her the disapproving "head-nun's look" – the look that the nuns reserved for girls of "good families" when they got in the smallest bit of trouble, the look that said "I expected better of you".

"Simon, it's always disappointing when a prospective client doesn't go ahead but I put the effort in and made *all* the changes you asked. You looked over the proposal yourself before I sent it off." He said nothing, so she continued her defence. "Sometimes you just lose accounts. I'm just as disappointed as you. I mean I'm the one who put all the work in, *including* overtime."

"Well, I just know this was one client that Joe particularly wanted to land and I'll have to tell him the disappointing news when he comes in tomorrow."

"Joe's coming in *tomorrow*?" she asked, already brightening at the prospect. Ali had always connected with her middle-aged Pierce Brosnan look-a-like boss; she had a way of getting Joe to see things from her point of view. Like the time she negotiated mileage for out-of-hours work projects and work projects down the country – it was a pity she had since got rid of her car.

"Yes, after eleven."

Joe was an elusive guy at the best of times, especially since his luxurious office was located upstairs, along with an architects' firm and a shared boardroom, and he had a habit of entering from the main door and not through the basement like the rest of the plebs. In the last week alone Ali had been told that she'd missed Joe twice and she was desperate to bump into him to see what kind of form he was in – and find out what his thinking was about employees doing courses.

Then suddenly Ali remembered something about the college brochure for her journalism course and she had a very devious thought. It was mostly intuition that pushed her into saying the next peculiar thing that entered her head.

"Now that I think of it, perhaps you could pencil me in for a meeting with Joe to discuss the proposal in more depth, all of us together. You know, in *fairness* to you, Simon, maybe it was lacking something in strategy or in overall vision. I'm sure you have some good ideas yourself on what was wrong with it and how I might have improved our submission, made it a bit more 'creative'."

The effect was instant. He looked stunned, as if the floor had just collapsed beneath his feet but he managed to blurt out a few bits of condescending advice and criticism before she cut him short.

"Yes, Simon, maybe so, but can we save this till tomorrow? If I don't catch this train I'll be waiting at least twenty minutes for the next one and the late train is always jammers."

Before he could open his mouth to object Ali was gone.

Praise the Lord but hadn't she seen the light and had what her self-help books would describe as an "insightful moment"! O'Grady's most unmotivated employee was going to prostitute herself and now all she wanted was to get home as fast as possible, for it was going to take quite a bit of time and a bit of creativity to get the new "Hooker Hughes" on the boil.

* * *

That evening Ali rustled up a stir-fry of chicken, crunchy vegetables and microwaveable rice. Such a healthy meal made her feel slim and in control, not only of her eating habits but of her life. Then she took a bath and shaved the undergrowth from her legs and under her arms, plucked her eyebrows, applied a mud mask and manicured her nails.

Later on she stuck on her Belly Buster, a battery-operated gizmo that helped blubber stick to muscle to give the illusion of a flatter tummy: only temporarily of course. After an hour of intensive pampering she began to feel so good that she was nearly tempted to phone Dave, to see what he was up to, but she knew the fecker was a bit lax about answering his mobile.

No, if she was planning to meet him she'd like to take him by surprise but it had been so long since she'd gone out with him, she didn't know if he'd be at home or at the Garda station. If she had enough nerve she could of course just show up and see how things went, maybe even stalk him a little and beg him for sex.

The Belly Buster was already convincing her that she had abs of steel and the physique of a woman who is so toned she needs sex every night just to keep her cardiovascular levels up. Her tight black skirt in the wardrobe, the one that was made from slightly stretchy fabric, hadn't seen a good night out in ages nor had her tight black top, the one which emphasised what Ali knew were her best assets, her boobs.

No, surely to God she had more respect for herself than to throw her body at that Neanderthal O'Connor again? Ovulation – that was it. Ovulation was the root of this madness, she decided. Hadn't she read somewhere that ovulating women had an irresistible urge to show off flesh and mate with the nearest thing that resembled a male? Good God, her hormonal state was driving her down the road of a good vibrator. Now there was a thought. Maybe if she had a good turbo-charged gizmo she might alleviate the urge she got every month to lose her dignity and self-respect by sniffing around for the scent of male pheromones, and any male pheromones at that.

Stiffening up, Ali gave herself a good talking-to – she wasn't ringing O'Connor and she wasn't going down the vibrator route either. Anyway, the walls of her apartment were so thin she was sure that if she switched a sex gadget on her neighbours would know what she was up to, and the thought of the cute guy in the next apartment knowing that she was so desperate that she had to resort to battery-operated pleasure was more than she could bear.

With sheer determination Ali weaned herself off all thoughts of sex – it would only keep her awake and there could be no sleeping in tomorrow – she'd need to wash and blow-dry her hair as well as put on her make-up. Smiling to herself, she half wished she could bump into her mother en route to work the next day to show her that from time to time she could pull off a polished look with her make-up – but only if the stakes were high.

6

The young good-looking guy on the platform gave her the eye as she paced up and down and acted like a savvy female executive who knows that time is money. It was hardly surprising really that he was staring her out of it. Posing around in her expensive high-heeled black shoes, which were polished for once, and her outrageously expensive designer overcoat, the one that was two seasons old but classic and well-tailored enough to last a decade, she looked and felt like a high-class hooker.

Her face was perfectly made up and her scarlet lips matched her nails exactly. Talons, she thought, as she splayed her fingers in front of her face. Underneath her expensive coat, flattering skirt and sexy but sophisticated top, she was wearing a favourite black-lace bra and black hold-ups with lace tops. Her Belly Buster and her light supper the night before had had such a good effect on her stomach that she'd even decided to forgo her safe big-knicker pants and wear a sexy black-lace g-string instead.

Carrying herself tall, with a conscious fuck-off air that reminded her of Lucy, Ali was like a tense cat ready to spring as she saw the train come through the tunnel and under the bridge, pulling into the station with a scream. By God, she'd get a seat today! She'd terrify the competition into giving way as she pushed through the doors with her best leather briefcase. Today Ali Hughes was unstoppable. Better than that she was hot. In fact she felt like a woman who could make deals or make love at the drop of a hat, or at least give the impression that she could.

Her heels clicked along the city streets and her scarf flapped in the breeze as she walked like a woman with a purpose. Another fine clear blue-skied day filled her with optimism as she swung her briefcase and looked forward to getting into the office early for a change.

No one was in yet. Since she was rarely first in the door Ali almost forgot the number of the alarm as it beeped its urgent call but from some remote portion of her brain she recalled the four digits and punched them in. Sleepy darkness hid the rooms. Pulling open the giant blind in the front room, she let the sunlight in. Today was going to be her day. She could feel it.

Lucy nearly died of shock when she came through the door and saw Ali already seated and busy working.

"Sorry, do I know you?" she said in mock surprise as she took in the rare sight of Ali the Professional Bombshell.

"Oh, leave it out, Luce! I do *occasionally* make an effort, you know."

"Yeah but on time *and* done up to the nines? That doesn't just require effort – that requires planning. You up to something?"

"No. Just the Big Fella himself is coming in today and I reckon if I look like I'm in control of my life he might actually think I'm in control of my work as well."

Lucy gave her a "I don't think so" smirk, then took off her coat and placed her funky handbag behind her desk. "Well, it's a good job Joe *is* coming in. I'm fed up telling people he's not here and I have a pile of cheques for him to sign, and now that I think about it I could do with a raise."

"Well, join the queue of the disaffected because I'm getting first crack of the whip!"

"Oh, I'd say that fecker would enjoy the whip all right, especially if you were doing the crackin' dressed like that!"

Ali snorted with sudden laughter and the paper cup of coffee began to shake in her hand and was in danger of spilling onto the pile of papers that she was thumbing through. "Lucy, it never ceases to amaze me how one so young and sweet-looking can have such a filthy mind."

"Not to mention the filthy gob."

"Oh, the filthy gob is a given, darling! Speaking of sweetness, isn't Pam coming back to work today?"

"Yep, far as I know, even though it's Friday and there's no logic to it."

"Oh good – a bit of goss about her holiers."

"You won't get much goss out of her – it's not as if she's been clubbin' in Ibiza," said Lucy dryly. "Didn't she bring that sap Tom on holiday with her and we all know she's taken the vow of celibacy with 'her Tom' till the ring's on her finger." With that, she stuck her nose into one of her favourite English celeb mags and immersed herself in the details of what was hot and what was not that season. Completely chilled, she'd decided to leave the post for half an hour, delighted that the despised Simon hadn't yet stuck his nose through the door.

Pamela and Maggie arrived in together, laden down with goodies, and Lucy's head whip-lashed round to greet the prodigal employee.

"Oh, you took a great colour, didn't you, Pammy? Jaysus, I thought you girls were on diets for Christmas! I'll stick the kettle on. Now hold off on the yappin' till I get back."

Tall and elegant, Pam Walsh took her seat at her pristine desk and in preparation for the day ahead took a deep breath, perched her dark frames on her nose and smoothed back her sleek chestnut hair which fell like a curtain to her shoulders. Her desk was bereft of clutter and shone like a mirror, which was not surprising since she had got the furniture polish out to wipe the lamination clean before she went on holiday. Still, she couldn't resist taking a wipe out of her bag and giving the surface a rubdown with her long, elegant fingers just in case a morsel of dust had dared settle in her absence. It was this kind of house-proud behaviour that had caused Lucy to christen Pam, "Pammy the Mammy".

When Pam would sigh and explain that she couldn't go for a drink after work or go for lunch because she was saving a big pile of cash to buy a predicable little starter home on a sensible commuter route with "her Tom", steam would come out of Lucy's ears and Maggie or Ali would have to steer the office diva into the kitchen before she blew a gasket and informed Pam of her Mammy nickname. "I can't help it, she's just such a bleedin' Mammy," Lucy would hyperventilate as Ali or Mags plied her with strong tea.

Today, however, even the dedicated, hardworking Pamela looked like she could do with a bit of rescuing from the predictability of the office life ahead of her and Maggie shot her a look of sympathy.

"Tell us, girl, did you have a good time?" asked Mags.

Pam looked up from the little angel she had placed on her desk and her face brightened.

"Oh Maggie, we had a ball! We had only one overcast day and we were nearly glad of it, it was so hot."

"Well, that's the beauty of Greece for you. The weather is nearly always with you."

"The holiers are cheaper and all this time of year, aren't they, Pammy?" said Lucy as she plonked a few heavy-duty mugs on her colleagues' desks.

Maggie shot the office nymphette a ferocious look and they all settled down to a good forty minutes of listening to stories of sun and sand, of boat trips and island hops and of cheap southern-European dining and Ali was torn between wanting to bury herself in her work and listening to the welcome female chatter.

For although Ali had felt cocky when she walked in the door, she was now feeling nervous of her impending meeting with her *real boss*, and it was these nerves, or else the chocolate cake that she had just wolfed down, that was making her feel sick to her stomach.

"Did you ever notice when you've been somewhere where there's blazing sunshine, how when you get to Dublin airport the sky seems to collapse down on you?" Pamela sighed.

Ali knew that feeling all right – she was feeling it every day. God, if only she had a job where she wasn't always stuck behind a desk and had the chance to go somewhere exotic from time to time, even if she had to dodge bullets or brave a few raging bushfires.

There was a sudden roar from Lucy and Maggie as Pam explained how she had flattened a Greek dancer on her holiday during a traditional night out.

"He was only a small lad and he was getting women to run at him and wrap their legs around his waist and then he would spin them around in a mad twirl. I kept saying to him, no, no, I'm too big, I'm too tall, but he kept saying 'no, you come, I big strong man'. Well, it must have been the few glasses of wine in me but didn't I run at him full pelt? The next thing I knew he was on his back and me straddling him and Tom looking on all embarrassed and everyone breaking their hearts laughing."

The ever-flexible Lucy was standing on top of her desk in a flash. "Jaysus! So he was wriggling his hips like this and you landed right on top of him and yer fella looking on and all!" Sensing a willing audience, Lucy gave a very dramatic and slow wriggle of her hips and it wasn't long before she had progressed into a full-blown sexy performance of Zorba's Dance from *Zorba the Greek* with the girls clapping in time and doing the "doo - doo - doo - doo - doo - doo - doo - doo" bit where the bouzouki music should have been. So involved was she in her performance that she didn't pick up on her colleagues' half-hearted attempts to warn her that her bosses were at that very moment descending the outside stairs. Moments later a startled Lucy was looking down on Simon and Joe from the vantage point of her desk.

Simon looked like he wanted her arrested on the spot but Joe seemed half amused at the sight.

"Good morning, Lucy," he said in that warm, deep, polished voice of his that was one hundred per cent male and sexy. He smiled and they all melted. Dead ringer for Pierce Brosnan all right, everyone said so.

Lucy paused for a second or two and then something seemed to ignite in her brain. "Well, I'm very glad to see you too. Do you know half the country is demanding to know your whereabouts?" She banged her foot loudly on the desk. "And I also want to talk to you about the shoddy office furniture in this place. See this desk? It's a health and safety hazard, no quality. I snagged one of me best pair of tights on this feckin' thing again only yesterday. I should be looking for compensation, I should!"

With a slightly dramatic toss of her head she eased herself catlike off her desk, slipped back into her seat, shot Joe a smile and Simon an outrageous look of contempt.

"Yes, I see you have some *issues*," purred Joe in a tone that had Ali thinking of vibrators again.

Joe leant over Ali's desk en-route to his private office, and she nearly fainted with pleasure when she inhaled the mixture of his natural scent and sexy aftershave.

"Alison, could I see you this afternoon? Simon mentioned that you wanted a meeting."

Ali spent the time until lunch poring over some statistical data for a large national bank, but she was so apprehensive about her scheduled meeting with Joe that she couldn't make any sense of the results. The afternoon came too soon and, with her enthusiasm almost completely zapped, she pushed the door open for her meeting in Joe's swish upstairs office.

She saw that Joe's heavy antique desk had been abandoned in favour of the L–shaped brown leather couch near the window. Half-drunk cups of tea, files and a newspaper were placed on the solid mahogany coffee table which formed an island between the couch and an oversized leather armchair. Hunched forward and twirling his manicured thumbs, Joe looked lost in thought when Ali entered the room, while Simon as usual just looked irritated by her presence.

As Ali walked the small distance across the luxurious patterned carpet, she was struck by how gorgeous Joe was in a roguishly sophisticated way. His expensive casual jacket was thrown over the back of the couch and his sleeves were rolled up to his elbows, showing off his manly hands and tanned forearms. Here was a man who was in his early fifties but had the animal physique of a man twenty years younger. He was lean and lithe from his frequent morning jogs, a necessity for keeping both his body and mind agile. In fact, he'd told Ali once, as he gave her a ride back in his green Jag from a meeting with a client, that he got his best inspiration for his business projects while out jogging.

"If you jog an area for six months you get to see changes in a way you'd never notice otherwise. Delivery trucks, new outlets opening, coffee shops and sandwich bars, you even learn a lot from the postman, get to know when 'bad' areas are about to go upmarket and good areas even more so. I've made a few sweet deals that way. But when too many people are in on the act that's when you've got to sell," he told her with a conspiratorial wink.

That was the moment when Ali really became aware that her boss had an impressive brain to match his impressive body. That was also the moment when she realised that for a select few in life making a couple of grand could be as casual and as instant as having a cup of coffee in the morning. She wondered what he was into now. Whatever it was, it would be something lucrative – she doubted if Joe ever got burnt on any of his investments – he was far too savvy for that.

Joe ran his strong fingers through his dark-brown hair, which was brushed with grey around the temples, and smiled at her warmly. "Alison, take a seat," he told her, pointing at the leather chair. Do you want tea?" He half-raised himself from his seat, making it clear that he was willing to personally boil the kettle and stick the tea bag in the cup to make her a cuppa.

What a difference from Simon who'd never offer to make anyone a hot drink, even if he was being tortured by having crabs clamped to his nipples! Graciously she declined Joe's offer and sat directly opposite him, making sure he could get a bird's-eye view of her boobs in one of her classiest low-cut tops.

Crossing her legs, Ali enjoyed the sensation of knowing she was wearing gorgeous underwear and was in the company of a mature, sexy and charismatic man.

"Okay, let's cut to the chase. The travel proposal, have you any idea why we didn't land that account?" Joe bluntly asked.

Alison shifted her weight in her seat for a moment, feeling uncomfortable as her lace g-string stopped feeling sexy and became what it was: a size too small and cutting into her stomach and bum. From the corner of her eye she could see Simon watching her like a hawk about to devour a mouse.

"Joe, I can honestly say that I pulled out all the stops. I brainstormed, came up with the most creative ideas I could that were within the client's budget and they just didn't go for it. I met with Simon before the submission deadline and took on board his suggestions but despite our *joint* efforts they just didn't go for *our* proposal." Alison smiled in the direction of Simon. If there was any shit going to hit the fan she wanted to make sure he was standing underneath the blades with her.

"Now, Alison, I think we have to take the client's word for it that they found *your* proposal to be lacking in creativity," stressed Simon.

"Well, we only have their word for that, Simon. We don't know what other company we were up against on this one and of course they might have got a more competitive quote from a bigger company."

Little Bastard was on the verge of interrupting but she got her next line in fast and had the pleasure of seeing his mouth drop open in amazement.

"However, in fairness, I have taken on board your recent suggestions, Simon, that I might need to learn a bit more. As you know, Joe, my background is actually in research. I've just sort of taken on more and more of a role in the commercial stuff since I started working here."

"That seems to be the way it's working out all right," he agreed.

"Well, I think we'd all agree that there is only so much you can learn from experience and on-the-job training and I think my skills would be greatly enhanced if I took some sort of college course. In fact I've found a marketing course that runs twice weekly and is generally well thought of." Alison pushed a brochure under Joe's nose and pointed with one of her specially painted red talons to the blurb written about the excellent marketing course she had found in a Dublin college, which coincidentally also ran an excellent journalism course on the same nights, for the same amount of money. "When I joined this company I was told that employees would be supported in further training which would be of benefit to the company."

"Yes, that's true," said Joe.

"Well, I was hoping that the company would be willing to back me on this marketing course by being flexible about working time and maybe even supporting me financially."

Simon leaned forward a bit and tried to dominate the physical space, breaking the intimacy between Ali and Joe. "Alison, while further education is all very well, I don't think we could spare you for two nights a week, especially when things get busy."

Joe held up his hand to stop Simon, as if to show that he was thinking over the matter in his head at breakneck speed and wanted no other distractions.

"When do you need to know by?" he then asked.

"Well, that's the thing – I really only have a few days left. I have to sign up early next week."

"Isn't this a bit short notice?" interrupted Simon snidely. "You couldn't have been giving it much thought if you're only getting round to discussing this with the company now."

"I wanted to do a bit of my own research first on the type of course that would be most beneficial to the company."

"Well, Alison, I'm sure we'll let you know and get back to you on this as soon as possible," said Simon dismissively.

"No, that won't be necessary, Simon. I'll tell her now. In fact, I was meaning to suggest you do some sort of skills update, Alison. It's good you took the initiative yourself. I'm happy to agree to this if you think you can handle it."

Simon was now becoming so agitated that he looked like he was genuinely trying to control a battalion of ferrets in his trousers and was squirming under the effort. "Well, in that case we'll have to get you to sign something to say that you will agree to work for the company for a year or two after you have completed this course and if you leave the company you will agree to pay the money back."

"You're not planning on going anywhere, are you, Alison?" asked Joe.

"No," she lied. "Not planning."

Lying was not one of her greatest strengths but Alison reckoned she could get good at it without much effort; she had better get good at it. Now that she had just got her boss to okay a marketing course that she had no intention of doing, she'd need to stay on her toes. Her hope was that she could get a general receipt from the college and that O'Grady's accountants wouldn't pry into the specifics of which course she was studying, so long as the amount looked okay on paper and tallied with the cheque. So as long as no-one asked for too detailed a receipt, Ali's deceitful and possibly even fraudulent plan should never be exposed. It was bloody risky and tomorrow or the next day she might regret her actions but, for today, everything was all right with the world.

Outside, she leant against the door, closing her eyes for a moment. She felt bad that she had deceived Joe but the guilt only lasted for a moment. Thank God she had worn the top; it always helped her pull, even if today it was only to pull the wool over her boss's eyes.

Maggie caught the beam on Ali's face as she strode past her desk and collapsed into her seat with barely controlled enthusiasm.

"You swung it then?" she whispered.

"Yep."

"They'll pay for it as well?"

"Uhuh."

"That's brilliant. How did you manage it?"

"I'll fill you in later."

From her vantage point Ali had spotted Simon and Joe descending from upstairs and she made a deliberate show of looking through the diary on her desk as they appeared in the main office.

"Well, it's the end of the week. How about we finish early today, ladies?" said Joe as he made a show of rubbing his hands together and looking at the clock which was registering four o'clock. If anyone's interested I'm buying the drink."

Needless to say there was a stampede out the door.

Joe's choice was a trendy little wine bar around the corner, which was bustling with the after-work drinks crowd by five thirty. Alison was bristling with such good humour and optimism that she decided to hit the shorts straight away and forgo her usual starter pint.

After a polite half an hour or so of communal chatter, Ali, Maggie, Pam and Lucy broke away from their two bosses and after that from time to time Joe would put a finger up in the air and strain his neck in the girls' direction in a gesture which asked, "Same again all round?" and they'd collectively smirk back in his direction to indicate that they were agreeable to his offer.

At half seven Maggie got up to leave so she'd be in good form to catch the early train back home in the morning.

"I know you're celebrating and all, Ali, but all the same you'd want to watch yourself with that stuff," Maggie warned as Ali knocked back yet another vodka.

"As long as he's paying, I'm drinking," said Ali with a giggle as she took a good-sized swig of her glass.

"All the same, you're already legless."

"*Almost* legless, Maggie, there's a *world* of a difference," Ali smiled.

7

On Sunday morning, having slept most of Saturday away in a painful stupor, thanks to Joe's free session of after-work vodkas, Alison decided to become a new woman. When she saw the state of her "professional" coat, which looked like it had been danced upon and saw the beer stains down her sexy top, she promised herself that she would moderate every aspect of her behaviour from now on. Her bathroom mirror didn't lie: one day on she looked like a tramp but definitely not of the sexy kind.

Delving into her store of self-help books designed to turn her into an independent, successful woman by the time she was thirty-five, Alison resolved to buy some index cards from the local stationery shop and fill them with positive affirmations about herself.

Then she washed, toned and moisturised her face, put on liquid concealer, foundation, powder and blusher and actually blended her eye shadow with brushes instead of just her finger. Her hair was blown dry, her eyebrows plucked and her perfume dabbed on between her cleavage and on her wrists. After an hour's pampering she was ready to meet her mother, to tell her of how well her life was progressing. Ali felt smug as she fished out her most fashionable and favourite clothes and headed for the old homestead.

* * *

Julie was in "marvellous form" when her youngest daughter arrived, and was glowing from her morning gym workout. Her arthritis was not a bother lately, now that she had discovered some "super" supplements of shark's cartilage from the local health shop. Feeling in sparkling form she had decided to increase her cardiac fitness levels by booking herself a personal trainer and was working out with weights instead of just doing her respectable middle-aged swim and forty minutes on the walker.

As her mother clasped her to her chest, Ali thought she could definitely feel some extra muscle tone underneath her expensive tightly fitted tracksuit top. Julie was looking fabulous, wearing a pair of high-tech sports trainers and a pair of slinky gym trousers that Ali would only have worn if she had just completed a week on a fruit and veg detoxification diet.

A glance was all it took for Julie to note her daughter's made-up appearance, but she said nothing, just curled her lips faintly into what Ali thought might even be a small smile of approval.

Looking like a lunatic who didn't even have the pleasure of being an escapee from the asylum, Ruth crashed through the door with both of her sons and their possessions just about intact. She looked like she'd just crawled out of a bin and Ali had no trouble putting her sibling rivalry aside for just a moment to feel genuine pity for her elder sister.

There used to be a time when Ali thought her big sister had it all worked out – marrying her college boyfriend, buying a home with the cash he inherited when his father passed on, belting out two kids while holding down a mentally demanding job teaching mentally unstable adolescents.

Big sister Ruth hadn't squandered a day of her twenties and had ploughed straight into the meaty, meaningful stuff of life while Ali busied herself in dodging life's responsibilities for as long as possible. On a bad day, and today was one of them, Ruth looked like she could be hitting forty, instead of her early thirties, especially when she had sole custody of her older, hyperactive son Conor as well as the ever-petrified Damien. Gerry was yet again at an antiques fair, buying God knows what overpriced crap somewhere down the country.

"Okay, Ruth, when are you going to admit that you have actually *killed* Gerry and that is why he never makes it to Sunday lunch," Ali said playfully.

"Haven't killed him – yet!" She threw her keys on the table and reached instinctively for her pack of Lights and a glass of wine. "Need to think of the best way to dispose of his body first."

Julie was already in the back garden kicking a ball around with her two nephews.

"We should really enter her into the Old Fogey Olympics. She's certainly making a most miraculous recovery in her twilight years," said Ruth snidely.

"Twilight my arse – she's only a babe by today's standards – wish I could look as bloody good," said Ali as she topped up her sister's glass. "For *once* be grateful – at least she's running the legs off your two sons for half an hour or so."

Liam's Sunday lunch was divine as usual; both Ruth and Ali were almost purring like kittens by the time dessert arrived.

"What do you know about computers?" Julie asked Ali suddenly as Liam went off to brew some coffee.

"Only that I sit in front of one for far too long every day."

Her mother looked cross and a small frown creased her forehead as she sat forward in the chair and looked intently at her youngest daughter. "There's no need to be smart, Alison. I'd ask Ruth, but I know she knows nothing about them. I'm thinking of buying a computer, that's all, and I was just looking for some advice if it's not *too* much trouble."

"Good God, what do you of all people need a computer for?" laughed Ruth.

"I'd like to have a few skills. I can type and I've kept the books for the ladies' club for years. Who knows, if I got a few more skills I might even go back into the workforce one day."

"What do you mean, go *back*? You were never *in* it," Ali reminded her.

The comment wounded more than she intended and Alison was immediately sorry for the apparent insult and tried to soften the blow of her words. "Mum, I don't mean to be catty but in fairness it won't be easy for you to find a job at your age. Anyhow, work is overrated. Trust me – I'd do anything to live your life of leisure with Dad doing everything for me."

Julie's posture stiffened and her demeanour told Ali that she was causing more offence rather than less.

"I got married young, I had two children. *Trust* me, it was no life of leisure," said her mother coldly. "As for Daddy looking after me, I did plenty of looking after him in my day, I'll tell you."

"Look, all I meant was –"

"It's all right, Alison. Maybe I'll just do a course in computers and get some *professional* advice while I'm there!"

Her mother bristled for the rest of the afternoon and the atmosphere was decidedly sour. It wasn't a day for boasting about one's future career path.

Initially, sensing a coolness between the three women, Liam hovered uncomfortably between kitchen and living room, then ended up spending an excessive amount of time in the kitchen listening to classical music and washing up any utensils he couldn't fit into the dishwasher – anything to avoid confrontation.

Ruth too was tetchier than usual and was chain-smoking without conversation, not even caring that her activity was attracting the most ferocious glares from her mother. Julie eventually left the room in a temper, snapped at her two grandsons in the next room to turn down the television and then stomped up the stairs.

"Taken to the bed for the afternoon, I'd say – no doubt it's all my fault," said Ali in an attempt to break the silence and raise a laugh with a self-mocking comment. There was no laughter.

Ruth said nothing. Large tears were welling up in her eyes and one rolled down her cheek silently until she brushed it away.

"Ruth! Oh fuck, what's wrong, are the kids getting you down?" Alison left her chair and put an arm tenderly around her sister in concern. "I know I haven't been the best of sisters lately but I *promise* I will baby-sit soon and give yourself and Gerry a bit of a break."

"It's not the kids I need a break from," Ruth snivelled and she grabbed Alison by the sleeve and looked her in the face with an intensity that was almost frightening. "Ali, promise me you won't get married too soon. Not because you're nearly thirty or because Mum would like you to or because your friends are settling down. Choose carefully," she warned. "Promise me."

"I won't. I mean, I will, yeah – look, I promise you, I'll be careful. Besides, I'm not thirty yet, Ruth."

"Have your fun first, that's all."

Alison hardly liked to admit it to her sister but ever since the family conversation had dried up mid-afternoon, she was actually having a riot of fun in her mind. For some reason she was thinking more than she should be about vibrators, Garda Dave O'Connor stripping her down to her g-string, and the cute guy in the next apartment whose eyes could peel the clothes off her back with one glance.

Now there was a threesome worth having. Wow, she'd love to mention this fantasy love triangle to O'Connor the next time he was going on about three-in-the-bed sessions. Another bloke would scare the bejaysus out of him. Shit, she was already thinking about the next time she'd see him! Was Karen really serious about him going to call or was it all just a wind-up?

"I'll have plenty of fun, Ruth. I promise you. Maybe we can even have some girlie time together soon," Ali said gently as she dreamt of starring in a porn video with a few brainless but well-hung red-hot studs and maybe Sexy Joe too.

8

It looked like an institution from the 1950s for the criminally insane: either that or some facility for locking up young offenders from the same era. There were grandiose plans to move the entire college into the city centre in the next five years, where everything would be all light and air, glass and sculpture, but until then the place where she was to learn her future trade was sombre and grey with corridors that reeked of disinfectant and windows that were draughty.

The seats were wooden, wobbly and ridiculously old-fashioned and the lecture rooms cold and pokey, but still Ali was full of optimism as she signed up for her journalism course, doubly so since O'Grady's was unwittingly paying for the entire programme. Thank God Simon had let her handle the booking herself and wasn't hounding her for a receipt . . . yet.

There were all types signing up for tuition: a few articulate young things who were looking for a "launch pad" into the world of the "Meeja" and who were eager to learn the basics and beat it as fast as possible, a couple of straight-out-of-school giggly types and a few middle-aged wannabees who underneath their easygoing jocularity were deadly serious about at least breaking into their local paper.

The woman in admissions took Ali's details and her cheque and a very proper-looking form was printed out from an adjoining printer. Then the college official tore along the serrated edge and handed one part to Ali as a receipt and the damn thing had all her details on it including her programme of study – journalism.

"Eh – I was wondering if maybe I could get a more general receipt from the college," Ali asked, aware that she was holding up the queue and that the students behind were getting a bit restless.

"This is a perfectly valid receipt," the woman replied briskly, eager to get on with the processing.

"Yes, but what I really need is something a bit more general – you know something just acknowledging that I'm doing a course with the college and that you have received my cheque."

"Well, if you want a letter we'll write you up one but we're so busy it will be November before we have time to do it – the letter would serve as a receipt if you preferred and would have all your details and your programme of study."

"Yes, you see, it's the programme of study thing that is the problem – could I get a letter without mentioning the actual programme I'm studying?"

The woman looked at Ali for a moment as if she was a bit touched, then pursed her lips together and said one word very clearly: "No."

"No?"

"No, the course you're studying has to be on all official documents and letters."

Stupid bloody nanny state, detailing every last thing! What happened to bending the rules and being flexible? So she could maybe stall O'Grady's till November, but after that she'd have to come clean, quit her job or have some journalism work lined up. Shit.

Momentarily she blanked her dilemma from her mind as she moved from the admissions office into the lecture hall and felt the buzz of anticipation from her fellow students. The head of the course was upbeat and professional, listing the programme of study that lay ahead: practical journalism, sub-editing, photography, writing, computer skills, law and shorthand to name a few. Alison felt the rush she always felt when embarking on new study or even occasionally a new work project.

There would be interesting things to learn, she'd push her brain cells a little bit further and she'd gain yet another qualification to add to her curriculum vitae, the CV which would one day fall on the right desk, in front of the right boss who would appreciate her and pay her well. Gnawing her pen she listened to the opening lecture, occasionally scribbling the odd note to herself in the new A4 spiral-ring pad, which she had bought for the occasion. Oh yes, she could hardly wait for the benefits to roll in!

Already the guy in front had a page of densely packed notes taken down. It wasn't going to be so simple, this journalism lark. Jesus, it was like they were all possessed, they were all so bloody eager. Still, there was no reason why fortune couldn't shine on her as much as the next. Feeling optimistic, she got down to business, racing to catch up on her shameful note-taking, feeling that her study plans were already exhausting.

* * *

When Ali rang in sick for the third day running, Maggie didn't believe her.

"Like, Ali, if you're having trouble balancing work with study already you'll have to find ways to get your act together, girl, and you'd better do it yourself 'cos I know you can't afford a life coach."

Ali moved around the bed a little to try and get more comfortable on her pillow while she held her cordless phone to her ear.

"It's legitimate, you bitch! I've been to the doctor and all and have a cert."

"Oh, are you *very* bad then?" asked her friend more sincerely.

"No, not really – I have some kind of stomach virus where if I eat anything at all I puke it all back up, but if I don't eat I'm fine, I'm not even hungry. Course if Simon is thinking of ringing me make sure you tell him I sounded *real* bad, won't you? Has anyone in particular been looking for me while I've been out?"

"If you mean have there been any calls of a personal nature from a certain member of the national police force then the answer is yet again no, but should he ring here I will pass on any messages all right, girl."

The pillow was digging into Ali's neck and she sighed and thumped it hard in frustration while Maggie laughed down the phone at her and then hung up. It really was very irritating that the bastard hadn't rung yet. Not that she doubted Karen's word. Hadn't Ali literally pinned her to the door to make her swear that she wasn't fabricating any lies about O'Connor? His week of nights had already been over a few days so he'd had more than enough time to ring her – unless something had happened on the job.

Suddenly Ali became very concerned that Dave O'Connor was lying in a hospital bed somewhere unconscious and in pain, having been beaten up or even shot by one of the city's vicious young thugs. An honourable excuse for his not calling, but an unlikely one. He was just being a bastard. Well, he could go jump – she had plenty of things to do.

Stretching herself out catlike, she yawned, got out of bed and hopped into the shower, enjoying the fact that she had time this morning to nearly scald herself into oblivion instead of just literally getting her skin wet like most weekdays. Afterwards she slapped on a green mud mask and, sitting in her white bathrobe and fluffy slippers, sipped some refreshing peppermint tea.

The loaded fridge in the kitchen was making her feel somewhat depressed since she had spent a fortune stocking it with healthy food and now wasn't in a position to eat anything without heaving up her guts. The pro-biotic yogurt would keep but the low-fat milk was probably a goner and the lettuce and the celery were limp from neglect and half-frozen from her fridge which only had two temperatures: arctic freezing or just plain broke.

Still, she felt a certain satisfaction when she closed the fridge door and took in the positive affirmations she had written: *I am slim and getting slimmer, I am in control of my eating* and *All my clothes in my wardrobe are the same dress size*. With satisfaction she patted her stomach: it was almost flat. A bit of unplanned malnutrition was proving very helpful in fulfilling her dream of becoming a svelte and sophisticated young woman.

Not that she would dream of starving herself full time, but a period of fasting had made her realise the amount of toxins she assaulted her body with on a daily basis and she had resolved to change her eating habits permanently. When she could eat again she would choose her foods more carefully and would introduce more fruit and vegetables and lemon juice. Ali had read somewhere that lemon juice in hot water was very beneficial to the constitution.

The loud banging on her sitting-room window frightened the life out of her and when she looked up she saw his dark eyes squinting though the gap in the curtains. He was grinning at her like a school kid and pointing towards the door.

When she had got over the shock of Dave's sudden appearance, Ali was overcome with a certain sense of fury that he hadn't given her any warning of his arrival, no doubt a deliberate ploy on his part to rattle her, a technique learned in the guards and employed by him as much as possible in every real-life situation.

"Well, *hello* there, you just out of bed?" he said as she answered the door reluctantly. He gave her the once-over in the impertinent manner she was now more than familiar with and put a finger mischievously to that sensuous mouth of his and grinned. "Jesus, you're green all over! You look like one of those white fellas who pretend they're black. What do you call them?"

"Minstrels," she said.

"Yeah – one of them – except you're –"

"Green – I know."

God, she hated him. His well-built frame dominated her doorway. He was looking great and she knew damn well he hadn't thrown on that casual well-cut jacket, those black jeans, charcoal fleece jumper and stylishly expensive leather boots with careless indifference. Her fingers yearned to caress his tightly cut dark-brown hair which she knew would feel both soft and bristly to the touch. His aftershave blended just perfectly with his natural scent and it almost made her swoon. But while he had evidently placed some thought into seeing her, she was stuck with green goo on her face and a pair of fluffy white slippers on her feet.

Drawing her dressing-gown tighter across her chest, she suddenly remembered that she was naked underneath. Then she remembered her unshaven legs. Christ, she couldn't let him see them! That would be just too much embarrassment for her to bear.

"Gotta jump into the shower, see you in a minute!" she said as she bolted for the bathroom.

Without hardly knowing what she was doing, she ran the shower again and stood looking at it for a moment, then frantically began to search for a half decent razor to shave her calves with. Two or three disposable razors were examined and binned on the spot until she eventually found one that wasn't quite as blunt as the others and had only a moderate amount of sludge and bristle stuck to the blade.

When she got up enough nerve she stuck one leg into the freezing cold water, soaped it up and attempted to shave it from knee to heel without crying out in pain. With two legs half hacked to death, she sat on the toilet and began to search for strays with a tweezers and tried to apply pressure with blobs of toilet paper to some cuts around her ankles. Brushing her teeth was strictly forbidden – he could be snooping outside the door and he might hear her and think he was on to a good thing – better to take a quick swig of mouthwash instead, just in case.

"Alison, where'd you hide the biscuits?" he asked as he banged on the door.

"Be there in a minute," she answered as she scraped the last of the green gunk off her face with a cotton-wool pad. Underneath, her face was glowing and the spattering of oversized pores on her nose had shrunk to a barely noticeable size. No, she wasn't going to need any make-up – the face-mask and her days of fasting, drinking nothing but water and herbal teas, had left her with a radiance that she rarely saw on her own skin. "In a minute!" she cried again as she zoomed into her bedroom and began to rummage through her underwear drawer, pulling out a two-piece black number and then discarding it for a newish denim set that seemed less presumptuous. Her denim jeans were delightfully loose and, as she slipped on a pair of leather zip-up boots and an oversized shirt, she knew she looked clean and fresh in a way most men couldn't resist.

Feeling a bit mad in the head, which might have been down to low blood sugar, she hardly questioned what she was doing and only felt an immediate urge to look as casually well-thrown-together as him. It was almost a game of one-upmanship. This was her territory now; he couldn't just barge into her apartment and play with her head without expecting her to retaliate in some sort of style.

"God, you look great! These things evidently work so," he said as he waved one of her self-affirmation positive-thinking slimming cards under her nose.

"Give me that!" She lunged at him to take the card away but he held it just out of her reach and laughed. "They're part of a project I'm working on with some teenage girls. They're notes to remind me about their problems with self-image – from an interview I did!"

"Oh yeah, I suppose the note inside your tea cupboard that reads, 'I am a professional and financially independent woman' is from a project you're working on with some stockbrokers then?"

"Will you stop trying to trick me! I'm *not* one of your criminals and I don't believe you have a search warrant to inspect my apartment," she hissed as she wrestled her flash cards from his hands.

He grinned at her again as he practically inhaled a low-fat chocolate biscuit with a cup of tea he had just made for himself, making himself at home on her kitchen chairs, resting his rear end on one while draping his legs across another.

"Speaking of criminals, did your nurse friend tell you I'd be dropping round a charge sheet on account of the fact that you were recently found to be in breach of the Public Order Act?" He made a show of pretending to look for a charge sheet in the inside pocket of his jacket which he'd draped over the back of his chair.

"Stop the legal-speak! If you came here to annoy me you can just feck off – I mean it too, Dave! I'm not in the mood!"

"Okay, okay, don't get cross." He, pulled his feet off the chair, sat properly and flashed his wide white smile at her, the one that made old ladies want to cuddle him and pat his head and made younger women want to do the same and more.

Ali kept the scowl on her face a while longer, determined to show him that she really was cross, but she was beginning to feel weak from lack of willpower or possibly loss of blood from her razor-scratched legs.

"Alison," he said softly and playfully as he reached for her arm and began to pull her to him.

Half-heartedly she tried to push him away, all the time aware that he was succeeding in reeling her in slowly and deliberately.

"Alison, no fighting," he whispered as he pulled her onto his lap and looked her in the eyes.

Ali tried her damnedest to keep a frosty look on her face as he tried to melt her with those boyish brown eyes which were full of mischief and fun.

"You're a funny girl," he said as he stroked a few strands of hair behind her ears and ran his forefinger lightly down the bridge of her nose.

"Oh yes, I'm a great laugh! I bet you told all your mates about how your ex was peeing in the street and how you had to take her home in the squad car drunk out of her head?"

"Well, it was very funny when you think about it – it's probably what got me here today."

"You mean you came to laugh at me even more?"

"No, but meeting you again reminded me that underneath that cold-bitch exterior of yours there's a really funny, sexy girl who has trouble getting her head together."

Alison rolled her eyes as if she disagreed with all he said but he kept looking at her and she began to laugh. "I'm *not* a cold bitch – you can take that bit back!"

"No, you're not cold now," he said as he started to kiss her on the back of her neck with his warm soft lips and she gasped as a familiar chill of pleasure chased down her spine. "You've missed me, haven't you?" he said with confidence as he nuzzled her and buried his face in her hair.

"No," she said, pulling away from him with supreme effort. "I've been very busy seeing lots of other guys, lots and lots, so you needn't think I've been spending my time pining for *you*, Dave O'Connor. I've been having three-in-the-bed sessions and all, you know!"

"Yeah, right – I bet you haven't had sex since we broke up." The edge in his voice was unmistakable.

For the shortest time they held each other's gaze and it was all there for the reading: the disappointment, the anger, the desire and the memories. Her body was tense from determination, determination to resist him, determination that her mind and not animal desire was in control of her body. Their lips were almost touching and there was nothing but the noise of her shallow breathing.

And then he smiled. Christ, he was too gorgeous, his lips were too special for a guy – she loved the way they curled upwards at the corner, dissolving into the most kissable dimples – and all of a sudden she couldn't help herself and smiled back. Slowly she edged her lips towards his, closing her eyes the better to savour his gorgeous mouth, but just as she was about to kiss him, he flipped her backwards over his knee, with one hand on her stomach, so that she had to use her fingertips to steady herself against the floor.

"Ha, bloody ha! Now let me up!" she demanded as she got a bird's-eye view of her kitchen floor and realised it was filthy.

"I'll let you up when you answer my questions *truthfully*."

"For fuck's sake!"

"I asked did you miss me."

"Are these your usual methods of interrogation? Because I doubt very much that they're lawful?"

"*Did you miss me?*"

"*No!*"

"No?"

She could feel the fingers of his left hand gently fondle her skin under the waistband of her denims and then she felt him gently pop the button. Very deliberately he unzipped her fly and as her stomach muscles tensed she was overcome with a fit of the giggles.

"Okay, okay, I missed you!" she told her floor. "Happy now?"

Slowly he pulled her upwards until she could look him in the eye. She straddled him, her lips and hair brushing against his neck, then raised her face to his and kissed him hard with a mouth that betrayed her body's sentiments.

There was no point in playing games with Dave or trying to pretend there was going to be any "romance" involved. Just seeing him was foreplay; he knew it and played upon it. Her desire for him was so strong that she was almost angry with herself for having such desperation, but she was excited too. She knew he must feel the heat of her skin through her clothes as he grasped her waist and kneaded his thumbs rhythmically into her abdomen. Hastily he searched out her lower belly and hips, then roughly pulled her blouse apart and squeezed her breasts with a familiarity she adored.

"Not here! If we stay here any longer we'll break the bloody chair," she told him as he reached to unclasp her bra.

He picked her up in his strong arms and carried her to the bedroom and she laughed as he threw her down on the bed and her body bounced then sank into the soft duvet. He was all over her in seconds, undressing her, kissing her, pulling her against him with his muscular arms and legs until she was filled with a constant ache for him that was agony and could hardly bear the waves of pleasure. He didn't once break the silence as he burrowed his mouth into hers in long, passionate kisses, then gently nudged her legs open with his knee and moved between her thighs with the intimate knowledge of a very special lover.

* * *

The rain drummed on her bedroom window and she listened to its soothing sound as she drifted into the most delightful snooze. Her bare bottom was nestled into Dave's crotch and lower belly and she could feel the warmth and hairiness of him when he moved. As she wriggled on the sheets she felt his arm tighten around her stomach and he clasped her against him with his thigh so that they were both still, both lying on their sides, perfectly together, skin to skin. He had been lion-like in his pleasure. She could hear his contented snoring and she tingled with excitement at the dead weight of his limbs about her.

A man in her bed; God, it had been an age. Just when she thought she had tamed her body and had become used to celibacy he had reawakened the demons within her. Without hesitation she bothered her sleepy lion and made him pleasure her all over again until she collapsed into a dead sleep of her own for several hours.

Somewhere late in the evening she awoke in an instant and was startled by the blackness of her surroundings. When she switched on her bedside lamp she found him already half dressed and putting on his wristwatch.

"Aren't you staying?" she asked in a daze.

"No, I know you women like to be held all night long but I gotta go. Besides, I'm starving and you haven't anything decent to eat in this place – it's all celery sticks and pots of yogurt, totally unlike the Alison I used to know."

"You could get a takeaway if that's all that's bothering you," she said, sitting up in bed.

"No, I gotta go."

"Were you planning to say goodbye?"

"Not if it meant waking you. Well, I would have kissed you goodbye," he said as an afterthought, noticing the frown beginning to appear between her eyes.

"I suppose I'll see you when I see you then," she said, straining to keep any feeling out of her voice and not wanting to meet his eyes.

"Here we go – now you're going all cold and bitchy again," he said playfully but she wouldn't look at him. Her pride didn't want him to know that she was disappointed at his leaving.

Suddenly, he grasped her by the ankles and pulled her roughly down the bed until he could push his face against hers and annoy her by nibbling her ears.

"And when I see you again you needn't go to such an effort," he said.

"What do you mean?"

"Shaving your legs; just for me! You've nicked yourself all around your ankles, you daft cow!"

Ali went to kick him but he fended her off without much effort.

"One of these days I'll have to show you how to shave your legs properly!"

His parting comment wasn't a definite indication that he would ring soon but it was somewhat promising nonetheless, thought Ali as she collapsed back into her bed and repeated the action she had performed earlier that day, that of banging her pillows in frustration. This time however she had a smile on her face.

9

It was eight in the morning on her first day back at work and Ali was actually at her office desk. It was evident Big Bastard, as she'd recently christened Dave, wasn't going to call and she was full of regret at having lost her dignity to him, yet again. The chamomile tea on her desk was literally getting up her nose and its dodgy silage smell was failing to act as a soothing tonic. She grew quite impatient waiting for the brew to cool down as she doused the teabag up and down in the cup.

Days of enforced fasting and absence from work had left her feeling wonderfully charged and alert but she was more sexually energised than ever and as cross as a ferret with no rabbit to hunt down. Why in God's name had she shaved her legs? If she hadn't wasted time crossing her pins with a razor blade she might have been able to string him along a while longer until he was dying for her instead of the other way around.

Tapping the desk with her pen in irritation, she read the title of her first college assignment and sighed. *Write a 400-word colour piece on your favourite sport.* There was only one sport she was an expert in – shopping. She wondered if shopping qualified. Of course she could always call Dave on the pretence that she needed help with her college work – Big Bastard wouldn't doubt for a minute that she would be utterly clueless about all things relating to sport.

Facing into the ton of work on her desk she now regretted taking the time off sick and, feeling sorry for herself, she decided to ring the one person she knew who was always on for a quick bitch. Karen would be just getting off nights from the hospital and would be shortly about to sit her ass into her girlie car to head home for her daily snooze.

"Seen any good willies lately?" she asked as her friend was called to the phone.

"Oh, it's you!" laughed Karen. "No, nothing too exciting happened in the willie department last night. Amazingly it was fairly quiet. We didn't have any broken jaws either. The most traumatic thing was when we had to get some lad's dislocated arm back into the socket."

"Why, what happened?"

"Ah, I just tried to lighten the mood by suggesting he take a run at the wall like Mel Gibson in *Lethal Weapon*. Well, he just started to cry – he thought I was serious. I had a grown lad of twenty-five in tears!"

"Well, I had a grown lad of thirty-two in my bed!"

"Oh Jaysus, not who I think, is it?"

"Yep. The very one. I was at home sick and he just kind of dropped by and he was looking gorgeous and I was feeling kind of sexy, well, desperate –"

"And one thing led to another but of course you knew it would because I bet you shaved your legs first."

"Right again – guilty as charged."

"Well, if you break up again I hope you don't think I'm taking you out with a couple of nursey friends to get you rat-arsed. God, Ali, Maggie will *kill* you. Didn't she spend weeks psychoanalysing you when you broke up the last time?"

"Maggie. Yeah, Mags will probably kill me all right – but the thing is, Karen, how can you break up when you don't even know if you're back together again?"

"Oh, it's like that, is it? Well, thanks for giving me your exciting news. I've gotta go concentrate on report now and then I'll have to drive my car home without crashing it due to the exciting news, and then I'll probably be too restless to sleep the morning away so I'll end up going on nights totally jaded. Thanks a bunch, Ali."

"What are you worried about?"

"That somewhere along the line I'm going to have to pick up the pieces – again."

* * *

The day was intolerably long. Simon was always cross when any of them got sick as he believed it inevitably meant that work got delayed and deadlines for projects pushed back – not that that should concern him as he never had to stay back late to work on any of his employees' deadlines. His dark sulky moods always had the effect of subduing the entire office. Today, as he passed Alison's desk, he made some sarcastic comment about her no doubt already missing one night of her course because she was sick and Ali flashed her eyebrows at Maggie across the room as if to ask, "What the hell is his problem?"

Over a toasted cheese at lunchtime, Maggie filled her in about Simon's black moods.

"You know the way when you go to the loos you can sometimes overhear a conversation in the back office if the window is open a bit? Well, yesterday evening when I stayed back to catch up on some work there was, shall we say, a bit of a heated discussion between Simon and Joe."

Ali sank her teeth into her ham, tomato and cheese toasted sandwich and groaned with pleasure as melted cheese, her first real food in days, dribbled on to her tongue. All thoughts of a future vegan lifestyle went straight out of her head.

"Go on, I'm listening."

"Apparently Simon found this course you could do over the Internet where you can do a diploma in marketing and can upgrade to a Master's. Well, would you credit it, Joe refused to go for it because it costs a couple of grand a year and he said he couldn't afford to give him the one day study-leave a week off which he wanted. Anyway, Simon was fuming. I guess that's why he's at you today. You're a bit of a reminder, yet again like, of his failed educational ambitions."

"For feck's sake, Maggie, I know my mere presence is usually enough to piss him off but he can't have that much of a problem with me."

"Well, I'd say he's sore about Joe okaying your course, especially when he wants to do one himself and get a few letters after his name on his business card."

"Oh God, Maggie, imagine if he got his precious online degree! I'd actually be happy for him – maybe the little fecker would even move on and leave us all alone."

"Maybe that's what Joe reckons too. He's useful to Joe where he is, always flapping around his heels but not really qualified to make the next big step upwards."

"He's lucky to have been able to work his way up from sales if you ask me," said Ali.

"Don't be such a snob, Ali – it shows he's got ambition and talent as well."

"Oh, come on, Maggie!"

"Well, let's be honest here, Ali. You're the one with the string of qualifications but he's still your boss and earns more money than you."

"True. I'd stuff all my qualifications if it meant I got more of his money."

"Well, isn't that the way of the world? We're all jealous of what everybody else has."

Taking her paper napkin in hand Ali wiped the corners of her mouth clean and, still chewing, gave her best attempt at a smile. "Maggie, ordinarily I might care a little bit about what that fecker thinks, especially if it affects me, but today I couldn't give a crap. Let's say I'm getting all my basic needs met and am feeling somewhat satisfied."

Maggie's blank stare met her across the table.

Ali pressed on. "Now promise me you won't go mad?"

"He rang? Oh God, it's worse than that, isn't it? You've had sex with him! After all the crying you did and promises that you'd never see him again, that you weren't compatible – and you had sex with him! Ali, girl, are you mad?"

"I like him. I know I shouldn't but I do and I feel happier than I have in weeks. Well, I would if he'd only ring. He's left me feeling desperate. I feel like a car ignition that has been turned on and the motor left running. I'm dying to see him again and I hate him for turning me into this – this – quivering heap of lust."

"What about all you said like he's too mysterious, he doesn't talk about his feelings, his job, he doesn't share any of his real thoughts with you – all the things that drove you mad about him before? Is any of that going to change, Ali, now that you're seeing him again?"

"I do know bits about him, Maggie. I know he's ambitious, that he owns his own house and has his mates renting from him, that he owns another house with his brother and rents that out, that he does up cars and sells them on, that he's drop-dead gorgeous. Did I mention that he's drop-dead gorgeous? Maybe he's not so mysterious – maybe he's just busy. Besides, I'm not exactly seeing him yet, Maggie. I just slept with him once and he did a runner."

"Well, what about the Ali Hughes who sat here across the table from me and swore blind that she wouldn't be turned into a helpless female by him or any other man ever again?"

"I'll say it again: I like him. He's different from me. I suppose that's the attraction, that I don't already know him inside out."

"From what you told me so far you'll never know that fella inside out nor ever be anywhere close to it."

"Mags, don't they say great sex is really a meeting of minds? Well, the sex between us is just out of this world so we must have some mind connection going on as well as some body chemistry."

"I'm telling you now, girl, I'll not let you cry on my shoulder if you break up a second time."

"Yes, you will, Maggie. You'll be there for me when I'm ninety and in the old folks' home and fancy some old codger in slippers with half his teeth missing. I'll be after the dirty bastard on the ward who doesn't wash and you'll be trying to convince me to set myself on the auld gent with the bowtie and the clean cuffs. Anyway, who knows, maybe me and Dave O'Connor are destined to be together for life."

"I wouldn't buy the wedding dress yet, Ali girl!"

"Oh, you're just an old cynic, Maggie. Isn't there a single romantic bone in that body of yours?"

"There's plenty of romance in these bones of mine, Ali, but sometimes common sense dictates that you override your instincts."

"Caution to the wind, Maggie, caution to the wind! You should try it some time. That's my advice to you."

"Be it on your own head then, Ali."

Both of them knew they had reached the point where offence might soon be taken, so they stopped with the banter and to lighten the mood began to gossip about celebs and their cellulite instead. Ali stuck her hand into her friend's basket of chips and began to rob some of her greasy fries but it wasn't long before she started to feel queasy. Perhaps she was throwing too much rubbishy food too fast at her recovering digestive system. God, she just wished he'd ring. No woman could stand feeling this way forever.

* * *

Back in the office Pamela was at her desk, finishing off her fruit gorge as part of a five-day detox that she performed on herself each year. Lucy somewhat snidely believed it was a cheap way to cut down on the sandwich bill, "so she can save for the house even faster".

Lucy was beginning to get on Ali's nerves these days. The office kitten was beginning to get work in one or two commercials and had just done a photo shoot for a city-centre recruitment agency. Lucy was in her element, telling them all that it wouldn't be long now till she was out the door with maybe a big part on one of the national TV soaps. While ordinarily Ali would be pleased for her, the little minx was acting up a lot, even getting snotty about taking any incoming calls from their friends if one of them was out of the office.

"You're looking very glum, Ali, what's up?" asked Pamela cheerfully from across the room as she saw Ali, chin on hand, staring past her computer screen.

"Nothing really, Pam. I'm seeing a guy, that's all."

Maggie snorted at her desk behind Ali but she didn't swivel on her chair to look round.

"Maggie doesn't approve, she thinks he's bad for me – that we're not compatible," Ali explained.

"Ooh, what's his star sign?" asked Pam, all eager.

"Scorpio."

"Ooh, the *sex* sign of the zodiac!"

"Me arse!" snorted Lucy. "I've dated some pretty hot Leos."

"Be quiet, Lucy! He'd also be somewhat mysterious," added Pamela. "Like an onion, all layers, you know."

He was that all right, her own private onion. Well, he wasn't going to make her cry, not this time anyhow, she'd be ready for him. Ali laughed as Pamela got into a passion mulling over their compatibility and offering to check their Chinese zodiac signs on the Internet as well.

"Oh, you needn't trouble yourself, Pammy. If he ever produces a ring I'll get you on the case."

Ali tried to concentrate on work, reviewing a questionnaire she had asked Maggie to look over. She noted her friend's comments in the margins that one or two of her questions were too vague and could lead to skewed data. There was nothing for it but to bring some of her positive-thinking flash cards into work: the ones relating to her career and professional ambitions.

It was time to focus on where her life was going in terms of money, prestige, success, getting a life plan together, a savings plan, a pension plan – all the things that really mattered. Men were like buses, her mother always said – there'll be another one coming along in a minute. Well, in Dublin every hour at any rate. Dave O'Connor would just have to wait.

10

The old lady who ran the shorthand and typing part of her course just didn't like her, Ali could tell that from the beginning. It began with the scream Ali had let out of her when she got her little finger trapped under the metal key of the typewriter. No matter that typewriters were dinosaurs in the modern world, the equally prehistoric Miss Leahy had decreed that no student should progress to softer keys until they had spent two classes learning the correct procedure for touch-typing the old-fashioned way. The evening class students had their own theory. Their guess was that the college couldn't cope with the demand for computers and that the prehistoric-typewriters ploy was a means to ease the pressure on the college's tiny computer room. All of them were busy making mental notes about the scathing comments they would write when it came to the end of term 'how was your college experience' survey.

Strapped in by its industrial-strength bra, Miss Leahy's ample chest heaved in anger when Ali pointed out that she had been typing for years and that the whole typing element of the course was pointless. Miss Leahy's dyed black hair had nearly turned white on the spot as she ripped her horn-rimmed glasses from her nose and let them dangle on a chain around her huge and intimidating bosoms.

"Miss Hughes, no doubt some day you'll be conveying something of *amazing* significance from the jungles of South America or the deserts of Africa and, with your own computer by your side, you'll file a completely inaccurate or totally libellous report to your editor. Why – because you have uneven touch. You'll have your fingers on the wrong keys and you'll create some mayhem of catastrophic proportions when you misspell some vitally important word or name. Uneven touch, Miss Hughes!"

The old dear emphasised her point by crashing her hand down on the desk in front of Ali's nose. Christ Almighty, this was worse than being back in secondary school with the nuns! At least then she wasn't paying to be verbally abused – here, she was. It was akin to some sort of sadomasochism.

Hungry, tired and cross, Ali wasn't even looking forward to the half-hour break between lectures. Recent college experience had taught her that she would be sitting in a cold and draughty canteen where the most an evening-class student could hope for was dried-out baked beans, soggy chips or ham, egg and cheese sandwiches with curled-up ends – bowel-clogging white bread only, of course, and a selection of tooth-rotting biscuits, cakes and desserts.

Not only that but the majority of the students didn't seem to be too friendly or normal, at least not to her. Their middle names seemed to be "busy" and "I'm networking, who are you?" If you didn't seem like the kind of person who could directly advance their career, they didn't want to know. Ali was alarmed at just how many were already cold-calling editors looking for work, submitting articles and generally behaving as if they deserved their place in the sun now and not at some vague time in the future. The odd time when she tried to start a conversation she felt that her fellow classmates were very guarded as if they feared someone else would steal their ideas or pinch their contacts.

Breaks were turning out to be cold and lonely so she decided if nobody was going to engage her in conversation she would just spend the time practising the illegible squiggles that were called Gregg's shorthand. It was another class that was run by the old woman in the ironclad bra and for the life of her she didn't know how people were finding the time to get through all their exercises. The shorthand alone – writing six lines of bat, cat, hat and other childlike words – was taking her an age, never mind the more complicated stuff like libel law and, God save us, the correct use of English grammar.

A tiny, smug little voice in her head began its usual pessimistic prattle. *Told you you wouldn't like this course, told you you'd get bored, betcha Big Bastard has another woman already and they're having more fun than you're having now!* Shut up, Head Voice! Ali screamed silently.

It was only October, but already she was beginning to think that Maggie's exercise goals were more interesting than the twice-weekly trek on the bus to the prized journalism course halfway across the city. Maggie was making great progress too on her plan to drop a stone in weight by Christmas, whereas Ali was afraid that the stress of this course was going to end in a marathon dash to the cookie jar and an expanded backside and hips that would put any office-party dress to shame.

There was nothing like a man to help keep the figure in trim, she thought, as she began her shorthand writing in the canteen, huddled up in her coat with a rather rotten sandwich and a powdery cup of coffee. When you were going out with a bloke you thought twice before attacking a packet of chocolate biscuits or devouring several handfuls of crisps before even getting round to making dinner. Then there were all the walks you dragged yourself on in the early days, the loss of appetite as the adrenaline of being in a relationship kicked in. And the sex of course. There was no doubt about it, being in a relationship was cheaper and more fun than going to the gym.

Why wouldn't the bastard ring? Her forehead furrowed deeply and she grated her front tooth against the nail of her thumb in the agitated manner she usually reserved for her monthly bouts of

PMT. Relationships were so bloody complicated.

Her mother and her sister would also be in the snots with her soon if she didn't give them a call. Her mum would be sulking because she would want an apology for Ali's insensitivity about her mid-life career ambitions and Ruth would be prickly if she didn't phone and ask her about the problems that were eating her alive. Why the hell did she always have to be the diplomat? Why the hell did everyone always expect her to pick up the phone first to plead, beg or say sorry? Well, to hell with the lot of them, she thought as she laboured to write the word "cat" for the fortieth time. She needed some fun herself.

* * *

From nine to ten on Saturday morning Ali spent the time looking at her phone and drinking one cup of tea after the other. At ten past ten she finally got up the nerve to lift the handset and deliver the line she had been rehearsing for the last two days, except it didn't come out right.

"Just wondered what you were up to," she said, trying to be cool and sounding awfully needy.

There was an awkward pause down the phone that seemed to last an eternity before he answered.

"I'm actually fixing the dishwasher for the tenants in the other house. Can I ring you back?"

Dave was always working on something – maintaining his property, working on his cars, playing sport or having fun with the lads, for he played just as hard as he worked, plus he was always checking out the actions of Joe Public for potential shifty behaviour because you never ever knew when a job might be going down. He was more exciting than drugs, although Ali would never ever tell him that.

"Okay," she said, trying to maintain her cool, and hung up.

Biting her lip in irritation, she went and made another cup of tea, this time a peppermint one to clear the headache that was already thudding in her forehead.

"Hiya, I was just working on a tricky bit when you rang there," Dave said when he returned her call.

"Oh," was all she could manage to say as she took a mouthful of tea. It was too hot.

"It's good to hear from you – I was thinking about you," he said.

"*Sure*, that's why you've been *busy* ringing me."

"Oh Alison, don't start. How about I just come round, say in about an hour – we could go for a walk."

Half of her wanted to make a sarcastic remark but with huge determination she bit her tongue. "Okay, that would be nice. I'll see you then."

The phone was hardly back in its cradle when Ali was lashing on her make-up and trying on a few outfits in front of the mirror before deciding on a tight top and a well-cut denim skirt that flattered all her lumps and bumps and emphasised the best part of her legs, the curvy bit from the knee down.

"Very nice," he said when he saw her, twirling her around for his benefit. "I'd keep everything the way it is from the waist up, just stick on a pair of trousers and boots or trainers instead. Have you had breakfast?"

Confused, she shook her head. Breakfast hadn't been tackled yet, she'd just had endless cups of tea.

"Good, you can work up an appetite so, burn off some of those resources," he said, eyeing her bum.

Ali was a bit cross at his suggestion. She had already worked up a fine appetite. Growing rumblings in her stomach alerted her to the fact that it was beginning to get grumpy. It wouldn't be long before it started to growl. "Couldn't we at least have a slice of toast or something here first?" she protested.

"No, come on, it's lovely out, real fresh weather. I'll buy you breakfast or maybe even lunch later."

It wasn't lovely out. It was hideous. The wind was mean and she had to keep her head down to avoid the pain of its icy chill. Every so often there was a spit of cold rain falling about her ears, nose and cheeks. He was storming ahead of her like an eager dog on a leash and every so often he stopped to drag her into a faster pace.

"Come on – let's go down by the sea. We'll walk the pier."

Furious, she wriggled away from his grasp to indicate that she didn't relish that amount of pain so early in the morning but he was insistent that she accompany him on his journey. In her opinion, walking the pier was meant to be romantic. Many a time she had eyed the couples, hand in hand or arms around each other's waists, walking the pier at a casual pace, sometimes stopping along the way for a quick kiss. However, this wasn't weather for walking but for snuggling up in a small pub somewhere with a real log fire roaring and a barman who knows your name within ten minutes. Reluctantly she followed his lead. The wind was violent in its outbursts, making the sea a swirl of anger, and the cold hissy rainwater bit at her face and hands with a callous indifference.

At the end of the pier, where there was no shelter from the elements, Dave stopped, stuck his hands deep in his pockets and gazed out at the choppy waters, noting any boats far off in the distance being tossed by the waves. Desperate for a bit of warmth, Ali huddled behind him and tried to use him as a windbreaker. The wind was blowing the smell of urine into her face from the nearby concrete shelter, its stench a nasty reminder of the gangs of weekend drinkers and young fellas fishing who threw their line out to sea for hours at a time, waiting for a bite.

He felt her nudge him, turned and pulled her to him, taking her red-raw hands in his and shoving one in each of his jacket pockets. Then he kissed her while the wind tore at her hair, whipping it round her eyes and nose. The heat of his lips was like a shock compared to the cold pain of the raging elements.

Ali threw her head back and laughed. This was so like him. He didn't want to talk, he didn't want endless conversation about where they were going as a couple or whether they had a relationship at all so he cleverly took her to a place where the wind was screaming and conversation impossible. She smiled, knowing that this silent display of affection was all he was prepared to offer; this was his apology for things gone wrong and this was the start of their relationship again, if she wanted it.

"Right then, fancy brunch?" he asked.

She nodded and allowed him chase her down the pier at a train's pace and into the nearest cosy pub where they ordered homemade soup and sandwiches and pints of Guinness and relaxed in each other's arms and acted like a couple who knew each other inside out and whom everybody expected would be engaged by Christmas.

* * *

In the afternoon he took her for a drive into the nearby garden county of Ireland, Wicklow, with its beautiful mountains, forests, rivers and lakes and he made a show of pretending that he was going to make her climb the Sugarloaf, a modest mountain popular with weekend walkers.

"Sure it's only a small hill, grannies walk it," he teased, getting great mileage out of the look of horror on her face.

He parked his car at a beauty spot, threw a light raincoat on over his jacket and took her up a lonely track, pulling her towards him every so often for a kiss and a quick grope, making Ali collapse into laughter.

He pulled her further and further away from the track and in towards the trees until she asked him was he thinking of doing her in and burying her in the Wicklow mountains. He didn't answer but started to kiss her more roughly and she could feel her cheeks being whipped by small branches as she moved deeper and deeper into the trees and finally collapsed onto the soft carpet of leaves and moss which were surprisingly dry.

Their noses, ears and hands were cold when they touched, but they were overwhelmed by their bodies' warmth and desire for each other. Ali couldn't stop laughing as Dave fumbled around her top, looking for her bra strap and breasts like a teenager on a first expedition, and she felt a thrill as he placed his hand on her stomach and then struggled to slide it between her thighs with all the layers of clothing getting in the way.

With her hand she caressed the soft hair on his neck and felt the strength of his arms all around her, holding her, keeping her warm. Suddenly she froze as she heard twigs crack on the track above her and through gaps in the foliage she could make out the feet and form of a woman walking a dog. The dog, a spaniel, came quite close as he rooted around in the dead winter leaves with his curious snout.

"We're going to be discovered," she whispered, half excitedly and half with dread.

"Then be extra quiet," he warned as he moved inside her slowly and deeply and covered her with long kisses that brought her body close to spasm while she stifled her cries of passion. Feeling the enforced silence like a delicious pain, she was utterly aroused by the chance of discovery as the animal wandered closer and closer.

"Come here now, Caesar!" cried its mistress in annoyance and the dog suddenly gave up its foraging, turned on its heel and broke into a sprint in the direction of its owner.

Dave never once stopped his torturous kissing until he felt her remove the steel grip from around his neck and shudder with complete satisfaction. He lay on top of her for a moment, smiling and picking the odd dried-up leaf from her hair before placing a smattering of small affectionate kisses on her lips.

"That was short and sweet if entirely unexpected," she laughed when he finished. "I'm filthy though and not fit to be seen – you'll have to take me home."

He didn't answer but laid his head on her chest and breathed deeply. Playfully she ran her fingers through his soft hair and nuzzled him and just as she was beginning to feel wonderfully happy she suddenly felt fearful, fearful that she was being too intimate, letting her heart rule her head, setting herself up for pain and an unpredictable relationship once more. Finally, her head overcame her emotions and she decided to be the first to break the stillness.

"You'll have to take me home," she said again more firmly as she pushed him away. She scraped the leaves and moss from her clothes and began the walk back to his car.

"Whatever happened to your car anyway?" he asked as she opened the passenger door and got in.

"Couldn't afford to run it any more and I kept forgetting about the tax. If we'd stayed together you'd have had to arrest me."

"Ah, you're just saying that 'cos you're hoping I'll get out the handcuffs!" Dave smiled mischievously.

"As I was *saying*," she said, pretending his handcuffs comment was too juvenile to respond to, "tax was a problem and then I kept forgetting to sit the driving test – so you see I was a *serial* law-breaker – not a good thing to be if you're constantly under the eye of the law!" She shot him a filthy flirty look and smiled as she put on her seat belt.

"Wow, you're a proper little delinquent – peeing in the street, forgetting about your car tax and now driving without a proper licence – just as well I didn't know you were so easily corruptible when we were seeing each other."

"Why's that?"

"I would have been tempted to corrupt you even more!" He slid a hand between her knees and laughed as she jumped.

She wanted to laugh too but his affection made her fearful. She didn't just want to be his constant on-off lover, wondering whether every encounter with him was the last – until he rang again, until he wasn't busy, until he wanted her.

"So *are* we seeing each other?" she asked slowly.

"Well, we seem to be seeing each other now," he teased.

"That's not a proper answer!" she snapped.

"Jesus, Ali, I don't know. You seem to think you were the only one who got hurt last time round. I'm a bit cautious of you too, you know."

Suddenly feeling on the verge of tears, Ali gazed out the passenger window and concentrated on the grass verges which were whizzing by at speed until eventually they got caught up in Dublin traffic and were forced to slow down to a crawl. The silence was embarrassing and Dave started fiddling with the radio until he got fed up with everything on offer, switched it off, sighed and began to drum his fingertips on the steering wheel. Ali's eyes were still firmly fixed on the window and now her hot tear-filled eyes noted that the greenery was being eroded by concrete pavements and buildings.

Then she felt him touch her knee very softly, and sigh.

"Yeah, okay then," he said, "I suppose we are going out with each other – that is, I'm willing to give it a go if you are."

Behind her eyes she could feel the tears beginning to build and she couldn't look at him. Afraid to speak in case her voice faltered, she continued to look out the window and then she reached for his hand and squeezed it hard in acknowledgement. Her heart was racing with relief, dread and happiness and she thought she recognised this feeling. It was lust, mixed up with hope and nostalgia, and if she let her senses run wild she might even be able to convince herself that she was actually falling in love with Mister Excitement all over again.

11

Karen's new male tenant Dermot answered the phone when she rang. Ali apologised for interrupting his Sunday sports viewing – she could hear the roaring TV commentary in the background. He was terribly affable, assuring her that the game was very dull anyhow and that it was no trouble to fetch her friend to the phone.

"Jesus, Karen, where did you get that guy from? He sounds like the ideal person to share a house with, like he wouldn't complain if you dropped a ton of bricks on his head."

"Isn't he great? Me and the girls found the one man in Ireland who cleans up after himself, pays his rent on time and is no trouble to live with. It's like having a husband around the place except he's actually useful – all we have to do is make sure no other woman gets her hooks into him!"

"Are you doing anything this afternoon?"

"Nope, not a thing except sticking on my laundry. Come on over – if you want we'll grab a takeaway or I have some frozen dinners and pizza in the freezer."

"Great, I'll pick up some wine and some goodies for after."

Thrilled that Karen wasn't heading out on the town or working,

Ali got her coat and her purse, set her house alarm and headed out the door. Her friend was always trying to explain her work hours to her but Ali could never remember if she was working full or half days, or even if she was working days or nights, weekdays or weekends. In truth, she hardly knew how Karen herself remembered, the working practices of nurses sounded so complicated.

Karen was doing some last-minute arranging of washed knickers, socks and other items on the radiator and began to fuss around with mugs and tea when Ali arrived. "You have a certain glow about you," she teased. "Has lover boy phoned?"

"No, I phoned him."

"Oh, Ali!"

"I phoned him and we had more sex, lots of sex in fact. You could say we had a weekend of sex actually."

Abruptly Karen put the clean tea mug in her hand down and her eyes bulged with amazement. "Christ, so have you come here for advice or just to give me a running commentary?"

"I don't know, maybe both. Do you think I was mad to do it with him again, Karen? I know some people might wait and see if they have a relationship first but what's the point in going out with someone only to find out that the sex is terrible?"

"True, true, but you've had sex with him before – you already knew what the sex was like, Ali – remember?"

Ali paused before answering and stirred her tea. "Well, don't you think good sex is an indication of something special – a sign that maybe you're compatible in the first place?"

Karen made a face. "Not necessarily. Sometimes sex is just sex. That needn't be a problem if you're just looking for a bit of fun. Are you having fun?" she asked archly.

"Oh God yeah, I feel wonderful. I feel alive."

"Then what's the problem?" asked Karen as she plonked a packet of chocolate-covered toffee biscuits on the table. "It's nice to have a man on the scene coming up to Christmas – you can always dump him after that if you get bored. Why don't you just go out with him till Christmas and take it from there?"

"What a callous bitch you are! Besides, you seem to think I have the upper hand in this, that I can decide when to start off with him and when to dump him." Ali was already munching through her second biscuit and reaching for a top-up of tea from Karen's stainless-steel pot. "You've seen him, Karen. He's a good-looking guy, he's ambitious, he's never short of cash *and* he's got a sense of humour. How am I supposed to know he hasn't got half a dozen women, and even if he hasn't he could get fed up with me in the morning."

Karen pulled her chair in closer to Ali's, put her arm around her friend's shoulders and gave her a squeeze. "Now, Ali, it sounds to me like you're just having a bit of a crisis in your self-esteem. I'm fed up telling you you're pretty. He may be good-looking but that doesn't mean he's out of your league, that you can't be the one to have him."

"Let's face it, he could have some skinny blonde in the morning with legs up to her armpits."

"Why do you always think *skinny* is better? There are plenty of women who would like a few more curves. Believe me, I'm one of them. Guys don't necessarily want a skinny woman either – there's a lot of truth in that old saying – you know, about it being nice to have a bit of flesh to cuddle up to at night."

"I guess the real problem is I'm not sure if I trust him."

Karen threw her head back and laughed out loud. "Ali, he's a man! Most women are always wondering if they can trust men – trust them to do the shopping, to pick kids up from school, to remember their birthdays. Your guy isn't likely to be much different from the rest."

"But surely you have to trust them not to break your heart? If you don't know if the other person loves you and you love them, then that's too risky. Maybe you're better not to invest all that time and energy in the first place."

Karen lit a cigarette and inhaled deeply. "Now, see, this is why going to bed with someone early on can be bad – you can end up thinking you're falling in love – well, you can if you're a woman. On the other hand I know you, Ali, and know you're not likely to put the brakes on this now, are you? So maybe the best thing you can do is slow things down a bit, maybe not see him so much – you know, be less available."

Ali snorted. "Well, see, that's the other thing. I'm not being that available because he's not exactly Mr Available himself. In fact it's kind of like having a relationship with the Bogey Man – I never know when he's going to show up. He's got so much going on you nearly have to ring his secretary for an appointment – if you know what I mean."

"So he's busy! There's lots of women would give their eye teeth for a man who was busy and ambitious and who just didn't slump in front of the TV every night."

"He *tells* me he's busy."

"So now we're back to the trust thing again. Either way, Ali, the solution is to keep busy yourself – that shouldn't be too hard. You've got a job, a new course, friends. Just don't give him the impression that you have nothing to do but mooch around after him. What does Maggie say about you seeing him again? I *presume* you've told her?"

"Oh Maggie, yes, she knows. It's not so much what Maggie says about Dave as what she doesn't say. I know she thinks if it didn't work out the first time it's not likely to work out the second time. Do you think that's true?"

Karen flicked a long ash onto her saucer and frowned for a minute. "Maybe all you need to change is your attitude. You know, keep busy like I said, stop worrying, just enjoy the time together."

"Easier said than done."

"Of course it isn't. Look, there's a big gang of us from the hospital going on a massive céilí and set-dancing spree to the west of Ireland soon. Why don't you come with us? It'll be great craic and it'll show him you're not dependent on him for a bit of fun."

"Set dancing! Isn't that a bit, I don't know, boring?"

"God, no, Ali, anything but! We're not talking the kind of Irish dancing the nuns used to force us to do once a week in school with girls paired off with each other!"

"Oh yeah, I remember. Hot lesbian action, that was!"

"Don't you know Irish dancing has got real sexy since then? You can't help but laugh and have a good time if you're being twirled around at ninety miles an hour."

"Oh God, Karen, I don't know. Isn't Riverdance a bit passé now? I thought the new thing was salsa, belly dancing, maybe even flamenco?"

"Oh, stop picking holes! It'll be great fun. It's fancy dress as well because it's an early Halloween thing. They do it every year and everyone lets their hair down."

"What will you be going as, then?"

"Oh, as a tarty nurse, what else?" said Karen, sticking her chest out and pulling up her skirt to her thighs in a mock show of how she saw herself.

"Well, I'll think about it."

"Do. Bring Maggie as well if she's around, why don't you? So that's your social life sorted – now all we have to do is think about your career. How's that course of yours going? Are you throwing yourself into it or are you letting this Dave fella distract you there as well?"

Karen rooted in a kitchen drawer for a corkscrew. With a practised air she pulled the cork from the throat of a bottle of red wine to allow it to breathe before dinner. Karen was always thinking of the next meal; it was probably because she was so skinny she hadn't enough reserves to keep going without constant food. It had never been proven, but Karen almost certainly had an unbelievably high metabolic rate.

"Oh, my course – oh, it's not so bad. Well, I'm a bit intimidated by some of them to tell you the truth. They're all so – so focused, so ruthless even – well, at least that's how I see it and I suppose it's not exactly shaping up to be what I thought it would be. I mean, *some* of it's interesting but they're teaching us stuff that I don't think I'll ever use, like how to write headlines for newspapers or how to type for God's sake. I have an assignment due on a sports piece which is such a *waste* of my time." Ali looked up to see her friend grinning at her ear to ear. "What's so funny?"

"Oh Ali, will you *never* learn? Do you know, when we were in school lots of the girls thought I was dead lucky to be your friend. Do you know why? Because *you* were always the one who put huge effort into *everything*. I was always a bit half-arsed but it didn't matter because I had a clever friend I could cog things off."

"So what are you saying?"

"I'm saying, just for once would you ever think smart?"

Slipping off her chair Karen pulled Ali by the arm and opened the door to the living room where the portly, ginger-haired Dermot was deep in concentration watching his football match.

"Derm, who's that playing?" asked Karen bossily.

Dermot told her and then cupped his hands over his plump belly and waited for them to leave.

"Do you mind if we pick your brains for a while," Karen went on. "Ali has to write a sports report for her course and she knows feck all about any sport I can tell you, so we need your help."

Ali blushed crimson as her sporting deficiencies were picked over but there was no stopping Karen when she was in full throttle. Within minutes she had extracted vital if somewhat superficial information from the obliging Dermot about the team, the players, how the game was shaping up and which reports in the next day's paper were the best for reading and cogging. Having shoved the phone pad and pen into Ali's hands, Karen made her take down every word that came out of his mouth.

"Dermie, you're an absolute dote! Would you like me to make you a cup of tea?" said Karen when she felt they had picked his brains clean. Despite his good form, she had worked out that he was getting agitated because he was being forced into a conversation with two annoying women.

"Tea? Yeah, great, thanks." Dermot barely looked at Karen. He was hunched forward in his seat in excitement as he watched the players chase down the field towards the goal.

"Chockie biscuits, Dermot, or would you like a Kit Kat?"

"What? Whatever – great, thanks," he answered although his eyes never moved from the box.

After delivering some consolation tea and a chocolate biscuit to Dermot, Karen closed the living-room door firmly, turned to Ali and asked, "Now, what do you fancy eating?"

"Oh, I'd love a takeaway but I'm watching the cash a bit. Let's say we just have that pizza you were talking about. Do you have any frozen garlic bread as well?"

"I do and just to keep you happy I can throw together a salad with some of my vegetables that need to be used or binned within the next twenty-four hours."

Ali helped her wash and chop the vegetables and make up a French dressing with vinegar and oil as they waited for the pizza to bake in the oven. The carrots were too limp to use and Ali was about to bin them when Karen lurched forward and grabbed them out of her hands.

"Hey, give them here! They'll be fine for my stir-fry tomorrow!"

"But they're limp!"

"Ah but I know how to make them stiff again!" Karen smiled as she savagely chopped off the tapery ends and stuck the butchered bodies in a jar of water.

"Now they'll suck up the water overnight and come tomorrow they'll be *firm* and *useful* again," she said smuttily.

"Karen, you really are a filthy individual. I don't think you ever turn your filth cells off, do you?" asked Ali as she stuck her nose in the oven and saw that the pizza was ready.

"You don't know what it's like. Every day I have to be *nice* to patients, no matter how I feel or how *annoying* they are, so when I'm not at work I have this urge to just go mad, say filthy things and just – go mad."

"Sounds to me like you might have Tourettes."

"Oi – don't you be going around making impromptu diagnoses – that's my area," laughed Karen, placing the deep-pan pizza on a plate and sitting down at the table.

As they munched into the food Ali sighed in satisfaction. Karen was eating with gusto. The cheese was running down her chin and Ali saw her lick a big blob of it from the corner of her mouth and knock back half a glass of wine in one go.

"Here's to us girlfriends!" said Karen, raising her glass. "And remember what I said, Ali – don't fall in love with him – keep some balance in your life."

Ali nodded and raised her glass to Karen. Naturally, she hadn't the nerve to tell her that she felt her life had keeled over since Dave O'Connor had come back into it and that she already felt she was on the path to ruin and insanity.

* * *

It was another Monday morning that Ali felt seriously tempted to pull a sickie but she did a quick mental calculation of the number of days she had been off in the last few months and reluctantly decided against it. Besides, she had already scheduled a meeting between herself and the graphic designer to go and see Dublin's plant hire king, Barney Kennedy, about his new line of trucks and Simon had decided to pencil himself in on her meeting.

The commuter train into work was even more cramped than usual and she was forced to stand the entire way into the city. The woman sitting down in front of her had shifted once or twice in her seat and given Ali the impression that she was about to get off a few stops earlier but she didn't actually stand up until the train pulled into the city-centre station.

Thank God she'd got a late-night taxi home and had refused Karen's offer to stay the night on her sofa again. The body must be getting old. In fact, the thought of wearing the same clothes including her knickers for two days running was enough to make her feel ill. Karen of course would have offered to lend her a pair of clean knickers, but you couldn't get one leg into Karen's knickers, never mind your actual bum, they were so small.

Lucy snared her like a spider when she walked in the door, her face red with excitement. Ali looked around the office and quickly took in that something had changed. There was a hushed air about the place, which was somewhere between death and anticipation.

"He's *gone*! Course you're the last to know!" gasped Lucy in a whisper.

"Who?"

"Little Bastard of course."

"*Simon*? You mean he's been fired?"

"No, not fired."

"He left?"

"He's taken holidays *indefinitely*, phoned in to say so. Awful strained he was on the phone. You could tell he was answering no questions. Joe is right pissed off. He wasn't supposed to be taking any holidays, I'm tellin' you. Anyhow, massive, isn't it? Joe can't be here all the time so we'll have just ourselves in the office without that little toe-rag being anywhere in sight."

Joe's face was purple when he emerged from the office, having been on the phone all morning. He all but barked at Ali that he instead of Simon would be accompanying her to her meeting with Barney Kennedy and she nodded silently in reply.

"I thought that went well," smiled Ali as she slithered into Joe's Jag after devouring some lunch-time tea and sandwiches on Barney's premises.

"*Did* you?" asked Joe shortly. He was still fuming with Simon – Ali could almost hear his angry thoughts rattling around his head.

"Well, he seems happy," she answered with a smile, trying to lighten the mood.

As Joe started the engine her bag slipped, her notebook from the meeting slipped out and his eye was attracted to the strange-looking symbols.

"I noticed when we were talking to him that you were writing down that squiggly stuff. Shorthand, isn't it?"

"Eh . . . yeah . . . I learned it in school. The nuns were very keen that we all left school with some secretarial skills."

"I've never seen you use it before."

"I've just started brushing up on it recently."

For a few minutes he said nothing and Ali didn't feel he was in the mood for conversation. He turned on the wipers and she watched the sudsy water squirt onto the screen and clean away the dust from the glass.

"How's your marketing course going?" he asked abruptly as he manoeuvred his beautiful car around a tight corner.

"Eh . . . fine."

"We must have a chat about what you're learning – see if we can't get some practical use out of it." He checked traffic in his rear-view mirror. "And don't forget to drop in your receipt to the accountants."

"Of course, no problem, will do, the thing is they're so busy in college that they can't issue me one till November – the *end* of November." Ali shot him a beaming smile but inside she felt as sick as if she had just consumed a dodgy Indian and was about to chuck up all over the place.

"Really? Well, if that's what they said."

Ali could see that Joe wasn't really paying her any attention – he was too caught up in driving. Their conversation was probably all going in one ear and out the other. What was her course to him anyhow? It was just peanuts money really. Still her guilty conscience and fear was wearing her down. All of a sudden she was haunted by visions of police stations and handcuffs – but there was no sign of kinky sex or Dave – the visions she was having were the real McCoy. If she was about to be fired or be prosecuted for fraud she had better at least get cracking on that new career she had promised herself before she ended up on the dole, or worse, in prison.

12

The phone rang in her apartment after seven one evening and Ali prayed that it would be *him* at the other end of the line. It wasn't, it was Ruth.

"Have you heard the news?" her sister hissed down the phone.

"No, the folks okay?"

"It's Mum. She's only decided to go and feck off to the Caribbean!"

"Oh, that's nice – are herself and Dad going on a cruise for Christmas?"

"Good God, nothing as normal as that – Dad rang me in a right state. The daft bitch has already gone – she won't be back till the middle of November. What do you think – she's only signed up to do a course run by this *guru* in the Caribbean who tells you how to change your life from the inside out so that you can 'fulfil your greatest potential'. Did you ever hear such shite? It's four weeks – four weeks of colon cleanses, counselling, relaxation, positive affirmations, releasing your inner wisdom, that sort of crap and it costs *thirty* grand! Can you believe it? Thirty grand. That would have knocked some hole in my house extension, I'm telling you. If there's any justice the silly bitch might get blown out to sea in a hurricane!"

Ali sighed. "Ruth, it's their money. You might as well accept it. You and I are never likely to see a penny. Maybe she's just going through some sort of mid-life crisis."

"It's Dad I feel sorry for. I get the impression there was no discussion about this. She just told him she was doing it and that was that. Ali, she's spending our inheritance money like it's going out of fashion and I blame *you*. You really rattled her that day when you said she was never actually in the workforce. Totally put her nose out of joint. She was sulking for days."

"*Me?* For Christ's sake, that's hardly fair! You're making a mountain out of a molehill. Talk to me again when you have calmed down. I'm in no mood for your ranting!" And Ali hung up.

It wasn't giving in this time, she thought as she immediately punched in *his* number. He had rung her since the last time. They just hadn't found time to meet up.

"Can I come round?" she asked as he said hello.

"Sure, if you want. Some of the lads are here though. Wouldn't you rather I came round to see you?"

"No, I'd actually prefer a change of scene. I'll let you drive me home though."

"We'll see how drunk we get first," he laughed.

Immediately Ali hung up and began dismantling her wardrobe, looking for something casual but stylish to wear on the bus-ride over to Dave's.

Sitting on the bus she practised some carefree lines which she hoped would mask her overall feelings of lust and excitement at being in his presence again. As she rounded the corner of his estate, she was met with the familiar sight of Dave's four-bed semi-d with converted garage. It was typical rented accommodation with a small front lawn overrun with grass and weeds, unkempt evergreen bushes and blistering paintwork on the windowsills and door frames. Outside the front door two wheelie bins were stuffed to overflowing, especially the recycling one, which was choked with empty cartons of convenience food.

Inside, the house was as untidy as ever, but today it particularly stank from stale food, drying clothes and sweaty trainers The smell hit Ali as soon as the door opened and as she passed the door of the front room she noticed that there were discarded cartons of Chinese food and tins of beer lying on the floor. The kitchen was worse than she ever remembered, with crumbs all over the table and work surfaces, everything out of cupboards and some nondescript goo engrained into the hob.

"I know this isn't exactly a showhouse but I really think you should teach your lads how to use an extractor fan," said Ali, wrinkling her nose in distaste at the smell of old cooking.

"Ah, I don't like to push it. They pay on time – after that I don't care."

In the sink, plates and dishes were stacked in a pool of greasy water.

"Did your dishwasher break down as well?" asked Ali in growing disgust.

"No, it's just full at the moment. I told you not to come round. This is a blokes' house – we're not into flower arranging."

"Or into using air freshener," said Ali as she noticed the odour of stale cigarette smoke as well.

One of the lads came into the kitchen and switched on the kettle. Then he looked Ali up and down as if he was trying to remember every detail of her appearance. Without a doubt, another guard.

"Larry, Ali here thinks we're all animals, that the place is in a state," said Dave.

"Ah, sure the place is pure shite, sure 'tis," nodded Larry as Dave grabbed Ali by the arm and shoved her out the kitchen door.

Upstairs in Dave's room, Ali pulled off her boots and plonked herself on the bed "Christ, I've always wondered how you manage to kip in this room. It's like sleeping in a laundry basket." A quick overview of the bedroom was enough to confirm that it was bursting with crumpled clothes, particularly socks and slacks, and at the moment there seemed to be no distinction between what was clean and what was dirty. In a corner she caught sight of Dave's dumb bells, almost concealed by a sweaty black singlet. He'd really let his room go to pot, she thought as she took in a pile of newspapers stacked haphazardly at the end of the bed and she pushed them impatiently onto the floor with her foot so she could stretch herself out.

"Hey, I was reading those!" he said, annoyed.

"*You* read business newspapers *and* business supplements?" she said in surprise as she lay on her side and looked at him, her head propped up by a hand.

"Sure I do – it's part of my life plan on how I can retire by the time I'm forty-five."

"What are you talking about, O'Connor? Nobody has a life plan like that – there'd be no point. Life just happens."

"Maybe if you're stupid it does but not to me. By the time I'm forty-five I want to have a string of lucrative rental properties pumping out cash, foreign pads and maybe here as well if prices are right. But picking the right places at the right time – that's the difficult part. At the moment I'm trying to brush up on bonds and precious metals. You've got to keep the money earning money. Only fools actually work for money, Ali. The rich get rich by having their money work for them. So what's your plan?"

Ali's brain didn't know what exactly it had been asked so it did what it could only do: it got her to giggle hysterically. "My life plan, I don't know, only to marry a fella like you, a fella who's gonna be a millionaire in the next few years. Then I won't have to do a thing, will I, only look good, have a few kids, be a cordon bleu chef in the kitchen and a whore in the bedroom – that kind of thing."

"Well, you wouldn't be the first woman to pick that as her life plan," he said as he pulled off her trousers roughly, knocking her off her elbow onto the flat of her back. Then he threw himself on to the bed, boots and all, and snuggled into her. "Of course, the woman I'd marry, I'd expect her to look after herself – you know, not let herself go after having the babies. A woman with an arse like yours," he said, playfully slapping her rump, "would have to go to the gym every day to make sure it wasn't down to her knees by the time she was thirty-five!"

"Is that a marriage proposal then?"

He smiled at her and said nothing.

"Oh, I wouldn't want to marry you anyway," she said archly. "I bet we wouldn't even have a joint bank account. I wouldn't know where any of your money was stashed."

"Rest assured, the woman I marry will know *everything* about my financial dealings. Naturally though, if she ever had an affair or planned to leave me and take the kids I'd have to do her in and bury her in the Dublin Mountains." Pulling her close, he started playing with her hair and biting her lower lip playfully. "Not that I'd have to worry about a woman like you knowing about my financial dealings. You haven't a clue about money."

"All I know is that it runs out too quickly and if I had a better-paid job things might improve," she sighed.

"Well, aren't you planning to be a journo? When does that course finish – after Christmas?"

"Only the first bit, the second part is after Christmas. Do you know, they don't even send you on a work placement! I don't know how I'm going to have time to become a journalist and hunt down stories without chucking in my current job and if I do that I'll starve."

"Sure I'd help you out!"

"Would you?"

"Sure. The next time we're caught in a riot with a bunch of gougers, I'll ring you first. Give you an exclusive you can give the papers."

"Now there's a thought – and maybe between us we can make up a few crime stories as well."

He looked at her in amusement.

"You know, I could make up some crime story about some Dublin underlord who is connected to some other underlord and how they're involved in drugs, prostitution, maybe even human trafficking. Sure the papers don't always use their real names anyway. Maybe we could call one fella 'The Weasel' and the other 'The Goblin' or something. You could help me with the terminology."

"Wow, that's a brilliant idea," he teased back. "Although maybe you should shy away from the outlandish stuff in the beginning. What about your mate who works in casualty? That dark-haired bird I met the night I took you home in the squad car."

"Karen?"

"Yeah – you tell her the first night she's working and a politician shows up with a hamster up his arse, she's to ring you with an exclusive."

They both laughed at the thought as they pulled down the blind on the window and buried their noses under Dave's smelly duvet. Ali could feel bits of biscuit crumbs chafing her bum as she wriggled to get free of a pair of his jeans which were tangled around the sheets. To hell with it, there was no point giving out to him. If he was going to be as rich as he said he was, they could always hire someone to do the cleaning and the laundry. With some paid help taking care of the domestic stuff, she wouldn't have any trouble being a whore in the bedroom seven nights a week. She wrapped her legs tightly around Dave and pushed her hips against his crotch with an alarming hunger.

* * *

The fact that Simon wasn't in the office gave her head some space. Even when he took holidays he usually rang in every day to ask how things were, but now he was positively shying away from giving any details at all to the staff about his mysterious disappearance, to say nothing of his exact global position. Joe was grumpy and in the office a little bit more but mostly he trusted his staff to just get on with things.

As she watched Joe get into his Jag one afternoon, Ali wondered how many rental properties round the world he already had pumping out cash for him, earning money for him while he wasn't actually there. He probably had gold investments too and God knows what else. No wonder the fecker never looked stressed and had time to go jogging while she felt too tired to even think about going to the gym any night of the week. He'd been smart enough to hire clever people and pay them a pittance for being "good employees" and all for the price of a smile, a bit of charm or a few free drinks down the pub on a Friday.

Dave had convinced her that night in his gaff that it was time to take control of her own destiny, to grab the bull by the horns and decide what she wanted out of life. After getting a "free ride" of his own he had the cheek to tell her that there are no free rides in life when she moaned that life plans sounded awfully hard. He'd chided her about her lack of focus, and told her that as no one was going to hand her a microphone or a job in a newsroom, she'd have to make it happen herself. She would too. She had already written out a positive-affirmation card stating as much and had stuck it in her tea cupboard.

Besides, in her new profession she could look glamorous all the time and she could retire in a few years, have the babies and become a Yummy Mummy and trophy wife, married to a millionaire ex-Garda or a nearly-there millionaire at any rate. Until then she'd develop a life where she was constantly busy and not in need of Dave for any emotional support so that he could get on with his plans to become some sort of global magnate by the time he was in his forties.

Finally she had a life plan, she thought smugly as she picked up the phone and rang Karen.

"Do you still have tickets for that Bog Ball dance this weekend?" she asked, referring to Karen's hospital céilí bash.

"You don't need tickets. You just turn up and crash in a hostel. Why? Do you think you'll go?"

"Yeah, why not? I'll check with Mags and get back to you."

Maggie, being a better employee than Ali, was deep in thought as she read a report at her desk with earplugs jammed in for better concentration. Ali leaned back in her swively chair, tapped her on the shoulder and mouthed "kitchen" very deliberately.

"Well, what do you think?" she asked as she stuck the kettle on to boil and plonked her mug on the table, ready and waiting with its teabag.

"Céilí dancing – oh, I don't think so, Ali! I could see how you

Dubs might go for it but for us Muckers, who were reared on it, it's not much of a novelty, girl!"

"Did I hear someone say dancing?" Lucy's curls appeared round the door of the kitchen as she caught a bit of the conversation.

"Oh Lucy, Ali wants me to go on this marathon céilí dancing session with her in the wilds of Mayo this weekend – I wouldn't think it would be your kind of thing."

"I'd love to go!"

"You're taking the piss, aren't you?" said Ali in disbelief. "I mean, don't you have something more fun to do this weekend? I don't know, like hanging out with Bono, getting your hair done, snorting cocaine . . ."

"Bono is an aul' fella, Ali, me hair comes in three styles only – curly, extra curly and like the arse-end of a dog – and I'll have you know I don't do drugs, never have done drugs in fact. I don't think you realise how serious I am about my career. Ever since I was the age of four or five and me da took me to the panto I *knew* I was destined for fame, not like these wannabees you have now who have only just got the notion for it. And drugs, well, drugs is a mug's game and I don't know how you can even imply –"

"All right, all right, I apologise!" Ali threw her hands up in the air in a show of submission. "Come if you want! Personally I think you'll be bored stupid but if the whole office wants to come –"

"The whole office? Ah Jaysus, don't tell us you've gone and asked The Mammy as well," groaned Lucy.

"Eh no, but if you're going I suppose we'll have to. I mean, you know she'll say no anyway because it's bound to clash with something she has on with Tom."

"Ah, here –" Lucy was out the kitchen in a flash, followed by Maggie and Ali who hung around the door of the office and watched Lucy in action as if she was some sort of big shot lawyer intent on immediate answers to very important questions.

"Pammy, do you like céilí dancing?" Lucy interrogated.

Pamela looked up from the satsuma which she was peeling delicately and eating so slowly it was beyond ladylike.

"Well, I've never really thought about it. If I had an hour or two to spare it wouldn't be my first choice of activity but then again –"

"Right – so if there was a céilí dance this weekend you wouldn't be that interested then?"

"Oh, this weekend would be out for definite, Lucy – you see, it's the anniversary of our first kiss and Tom and I are –"

"Grand, Pammy, grand so. Tea? We've the kettle on – back in a sec."

Lucy dragged Maggie and Ali back into the kitchen, just as the kettle started screaming.

"Right, now that I've asked and she's not interested, where and when do we meet?"

"Just a sec, Luce," said Ali. "I don't mean to put you off or anything but it's fancy dress as well. I know someone as shy and retiring as you will find this a bit difficult but you'll have to really put yourself out there, find the actress in you and let yourself go. Do you think you're up to the challenge?"

"Bleedin' bitches! Just you wait! I'll dance youse off the dance floor, I will!"

Ali couldn't stop laughing – a marathon fancy-dress bash in the wilds of County Mayo, three wild women and a bunch of rabid man-eating nurses! Life was beginning to look promising again. Oh yes, Ali Hughes knew where she was going all right. Roll on the life plan!

13

The big hire bus was packed to the brim with dodgy-looking characters en-route to the west for the early Halloween shindig. Ali unwittingly flashed her suspender belt and stockings as she ran across the road to greet a wildly ecstatic Karen who was waving furiously out a window.

"Jaysus, this is just like being back on one of those school tours," wheezed Ali. "Who the hell are you supposed to be anyway?"

Karen was dressed in a tight black dress, zipped down low in front to show off her cleavage.

"Hang on now till I get the extra props."

"Mother of God!" said Ali as Karen slipped on a crucifix and a short black veil.

"Yeah, something like that – you could say the nuns made a very definite impression on me!" Karen gave a devilish smile. "What do you think? Will I get my arse felt tonight?"

"I thought you said you were going as a tarty nurse?"

"Don't be daft! I can hardly go as a nurse when I *work* as a nurse, can I? That's why it's *you* and not *me* wearing that really old nurse's uniform, you twit!" Karen pulled the ring on a can of beer and handed it to her friend with a stiff warning. "Not too much of this stuff, mind. Set-dancing céilí bashes are all about dancing not drinking. Too much beer and you'll miss all the craic."

"Are you sure this is going to be fun?" asked Ali, a little bit concerned that the weekend was going to turn into a damp squib.

"Oh absolutely – dancing is a different kind of a drug in itself," said Karen defiantly.

"It sounds like something the nuns would say," Ali snorted.

"Sounds like something *I* might say," said Lucy as she plonked down beside them dressed in black leggings, fingerless lace gloves, netting in her comb-backed hair, a pink ra-ra skirt and a lacy bra over a sexy top. "Madonna," she said, seeing their confused looks. "The early years of course – she's me heroine, she is, a real bleedin' icon – if I could have a career as long as hers I'd be well happy, I would." Lucy got it all out in one breath and Ali and Karen nodded with the reverence that Lucy expected whenever the subject of her own career was mentioned.

Maggie wasn't long turning up – as a Spanish gypsy, which Karen said was cheating really, considering she looked so Spanish as it was.

As the driver pulled out of Dublin's inner city, Friday-evening commuters waved at the busload of panto dames, trollops and dolly birds of both sexes, who were heading west for a weekend of boisterous behaviour on the sand dunes of the Atlantic coast.

It was just like being back in school again as the big engine chugged along and the miles of roadway slid by but instead of stupid bus songs the air rang out to the noise of tapping feet, accordions, tin whistles and bodhráns as the hospital revellers geared up for an all-night hooley.

"So are there any doctors on this bus? My dear departed mother, her that has fecked off to the Caribbean, would be 'delighted an' excited' if I met a doctor at a respectable hospital dance," laughed Ali as she got stuck into her second can of beer.

"There are but you'd be better off staying well away. They all think they're God's gift and that nurses are something you scrape off your shoes," snorted Karen with a toss of her veil. "But if you're looking for a medical man we've got technicians, radiographers and physicists on board amongst others. Not that I would fancy going out with someone from the hospital. There's also a few heads here from the Wednesday-night set-dancing crowd that I meet now and again, teachers most of them, but what keeps things interesting about these hooleys down the country is that there's always a few dark horses who wander in for the night. Locals – big-shouldered, hot-lipped fellas of few words who'll be down from the mountains. And, as Elvis says, 'a little less conversation, a little more action' is fine by me. That's where I'm hoping I'll get my shift tonight, girls – a nice young mountainy man!" Karen winked lewdly.

"You're sex mad *and* dangerous, you are," said Lucy as she glared at a 'priest' across the aisle who was eyeing up her cleavage.

"Oh, tell me about it!" Ali groaned, rolling her eyes. "I learned everything I know about sex from Karen. Wasn't she the first one to bring her mother's tampons into primary school and all and scare the living daylights out of a whole class of eleven-year-olds!"

"Oh, now, you needn't be giving me a hard time just because I was showing an interest in medical matters from an early age," said Karen.

"Ah sure, we figured out everything we needed to know from the cows," joined in Maggie, totally deadpan.

Stupid conversation and great music made the ride to the rugged landscape of the west an effortless affair. Only half an hour into the journey Ali and co got the munchies and began to scoff a huge bag of egg-and-raw-onion sandwiches that Karen had buttered up that day.

"Do you remember, Ali?" said Karen. "How me mammy always made me 'smelly sambos' for the school tours when we were kids?"

"Fuck, who would have known they go so well with beer," said Ali as she munched through her third one. It wasn't long before the vile smell of burped egg-and-onion sandwiches was choking the air down the back of the bus.

"Ever so unladylike," said Karen as Ali produced another ear-shattering smelly burp.

* * *

The hostel reminded Ali of her jaunt straight after college when she had gone travelling on a J1 visa with Maggie and a few others down the east coast of America.

"Do you remember the last time we were together in a hostel, Mags? There was a hurricane brewing just off the coast of Miami."

"My mother was saying novenas," said Maggie. "I remember being a nervous wreck when that Italian waiter told me the planes had stopped taking off from the airports. What was his name again, Ali? He took a shine to you and your 'Irish freckles'."

"Roberto. I remember he scared the shit out of me one day by telling me there'd been a shark attack on South Beach and then he tried to wrestle my bikini top off in the waves."

"Oh yeah, I remember. Well, thank God the 'bashtard wind' swung back out to the Caribbean at the last minute." Maggie checked her reflection in the mirror, topped up her lip-gloss and adjusted her black curls so that her large gold-hooped gypsy earrings were even more obvious.

"Wind, wind, the only wind tonight will be from all the fartin' after youse three eating all them egg-and-onion sandwiches," quipped Lucy as she finished painting her nails black.

"Right, give us a look at you ladies!" said bossy Nurse Karen as she adjusted Maggie's Spanish blouse until her milk jugs nearly fell out. "I just want to see that you all look like brazen hussies. Not bad, not bad, except you could all do with showing a bit more cleavage."

"Fantastic. Let's go and kick up some dust!" said Karen with a flounce of her veil.

* * *

The bar was just beside the wooden dance floor and it was peculiar to take in the sight of barmen pouring ferociously expensive pint glasses of fizzy orange and lemonade, which were knocked back by sweaty dancers in seconds. Everyone probably had one real drink to begin with but that was about it. You didn't exactly need to get too tipsy when you were chatting up blokes dressed as Wonder Woman or as the Mother Superior.

Charlie's Angels, ballerinas and panto dames also abounded, and that was just the men. Everybody felt outrageous and not for the first time Ali noticed that men, even so-called heterosexual ones, seemed to thoroughly enjoy dressing up as girls, placing particular emphasis on the stockings, heels, outlandish make-up and doing "handbag dances" in the middle of the dance floor.

"You look familiar," said a guy dressed in a tutu, pink tights and black brogues as he leaned into Ali at the bar.

"Oh, that's because I'm a weather babe from RTÉ *and* I'm a former Miss Ireland as well," she said, smugly grinning from ear to ear.

"I'm Ireland's youngest plastic surgeon myself," said the baby-faced ballerina.

"Right, it's obviously a night for telling porkies so."

"Wanna dance?"

"Ah no, I couldn't. I don't do this kind of thing on a regular basis," Ali shyly explained. "I mean, I learnt a few steps in school once but I don't know if I can remember them."

"Oh, for God's sake, it's not exactly synchronised swimming! It's just about getting pulled around the place and throwing a few well-aimed kicks into the bargain," said Nureyev as he took her drink from her and dragged her by the hand.

Before she knew it, Ali was being twirled around so fast she could have been in a fairground, being pushed and shoved from one pair of big hands to another, forming lines in and out, kicking, stamping feet, joining hands and generally behaving like one confused cow in a stampede of cattle.

Two dances later and a hot and sweaty Ali was being propped up by her friends and gasping at the bar for pint glasses of tap water instead of pints of Guinness.

"Will you look at those lads over there – aren't they gas with their 70's nylon shirts and ties and their hair greased back with Brylcreem," Ali said after she had recovered enough to spit out an entire sentence without wheezing.

"They're not part of the fancy-dress crowd. They're some of the mountainy men down for the night to see the talent," said Karen in a hush.

"Christ Almighty! You're kidding me – nobody still has clothes like that in their wardrobe!"

"Oh, some of the old country lads would, especially if they never threw them out in the first place," said Maggie knowingly. "They've probably had those rig-outs for the last twenty-five years. Sure look at the age of them, fifty plus if they're a day."

"*You* said they'd all be young studs from the hills," hissed Ali at Karen, making the mistake of returning a smile from one of the middle-aged hillbillies who was staring in her direction.

"Oh Jesus, would you credit it! It only looks like Ali has gone and pulled one of the old codgers," laughed Maggie as a sweaty nylon shirt crossed the floor in their direction and announced itself as Dennis.

"Are ye all from Dublin, girls?" the gap-toothed Dennis asked as his opening line.

They all replied in the affirmative and you could see the smile break out on the little man's face as he reasoned that they would all be good-time girls so, experienced no doubt and into all sorts of debauched behaviour.

"So are you a proper nurse then or are you just dressed up for the night?" Dennis asked with a nervous laugh as he took in Ali's outrageous costume. His little piggy eyes were firmly glued to her ample chest and her black bra showing underneath.

"To tell you the truth, Dennis, I'm actually a very special kind of nurse who deals exclusively with people's sex bits," said Ali authoritatively and with a hint of badness. "In fact I work with one of Dublin's *leading* plastic surgeons."

"Are those yokes for real then?" he asked with a guffaw,

gesturing at Ali's heaving bosoms, which were even more impressive than normal as they fought to get free of her Wonderbra.

"Oh no, not at all – these represent some of my boss's, Doctor McCarthy's, best work in progress – he handles them *personally*, you know. Well, you've got to look the part for the patients, Dennis. In actual fact we're doing a roaring trade in penile extensions right now. If you mention my name at the surgery I'm sure we could *cut* you a good deal if you're interested!"

"Oh God, I wouldn't know about that," he said, spluttering some stout all over his psychedelic shirt. "Sure how would I be able to drive my tractor if I had one of those extension jobs?"

"You drive a tractor?" asked Karen in her poshest accent.

"Oh Jaysus, take it everywhere! Isn't that how I got here tonight?"

"And what's the top speed you can get out of a set of wheels like that, Granddad?" Lucy asked in mock earnestness.

"Oh, you'd be surprised what that baby can do," said Dennis as he eyed Lucy's slim legs up and down and copped a feel of her firm thighs with one of his sweaty hands before she clocked him one.

"Well, aren't you a dirty bastard testing the morals and the intellect of my poor city friends – tractor indeed!" said Maggie in her thickest country accent as she swept Lucy and Ali away from the groper and roped them into the start of *The Walls of Limerick*.

Karen started to make faces over Dennis's shoulder, pretending that she desperately wanted to be rescued as well, although she looked like she was getting great mileage out of her conversation, especially as one of Dennis's friends had joined in the craic.

"Oh, sure we'll leave her where she is! Isn't she a dirty bitch anyway and well up to the challenge?" laughed Ali.

At half four in the morning the hardcore hooley dancers were still at the stamping and whooping and naturally Lucy had become the star of the show with her energetic enthusiasm, amazing flexibility and her mock-lesbian talents, but the majority of the crowd had retired to the nearby lounge area and were singing traditional Irish songs from around the regions, a loud cheer going up when any particular county got a mention.

"I love this song," whispered Karen hoarsely as someone sang a moving rendition of *Raglan Road* and then Maggie made a fair stab at *The Lonely Woods of Upton*. The tapping feet of the musicians were infectious as they played their instruments with obvious love, pints of drink almost untouched at their feet as they swooned to their own music.

Close to six, only those with matchsticks propping open their eyes were still in the lounge drinking and listening, and surprisingly the normally hyperactive Karen and the irrepressible Lucy were the first to make their excuses and crawl into their bunks.

Maggie, being from the country, laughed when it was suggested to her that it was getting late. "Down home sure we'd only be getting going," she said with a nod and a wink.

As the mood mellowed a nearby panto dame, with rosy-red cheeks streaked with dirt and perspiration and his wig of blonde curls askew, picked up the guitar and started to strum out a soft classical tune, smiling from time to time in Ali's direction.

"I recognise this. Where have I heard it before?" asked Maggie.

"Sshh, it's the theme song from *The Godfather* – Al Pacino's son plays it on guitar in *The Godfather 3* when he goes to Sicily."

"You certainly know your gangster films, girl."

"Shut up, you're ruining it," said Ali.

Closing her eyes, she lost herself in the beautiful music being strummed by the long slender hands of the strange-looking guitarist who was still smiling at her.

"I could make long passionate love to a man who played me songs like that," mused Ali as she closed the door to the room where Lucy and Karen were already snoring in unison.

Maggie wasn't listening – she was so tired that she just about pulled off her shoes and fell into the bed.

"Well, I could," said Ali sleepily. "I wonder who he was? Karen might have known if she'd been there."

In her dreams Ali became the impossibly beautiful wife of Al

Pacino, except in her version of the film she didn't get blown up by a car bomb but got to make mad passionate love to the young Pacino forever.

Still revelling in her fantasy the next day as the bus pulled out for the capital, Ali realised she'd spent the entire weekend trying to forget all about Dave, and had almost succeeded, but as the big bus chugged its way nosily back towards the city she could think only of the one man who had got her own motor running. Mother of God, she really had to do something about this sex drive of hers – its ferocity was getting to be embarrassing.

14

It was still days away from Halloween but the city was bustling for Christmas everywhere one turned. For God's sake, couldn't the traders wait, Ali thought as she struggled with her umbrella which had developed a life of its own. Damn work. Knowing her luck, Little Bastard might even be back from wherever he had disappeared to over the last few weeks. Maybe not exactly full of sunshine, but energised no doubt from his break and even more full than ever of his own self-importance.

Ali was still fighting with her umbrella and muttering to herself when she had the pleasure of seeing her feet lifted from under her and feeling her bum take flight with the force of an unknown impact. Suddenly she was lying on the wet ground on the flat of her back, totally winded, with a crowd of onlookers peering into her astonished face. Their collected umbrellas formed a kind of tent around her and she felt like some sort of freak being scrutinised at the fairground.

"*Jaysus*, that must have hurt," she heard an aul' wan in a headscarf mutter as she towered over Ali's paralysed form and shook her head slowly.

"Do you think you might need an ambulance, love?" a middle-aged man in a dirty camel coat and too-short trousers asked excitedly.

"I don't think she's half as bad as the poor fella who hit her – he looks like he's having a heart attack altogether," said another annoying accident groupie who was gesturing in the direction of a winded old-age pensioner in crumpled clothes leaning against his offending moped. The old codger was drawing his own sideshow and the most annoying accident buffs were drifting between Ali and him, trying to decide which of the two was the most exciting.

"Sure we'll get her an ambulance anyway," decided the aul' wan. "Do you have a phone in your handbag, love?"

"I do, but it's not charged up," Ali apologised. "Look, I'm sure it's not necessary to get me an ambulance. I don't think I'm that bad and anyway my boss will kill me if I don't show up for work. I'm sure I'm fine."

With monumental effort Ali sat up in the middle of the road and screamed a scream of pure hell as pain ripped through her lower back. She was then in a dilemma as to whether to try and lie back down again or to try and stand up – either option seemed terrifying and she was surprised she was thinking so much, considering she had just been mowed down.

"Take it easy, sweetheart. Don't be in a rush to look too good. Think of the compo," whispered the middle-aged bloke in her ear.

Ali was horrified at his suggestion but she didn't have any time to be indignant as the ambulance arrived at high speed and its mere presence was a signal to many that the morning drama was over.

A flustered Ali apologised to the handsome forty-something ambulance man who came to her side. "I'm sure you have more important things to do," she said. "I think I might even be all right. I'm probably just a bit bruised."

"Oh now, love, since we're here I think you should get into the ambulance anyway and be done with it. Believe me, I've seen people walk around on broken legs after an accident. You don't really know you're okay till you've been checked out by the doctors and nurses." He spoke to Ali gently like one would do to a sick child who was protesting against taking any medicine. "Now just fall back into this stretcher here and we'll belt you up. That's great. Good girl. We'll have you at the hospital in no time."

* * *

Clutching her handbag for what seemed like an eternity – she'd read somewhere that hospitals were full of opportunistic criminals – Ali lay strapped to the rigid board until someone finally came to talk to her. She'd barely had time to state what had happened to her and where she'd been injured when the white coat disappeared and left her wondering if he was likely to return any time soon. After all, the mere fact that she could talk was probably an indication that she didn't need any medical attention for another few days at least.

The intense electric lights in casualty were beaming down into her face, hurting her eyes, and she might as well have been a speck of dust as she lay there strapped to her board desperately trying to catch the eye of anyone who was passing. It wasn't long before she got the feeling that these doctors and nurses were skilled in the art of not making eye contact, particularly with people whose state of consciousness was in itself a sure sign of their being malingerers.

Panic took over as more than an hour slipped by and Ali realised that she was powerless to move, powerless to be heard and stuck to a heavy-duty plastic board for as long as these medical people deemed necessary. Christ, this must be what it was like to be in a coma or be operated on when the anaesthetic hadn't worked, she thought.

Would these medical people notice if she died or started to suffer from severe dehydration due to neglect? It wasn't looking very likely. They were practically exhibiting signs of attention-deficit disorder when it came to answering any of Ali's increasingly loud "Excuse me's!" Sure it wasn't entirely implausible that she could choke to death on a lump of phlegm and wouldn't be able to sit upright to clear her lungs, or maybe she'd have a coughing fit and wouldn't be able to breathe and would asphyxiate on the spot. What if she needed to go to the loo and she lying there completely powerless?

All she wanted was for these bastards to contact a friend or relative so that there would at least be someone reliable by her side to fight on her behalf, should it look like her vital signs were going down the tubes. Why, oh why had she let her mobile power down?

Then she saw him, like Lawrence of Arabia: a distant white-coated figure approaching down the long corridors, a slow-moving form which seemed in complete contrast to the hurrying figures of these antlike medical personnel, a body which was taking its time meandering through life amongst all the madness. He was taking casual sips from a bottle of mineral water as his long slender legs approached her trolley.

Something told Ali that she must communicate with this individual, tell him her name at least so that he could contact Karen or Dave or her family and friends before she expired on the spot. If she stared at him long enough he just might return her gaze. It was worth a shot. *Look at me, look at me*, she tried to telepathically communicate with him as he replaced the cap on his bottle of water while walking hypnotically in her direction.

"Help me, please help me!" she cried in the loudest whisper she could summon as his figure just drew level with her accident trolley.

He looked stunned for a minute, as if some unseen ghost had just communicated with him from out of the blue.

"Please help me! I've been stuck on this trolley for nearly two hours and nobody will talk to me and there will be people who will be terribly worried about me, who don't know I'm even here!" protested Ali in a breathless rush.

For a moment she wondered if he was foreign and unable to speak English. He was right over her now, staring down at her somewhat benignly but puzzled. His piercing blue eyes seemed to be scanning her panicked face for information. His fair eyebrows knitted together and she saw him run one hand through his mass of long fair curls, as if he was troubled by her very presence.

"My friend works here, she's a nurse," said Ali. "She's not working today but she doesn't live far away. I just need someone to call her, see? Would you call her if I gave you her number?"

She was just about to give her pigeon French and German a shot when his face broke into a smile.

"I know you," he said suddenly.

Jesus – now wasn't the time for her to run into someone she had obviously met around town and probably in a drunken state. She hoped to God whoever he was and whenever she had met him she had been nice to him in any sense of the word.

"Yes, you went céilí dancing with the hospital crowd. You were dressed up as a nurse."

"Are you a doctor then?" Ali asked, somewhat relieved. Maybe this guy could make a quick diagnosis and discharge her with the minimum of fuss.

"Well, yes, I am a doctor actually."

"Oh good. Look, I have just a bit of pain in my back and my thumb is really sore. Will I need X-rays? Do you think maybe I could leave soon?"

His puzzled look returned. "I couldn't possibly say."

"But I thought you were a doctor?"

"I am. I'm a medical scientist."

"Is that the same thing as a medical doctor?"

"No."

"Well, what do you do around here then?"

"Well, I analyse blood in the lab but sometimes I'm out and about testing blood-glucose equipment or maybe having a look at the blood/gas analyser . . ."

Ali was beginning to feel quite cross but still, sensing that she should be nice to this boffin, she smiled at him sweetly, rattled off Karen's number and begged him to ring her immediately or at least as soon as possible.

"Aren't you going to write her number down?" she yelled after him as he began to disappear back into mirage status.

"No need, I've memorised it," he called back to her.

Certain that no help would ever come and that the twit wouldn't remember Karen's number when it came time to dialling it, Ali closed her eyes and folded her hands on her chest over her handbag. Thank God hospital environments were always hot and made one feel perpetually thirsty. It was the only thing that might save her bladder from bursting at any minute.

* * *

When she next looked up she saw Karen panting over her, hardly able to breathe from running down the corridor to get to her. Also present was a very cross-looking Ruth who was biting her lower lip in irritation.

"Oh thank God! Your jaw's all right anyway!" Karen sighed deeply in the greatest relief.

"Of course my jaw's all right. What the hell are you on about?"

"Oh well, when they rang me to tell me you were in a traffic accident and couldn't speak, I just ran out the house. I thought you couldn't talk because your jaw was broken and they deliberately weren't telling me over the phone in case I panicked."

"Well, it looks like you've worked yourself up into a sweat for nothing. I couldn't speak to you myself because I was strapped to a board, you twit! Jesus, Karen, I thought of all people you were most likely to be a cool head – what with you being a nurse!"

"Oh Ali, it's not the same when it's someone you know and I knew you'd recently given up your health insurance and I wondered who would operate on you and would they do a good job."

"So, you're all right then, Ali?" Ruth asked tersely, ignoring Karen's rant.

"I don't know. I haven't been seen yet. Well, I'm obviously not about to die if that's what you mean. What are you doing here anyway? I didn't ask anyone to contact you."

"Karen, having decided in her professional capacity that you were obviously at death's door, thought she should break the news to a family member. I've been dragged out of school to rush to your side and you don't even look like you have as much as a scratch on you. Jesus, Ali, I thought you were old enough now to cross the road by yourself *without* getting knocked down!"

Karen blushed a bit and at least had the decency to look a bit sheepish, as if acknowledging that she might have overreacted by calling in the cavalry in the form of Ruth. Ali didn't really like her older sister knowing any of her business unnecessarily.

"I'm really sorry, Ruth, okay?" said Ali. "But it's not as if I've just pulled a big spoof on you. I have *genuinely* been injured, you know."

"Oh, she has – that wrist is definitely broken," Karen said authoritatively.

"It is?" said Ali in amazement. "It only hurts a little. I thought it might be sprained – but broken, are you sure?"

"Definitely – it'll be in a cast for four weeks minimum – you'd better take off your rings."

Karen had slipped back into nursey mode and Ali felt relieved that someone was taking care of her.

* * *

When Ali was finally seen by a doctor, her wrist was indeed encased in plaster and she was given a neck brace because of soft-tissue damage to her neck and back. Then she was discharged with some painkillers.

Outside in the car a very cross Ruth decided that Ali couldn't return to her apartment and that she had better sleep in her spare bed in her tiny three-bed house for the next few nights. "We'll throw the two boys in together even though they'll probably kill each other. Christ, it's almost as if you *knew* to have an accident when I'd be getting my holidays!" she said in irritation as she lit a cigarette in her car, causing Ali to develop a throbbing headache.

As they drove Ali was tempted to think that her sister was deliberately braking late at traffic lights to cause her maximum discomfort as her neck jerked but she kept her mouth shut and didn't complain.

"Well, don't think I'm going to mammy you – there'll be no chicken soup," Ruth continued to rant as she almost dragged Ali out of the car and frogmarched her into the house. "And what's this about you not having any private health insurance?"

"Considering the state of our health service, would it make any difference anyway?" protested Ali and a torrent of abuse followed. The little sister withered inside as she got the schoolteacher dressing-down complete with bossy tones. It was with relief that she squashed herself into her nephew's child-sized bed where she prayed that the painkillers would knock her out cold till morning.

* * *

In the morning she awoke screaming, much to Ruth's consternation, as she realised that her neck had locked and she couldn't even get it off the pillow.

With her sister's help, an inflexible Ali rolled out of bed.

"Feck it altogether – it looks like I'll have my work cut out for me looking after you," snorted Ruth as she reluctantly tried to make Ali comfortable in the bed by bundling a pile of pillows under her neck.

Dave came to visit, but only once on Ali's insistence. For Ali didn't relish her sister knowing her dating habits and it felt weird to be groped by your boyfriend while lying helpless in your nephew's single bed surrounded by pictures of *Batman*. Dave attempted a quick fondle to put her in better sorts but she was in so much pain she couldn't manage more than a childish kiss on the lips in return, even though her body was aching for his touch just as much as it was aching from the accident. Then she couldn't stop laughing as she tried to snog him and her giggling left her in spasms of pain which ironically set her off laughing again so she was forced to throw him out the door within half an hour in case his visit landed her back in hospital.

"So you're seeing a guard," said Ruth smugly as she helped Ali downstairs to watch some much-needed TV.

"Evidently."

"Well, I suppose it's nice to have a bit of rough," Ruth sighed, throwing a glance towards her slippered husband reading a book in the corner of the living room with his glasses perched on his nose.

Gerry was hardly the picture of excitement. In the few days that Ali had stayed with her sister and brother-in-law, she had learned that Gerry's socks rarely matched and that his feet often smelled and that married couples with children hardly said two words to each other at a time and when they did complete sentences they usually came dripping with venom. It was enough to make Ali consider going to her dad's to be nurtured – he'd offered to now that Julie had gone AWOL, but Ali turned him down, thinking he just might kill her with kindness.

"Your fella drives a nice car too."

"Oh, I hardly know what he drives – he seems to change it by the week," yawned Ali, being deliberately malicious.

"An exciting man so," said Ruth snidely.

"Absolutely *and* he's terrific in the sack," said Ali as a means of deterring her sister's snide remarks once and for all, although she felt a bit bad afterwards as Ruth genuinely looked more than a bit hurt. It probably was hard to feel romantic when both you and your partner were working and had two young excitable boys to feed, bath and scold every minute of the day.

Seeing her sister's worn-out face, Ali made a mental note not to get married, or at least to get her tubes tied first so that she wouldn't be tempted to see what her genetic material would look like when it came out in the wash with some future mate. Part of her felt sorry for her big sister, lost these days in the role of mammy, wife and general drudge. Ali vaguely remembered that Ruth used to be fun but all of that had changed with the arrival of the two brat nephews.

At that moment the two brat nephews ran into the kitchen screaming and tugging a toy which both claimed to be sole owners of. Conor let go at the last minute, leaving his brother to crash into Ruth and causing her to knock warm tea down the front of her top. Ali was sure Ruth was about to flip the lid but instead she saw her sister fight back the tears.

Christ, going back to her one-bedroomed apartment, even if she had to fend for herself, was preferable to living in this cuckoo's nest! She decided her body was going home, even if she had to get there by will power alone.

15

Turning down the volume of her TV set, Ali let the picture illuminate the room as she took Karen's call. The old Doris Day film she was watching was nostalgic heaven, but her injuries were still niggling and she couldn't get herself comfortable on the couch, not for all the pillows and cushions in the world even when they were propped up in all sorts of outlandish positions.

"I'm on a break, how ya doin, buddy?" Karen chirped down the phone line.

Munching on her fourth chocolate biscuit in succession Ali could only manage a half-intelligible mumble. "Uhm, well, you know the way you fantasise about staying off work when you're sick but still well enough to eat chocolate and ice-cream and watch TV at the same time?"

"Yeah . . ."

"Well, the fantasy isn't much good when you're in pain."

"Oh, if it's only pain that's bothering you maybe I could get you something a bit stronger for the next few days."

"Spirits would be good. Listen, I'd settle for some vodka if you're thinking of coming round. Maybe you could just pour it straight into the chicken soup that I know you're probably making for me at this very moment."

"Sorry. No time for chicken soup unless you want me to grab you some from the hospital trolley on one of the wards."

"And to think as a taxpayer I'm paying your wages!"

"You don't *earn* enough to pay my wages and stop trying to make me feel bad. I feel bad enough as it is what with arriving into casualty like an eejit and dragging your sister there unnecessarily . . . "

"*And* telling her I had no health insurance. Do you know how much bossy-big-sister lecturing that cost me?" snapped Ali as she turned the TV to mute and juggled the phone from ear to ear in an attempt to ease her aching neck.

"Sorry about that but to be perfectly honest I think you should have kept your health insurance."

"Oh, for God's sake, I'll take my chance! I'm healthy, I'm young, bar this minor incident I'll never be in sight of a hospital again any time soon unless of course I get preggers and that is *never* gonna happen."

"Pregnant – oh, believe me that is the one time you'd *definitely* want to go private – I heard this story once of a young wan whose entire vagina was stitched up by mistake after delivery and –"

"Karen, will you ever shut up with your horror stories and leave off about the health insurance? I really can't afford it. Did you ring just to give out or do you have any consoling words for your bruised and battered friend?"

"Excuse me! I was ringing to give you some good news actually. Something that will help you in your future career as a journalist no less – well, it might, I'm not guaranteeing anything, mind."

"Let me guess – you've sleeping with a top-notch plastic surgeon who is willing to do some work on your best friend at knock-down prices. This would be good because I think I'm going to need some sort of a radical makeover if I'm to compete with these birds off the TV," moaned Ali as she flicked through some of the 24-hour news channels with the sound still off.

"Shut up and listen, will you? When I was working today this guy came in looking for a tetanus – apparently he's a well-known photographer. Well, he was caught up in a bit of a riot with a yobbo and a dog and he got bit on the thumb, wasn't exactly sure which species did the damage, and I just *happened* to tell him that my best friend was trying to become a journalist and didn't he give me the name of some newspaper editor and said you could use his name to ring up and see him! He said this fella would be willing to go through a few ideas with you if you mentioned his name."

Ali could nearly feel the excited glow coming down the line.

"Well, amn't I brilliant, getting you your first job and all?"

"Is there *actually* a job involved or am I just to turn up and meet this guy so I can dig up a few ideas that he might pinch?"

"Jesus, Ali, don't be so cynical! It's a possible foot in the door, isn't it?"

Rearranging her cushions, Ali switched the sound of the TV on again to get the headline update on one of the satellite news channels and all at once she felt tearful and began to sniffle a little down the phone.

"Hey, Ali, what's up with you?"

"I'm just watching the news and all these women are just so beautiful – not a hair out of place, mad white teeth, perfect make-up, lovely clothes – I don't think I could ever compete with them. I know I've got the brains naturally –"

"Probably."

"But my eyes aren't as big as theirs and my nose is way too big and even in the newspapers now they show pictures of journalists and they're all dead attractive."

"Couldn't you become a war correspondent? Nobody would care what you looked like so long as you were mad enough to dodge a few bullets."

"Are you insane? They're *all* good-looking and brave and articulate and they have a 'fuck-off attitude' that you just couldn't put on!" Ali wailed.

Ali heard Karen take a sharp breath in, the way she did when she was trying to analyse a situation before coming out with something reassuring if somewhat implausible.

"Sounds to me like you've got post-traumatic stress syndrome. Look, calm down for Christ's sake. I'll come over after work but I'm not bringing any vodka – you sound depressed enough as it is."

"Will you bring chocolate?" sniffed Ali.

"I thought you wanted to be as good-looking as the women on TV? If you keep eating chocolate you'll get a flabby arse and fat thighs."

Ali started to cry again and made big snorty sobs down the phone line.

"Okay, okay, I'll bring the chocolate."

"Big sizes?"

"All right – if you must – I'll even bring ice-cream."

"Well, don't expect me to share. I'm depressed *and* in pain."

"Oh for God's sake, I'll bring a whole tub just for you!"

"I love you, Karen."

"Why wouldn't you? I'm fucking marvellous, I am."

* * *

Things seemed to brighten up once Karen called round, stocked up the fridge, tidied the apartment and told Ali that her high-sugar diet of recent days was probably adding to her crying bouts. There was even a medical reason for Ali feeling madder in the head than usual as apparently a near-brush with death could take a few days to get through to the brain. In the simplest layman's terms Karen explained that Ali's brain was shocked at her body's recent trauma, and in a delayed reaction was having a mini nervous breakdown for itself. Her blubbering and madness would last until the brain finally learned to accept the awful near-death experience.

"Jaysus," said Ali out loud as she hooked another chocolate fish out of her Phish Food ice-cream with her spoon. Karen's pseudo-medical explanations were always riveting, especially when they could explain why life was going pear-shaped at any one time.

Sugar overload, PMT, pheromones, toxin-induced cellulite, Karen knew them all and about their effects on the body and the mind but this Post Traumatic Stress thing was even better – it even kind of made Ali feel a bit special. She couldn't wait to tell a few people that she was suffering from temporary insanity. After all, it was okay to admit that you were mad if you were able to stress its fleeting nature.

"And you *seriously* think all those anchor women on the TV news, although admittedly fabulous of face, have big arses just like me?"

"Of course," Karen nodded. "Sure they're on the TV twenty-four hours a day – when would they get time to exercise? They probably have loads of cellulite too from sitting on their arses, but it doesn't matter 'cos the public only gets to see their mugs and even you would be easy on the eye if you had someone doing your hair and make-up every morning."

"So what you're saying is that a big arse is not necessarily an impediment to my career?"

"Not at all."

"And bar the temporary insanity, there's hope for me?"

"Well, you might have to get veneers on your teeth."

"Fuck that – could never afford it. I'd better stick to print journalism – at least I could keep my gob shut when they're taking my photo. So what's the name of this photographer you met and who did he say I should give a call?"

"His name was Ray O'Mahony and he said you should give a fella called Donal Dineen a shout. He's a news editor with the *Chronicle*."

"Oh Jaysus – a national! Should I phone him tomorrow?"

"Why not now?"

"It's too late. Besides, I don't want anyone to wreck this warm chocolate-and-ice-cream buzz," said Ali. She wriggled her curvaceous backside into the settee cushions for the evening and for the first time in a long time thought of her derriere more as an asset than a hindrance. Propped up with several pillows she began to make serious inroads into her tub of ice-cream while her friend laid on the bossy but comforting nurse-knows-best routine, fussing around making cups of tea and tucking Ali in with a blanket.

"Oh, by the way, your 'Lawrence' says hello."

"Who?"

"The fella you called Lawrence of Arabia, him of the tall slim build with the longish blond hair and blue eyes. The guy you stopped in casualty – Lawrence, well, actually, his real name is Karl, Karl Hunter."

"You know him?"

"Of course I know him – doesn't he work round the corner from A&E in the medical lab, but he's always around looking at equipment and calibrating machines and drinking mineral water. He was at the Bog Ball fancy dress."

"Karl – so that's the panto dame's real name. He plays guitar, you know."

"How do you know that?" asked Karen

"Oh never mind, you were asleep. Do you think he's asking after me because he fancies me?"

"*No.* I don't know. I think he just wants to know how you're doin'. Why? Do *you* fancy *him*?"

"He can play the guitar, classical guitar at that, and he did sort of save my life, Karen. Yes, I have given him *some* degree of thought."

"He did *not* save your life. Me now, I'm forever saving your life. Oh for God's sake, Ali! Hey, you didn't answer my question! *Do* you fancy him?"

Ali smiled but didn't answer. She was enjoying Karen's questions and the gorgeous ice-cream. There was no doubt but that the rotten day was turning out nice. Karen rambled on and on and Ali lost herself in thought. Sometimes there really were advantages to being incapacitated. Ali immediately checked herself – she didn't want to develop a victim mentality, especially if she had to ring this head honcho on a national paper. Something told her he'd be as tough as nails and she'd have to pretend to be as tough as nails too, one gunslinger facing down another, that kind of thing. Her inner bitch would need time to develop a hard-sell in-your-face attitude and she wondered if the Ali who ate men raw for breakfast would be agreeable to putting in an appearance any time in the near future.

Naturally, under such tremendous mental pressure, it wasn't long before Ali had cleaned out the ice-cream and was munching her way through half a giant bar of milk chocolate. It was nice though to think about "Lawrence" or Karl as he was really called. She was glad he wasn't called something typically Irish, it would have ruined the way she thought about him. Karl sounded a bit more exotic and strong. Why, he had even swanned into her life like her own personal Jesus. Come to think of it, he even looked a bit like Jesus, well, the traditional North European version of Jesus with the long blond hair and blue eyes. Ali started to chuckle to herself. Imagine if she brought *him* home for Sunday lunch! Hey, Mum – meet my special friend *the doctor*, oh and yes he just happens to be *Jesus* as well. Speechless, she'd be. Gobsmacked for sure.

* * *

She didn't ring Dineen the next day. That was perfectly acceptable, she told herself, Karen had only just told her about him and she'd need time to prepare a good phone routine. Anyway, she felt rotten. She'd eaten so much sugar the night before that she felt like she was hung-over and several cups of coffee couldn't lift her headache or her mood.

In truth Ali felt fat and sluggish, the way you do when you've been moping around a confined space for days on end with time to kill and nothing to do but eat and watch TV. Besides, even though she had begged 'Ali who eats men raw for breakfast' to make an appearance, the prima donna steadfastly refused on the grounds that she had "standards" and Ali's body currently was not meeting them. Hopefully, Ali could eventually tempt her inner bitch out with a few more rounds of chocolate. It was worth a shot, she thought, as she unpeeled the gold foil of another giant bar.

Much poor-quality chocolate was scoffed over the next few days but none of it helped her pick up the phone to dial the newspaper guy. Ali told herself procrastination was completely reasonable. After all, she was still a walking cripple – there was no point in Dineen scheduling a meeting with her while she was hobbling around with a bad back, a broken wrist and wearing a neck brace, not unless she was willing to fabricate some exotic lie to explain her banjaxed condition. Simply explaining that she was just back from the war zone that was her local hospital was unlikely to make any impact on him.

It was only when Karen rang and told her to get off her flabby arse and stop putting things off forever that Ali summoned up enough nerve to phone the paper and she was surprised when she got straight through without much hassle from the receptionist. Something told Ali that this Dineen fella would be brusque, rude even, but he was so short and impatient that it made her draw her breath.

"Come on Thursday at three and bring ideas," he said and hung up the phone.

Jesus, she hadn't expected that. In her head she thought it would take months before you'd get an appointment with these paper guys, before they might have a "slot" free to see a complete nobody like her. In a panic Ali rang Maggie in a bid to get some steady advice from the one lady who never lost her cool.

"Well, girl, who's the budding reporter here, you or me? What do they say – give them what they want and write about what you know. You're not going to be fit for work for a while so you may as well use your time wisely."

At quarter to three on Thursday, she arrived on the premises much recovered and minus the neck brace, wearing her good work-coat, knee-high flat-heeled boots (on account of the bad back heels were not an option) and of course her lucky red talons. The receptionist gave her a much-practised snotty look and led her to Dineen's desk inside the newsroom.

It was much quieter than she expected inside the office. In fact it was deathly quiet and as she crossed the floor, a journey which seemed to take a lifetime, she was aware of several heads lifting from their desks in a discreet attempt to glean something from the stranger's appearance.

He was stuck to the phone when she arrived, his head bowed into his chest and his voice dropped in a low murmur. Mesmerised, she watched as his chair swivelled back and forth in time with his conversation. He acknowledged her with half a smile and a raised hand in the air, but then went back to his low mumbling and swivelling so that she felt embarrassed and participated in the ludicrous game where one looks all around taking in numerous details while at the same time giving the impression that one is taking in nothing at all lest one be mistaken for being nosey.

"Alison, Donal Dineen, hear you want to be a reporter."

"Yes, yes, I do, I'm doing a course at the moment – it's not finished but –"

"Don't put a lot of store in courses myself – more interested in what a person can do. What can you do for me, Alison?"

Taken aback by his blunt candour Ali cleared her throat and when she spoke she heard her voice squeak. "Well, I thought maybe I could concentrate on local stuff, you know, things I'd know."

"Fine, what do you have in mind?"

"Eh . . . well, my local girls' secondary school is setting up an organic vegetable patch and selling their produce to the community to raise money for charity."

"Hardly cutting edge – but okay, maybe we're talking early Britney Spears here in terms of uniforms – schoolgirls get down and dirty to raise money for charity. Maybe we could get them to water the plants a bit and get in a hint of mud-wrestling as well. What do you think?"

Ali thought he was taking the piss – either that or he was a serial killer.

"What? No, I don't think you understand. I mean they're only kids. I wouldn't want them to be exploited, I mean misrepresented," she stammered.

"You've got to see things in terms of pictures, Alison – we're a pictures paper, see? I'm always thinking in terms of pictures. What else do you have for me – tell me it's something exciting?"

"Well, we've, ahem, got a marathon set-dancing competition coming up to promote Irish culture in the cities and across nationalities. That takes place the whole of next weekend."

"Irish – is that still sort of sexy in a weird kind of way? Think we might have run something about that recently. Okay, maybe we could go with the international twist on the set dancing – you know, the Irish teaching the Chinese and Russians or whatever to kick up their heels. I see a twenty-first century take on the traditional set dancing at the crossroads. Are there any crossroads in the locality?"

Alison found herself looking at this Dineen chap as if he had four heads. "Well, I can only think of one crossroads in the entire area and it's at the junction of two dual carriageways. I don't think you could arrange a photo shoot there, not without killing a few people at any rate."

"Right, okay, see your point. I'm still thinking here. Will there be any good-looking young-wans at this bash in short, sexy skirts? I'm thinking particularly Polish, Eastern Europeans – our male readers really go for that kind of thing."

Alison raised her eyebrows and heard herself make a half-strangled gasp.

"You find what I've said offensive?" said Dineen.

"Well, er, I . . ."

"I'm sorry you're offended but we can't have any women in the paper who aren't easy on the eye. Cellulite and stretch-marks are not what our readers want to see – fact!" He shrugged. "So, what about drugs, joyriding, shoplifting, crime, anything with a hint of horror in it, can't get enough of it. Can you horrify the readers, Alison?"

Ali, the obviously crap wannabee journalist, was struck dumb. He was waiting, waiting for her to say something momentous and she found herself starting to talk off the top of her head, not knowing where, if anywhere, it was leading.

"Well, a friend of my dad is a beekeeper." She could see that he was waiting intently for the punch line, the package, some kind of wow factor. "Well, apparently he says it has been a very mild autumn and early winter."

"Yes?"

"Well, apparently . . . well, apparently it hasn't been this mild in over a decade and the conditions are just right for wasps, lots and lots of wasps to survive the winter and make it into summer. Apparently we could be in for swarms. That's it."

Nervously, she watched to see what he would say and he said nothing. He showed no sign of emotion, no sign whatsoever of approval or disapproval on his face. Oh shit, she had blown it, blown it big time.

Then suddenly he smiled. "I like it, I like it a lot – in fact, now that I think about it I *love* it – killer wasps on the way – big, big picture of a wasp. The cast, not a problem for the typing, is it?"

"Oh no, I can type with one hand if I have to."

"Brilliant. Go for it! Three hundred words on my desk ASAP!"

"You want me to write something?" she gasped in excitement.

"Yeah – didn't I just say as much?"

He turned his back on her again and started some more mumbling into his phone and then turned around and waved a hand at her. This was clearly both his hello and goodbye signal wrapped into one. It was time to leave and for some reason all she could hear was Maggie's voice in her head. "Well, well, well, wasps, would you ever credit it?"

* * *

Exhilarated and a bit confused, Ali got a taxi over to see her father to ask him how to contact his beekeeper friend. It would have been cheaper to ring him, but frankly she wanted to see him to ask how things were going with Julie being in the Caribbean.

His ashen face told her that all was not well. She followed him into the kitchen, filled with sympathy for him. He was like a big collie moping about, pining for its absent owner. The place was immaculate, the homemade soup was still in the pot, the warm baked brown bread on the counter, but Ali had to admit that without the human tornado that was her mother, the place was like a funeral parlour.

"She's not listening to any reason," said her father wearily. "One phone call, one phone call is all she's made and she's left me without any means of ringing her back. She says she can't have *any* negative influences in her life at this crucial stage."

"I'm sorry, Dad. Ruth says it's my fault, that I pushed her over the edge with my comments that she never had a real job. I didn't think she'd do anything out of the ordinary though, certainly nothing as crazy as this."

"It's not your fault, sweetheart. Your mother has been restless for some time now. Oh, to be honest I've known for several years that she's been frustrated with her life but she's spending *thousands* just for some guru type to tell her to maximise her potential. She could have bought herself some nice jewellery for the same money." He sighed as he poured Ali some percolated coffee and offered her some luxury bickies from Marks & Spencer. "I'm sorry – I'm not up to baking any of my own biscuits or macaroons since she took off," he whispered.

"Do you know what she's doing exactly?"

He shrugged his shoulders sadly. "Yoga, colon cleanses, group counselling, positive life change workshops, who knows. She's told me she's throwing out all my 'non-living' ingredient sources when she gets back. It's all bean sprouts and red-skin peanuts when she comes home, she says. Imagine, she insulted my chocolate soufflé pudding by calling it devil's manure to the digestive system! Oh, and she won't tolerate any questions as to why she's taken off exactly. I can only hope it's a phase, Alison, that she'll come to her senses – eventually."

It was awful being in his presence. Normally she could have hung around the house for hours but she couldn't stand this pitiful version of her father. For years she had thought that her mother was like a giant mushroom feeding off her father, but maybe their marriage was more of a symbiotic relationship than she had realised. It seemed he needed Julie much more than she'd thought. He needed her to make him feel needed. She made him feel alive and without her life-force about the place he was strangely dead.

Without any fuss Ali got the contact number off him for his beekeeper friend, who knew about wasps, finished off her coffee and left.

Marriage was a funny thing, she thought, as the bus took her back out towards the coast. Relationships, marriage and need itself took you far away to a place where you as an individual hitched your fortunes and your happiness to those of another. Struck by that thought, she opened the door of her apartment and glared at the phone. In all honesty the damn thing didn't ring as often as she would have liked.

Had she been happier when she was out of the Dave O'Connor relationship and pining for him or was she happier now that she was back in the relationship but still without him, at least most of the time? "Jesus, Ali, you're as cracked as your mother," she said as she threw her keys on the table, switched her kettle on and dialled the beekeeper.

* * *

For an entire week Ali bought every single edition of the *Chronicle* that hit the streets without any sign of her wasp story. It was costing her a fortune and still there was no sign of the damn thing even though Dineen had said it was a nice little story and that it would definitely appear. Then on Wednesday she came across a giant picture of a wasp on page seven and she was disgusted to see that they had rewritten her first paragraph to give the impression that giant wasps would soon be hitting the coast of Ireland and might even be arriving as early as January.

"That's not it, they've got it *completely* arse-ways," she said angrily as she threw the paper across the floor at Dave's feet.

"Oh, isn't it a start? Don't be so *waspish*," he teased.

"Can you believe they didn't even give me a by-line," she sighed.

He consoled her with a hug and told her that maybe her anonymity was a blessing in disguise.

"At least Simon and Joe won't know that you're using your time off work to advance your career," he placated her. "Anyway, in years to come you might find it embarrassing to remember that your first published story was about wasps!"

"What I do during my time off is my own affair – besides, neither of them would read the *Chronicle* – it's a tabloid and too trashy for the pair of them. Still, I thought if I got a few stories published it would be a nice source of cash but I've made so many phone calls for this damn article it's probably ended up costing me money. First Dineen wanted one expert opinion, then another, then he decides to cut their opinions out completely, then I had to get a taxi across town to meet that damn eccentric beekeeper who refused to talk to me over the phone, he wanted me to meet the bees in person so I could really get a feel for them. Bees don't even leave the feckin' hive in winter. Talk about a total looper!"

"I meet them all the time – loopers, I mean, not bees. Come to bed and forget all about it," Dave advised.

Like a kitten she gave in. Dave had been sweet over the last few weeks, staying over when she was too sore to clean or shop, cooking the odd meal which generally involved pasta, meat and something out of a jar – but she was grateful to him. Right now it felt good to have a boyfriend.

* * *

In the morning he was gone before she got up and when she did she noticed that he'd left his dirty underwear and T-shirt on the floor for her to wash, yet again. Ali didn't like that. He was getting more and more presumptuous of late and she wasn't his damn trophy wife, yet. In a temper she kicked his jocks across the room in a fury, sending a jolt of pain up her back, and then scowled at the alarm clock. It wouldn't be long before it would be screaming out its hated daily dawn chorus. Soon she'd be well enough to return to work and the thought did not fill her with any sense of joy.

16

It was a bright and cold winter's day. Over the sea, the blue sky was streaked with white and pink and it was the kind of morning that made one glad to feel alive. The modern hunk of steel and wheels known as the Dart was stalled in Connolly Station for fifteen minutes and its delay was a fantastic bonus as Ali's enthusiasm for work was zilch, especially since Simon was expected back into O'Grady's that morning. Ringing ahead to tell Maggie that she was on the way, she was perplexed to find her friend talking to her in strangled tones.

"I can hardly hear you, what did you say, Mags? Oh, let me guess, you can't talk because now Little Bastard is back and he's issuing orders as usual."

"Stranger than that."

"What, don't tell me he's flipped the lid and has arrived into work in his shorts and flip-flops?"

"Close."

"For fuck's sake you're driving me nuts! What's up?"

"Eh, gotta go – so you'll be in shortly? Right so – bye."

The tension when she walked in the door was unreal. Maggie

and Pam were making wide eyes at each other across the room from behind mugs of tea. Before long Ali found herself making cows' eyes back at her two colleagues, followed on their part by the mouthing of incomprehensible words and nodding gestures towards Simon's door. Finally, when she could stand it no longer she bundled Maggie and Pam into the kitchen.

"What's going on?"

"It's almost indescribable. You'd need to see it with your own two eyes, wouldn't you, Mags?" gasped Pam.

"It's himself – he's gone and reinvented himself. I think I preferred him the way he was to tell you the truth – you know, better the bastard you know than the bastard you don't," said Maggie.

The door opened.

Ali gasped.

Simon was standing there with bleached-blond highlights in his hair, wearing designer stubble, a suntan and a casual cream linen suit and shirt that Ali could tell even from a distance were very, very expensive.

"Alison, you're back," he said with a beaming smile. "Come in, won't you, for a cup of tea. I want to hear *all* about the accident and how you're doing now."

Maggie gave her a sharp nudge. The dig she took as a signal to keep her mouth, which had locked into open position, shut and to be on her guard against revealing anything to this strange boss.

"Maggie, could you bring us some tea, please? My usual if you don't mind."

Maggie shot Ali a look as if to say, "*Wait till you see this, girl!*"

To Ali's amusement, Simon took off his jacket and slung it over a chair, making sure that she could read the label on the back: *Armani*. Christ, he'd either been somewhere where you could buy counterfeits or he must have re-mortgaged his Aunt Betty's house. There was no doubt about it. He was also sporting a Breitling on his wrist. He must have been to the Far East or some such place to buy such an expensive-looking fake. Naturally, she knew Simon was paid a hell of a lot more than her but he couldn't afford this gear he was wearing, not on what Joe must be paying him, could he?

"Have you been badly hurt, any pain still?" he asked her as he clasped his hands together and placed them under his chin.

"Oh, you know, some stiffness and soreness. My wrist will be out of the cast soon – it wasn't a bad break but I think typing will be a bit slow for a while."

"I hope you're suing the bastard who did this to you. I know a good solicitor who could help you. I know quite a few influential people, you know – many of them would be my associates."

Ali smiled a tight little smile. Who the hell was he kidding?

Maggie arrived in with the tea and she had the slightest smirk on her face, so faint that you'd really have to be a close associate of Maggie's to know it was even there.

"Your *green* tea, Simon – don't you know I nearly put the milk in it again!"

Simon beamed as Maggie scooted out the door.

"Er, so did you enjoy your holiday then?" Ali asked politely. Her limbs were dying to escape. This enforced banter was killing her.

"I wasn't on holiday actually."

"No?"

"No."

The super-cool image faded a little as Simon played with his new watch and ran a hand through the new highlights. "This is a tiny bit awkward, Alison. I was, in fact, away on a personal development course in the Caribbean and while I was there I met someone you know very well. So I'm letting you know, because you'll probably hear from her anyway. I met Jules, fabulous woman. Can't believe she's in her early fifties, she's such a young spirit."

"*Jules?*"

"Yes, your mother."

"My mother Jules, er, Julie?" gasped Ali. Her jaw nearly bounced on the floor with the horror of it all.

"Yes. Well, you see, while we were there we became rather close, I suppose you could say we bonded."

Oh Christ no, he wasn't going to tell her that they were an item, was he? Her mother hadn't been so stupid as to shag her nerdy little boss just so she could tell people she had a toy boy, had she?

"Oh, yes?" she gulped back her tea.

"Well, some of our sessions – group counselling/group visualisation sessions, that is – were a bit, how shall I put it, I suppose *intense* is the word and she was really there for me. Jules became my *special* buddy."

She was surely dreaming. Any moment now Dave was going to wake her up and he'd be telling her that she had overslept and he would try and throw her into the shower, either that or she had just smoked a huge joint and in that case this awful dream was likely to continue for much, much longer.

"I'm sorry, Simon – you were saying that my mother, er, Jules, is your special buddy?"

"Yes, well we, all of us who were there, we became each other's support system. We're called the 'farmers' – we reap what we sow and –"

"Er, Simon, my mother – how does she fit into this reaping and sowing exactly?"

"Oh yes, well, as I said, she was the one that I formed a special bond with. Basically we're each other's support system, to bolster each other, encourage each other like in the AA. Jules *really* is an *amazing* woman – you're so lucky that she was always there to nurture you. Well, anyway, that's what I wanted to tell you, because you might find that Jules mentions me or meets me now and then and I just wanted to explain our relationship."

He fumbled around at his feet, opening a drawer in a filing cabinet, and took out the biggest bag of nuts that Ali had ever seen and threw a whole handful into his mouth.

"Would you like some? They're red-skin peanuts, a great natural protein source."

"Ehm – no – thanks."

Ali got up to leave but found her legs a bit wobbly and sat down abruptly again.

"You're probably still a bit stiff from the accident," said Simon, leaping to his feet. "Here, let me help you up." He gave her his arm. "All right then?" he smiled.

She watched as the smile suddenly turned to a frustrated scowl as he tried to dig out some nut skins from his gums.

All right? Mother of God, was he mad?

Somehow she staggered back into the front office.

"It's a strange experience, isn't it, seeing Simon the Archangel?" said Maggie in a low voice as Ali returned to her desk. "Personally, I think it's the streaked hair that is most frightening, that and the stubble. All right then, Ali?"

"No, Maggie, I'm not all right. My life is in ruins. My silly mother and Simon have only been on the same self-indulgent course in the Caribbean and are now best buddies."

Maggie's eyes opened wide and her jaw dropped but, being Maggie, she recovered instantly. "Oh, you'll be on for a Diet Coke and a panini at lunchtime so."

"No, Maggie, I don't think even a panini will fix the problem," sighed Ali as she stared at her computer screen and felt her stomach clamp down with utter dread and loathing.

* * *

All week Ali could only think of her mother being home and of her dad having to put up with any nonsense that she had learnt on her self-discovery trip. When Ali told Ruth of her mother's antics in the Caribbean her older sister was livid and busting for a fight, so much so that she was determined to go over one evening to have it out with Julie. Ali decided she had better go along with her in case there was a bloodbath.

"Well," said Ruth, her hands on her hips, all teacher-attitude-outside-the-staff-room-door style, "what have you got to say for yourself?"

Julie was sitting at the table in the kitchen eating a huge bag of peanuts and Liam looked as miserable as hell.

"How *could* you, Mum?" Ruth went on. "How *could* you take off like that? Dad says you're giving up *all* refined sugars and *most* carbohydrates to boot – how could you when you know how much he enjoys making Christmas cakes and puddings *for you?*"

"Well, perhaps Daddy has been co-dependent on me for years," her mother said frostily. "Ruth, would you mind not lighting that cigarette, darling? Babette says I'm to maintain a completely toxic-free environment for the next month at least."

"Babette? Babette who?" said Ruth with a snort.

"Babette Meehan, the woman who has saved my life by pointing out that *I*, yes, even little old *me*, has a life to live!"

"Is it true that you have spent over 30,000 euro just to do this – this insane mid-life crisis course?"

"Yes, it's true."

"And this money, did you get it from selling *our* home to one of those institutions?"

Their mother suddenly went very quiet and almost regal and then, when she opened her mouth again, she spoke so quietly and calmly that Ali was sure she must be on tranquillisers. "Ruth, this is *my* home, mine and Daddy's. In reality it ceased being *your* home when you left it, got married and bought your own place. And where I got the money from to do this course is *my* business. I will not take any more criticism from you. Babette says criticism is just a means of keeping a person down. I think perhaps you should leave."

God, she was brilliant, thought Ali watching her. When she wanted to, Julie could really do the Bette Davis act with conviction. For a moment Ali was filled with admiration at the hedonistic selfishness of her mother who had just decided that she was going to take her boring life into her own hands and give it a good squeeze to wake it up a little.

"And *you*, do *you* have any issues with my recent behaviour or my new life?" asked Julie as she turned slowly and deliberately towards Ali.

"I only wish I'd taken the time to explain a bit more about computers to you."

"Oh *yes*, when I told you I was looking for a career. Well, let's say then I was just into putting sticking plaster on my life. Babette has made me realise that I have to *completely* change my life from the inside out." She stopped, patted her hair and smoothed her painted hands down her dark-red trousers. "Anything else, Ali?"

"Well, yes, actually. I hear you've become a special buddy to my boss, well, supervisor. Simon, Simon Webb. I'm just wondering, did you discuss me much on holiday? And this buddy system, where you meet him to boost yourself up, is there any way that can be reversed? Could you get a new buddy – you know, one that I don't work with – by any chance?"

"Oh, Simon! Lovely, lovely boy! I just couldn't help but take him under my wing – maybe it's because I never had any sons of my own."

Ruth shot her mother a malicious look which Julie saw but ignored.

"No, darling, I don't think I mentioned you much except to say that I was glad you had such an *exciting* job and that I hoped you would find a nice man some day soon."

Ali cringed – the thought of Simon being privy to such comments made her stomach churn. "Right. Anything else, Mum?"

"Well, maybe I mentioned my own personal relationship with you and the kind of relationship you have with Daddy, the trouble you have had holding down any kind of job, until now, but nothing more than that."

Right. Her whole life so.

"Okay, well, this buddy thing then. As I was asking: could you perhaps get a new buddy, maybe get on to this Babette person and explain that Simon is no longer suitable?"

Julie looked genuinely offended and squinted her eyes in a manner which told Ali that her request was just not an option. "Darling, you see, we *bonded*. I can't undo that bond or force a bond on someone I didn't bond with from the first. You see that, don't you?"

"Of course, Mum, yes, I see."

* * *

Ruth was fuming when they left their parents' house in the evening. She snorted furiously and thumped her hands hard on the steering wheel.

"The stupid, stupid bitch!"

Jesus, maybe Ruth should give up the teaching game, thought Ali. It seemed to make her extraordinarily violent – but now that she thought about it, Ruth was often prone to violent outbursts even during the long school holidays. Well, at least it was dark, less chance of any nosey neighbours noticing her grown-up tantrum.

"Don't you *care* that she's spending all that money from the house on stupid things like holidays away, that there's no house left to leave us?"

Ali shrugged. "There's always the jewellery."

Ruth laughed heartily, so much so that she couldn't stop, and Ali found herself joining in.

"Oh yes, the jewellery!" Ruth snorted.

"Unless of course my boss, her new Best Buddy turns out to be a fairy with a liking for baubles and she leaves the whole shaggin' lot to him. The way our luck is running it could happen."

A smile was etched on Ruth's face but she was still annoyed – Ali could tell that by the way she was twitching in her seat.

"All the same, why didn't you say anything?" said Ruth. "You just let me do all the talking! Why didn't you criticise her even a bit?"

"Because there was no point – I was there looking at her and I was struck by something Karen once said to me, that there's no point arguing with the drunks and druggies in casualty because no one has a chance of getting through to them when they're high. Mum might not be on something like a real drug but she's on something all right, maybe a power trip or a mid-life crisis but it is getting her off her head and there is no point arguing with her until she comes back down to earth."

Putting on her seat belt, Ali's stomach lurched as her furious sister revved the engine, put her foot to the floor and sped away. They were mostly silent on the drive home and Ali was surprised at how stoically she was reacting to her mother's complete transformation into a selfish cow. Though only part of her was indifferent – a large part of her was still furious. Karen was right though, there was no point in trying to get through to drunks and lunatics – her mother would have to come to her senses herself. Then, remembering Karen and her drunks, Ali decided that she'd better ring her soon to invite her and her nurses to Dave's Early Bird Christmas Party.

As the coastline came into view Ali stared out towards the blackness of the sea where a million twinkling lights were reflected on the water: the lights of stars, of other people's homes and of distant ships passing in the night.

Ruth dropped her at the door. Then, nearly mounting the tasteful little rockery at the front of the red-bricked apartment block, she reversed and, with a toot of her horn, she was gone.

Rubbing her still stiff back, Ali opened her front door, walked to the kitchen, eyed her slimming affirmation cards and stuffed a huge slab of chocolate into her mouth. Parents can be very stressful, she thought as she demolished her drug of choice in two minutes flat.

17

Dave was kicking off the Christmas season with a mid-November party in his smelly 4-bed semi-d and Ali was half-dreading, half-looking forward to the affair. For it was planned for that Thursday night and Ali would have to drag herself out of bed the next day and go to work bollixed, which kind of took the fun out of an evening bash. There were no more sickies she could pull and days off were strictly reserved for Christmas.

When Ali arrived at Dave's house in the late afternoon she was amazed to see him with his sleeves rolled up and a pair of too-tight yellow washing-up gloves glued to his spade-like hands.

"Oh, I *see*! You expect me to be your charwoman when it comes to your dirty laundry but when you *have* to be you're a secret cleaning wizard!"

She'd had it out with him about his annoying habit of leaving his jocks and socks in her apartment: but of course Dave had squirmed out of any blame by disarming her with his cheeky smile.

"Why *exactly* are you putting so much effort into cleaning the joint anyway?" she asked. "Bloody hell, I don't believe it! Your worktops are sparkling! Let me guess – you've *finally* whacked

Larry for leaving his dirty dishes in the sink and you're just doing a clean-up before forensics arrive."

"It's just, Miss Bigshot Reporter, we kind of reasoned we were probably immune to our own dirt by now but maybe our guests wouldn't be. We wouldn't want to poison some poor fecker and have him putting it down to getting a bad pint in the pub before he arrived."

"Are you going to wash the kitchen floor as well?" she asked, sickened by the bits of blackened goo flattened into the lino and by the way the floor literally stuck to the soles of your feet.

"Ah no, I'm just giving the work surfaces a rub around with a cloth – any bastard who drops some food on the floor and then decides to stick it in his gob takes his chances."

Ali opened the fridge to get out some milk for her tea and was nearly flattened by an avalanche of beer, bottles and cans that were crammed into every corner and even into the space where the eggs should be. Bags of Basmati rice dominated the work surface along with bags of onions, bell peppers, chillies, mushrooms, crisps, popcorn and mini-sized chocolate bars.

"See you're doing the old reliable Dave O'Connor curry, the one that has everyone guessing what the exact ingredients are. Great – all those farts in a confined space – can't wait."

"Smartarse!"

"Yeah, I guess everyone's arses will be smarting with all the chilli you'll be adding in too."

He threw a dishcloth at her. She knew it was a dangerous manoeuvre but she retaliated by squeezing dirty-sponge water down the front of his shirt. In an instant he was grabbing her hair and pulling it out of the way so that he could drip dirty water down the back of her neck and then he rubbed her face hard with the greasy, smelly, sponge.

Her screams drew in a few of his garda tenants to the kitchen, but not one of the feckers were willing to rescue a damsel in distress although they were all only too willing to crack open a beer can, watch the commotion and throw in a few suggestions for fighting dirty. Dave didn't really manhandle her though as he was still mindful of her injuries – she'd only got the cast off her wrist that very day. Still Ali got the fright of her life and screamed like crazy as Dave poured the entire bowl of greasy sludge water over her head.

"Feck it, I'm going to have to wash the floor after all!" Dave lamented as he stared at the sopping linoleum.

"Erra, sure I'll clean it up," said Larry and he took the mop and in slow motion began to give a rub around the floor with his fag dangling out of his mouth, totally unaware that he was trailing cigarette ash right around the kitchen.

Dave took the opportunity to haul Ali upstairs and into the bathroom.

"Right, take your clothes off," he said as he shoved her into the shower and before she could say a word he had undressed himself and was shampooing her hair. "I do a great shampoo if I say so myself," he said to the back of her neck as he smoothed back her hair and rinsed the bubbles away, "and as you know yourself I'm *famous* for my wash and blow."

"I'm cold!" she moaned. "Please, please, turn the temperature up before I freeze?"

"No, it's hot enough. If you're cold – I'll warm you up." He pulled her backwards into his stomach and chest and kissed the back of her neck playfully, his hands instinctively reaching for her full breasts. Slowly, he began to rub shower gel onto the curves of her body and she bristled with excitement and desire. Not being able to see him heightened her pleasure – she was acutely aroused as she wondered about the destination of every touch. Then, after his hands had travelled up and down her several times, he turned ninety degrees, pushing her against the wall so she was locked in his embrace and shivering with anticipation. Straining on her toes with her hands pressed hard against the grimy, scuzzy tiles Ali had a strange realisation – this bunch of lads badly needed a cleaner.

* * *

Trickle by trickle they arrived later that night and then Karen sauntered in, looking fabulous as usual, wearing a size-eight, maximum size-ten mini-dress, the one dress that was to become *the* dress for that Christmas season. Smiling, Dave welcomed her warmly and the four nurses who flanked her like minders.

"Fucking Christ – them's the pants all right," one of the lads whistled as one of the said nurses filed past in a skin-tight pair of trousers.

There was no doubt about it, Ali would be in the good books with Dave. As he said, the lads always liked a few hospital angels about the place, especially ones who looked like they might want to inflict a bit of damage and then nurse the lads back to health afterwards.

Dave's curry went down a treat and anyone even half-sober spent the night with tight smiles on their faces trying to pretend they couldn't hear, never mind smell, the noxious farts that were ripping around the room.

Snogging and monotonous CD-playing abounded and needless to say every utensil, whether saucepan or fireplace, was not immune to the odd spate of barfing. Well into the night, when the revelling had died down a bit, Ali happened upon the sight of a blonde nurse inflicting the kind of damage that lads are supposed to like. A big-boned girl, she was doing her mightiest to flatten the unfortunate fella whose lap she was sitting on, only allowing him up for air when he couldn't hold his breath any longer.

Sometime around four Dave grabbed Ali's hand and pulled her up to his room, but when they burst through the door in a fit of snogging and turned on the bedside lamp, they were faced with a vision of Karen spread-eagled across the bed. Alarm bells rang in Ali's head. Years of experience had taught Ali that Karen was always the jammy bitch who managed to ferret out a bed at the end of a night's partying.

"Oi, you get up out of there!" Ali screamed at her, but she didn't move, not even an inch.

"You needn't bother, she's dead to the world," said Dave.

"She is in her arse. I know her. Wakey-wakey, Karen – I know you're spoofing!" said Ali as she took off one of Karen's shoes and tried to tickle her feet.

"Comatose, didn't I tell you," said Dave as he tried to unbutton Ali's top.

Completely horrified, Ali soon found herself lying on his dust-laden carpet on top of a pile of dirty smelly clothes, sharing one pillow, a blanket and his spittle.

"I'm telling you she's awake," Ali whispered as Dave squeezed her breasts and pulled aside her knickers.

He didn't care. She did: the floor was terribly hard despite the layer of dirty clothes and if it weren't for all the alcohol she'd knocked back she knew her recent injuries would be plaguing her. Next door it was evident that one of the lads had pulled one of the nurses and if the loud moans didn't give the game away the sound of the bed belting against the radiator was a sure sign that action was afoot.

Oh, definitely, a night for any girl to remember.

18

In fairness to him, Dave did hold her hair back from her face while she vomited into the bath and he did call and pay for the taxi the next morning so that she could get into work roughly on time. Ali was sure Maggie would be waiting for her with her lips pursed in disapproval, saying nothing, acting like the mother that her mother had never been. Instead she found the office eerily quiet when she dragged herself across the doorway, which was an extremely difficult task considering she was fighting the spins.

"Where *is* everyone?" she croaked to Maggie, her voice worn out from the vomiting and the smoking both passive and active the night before.

"Pam's on a job, Joe could be on a suicide mission for all I know and Lucy and Simon have gone for coffee."

"*Fuck off*! Lucy wouldn't willingly put herself within a mile of Little Bastard – you're pulling my leg, Mags."

Ali plonked herself on her swivelling office chair and tried to swivel the same way as her spins to feel better, but to no avail. "Maggie, pet, will you put some foundation on me to give me a colour? It's in my drawer?"

"No, I won't," said Maggie crossly.

It was just then that Ali noticed that Maggie's hands were working furiously, folding sheets of paper and stuffing envelopes with them in a sort of frantic indignation.

"What in God's name are you doing?"

"Same as you," said Maggie as she plonked a pile of letters and envelopes in front of Ali.

"I can't. My wrist still hurts from my accident and eh – from some shower action last night. Besides, I didn't go to college and earn *two* degrees to stuff shite into envelopes," said Ali with a haughty wave of her hand.

"Well, neither did I but that's what happens when your receptionist quits because she's landed a plum job on the nation's favourite soap."

"What? *Me Auld Flower*? Lucy's going to be on TV?"

"Well, not if Simon has anything to do with it, girl. Grovelling he is, singing her praises, telling her she's the best thing since sliced bread, trying to talk her out of it, increase her wages, that sort of thing I'd warrant, but she says it's too late."

"*Our* Lucy going to be on TV! She's escaping! She'll never look back I bet," sighed Ali.

The little miss arrived back half an hour later all purrs and smiles as she lounged in her chair and casually flicked on her computer. Simon walked by with a forced grimace of a smile on his face – his upbeat demeanour no doubt part of his positive-thinking big-bucks course. The door of his office shut and it wasn't long before they noticed a red light on the phones. He was probably giving out yards to someone about Lucy quitting. Ali desperately hoped it wasn't her mother.

"He offered me a five grand raise, he did, but I just arched me eyebrows – you know, just to show him that he couldn't afford me no more, no matter what he was paying."

"You're really, really going to be on TV, Lucy?" Ali gushed.

"Course I am. I'm to play the new young temptress on the block, the slapper that pushes what's his name over the edge, you know that aul' guy, he must be forty if he's a day, get him to leave his wife and all for me. I've been hired basically to drive the men of Ireland wild with lust, that's what they said."

"It will be a difficult role for you then, girl," said Maggie with a mock smile. "Ah no, more power to you, Lucy, you're living your dream – we couldn't but be happy for you."

Lucy told them she was leaving at the end of the week and that Simon was livid at her rapid departure, saying he'd find it difficult to replace her that quickly. Acting even more like the cat's pyjamas than usual, Lucy recounted how she'd told him she'd only stay till the end of the week if he let her do a few important things during work hours such as getting her hair cut and nails done and let her out on extended lunch breaks to go shopping.

It was only after her smug little rave on The Importance of Being Lucy that their former receptionist actually took in Ali's utterly decrepit appearance

"Jaysus, you look like the dog's dinner – you'll scare the bleedin' customers, you will."

"Maggie won't put my foundation on."

"You're getting too old for the gargle. At your age you should be finishing with all that shite and getting a belly on you, havin' a few young wans of yer own."

"Feel like I have one in there already – you know, the morning sickness."

All of a sudden something changed in Lucy's eyes – it was like throwing a switch – and full of devilment she grabbed Ali and snogged her full on the mouth. Ali felt like she was suffocating as Lucy locked her in an iron embrace, stroked a lock of her hair and super-glued their lips together for what seemed like forever. Then, pretending to be startled, and still holding Ali, Lucy turned abruptly and narrowed her eyes in pretend annoyance.

Simon had left his office and was standing there staring at them. He turned puce, coughed, cast his eyes down to his feet and shuffled back into his office again.

As Lucy released Ali from her grip, she laughed her trademark dirty laugh. "Me parting present to him – just a little somethin' to keep him *warm* on the long, cold winter nights – 'cos you know that's what that little weasel fantasises about when he's out of the office – *us* – all of us together!"

Ali still couldn't move or speak – it was like someone had pulled out all the vital wires connecting to her brain.

"Ah Jaysus, you didn't think it was real, did you? I'm an actress – I'd kiss the back of a bus for the right money!"

A mute Ali frantically shook her head.

"You weren't meant to *enjoy* it – you didn't enjoy it, did you?" Lucy asked threateningly.

From Ali's strangled throat came a very raspy "No!"

"Good, 'cos if I thought you'd enjoyed it . . ."

"Lucy, you know what you said about kissing the back of a bus for the right money?" teased Maggie.

"Yeah?"

"Well, how much for Simon? How much would it cost to snog Simon?"

"Ah Jaysus, Maggie, it would want to be a very big paycheck – a *very* big paycheck, I'm telling you!" Lucy visibly shivered. Then she turned to Ali. "Oh, come on down the jacks and I'll put the feckin' stuff on your gob then! You look like you're goin' to hurl anyways."

Not for the first time, Ali wondered why everyone thought they could talk to her as if she was a little girl as she let a real child, Lucy, rub cheap moisturiser and brown sludge foundation onto her wretchedly pale face and lecture her about responsible adult behaviour and of her need to give up "the sauce".

* * *

Tears were shed, some of them crocodile, cheeks were air-kissed, drinks were knocked back, cleavage was flashed, tights were snagged and speeches were made as Lucy disappeared from their lives and beamed herself onto the national airwaves.

A straightening iron had been part of the going-away present from Simon and the contemptuous look that Lucy had given the item was enough to strike the fear of God into its giver. "Doesn't he know me curls are me bleedin' trademark? What would I want to be straightenin' them for?" Lucy seethed.

The girls had the sense to get Lucy a voucher for a designer handbag and shied away from buying the actual item itself for fear that the bag would be given the rolled-eyes treatment. Joe, who always backed the winner, threw €200 behind the handbag-purchase scheme, much to Simon's annoyance.

Fearful that the little minx would sabotage the computer system by introducing a Lucy virus before she went, in revenge for low pay, they all breathed a sigh of relief every time they switched on a terminal and it didn't blow up.

"I suppose we couldn't expect her to stay forever – the year she spent here was just research for her really," smiled Maggie, the morning after Lucy had left, as they all shared some funny Lucy memories.

"It's awful quiet though without her, isn't it?" sighed Pam as she participated in the current office obsession of stuffing letters into envelopes.

A mailshot they called it – a shot in the dark more like, thought Ali as she rolled her eyes skywards. Both of her thumbs were beginning to ache with the repetition of folding, shoving and sealing. Maybe she shouldn't have come back to work so soon. Blast that OAP and his shaggin' moped.

* * *

The doctor stuck the X-ray in front of her nose and after a bit of "hmming" declared Ali's wrist to be a fine specimen of bone-setting.

"As you can see it's in a perfect anatomical position. There should be no long-term problems from the break to your wrist."

All right for him to say, thought Ali as she left his office – her thumb still had the tendency to throb unmercifully, especially if she had been spending any length of time typing.

Annoyed with her public consultant's brusque pronouncement on her bone-setting and muttering to her toes, she took a wrong turn somewhere and ended up in casualty.

When she looked up there was her tall Lawrence of Arabia again, drifting cloudlike down the corridors in her direction. If truth be told she would have preferred to keep her head down and turn on her heel but he caught her eye and smiled at her and she was forced to stop and acknowledge him.

"I know you," he teased.

Smiling catlike, she acknowledged the joke. "Yes, we've met twice so far I believe, both times under unusual circumstances, you being dressed as a woman the first and me being a screaming woman the next."

"How've you been?"

"Oh you know . . . in pain."

He laughed. "If you want real pain you should try hospital lunch – that's where I'm heading right now. I don't suppose you'd like to join me?"

For a moment she thought of manufacturing a lie but she had to eat somewhere and the longer she was away from the office the better. Her lack of an immediate answer either way told him that she was hovering.

"Oh come on, you haven't lived until you've survived hospital sandwiches and soup!"

They'd got past the soggy sandwiches and chips and on to tea when he took her injured paw in his long slim fingers and examined it tenderly.

"Your poor wrist, does it still hurt?"

"Yes, but the doctors think I'm some sort of a malingerer for saying so," she laughed.

"I hope everyone has been *especially* nice to you since your accident and have been pampering you loads."

"Well, my sister did her bit I suppose, my mother was useless as usual, wasn't even in the country to tell you the truth and Karen, well, Karen was great – a good friend in a crisis, she always has been."

"Oh, it doesn't sound to me like you were pampered half enough. Maybe you could do with some more. In fact, maybe you'd like to go out to dinner with me sometime?" Lifting his eyes from her hand, he smiled directly at her in a brazenly confident way.

"Maybe," she dithered.

His candour unnerved her and yet it excited her. She could feel herself blush from her throat and wondered should she just make some excuse about needing to get back to work and then running away. For a moment she hesitated and thought about ranting off the wrong number, the one that ended with 4 instead of 6, but if she did he might start pestering Karen. Besides, she might see him in the hospital a few more times if things didn't heal properly. So, for some extraordinary reason Ali gave "Lawrence" her real number and then prayed he wouldn't ring it.

* * *

After what seemed like an eternity without Lucy (a few days) the staff demanded a meeting with management to protest that they couldn't cope with doing administrative and reception tasks on top of their own work. Besides being downright ridiculous, it just didn't look too good either. What office in the city for God's sake hadn't a receptionist, they moaned. At least they extracted a commitment from Simon and Joe that they intended to replace her, even if they couldn't pin them down to exactly when.

Ali was already in a bad mood on Friday afternoon when the shit hit the fan.

It wasn't every Friday night that Dave was free and she was looking forward to spending a normal weekend with him but he had infuriated her no end by telling her he was going to a sergeant's going-away party instead. She banged down the office phone and resigned herself to the usual few drinks with the rest of the staff.

Then she heard the familiar, high-pitched, rippley laugh and the hairs stood up on the back of her neck. Before she even raised her head Ali knew she would be met with the vision of loveliness that was her middle-aged mother.

"Alison, darling," cooed Julie and Ali cringed as her mother waved her "royal wave" across the office, shaking her chunky gold bracelet in the process.

She must tell her mother that under no circumstances was she ever to meet Simon in her workplace ever again, no matter how much Simon needed to meet her for his "buddy building".

"Jules is coming for drinks with us," declared Simon as he grabbed his coat and pushed the smiling granny out the door.

Mortification was the only word for how Ali felt and Maggie shot her a look of concern, although then again it could also have been pity.

"What's that, darling?" asked Julie as she stuck her nose into Ali's glass in the pub.

"A Bacardi Breezer."

"Oh, I think I'll have one of those so."

"Mum, it's *spirits* for God's sake!"

"Alison, you must take me for an innocent. Haven't I been drinking G & T's all my life? It's hardly holy water, you know."

"How you holding up, girl?" asked Mags surreptitiously.

Fortunately Julie was so loud that you could easily hold a dual conversation alongside her and not be overheard. In Ali's opinion her mother was never much of a shrinking violet but since she had completed her positive life-enhancing course in the Caribbean she had developed the fortitude of a WAG when it came to public brazenness.

"Ssh, can I have a bit of quiet, please?" said Simon loudly.

All staff eyes were directed towards him.

Simon was beaming. "Now, as you all know, we have been down a receptionist this last while. Well, I'd like you to meet our new receptionist, Jules, who will be starting with us from next week!"

Rooted to the floor in shock, Alison hoped this was a nightmare. She stayed a while longer for the sake of decency, then, hang the expense, got a taxi to see her father. En route she had time to think and the enormity of the situation hit her: *her* mother in *her* workplace, *her* mother being one of the "girls", *her* mother possibly on the side of Simon. How would she ever be able to bitch about her boss ever again? There was only one possible option, she'd have to quit, she'd have to tell her dad that the new Jules was suffering from temporary insanity or blind ambition but either way she couldn't possibly work with her for a moment. Dad would let her borrow a grand to tide herself over until she got a new position and, if she quit, O'Grady's might forget all about her course. November would soon be at an end and that was the ultimate deadline she had for stringing Joe along for her "marketing receipt".

"I'm sorry, love," Liam sighed as he got out the cheque-book and without any hesitation wrote her a cheque for two thousand euros. "She's impossible to get through to these days, talking of botox injections for her crow's feet and maybe even a boob job – saying things like she missed the swinging sixties, the hippie seventies and now the Celtic Tiger and she's got to do something to show the world she's still alive."

"Well, if it's excitement that she's looking for she'll come to her senses after a few weeks working with Simon – it's deadly dull in that place."

"Don't joke, Ali – I really don't know what's come over her. She's hanging out with these 'farmers' now who 'reap and sow'. If she was that much into horticulture I would have got her a greenhouse."

Ali was uncertain whether he was serious or being ironic. She felt so sorry for her poor father, the innocent victim in all this.

"I just hope that one day the Julie I married comes home to me," he said as he shook his head sadly and saw Ali off at the door.

Karen was thinking of popping over to Ali's apartment with a straitjacket when Ali told her later that day that she was quitting her job. "You can't! You have a *plan*, remember? You're going to work towards a new career and then leave."

"Well, my mother screwed that one up for me. I *absolutely refuse* to work with her for even a day."

"Look, is your mother even qualified for this job? Maybe she won't even last a week."

"Oh, she's qualified all right. Crafty thing did a computer course with the community network and she's even bought a PC. You know yourself she's always been razor sharp. Before she married Dad she worked in Granddad's drapery shop and she's been doing the books for her ladies' club for years. And when she gets an idea in her head there's no shifting her. She's looking for a start and is probably willing to work for very little, and believe me around O'Grady's that's a very big selling point."

"Then you'll have to tell this Simon fella that it's you or her. Call his bluff."

"Oh Karen, don't you see? Simon *wants* me to leave. He can't fire me and he's just got the ultimate reason now for me to quit."

"Wasn't that the *old* Simon? I thought the *new* Simon was very touchy feely?"

"Yeah, well, you know what they say about leopards and spots."

"Speaking of spots, what about Joe O'Grady himself? Hasn't he always had a soft spot for you? I'm sure he won't let this happen."

"Believe me, Joe won't take my leaving too hard. What he values is low-paid workers and as I said I bet my mother is working for a pittance."

"So what'll you do now?"

"Quit, and take some time off."

"Oh Jesus – do you really, really think that's the only option here?"

"If your mother was a nurse would you work with her on the same ward?"

"Well, I suppose I could always put in for a transfer."

"Well, I can't put in for a transfer."

"No, I don't suppose you can," sighed Karen.

* * *

Ali was lounging in front of her TV in a state of bliss, drinking hot chocolate in the middle of the day, delighted that she didn't have to go to work. Under cover of darkness, she'd already gone into O'Grady's and cleaned out her desk of all her belongings and copied any important files off her computer and then her P45 conveniently arrived through the post stating her earnings for the taxman. The girls had begged her to come in for going-away drinks and she would, eventually, but right now she was content to be alone – being alone felt good. Outside the wind was howling and she knew if she could see it the Irish Sea would be swelling and monstrous grey waves would be pounding the sea wall and the pier. Heavy rain and high tides had caused floods on the north side of Dublin but there were no floods expected for the south-east coast – at least that's what the weather people were predicting.

Next day the fog lingered till noon but after that the promised high pressure materialised and the bright winter sun cut through the cold white clouds. Having been confined to the apartment for ages, bar attending her course, Ali decided to make the most of the fine weather and head towards the city centre for a bit of window-shopping and a bit of posing in the large coffee rooms off George's Street where one could lounge for ages over a newspaper and a pot of tea without being kicked out by the staff.

There she treated herself to a large fry of bacon and eggs and stuck her nose in the paper, reading a convoluted article that she couldn't understand despite her third attempt. Giving up on that, she attempted to wrangle answers from the crossword clues.

She was startled when she heard a "Hello!" whistle past her head.

"You look a bit flummoxed, can I help at all?" Karl asked, smiling at her. His long fingers held his tray steady while he ran the fingers of his other hand through his blond hair. "The answer to 17 down is Plato."

"Oh."

All Ali wanted was some private time, time where she could just sit and observe people's comings and goings, and she wished he'd just leave.

"I'm sorry, I'm intruding," he said and was about to leave.

She immediately felt guilty, closed over her paper and smiled, although she wasn't quite sure why – after all, he hadn't even phoned.

He smiled back and sat down.

"Em, sorry for not phoning," he said. "I wasn't sure if you really wanted me to. You seemed a bit unsure that day, that day we met in the hospital."

"Well, to tell you the truth I have a boyfriend."

She blurted it out, waiting to see how he might react, whether he'd be relieved or maybe even genuinely disappointed, but he seemed just a little taken aback at her candour.

"Naturally we're just *crazy* about each other – we're always on the phone confessing our love and are out on the town every other night," she continued with a playful arch of her eyebrow and a roll of her eyes.

He looked at her for a moment as if she was mad in the head and then he just laughed. "So he doesn't phone you as often as he should and you'd like to go out more."

Okay – so his powers of perception were evidently superb.

"Oh, it's just, you know, he's always working. To be more exact, he's always working when I'm not – that's the worst thing about people who don't work regular nine-to-five jobs – when you're off they're not – and sure when he's not at his real job he has a million other jobs to do. You should know what I mean. I bet you work lots of antisocial hours at the hospital."

"No, I work regular nine to five, five days a week, except today I've taken a day off just for the hell of it."

Ali smiled. She wondered what he would think if she told him that she'd given up work completely. Maybe he'd run a mile like most men once they smelt the whiff of unemployment. In her experience two words scared the hell out of all men: commitment and dependency – oh and pregnancy of course.

She couldn't resist telling him. "I'm suddenly unemployed – by choice of course."

"Good for you. What do they say – life isn't a dress rehearsal? Tell you what – come and help me celebrate my own mental-health day," he said with sparkling eyes, and went on to explain: "A day you take off when you just need a break."

It was a surreal few hours. They lounged around Grafton Street and St Stephen's Green, talking about ridiculous things – about whether it would be possible to lure a duck from the pond there and then so that it could become crispy fried for dinner, about the secret life of belly-button fluff, about abseiling naked and about growing old disgracefully.

After a long, slow walk, slowed down even more by intermittent convulsive laughing, Ali found herself in his rather grand old-world city-centre flat. It wasn't trendy or ostentatious, had a quiet self-assurance about it, almost student-like but more grown-up. Essentially his pad oozed style without even trying but it was a man's environment bereft of frills or any kind of girly clutter.

"Do you own this place?" she found herself asking cheekily as she stared out the big sash window at the evening commuters vying for buses on the road.

He laughed and his dark blue eyes laughed too and caused tiny wrinkles to form around their sockets. "I wish. No, I rent it along with Hugo. He *is* a doctor, a 'real' one – you know, a medical doctor as opposed to me who only has a doctorate. Wine?"

Ali strained her neck looking up at the high ceilings while he went off to ferret out some wine from his galley kitchen. It must cost an arm and a leg to rent this place, she thought. Dave would never have approved of wasting so much cash on such extravagant living. Two enormous white bookcases, carved to match the Georgian cornices, held his book and CD collection. Eclectic was the only word to describe his literary and musical possessions.

Books varied in topic from history to biography, archaeology to modern literature and poetry.

As she picked up a few and flicked through the pages she noticed tiny dog-ears which told her that his books were not for effect but were well-loved treasures. A bookworm, she thought, and a man who clearly loved music too: Bach, Handel, Beethoven, Chopin and so on, and a heap of truly weird stuff she had never even heard of including some African tribal music – and, of course, the eternally weird and eternally fashionable Leonard Cohen.

"I see you're into a lot of old, heavy stuff," she teased, waving her arm at his music shelves when he walked back into the room.

He handed her a glass of white wine and with a furrowed brow began to dissect his music shelves.

"I'm sure I have some regular music in here too," he said, fumbling among his CDs. "Kate Bush?"

"You must be joking," laughed Ali.

"U2?"

"Not in the mood."

"The Smiths?"

She raised an eyebrow.

"Oh hang on. Ah yes, a fine piece of music here – in its own way as perfect as anything that Beethoven or Shostakovich ever composed."

After he placed the chosen CD in the stereo he seemed to tense for a moment, his ears straining for the very first note and then all of a sudden his entire frame began to spasm and shake in time to the awful wail of music that filled the entire room.

"Metallica!" he cried with a flourish as he played an imaginary set of drumsticks. "Isn't it just fucking brilliant?"

It could have been an incredibly nerdy moment but it wasn't. It was genuinely funny, so much so that a spray of wine shot out of Ali's mouth as she gasped with laughter. Then they jumped around the room, on the mat and all over the couch, punching the air, head-banging and playing air guitar like two idiot teenagers.

* * *

It was a strange feeling to be in a strange man's bedroom that night, even if not in his actual bed. There was no deliberate planning involved – the hours just whiled away all by themselves until all the buses and trains had stopped running. Karl's place was a neat but manly space and so different from Dave's tip of a room, with not a dirty sock or pair of jocks in sight. Then it hit her that maybe "Lawrence" could be a serial killer and that at this moment nobody on this planet knew where she was staying. In theory, and maybe even in practice, she could be murdered in her bed (correction, one of his beds) and nobody, not a single person would ever know.

Suspicions should have been aroused when he cooked her dinner: something wonderful made of chicken fillets, cream and basil, a good dash of the white wine they had opened, a few grapes scooped from his fruit bowl, and pasta.

Cooking wasn't normal amongst young blokes, was it, she wondered now. Granted her father could cook, but in a young bachelor it was surely a sign of abnormality – or maybe he was just a bit eccentric.

Stretching her arms upwards, Ali stifled a yawn and then heard him playing his guitar in the other room.

It was the classical piece of music that she had first heard him play the night of the fancy-dress set-dance, the piece from *The Godfather*. Was he doing it on purpose? Didn't he know the effect that piece of music had on women? Ali felt like a rat being lured to the sweet music of the Pied Piper. Well, if he thought that would be enough to lure her in for a shag he could feck off. Still it stirred something within her – if not lust, it was at least interest.

19

Maggie rang the next day and told her that she was seriously, seriously worried about her. Nobody, absolutely nobody quits their job without a plan of action, she said. Had she sent out CV's, rang recruitment companies, done anything at all towards furthering her career?

Dave had already figured out that there was something wrong and asked her why she wasn't going to work. He nearly exploded when he heard the answer.

"How are you going to pay your rent? Not that you should be renting a place like that anyway – it's *way* out of your league even if you do get it cheaper than you should because your clueless landlord lives in Australia. When are you ever going to grow up, Ali? If it had been me now I would have been in there raising hell, demanding that they *un-hire* my mother and if I had to leave I would have stayed there as long as it took to get a new job first."

The more Dave ranted and raved at her, the angrier she became. It didn't take long for a full-scale screaming match to break out where she accused him of being obsessed with money and he told her she was a spoilt child and it ended when she told him to leave the apartment and not to bother coming back. Part of her even meant it too.

Ruth called in after school and asked her how she was doing and reiterated how appalled she was at their mother's behaviour, citing it as proof positive that Julie really was a sociopath.

"Apart from hiring a hit-man to do her in, what are you going to do for work?"

Ali shrugged. "Don't fancy waitressing, teaching or doing what I'm doing at the moment. I don't know. Something will turn up, something always does. Anyhow I can go on Social Welfare after a while – I'd say I won't get it immediately because I quit my job voluntarily – and Dad has loaned me something to tide me over for a bit."

When Ruth left Ali lost herself in ice cream. The phone rang. It was Karl.

"I know this is a bit forward," he said, "but do you want to come down home with me for a few days? I didn't tell you yesterday because I didn't want to take the shine off your own news but I'm leaving my job as well and one of the things I'm doing is renovating an old house that a maiden aunt left me. Now I don't want you to think I'm just looking for you to come down to help clean my house – but it could be fun, would take your mind off things while you're at a loose end – we could scull a few pints in a few pubs off the Shannon. What do you think?"

"And where *is* home exactly?"

"Well, technically Tipperary, although if you spit one way you're in Limerick and the other you're in Clare and, if the wind is really behind you, you're not that far from Galway either. Well, are you on for it?"

Ali laughed at the audacity of him but she couldn't deny she was tempted. Outside the window of her apartment dirty grey rain splashed into the puddles of the tarmac driveways and dirty grey clouds loomed in the sky, rolling in from the sea. If it was raining and one was unemployed, then it was a great idea to head west and ensconce oneself in a quiet little pub somewhere.

"Isn't it the wrong time of the year for renovating, Mr Big Property Owner? I might be a silly city girl but even *I* know you can't put a roof on in this weather."

"It doesn't need a roof put on. Do you own a sleeping bag?"

Ali half-changed her mind when he pulled up to collect her in his cramped little Volkswagen Polo. Evidently she was just a big as snob as her mother or maybe she'd just been spoilt getting her bum in and out of Dave's exotic motors. When Karl got in he had to hunch up and his legs were around the steering wheel. She was reminded of a long-limbed circus clown riding a unicycle. Thank God the motor-mad Dave wasn't here to see her occupy the passenger seat. To hell with that bossy bastard! She'd show him she wasn't dependent on him for a life. She was going to apply for her driving test too as soon as she got back, just to be even more independent.

"I know it's not much," he said by way of apology. "Spending all those years doing a doctorate eats into your cash base."

Embarrassed that her face had obviously twitched at the sight of the car, Ali made reference to the fact that she had no set of wheels herself and that it really was a treat to be in any kind of motorised vehicle at all. The seats too were extremely comfortable, she told him and she bounced her back into the chair a few times as if to emphasise the point.

The drive was easy and fast. Even though it was wet, she loved the stretch through Kildare and the greenness on either side of the motorway. North Tipperary was upon them in a flash and surprisingly there was no rain, there was even some sunshine, and she was struck by the prettiness of the county, which seemed at first glance to be all trees and mountains. The change in the weather and the freedom of shaking off the city helped lighten Ali's mood.

After a while Karl swung his car off the N7 and up a winding road, climbing a hill and then parking between two massive four by fours.

"Gas guzzlers," he said in a jocular but envious tone, gesturing at the two majestic vehicles which were wedging in his small car.

Ali didn't hear. She was lost in admiration as she gazed down at the River Shannon, viewing from her elevated position the pretty stone bridge which crossed the wide waterway and taking in the stunning backdrop of mountains and the pretty little village below.

"Longest river in the British Isles," he told her.

"I know."

"Fancy a pint?"

Inside, the pub was bliss. Stone floors and walls and wooden beams with bits of fishermen's pots and yellowed pictures hanging everywhere. At the back was a real stove fire and various trinkets were hanging out of the high old-fashioned mantelpiece. It wasn't busy and they got a prime spot overlooking the river and bridge below.

Ali could see how you'd throw up city life for this; even the drink was considerably cheaper, although she didn't get to feel the difference in price herself. Karl was buying – insisted upon it, in fact. So Ali just sat back and enjoyed being treated like a queen. They ordered some mussels in white wine and chips and he paid for that too. His attention to her seemed charming if a bit old-fashioned. Part of her knew she shouldn't be in his company and part of her wondered was she only there to spite Dave but after several pints she relaxed and found herself laughing and taking his long slim fingers in hers, turning them over to make a pretence of reading his palm.

"I see a *troublesome* woman coming into your life – she will cause *much* confusion," she laughed as she wagged her finger at him in stern warning.

"Does she have pretty brown hair and expressive eyes?"

The frankness of Karl's question made Ali uneasy and excited. Feeling like he had hit some kind of inner funny-bone which was making her squirm, she tried to joke her way around his intense stares and questions.

"No, this woman will be a definite redhead."

"Oh God, no – the mother would never approve. Redheads are *fierce* unlucky. Let me read your palm. Oh yes, see here. I see a strange man coming into your life very soon."

"Will he be troublesome?"

"Very."

Several hours later, when they fell out of the pub and into the nearest bed and breakfast, both parties were far too incapacitated to be in any way troublesome.

* * *

The fry fixed her the next morning. It always did. He on the other hand looked a bit shaky but a couple of effervescent vitamin C drinks bought from a local pharmacist's and knocked back in quick succession seemed to bring a bit of colour back to his cheeks and his enthusiasm returned as he offered to show her a few of the local beauty spots.

There were times when she thought his car was going to pass out on the steep ascent towards Lough Derg but when the large blue lake made its first appearance she took a sharp breath inwards. Its beauty was almost spiritual and its influence completely calming.

It was a morning of saying goodbye and then hello again to the lake's shores as they stopped at the pretty little marina of Garrykennedy and later Dromineer where they got out for a walk to see the cruisers. Two beautiful white swans and a mucky grey cygnet circled each other on the glassy water and Ali was mesmerised at the tenderness of the little family as they glided close to the lake's shore.

Gazing at the lake's shoreline, Ali thought of the day when Dave had chased her down the pier, and the choppy waters of the Irish Sea and the hissing wind had thrown them together again, into the second phase of their relationship. A frown crossed her forehead as she remembered.

"Don't you like it here?" Karl asked, seeing her forehead wrinkle.

"Oh yes, I love it," she said quickly.

He next took her to see his "shack" on a field two miles from the nearest village.

"Do you want to come and walk the land with me?" he asked as they pulled past a gate and up a winding and overgrown driveway.

"You'd better stop with that talk or you'll be giving me notions. Walking the land indeed – isn't that virtually a marriage proposal?"

It wasn't a shack either. It was a stone-built farmhouse, complete with an imposing doorway and sash windows and when they pushed open the heavy wooden door she saw the most amazing hallway with a sweeping wooden staircase ascending into a ceiling so high she had to nearly bend her neck backwards to take it all in.

"Janey, it's impressive all right."

"Ah, it's not that special – it's only over 2,000 square feet."

"That's huge – you should have seen the inside of my flat!"

"And it mightn't look it but it needs lots of doing up in places," sighed Karl.

"Well, if you can't afford to do it up you could always rip out the fireplaces and the windows and sell them on for a few bob. You'd raise enough that way to clear a hefty credit-card bill at any rate. Only kidding, obviously that would be *totally* sacrilegious."

He led her inside and, as he stopped for a moment to close the door, she saw that the house was not nearly as pristine as she had first thought. The front door was partly held together by putty, the fanlight was cracked and the walls in the hallway itself were peeling and damp in parts. The floorboards were solid enough, although they were badly gapped in places, and peering into the front rooms she noticed that when the wind blew from time to time the old windows rattled unmercifully behind the faded shutters and the dust rose up in the two adjoining front rooms like something out of the Wild West.

"The kitchen is newer and a bit more homely," he said, leading her by the hand down two steps into a room to the rear of the building, which was flooded with light from three windows and a pair of wooden French doors which led out to a wilderness of a garden. The teak-stained floorboards were warped in places, the

Belfast sink cracked and the white wooden ceiling was peeling, but he was right – it was more homely.

In a corner, lying on some old newspaper, was a mound of chopped wood. Karl took some and got the kitchen stove going, saying that when it was in full burn it would take the chill off the walls.

He told her again that the house was inherited from a childless great-aunt, who had taken a shine to him before she died and that he was now itching to have a go at renovating the place.

All the while, as he talked, Karl was making himself busy while Ali sat on an old rocking chair and listened and smiled. Intently she watched as he fried red peppers and onions in olive oil mixed with curry powder. Then he opened a couple of tins of salmon and tins of leek soup and added them to the pan, casually threw in some milk and hot water and made up the most gorgeous-smelling chowder.

He lit some candles in old wine bottles and placed them on the scrubbed wooden table and set down mismatched cutlery and bowls along with salt and pepper cellars. Moving across to a paint-spattered wooden chair, she gorged herself on the chunky fish soup which was served up with hunks of home-made brown bread and butter and a bottle of red wine.

After they'd eaten he plucked some songs from his guitar, humming to himself as he fine-tuned the strings, and every time a strand of fair hair fell in front of his eyes he pushed it back with a long smooth movement of his hand that mesmerised her. Deep in concentration he tried out some chords and then replayed them as he tried to remember a piece.

Then his eyes caught hers and he laughed. "It's been a while since I played this one. I'll play something else."

Then he played something classical and started to sing in Spanish and Ali could feel the hairs on the back of her neck stand up in delicious shock. Tingles of pleasure seemed to tap up and down her spine and she gulped down a mouthful of wine to drown out what otherwise would have been a gasp.

* * *

In the half-shadowy light of the kitchen with a throw draped around her shoulders to keep her warm, she made love to him, moving on top of him as he sat in one of the battered old chairs, kissing him with tenderness, feeling his long slim hands gently caressing her body as their energy merged. Body, mind and soul flowed into one – like electricity, sometimes certain and steady and sometimes jolting them to unexpected places of pleasure.

What the hell are you doing, Ali Hughes?

Shut up, Head Voice – you're ruining it, Ali chided.

20

Back in Dublin, Ali decided to put Karl, his body, his mind and especially his guitar out of her head for good. For starters, he wasn't her type; he was a bit too "other worldly", too deep and just plain different from her. Besides, she could never really abide longish hair on a bloke. If she had to introduce him as her boyfriend to her friends, well, she might be a bit embarrassed.

Anyway, Karl had decided that his future would take a certain path and was moving down the country to work in a start-up pharmaceutical company, and Ali wasn't planning to join the welly-wearing brigade any day soon. Her mother might have effectively ruined her life but Ali decided to move on with her own plans to make something of a name for herself in the world.

Making a name for yourself was scary though. In fact, all the way back from Tipp Ali had hoped that her answering machine would be clogged up with messages from O'Grady's begging her to come back, but that of course was just fantasy. So having written her first piece on the killer bees making their way soon to Irish shores, Ali tried to pitch a few more ideas to Donal Dineen but he wasn't bitten with enthusiasm and nothing she researched made the December papers.

Not the best time, Dineen told her – anything "featurey" was planned weeks in advance for Christmas. There'd be plenty of soft news items around nights out, Christmas parties, that sort of thing, but nothing she could cover as assignments, and shift work would be given to the paper's more regular freelancers. Of course actual hard news, such as Christmas drunken riots, that sort of thing, they'd be very interested in that. January would be a better time to get back to him with ideas.

Right, it was feck off so unless she could come up with something with a criminal slant to it – like something Dave could throw her way and that wasn't very likely, not after their big tiff. Dave hadn't left any messages while she was away and the liberated woman in her didn't care. The liberated part of her didn't even care that she had slept with another man. Why should she care? Dave could be cheating on her any day of the week on his job and Ali would be none the wiser. She could see it now: "Well, missus, it seems to me you're running a brothel . . ." "Oh, guard, why don't you come inside and we'll come to an arrangement?"

Oh yes, men who didn't keep regular office hours, who didn't even have an office, could be up to all sorts of shenanigans and a loyal girlfriend would be none the wiser.

From now on, Flighty be my middle name, thought Ali as she squandered the whole month of December. She spent a pleasurable few days before Christmas pretending she was loaded while consoling herself with the notion that she had already made some progress on her future career, and come the New Year money would be rolling in from a new life as a journalist, although she might need something more stable too. The prospect of another real boring job put chills down her spine but her dad's tide-her-over money was running out fast.

It had been nearly a month since she saw Karl and he rang only once. Ali could hear the slight hesitation in his voice as he dithered over whether or not to leave a message on her machine. He did and she played the recording more than once, but she wasn't going to call him.

Christmas was destined to be a miserable affair with no proper boyfriend on the scene – she should have heeded Karen's advice to dump Dave after the festive season – and her mother had appalled her two daughters yet again by insisting that herself and Liam take off to a flash country hotel for "the bird and the pud". Naturally Liam was traumatised at being wrenched from his kitchen at such an important culinary time of the year, but Julie was adamant that she needed some aromatherapy treatments and maybe a round of golf with the possibility of a bit of celeb-spotting at some exotic spa in the west of Ireland.

Christmas with Ruth, her slipper-wearing husband and their two brats was an impending nightmare, but it was either that or sipping wine on her "ownio" in her apartment which was decorated with just one midget Christmas tree and cheap accessories.

* * *

On Christmas Day Gerry greeted Ali at the door in a pair of fluffy slippers – a present from Santa, he explained in embarrassment – and Ali was hardly in the door when she heard the two boys having a tantrum about who was meant to get Percy the Train for Christmas.

"Santa meant it for me!" wailed little Damien.

"No, no, Santa left *you* James the Engine, not *Percy*," explained his mother.

"No, he didn't! Percy's mine!" screamed Damien. Then the first bite of the day was placed and after a wail of pain Conor retaliated with some shin-kicking and head-butting.

"Drink?"

Before Ali could reply, Ruth poured her a monstrous vodka, rolled her eyes heavenwards and then drank it herself in one go.

"Little bastards, they won't even be any good to me in my old age. Boys just shunt you off to the old folks' home without a twinge of guilt. Sausage roll?" Ruth was cramming the pork treats into her mouth in an attempt to stuff down the silent screams.

The telly was switched on the entire day to remove the need for the adults to engage in any meaningful conversation.

Faced with the prospect of more of the same on St Stephen's Day, Ali made her excuses after dinner and literally charged for her own apartment, which felt cold and lonely as soon as she entered the door.

Quietly she made tea and then cursed the fact that she hadn't bought any milk. Leaning against the kitchen counter-top, she downed two mouthfuls of scalding brew, knocked back some Christmas cake stolen from Ruth's, took a deep breath, read the instructions once more and took the test. The blue line showed up. It was positive or then again maybe it wasn't.

Rooting through her bin to find the outer cardboard casing, Ali reread the instructions.

Yes – it was positive.

Ali climbed into bed, covered her head completely with the duvet and tried to remember when exactly she had stopped believing in Santa Claus. Was it nine or was it ten?

* * *

Naturally Karen had to be called in like the cavalry – that had always been her job when disaster threatened. The day after Stephen's Day and still in her pyjamas Ali opened the door to her best friend.

"Show us."

Karen's long taloned fingers took the plastic wand from Ali and held the dreaded thing up to the light. "Oh yeah – these are very reliable. Yeah, you're up the duff all right."

With clinical professionalism she handed the urine-soaked stick back to Ali then, realising that her brutally direct approach had totally taken the wind out of her best friend, she apologised and began to fuss.

"Sit down. You look pale. Do you want a cup of tea?"

"No milk in the house."

"Something stronger then: a real drink?"

"Do you think I should since I'm – you know?"

"The word is pregnant and in my experience most nippers are steeped in booze their first few weeks of life. It's usually the booze that causes the nippers in the first place. Go on, one beer won't kill you if you want it and if it helps you get over the shock."

Taking the cold bottle from her friend Ali could only manage one disgusting mouthful as her taste buds rebelled against the alcohol. The shock of pregnancy was enormous. Somehow she'd imagined only sixteen-year-olds were distraught to find out they were unexpectedly expecting, whereas here she was nearly twice that age and she was absolutely rocked to her core.

"Bollix. Now that I'm not working I'm not entitled to maternity benefit either," Ali moaned.

"It could be worse, Ali," Karen placated. "I know you're not getting on great at the moment but at least Dave is a decent as well as a sexy guy. I'm sure he'll stand by you no matter what you decide to do and help out."

Ali shut her eyes and stroked the space between her brows in a rhythmic manner. Taking a deep breath, she said it out loud: "The thing is, it's not his."

It was Karen's turn to be in need of the beer when Ali told her about her little three-day sojourn in Tipperary.

"I never told you because I didn't think it mattered. It was just a fling."

"Like hell! Oh Ali, what are you at? Now just think a minute. Are you absolutely sure it isn't Dave's?"

"Oh yes, absolutely certain. I haven't had sex with Dave since his Christmas party and then my 'little friend' arrived and then we had a big fight and couldn't stand the sight of each other – so yes, I'm certain."

Bar the admonishment for not using contraception, there was not much that Karen could say and she left her friend at three in the morning hugging a water bottle and watching a DVD of *When Harry Met Sally*.

So what if Ali's life wouldn't end up as happily as a movie? It didn't stop her wishing for it to happen.

* * *

There was no two ways about it: she was running out of money. She was running out of money and she didn't exactly work in an area where recruitment consultants were on the phone every day headhunting her for some major client. At this rate she might have to go back to waitressing, just as a stopgap or maybe even a bit of substitute teaching if she could get it. But she felt horrified at the thought of returning to haphazard student-type work. Part-time badly paid work would cripple what was left of her self-esteem.

No, January would be a better month; Dineen had said that. January would be a better month all round. New Year, new career: new baby? Oh God. It was looking like "new somewhere to live" as well.

Deep down Ali knew there was no way she could keep on her apartment, which was due for renewal in January as well. Worse still was the thought that she had to leave the lovely location of the sea and the pastel ice-cream coloured buildings, the trendy little cafés and bars, the people in stylish clothes, the glittering yachts in summer and big fuck-off cars. It had all made her feel part of a scene that was bursting with optimism and style even though she was mostly an observer and not a participant.

A few days after Christmas Ali sat on a bench overlooking the sea and cried for the impending loss of her beloved apartment, cried for Dave and cried for the loss of her detested job. Ali even cried for the cute guy in the next-door apartment who had produced a girlfriend over Christmas – she'd seen them kissing in the hallway and felt strangely gutted. Karen said it was all just hormones and the New Year blues, but Ali didn't think that that was quite the case. It seemed to her that she was going through more of a life crisis than a crisis pregnancy.

Perhaps she was just an all-round saboteur, someone who for whatever reason had to screw things up just as they were going right. At any rate she was going to need a new roof over her head soon and she couldn't even stay with her parents, thanks to Julie's monstrous behaviour.

So when Karl rang and asked her would she come to his New Year's Party down the sticks, she accepted. Why wouldn't she? It fulfilled her need to both run from and collide with impending danger all at once.

It didn't make sense, sure she knew that, and Karen pleaded with her to stay in Dublin and not be running down the country to a party where she knew nobody except the father of her foetus, and even then only briefly. Her hormonal state was going to be her undoing. Karen went into nursey mode and told Ali that at times like these there was a need to be a bit rational. Besides, Karen added, how was she going to feel relaxed in the company of strangers when she couldn't have a drink – the thought of booze made Ali feel quite nauseous – and how could she stand up straight in a room for more than twenty seconds when she felt like fainting all the time?

"I just feel like I have to do something, anything – anything is better than being here going mad worrying about it. Can't you see that, Karen?"

"Well, I think you might feel a bit of a sap surrounded by a lot of people you don't know but sure if it all goes arseways won't Auntie Karen still be here for you? Auntie Karen? I'm not sure if I like that – Jaysus, you having a baby is making me feel quite old."

"You old? Never! I'll text you at midnight to wish you a Happy New Year. It'll be the first New Year's Party in yonks where I'll be stone cold sober, but I'll just spend the time stuffing my face instead – sure I'm going to get as big as a house anyway," Ali quipped with a happiness she didn't really feel.

Karl had a friend who could give her a lift and, because she wasn't sure what state public transport would be in on New Year's Eve, she accepted. Walter was a nice but dull computer analyst who talked enthusiastically about his work the whole two and a half hours from Dublin. Smiling now and then to feign interest in his conversation, Ali was relieved when he stopped for petrol en route and bought her two bags of liquorice without any comment. All the way towards Tipperary she scoffed the sugary sweets as the smell and taste of liquorice seemed to curb her waves of nausea. Now and again Walter looked at her as if she was bats. That was all right, she felt bats.

When they had put many more miles behind them, and travelled the bendy road up to Karl's stone farmhouse and saw the windows lit up with candles, she felt a rush of excitement. She almost felt like a character from a Jane Austen book about to meet the ladies and gentlemen inside.

Not that the crowd inside looked at all like ladies and gentlemen. They were a mixed bunch, like the crowd at most parties she supposed, but she was struck by the numbers of people there and at the diversity of ages, ranging from those in their late twenties to maybe late forties or even fifties. They were all drinking punch, some in front of a roaring fire in the living room, some mingling in the adjoining dining room as the two dividing doors were flung open between the rooms for the night. The punch smelled divine – maybe it was the soothing cinnamon – but still Ali didn't dare try it.

Now the poured champagne, that was a different matter. It wasn't the cheap paint-stripper stuff with bubbles in it that is often passed off as champagne – this was the real McCoy and strangely it tasted good with the odd piece of liquorice as well. Maybe the future father of her baby was actually very well off, she thought as she munched through some yellow and black rings. Then she heard herself say that sentence out loud and cringed at its mercenary tone. For a moment Ali put out a hand to steady herself against a wall – the thought of Karl as a father to anything inside her made her sway.

Looking around, Ali noticed that he'd done a bit of cosmetic stuff with the place over the last few weeks, painted some of the woodwork, cleaned down the fireplaces in both rooms, put up one or two lights. It looked like he'd succeeded in moving down his entire music collection from Dublin and CDs and books were now in open boxes in the living room, pushed to one corner. As her eye fell on a CD by Bach she was struck by the stupidity of her situation.

All of a sudden she wanted to run, to be back in Karen's with a few acquaintances or maybe ringing in the New Year with Maggie down in Cork or even in Ruth's, listening to her moan about how crap the previous year had been. This place seemed so quiet. Dave's crowd were probably trashing the place by now, pouring beer everywhere and eyeing up the future bonkfest. Maybe Dave would be eyeing up some young wan at this very moment. Ali didn't know how she felt about that and she tried to banish Dave and all his mates from her mind.

It didn't take her long to register that Karl had entered the room. He was so much head and shoulders above everyone else and with his long stride he was across the floor to her before she knew it. Eager, that was the word for it. There was a sparkle about him. Ali could tell he was genuinely glad to see her, but she didn't know how she felt. Perhaps it was just the awkwardness of the situation, but all she could feel was numbness. Evidently he was interested in her and he was probably further encouraged that she had travelled all this way to see him, but under the circumstances she found chit-chat impossible.

After a few attempts at getting her to relax, warm up, be funny, relate to him in any way, he became politely irritated and the light inside his eyes dimmed a bit, the way it does when you realise the person you have greeted enthusiastically isn't as keen on you as you are on them. As his mouth became tighter and the smile left his eyes completely, Ali began to panic.

Clearly puzzled by her lack of warmth, he eventually left her with her glass of champagne and greeted a couple who had just turned up with a bottle of wine and some chocolates. Then she was left to the mercy of the room and she felt her stomach tighten as she noticed some middle-aged fogey with a beer belly walking towards her. He introduced himself as Nigel and attempted to jolly her into a better mood, telling her not to be a stranger. He took her by the elbow and introduced her to Deirdre, a forty-something woman with greying hair and nice but sensible clothes and glasses. Oh God, how she hated when people not your type tried to include you in their banal conversations and then introduced you to other people not your type!

Time crawled by and, although the room was now buzzing with voices and she recognised that people were having fun, she herself couldn't get in the mood and at one stage she was aware that she was being stared at. Not that that was exactly a surprise as she wasn't exactly being a social butterfly and neither was she getting drunk off her head.

Close to midnight people streamed out of doors and headed towards the back of the house. Ali gingerly followed the rest of them and, as the countdown to the New Year began, Karl and some of his friends started letting off fireworks. Explosive lights of every colour tore into the black sky and their screams totally drowned out the screams of the revellers as they hugged and kissed each other and wished each other well.

Feeling like she was having an out-of-body experience Ali watched while everyone was lost in the sky festival.

It was then that Karl grabbed a moment to take her aside.

"What's going on?" he hissed.

"I'm sorry. I shouldn't have come. I'll get the first train, bus, whatever out of here as soon as I can."

Impatiently, he dragged her round the side of the house and, in the shadows where they couldn't be seen, he pushed her up against the wall and stared in her face so she could see his fury.

"Look, if you're not interested in me, that's fine, but I think you're playing a strange game. Not returning my calls, then accepting my invitation to come down here and then not saying two words to me all night."

"I'll say two words to you now. I'm pregnant."

For a minute Karl's face went blank, then he let go of her abruptly. She watched as he clasped and unclasped his hands and then smoothed his eyebrows back with his fingertips as if he was lost in thought and she wasn't really there.

"Okay," he said at last. "You're obviously not up to partying. You need to take care of yourself."

Leading her into his house and up the stairs he showed her into his bedroom, took her shoes off and tucked her under the blankets. Caught up in the mechanics of looking after her, he didn't once ask "Are you sure?" or "Is it mine?" or "What are you going to do?" or worst of all, say "I'll support you in whatever you decide to do." How weird is that, she thought as he quietly left, but then there was a touch of the old-fashioned gentleman about Karl – she'd thought that the day he'd paid for everything in the pub. Maybe he knew she wouldn't be here if she had any doubt about the child's father.

Then there was no more time for thought as she fell into a deep exhausted sleep.

* * *

Around midday the next morning she awoke and when she went to put her foot on the floor she was overcome with a terrible wooziness. Downstairs she could hear movement, then she heard the sound of an engine turning over and tyres crunching on the gravel outside.

Her stomach cramped when she entered the kitchen and the smell of bacon hit her in a wave.

"Last of the revellers," Karl said, gesturing towards the front of the house.

He didn't bother offering her breakfast – obviously he could tell by her scrunched-up nose that she wasn't interested in a fry.

"Tea would be nice," she told him, "and some dry toast. With marmalade, maybe."

"Right."

After that exchange silence reigned as Karl switched on the kettle and put bread in the toaster.

Ali was trying to think of something, anything to say to break the silence when Karl beat her to it.

"I was awake most of last night. I came in and lay on top of the duvet for a bit, beside you, but you were dead to the world."

"I was just exhausted. I seem permanently exhausted at the moment. It's part of my overall condition, I think."

"Have you seen a doctor?"

Ali shook her head. "Just did the test – two in fact – just to be sure to be sure."

"And are you? Sure to be sure?"

"Yes."

"Right."

"Karl, I'm sorry to be landing all this on you – I didn't think this would happen after our time together – it shouldn't have happened – I thought I was safe . . ."

"Yeah, well, don't beat yourself up – there were two of us in it – it's not like I don't know how babies are made."

He busied himself with kitchen tasks and, watching the back of his head, Ali wondered if he was asking the same question as her: why the hell didn't they use a condom?

Karl's blond head turned round as he heard the toast pop up and it wasn't long before he served her up some plain toast with marmalade on it, just the way she liked it with the peel scraped off, and a mug of tea with just the right amount of milk in it. Just at that moment, she felt like she had been married to him for years and she thought about that as she went back upstairs and read an out-of-date Christmas magazine supplement in his bed with her head propped up against several of his stout pillows.

21

Ali stayed – and then she stayed some more. And suddenly it seemed as if she was on everyone's most wanted list. Karen was threatening to pull her by the hair back to Dublin if she didn't return her text and voice messages soon. It wasn't as if Ali was avoiding her exactly, it was just that Karen would be plaguing her as to what she was doing and what she was planning and Ali just couldn't answer any of that, not yet.

Maggie, normally ever so laid back, was also threatening, albeit very nicely and calmly of course, to make a detour from County Cork to find out what she was doing and even Ali's mother sent her a text to say she had been "missed" for the traditional New Year's roast. On the surface it seemed like quite a nice message, but reading between the lines Ali knew what it was really saying: that she wasn't at the family homestead and that she should have been. Although Ali didn't know why Julie should be so miffed, it wasn't as if she had done the cooking herself.

More beep, beeps emitted from her mobile and Ali realised Dave had left a voice mail, which surprised her. All it said was "Happy New Year!" No how are you doing, where are you, I love you, I miss you, or even I hate you – just Happy New Year. Maybe he hadn't scored over New Year's and was feeling nostalgic, crying into his pint, that kind of thing. Still, his voice was comforting somehow. She played the message over and over, trying to tease out any emotion from his voice. Was he angry? Was he sad? She thought of his impish grin and infuriating behaviour. Evidently she was feeling nostalgic as well. Well, there was definitely no going back now. One might have been able to conceal a fling, but not somebody else's baby – not that she would have concealed a fling – she would have told him.

It was ironic though. Now that she had broken off with Dave she was thinner than ever before. Now that she was preggers she could have been that out-and-out babe she imagined he always wanted. Just one whiff of pregnancy hormones and the fat was literally melting off her. If it wasn't for her lank and greasy hair and her itchy, dry but spotty face she could have looked damn desirable even.

Dunking a teabag in her cup, Ali sighed and went to root out a dry biscuit from a cupboard. In just over a week she had become familiar with the essential nooks and crannies of Karl's house and apart from constant nausea she was beginning to feel quite at home, a thought which alarmed her just a bit. Next she'd be wearing wellies, growing potatoes out of her face and letting all her womanly body hair grow into a thick black mat. Sure, what else could you do in a place miles from the nearest pharmacist or beauty parlour?

Karl was so busy going to endless meetings, training sessions and "getting to know you" do's with his new company, going to work before she got up and falling into bed long after she had gone to sleep, that they managed to avoid having a proper conversation about their dilemma – or the question of sex – and that suited both of them for a while because both of them were shell-shocked.

After two more weeks of her drinking tea and eating nothing but dry crackers, ginger-nut biscuits and liquorice, he came to sit on her bed looking pale and nervous.

"Look, I know you're sure and all and you have all the

symptoms. It's just, well, I was wondering if you'd go and see a doctor anyhow just to confirm it. Besides, I'm worried at how sick you are. There's a doctor I know in Limerick who's very good. I could get you an appointment if you like?"

It was evident that the young doctor who greeted them thought that they were a long-established couple. Beaming from ear to ear, he asked Ali if she wanted to repeat the test and when she shook her head he asked her to lie on the table so he could feel her abdomen. Then taking out a foetal Doppler he rubbed some cold gel on her tummy and said they might just be able to pick up a heartbeat and suddenly there it was like a little horse running fast in the Grand National, a magnificent little heartbeat which took her breath away.

Before Ali knew it she was being drained of blood for tests and being signed up on the regional GP/hospital maternity scheme. It seemed she was having a baby.

On the way back to Karl's farmhouse she made him pull over at a petrol station for a bumper bag of liquorice, and he asked her if she was all right. Then, with a quiet concentration that let Ali know he was also struck by the sound of that baby's heartbeat and was probably shook to his boots by it all, he drove in silence all the way home. Ali was quiet too. Today she was twenty-nine, although she said nothing to Karl. It didn't seem appropriate.

* * *

Somehow she stayed a few more days and a few more days again and then Karl drove her to Dublin to collect a few things she needed from her flat and then it was February and Karl was still flat out working for his new pharmaceutical company.

But then, at last, they had the discussion that neither of them really wanted to have.

"You're happy then with how things are going so far with . . .?" Karl faltered, struggling to find the next word, the appropriate word to finish the sentence.

"With the *baby*?" Ali tried slowly.

"It is a definite baby in your mind so?"

"Yes, of course."

He sighed, relieved that he didn't have to choose the word, whether it be baby, foetus or heap of developing cells and Ali was struck for the first time that even choosing something as simple as a word meant choosing a course of action.

"You can stay here," he went on. "But it's a bit remote and I'll be working all day and travelling a good bit in the new job and I don't know how you'll get to appointments in the hospital when they come up. Maybe my father could drive you – he's retired, he's always looking for something to do."

Ali felt quite alarmed at the thought of his parents knowing about her predicament at all. "I wouldn't want him to know . . ."

Karl shrugged. "They're going to find out sometime. What difference is it if it's now or later?"

He was right. It was logical that somebody should help take care of her while he was away. The problem was things weren't at all logical. Nothing seemed at all logical these days.

* * *

Of course it had to happen. Ali had told her father where she was staying, saying that she was starting a wonderful new life: New Year, new career, that kind of thing. So her mother just had to stick her oar in.

Early one afternoon just as Ali had thrown up in the toilet and was praying to God to return some power to her legs, she heard the heavy crunching noise of a car on the driveway outside.

From the top bedroom window she caught sight of her dad's reliable old Volvo and she could see her estranged mother making her way to the doorway, fluffing her hair as she wiggled her way up the path. Christ Almighty. Ali raised her eyebrows in annoyance. The vanity of it all! The woman's ego was positively massive. Julie was always acting as if the paparazzi were waiting for her at every turn.

For about thirty seconds Ali thought about hiding upstairs but she knew she couldn't avoid her mother forever. Far better she threw her a few bones to satisfy her appetite so she would feck off back up to Dublin and out of her world.

"Darling!" cooed Julie as she clutched Ali to her bosom and air-kissed her spotty cheek.

"Mum. You came all this way to see *me* – how *sweet!*"

Her father shot her a look of apology. He didn't need to explain. It was certain that Julie had worn him down and extracted the information from him about her daughter's whereabouts, then planned the whole military operation to look like a casual visit. Keep that in mind, Ali told herself. She's got a razor-sharp military mind, no scruples and has come to pry and spy. Tell her nothing.

"Isn't this a *lovely* part of the country? You'd never know what a jewel of a place this was unless you had a reason to be here, sure you wouldn't, Liam? But you're looking very thin, Alison darling. Thin, but spotty. Now a bit of make-up would cover up those blemishes although they say that that isn't very good for the pores."

"I'm detoxing, Mother – you know, post-Christmas penance," lied Ali. She couldn't mask the anger in her voice at having to suffer the impertinent figure of her mother, invading as always her space, even this new space in this house in the middle of nowhere.

Sensing the tension, Julie sweetened her voice and adopted her naughty but lovable-little-girl demeanour. "Oh, sweetheart, you're not still cross with me for taking a job in your old workplace, are you? From what the girls tell me you were looking for a new position anyway."

The girls! The girls! Was she now best chums with Maggie and Pam? What exactly were they telling her?

"And isn't Lucy a scream? She said I looked more like your sister than your mother! She came to lunch with us one day last week, a bit of a reunion. She's going to be on TV soon. Very pretty girl – her make-up alone is an art form."

For the first time in her life Ali felt pure hatred towards her mother. It was as if she had robbed her life – working in her old job, having drinks and lunch with her colleagues, having meetings with the gorgeous Joe himself no doubt. Hearing it spewing from Julie's excited mouth, Ali wondered in a panic if she had actually had a great life but had just thrown it all up. Then she heard Karen's voice repeating that Dave was a sexy fella too and she suddenly felt cold and very, very sick.

"You've gone green, Alison," her father said as he placed an arm around her and made her sit in an armchair in the kitchen.

"I think one of the herbal teas I was drinking isn't agreeing with me."

"Enough of this herbal-teas nonsense – we're taking you out for a nice pub lunch," said her father firmly. "Get some real food into you."

It was a disaster. The ride in the back of the car made it impossible for her to hide her nausea. When she got to the pub she picked at a chicken salad and drank mineral water while all the time her father shot her looks of concern. She could tell that her mother was burning to ask her what she was doing marooning herself in the middle of nowhere but that her father for once was being firm and was insisting that at least some of her privacy be respected.

* * *

Two days later and a phone call from Karen told her everything about the inner workings of her parents' minds.

"They cornered me yesterday in the car park of the supermarket. Me ice cream was nearly melted in the boot of the car. Well, look it here, Ali, your mother figures you're up the duff and she asked me straight out if you were."

"Jesus Christ, Karen, I hope you denied it?"

"I did. I did of course but it wasn't easy. Your mother has a way of looking right through you that makes it dead hard to tell porkies. But I didn't tell, that much I swear."

"Thank God for that."

"But your mother she wouldn't let it go. She kept on about your appearance and your lack of appetite and your nausea and your irritability. She kind of put me on the spot. So I knew I had to do something to throw her off the scent and explain your symptoms so I hope you don't mind but I told them that you had a stomach ulcer. I was quite proud of myself actually coming up with something like that on the spot – you know, a medical condition which fits with your pregnancy symptoms."

"My God, Karen!"

"Well, then I kind of added in a few bits to make it more believable, like that you were probably irritable because you were worried."

"Worried about what?"

"Well, that maybe you were going to need surgery and were worried because you had let your health insurance go and you might be waiting a long time on the public. Well, that's when your dad said he'd just give you the money up front for you to go private and then your mother said something about you never thinking ahead and it always costing them money. So then your dad started to shout that no one would hire you now when you're sick and that you wouldn't have needed a new job if your mam hadn't nicked your old one and that's when I kinda sneaked home to eat my melted ice cream."

Ali dug the phone into the side of her head and groaned silently.

"I did the right thing, didn't I, throwing them off the scent, Ali?"

"Oh, as *always*, Karen."

Putting down the phone, Ali stared down the wooden hall at the old-fashioned fanlight in the door. Her family would be trying to casually arrive down all the time now, her father to find out if she was at death's door and her mother to find out how much all this illness business was going to cost. Suddenly living in the middle of nowhere had become far too public.

Consumed by her thoughts Ali hardly heard the fat envelope dropping through the door. Picking it up, she ripped the brown envelope asunder and stood staring at the folded sheets of yellow paper. Her college assignments from the night-time journalism course. She'd done well with the first module, thanks to all the time off she had for cramming and catching up on reading because of her broken wrist. As always with Ali and courses, on paper things were looking beautiful, but what good was it all to her now, especially as there was always the threat of discovery hanging over her? It couldn't be long now before O'Grady's started insisting on their stupid receipt for her course. Between quitting her job, Christmas and the New Year they must have been distracted but if there was one thing Ali had figured out it was that paperwork always caught up with you in the end – it was always just a matter of time.

22

Karl's new company had sent him away for a couple of days on a training session to Amsterdam. Naturally the expectant father was worried sick about Ali and he made sure that the house was stocked with food, that there were masses of logs on hand for the stove, that all the bills were paid and then he dragged her out to the hall and showed her the fuse box and made her repeat after him again and again about electrical sockets and flipping trip switches.

"No, on second thoughts – don't touch anything. If you think anything at all is wrong you should ring my dad."

Her face must have shown that she wouldn't be too happy with a visit from his parents because he continued to try and reason with her.

"They're going to show up eventually."

"Do they know I'm here?" Ali asked anxiously.

"I told them you were a friend of mine doing a bit of research and writing for a government project and looking for a quiet place to stay for a while."

There was no doubt about it, she was rapidly losing track of reality. Not only was she apparently suffering from a chronic stomach ulcer, thanks to Karen, now she was doing research for the government as well – half the locals would probably think she was some sort of Irish FBI agent to boot. It reminded her of a stern warning one of her primary school teachers had once issued that lies beget lies until before you know it you are being swept away by them.

"I'd better hurry. Don't want to be late. I'll give you a bell when I land."

Clasping her hands in his, Karl placed a small kiss on the bridge of her nose before gazing anxiously at her again.

Ali read his look and sighed in exasperation. "I promise I won't do anything too daft or too strenuous and if I need information about anything *remotely* dubious I promise I'll call you first."

"Or my dad."

"Or your dad."

It was only when she was on her own without anyone to chat to that day that she noticed that this great old house was like a ship. It had a life of its own and creaked and groaned and sighed and the prehistoric sash windows sounded in agony when they rattled in the wind. As she walked through the half-empty rooms, she hoped there weren't any ghosts. Her footsteps rang hollow on the old wooden floors as she strolled absent-mindedly around the rooms. His home might have old-fashioned charm but when the winter sun streamed through the large windows she saw just how much it was in need of repair. The dust clouds reminiscent of the Wild West that she had noticed the first time she came would sweep across the floor no matter how many times the floor was brushed, and when you moved the shutters of the downstairs front rooms little bits of plaster would crumble to dust in front of your eyes. Spiders and their webs were everywhere enjoying the feast of woodlice and when Ali stared downwards into the cracks between the floorboards she shuddered to think what kinds of animal life inhabited the crawl area beneath.

The kitchen cupboards had seen better days and were literally falling off their hinges and there was a funny musty smell coming from one cupboard in the corner. Ali didn't think the peculiar smell was just down to her pregnancy and her keener sense of smell. There was what could have been a beautiful hardwood floor throughout the kitchen dining area but it needed a good sanding and polishing and was buckling to breaking point near the kitchen sink.

Upstairs one of the bedrooms was nearly uninhabitable and when you opened the door it seemed like a perpetual gale was crashing through the room. The windows rattled angrily and when Ali approached them she noticed there were even a few small bits of glass missing from one pane. Christ Almighty, the cold wind was like a knife through her bones, she thought as she pulled her heavy cardigan tighter around her waist.

Even in the so-called "habitable" bedrooms there were some large cracks and some damp. A large wardrobe was pushed against one corner to conceal the worst of it in what had become Ali's bedroom, but still she knew the dampness was there – she could smell it and no amount of pot-pouri, essential oils or air-freshener spray could lift the mustiness from the air.

On the landing there was ancient, stained wallpaper hanging from the walls, and in one of the corners of the frame of the landing window she noticed some grass growing in a tiny mound of earth.

The bathroom was the worst of it though. It was beyond freezing; its icy breath cruel. The radiator never seemed to get past lukewarm and Ali craved heat so much that in the weeks since she had come to stay in his home she had developed the habit of staying in the shower so long that her flesh was nearly burning.

All alone, she made a plain supper, read a little, listened to music and went to bed to lie with her eyes wide open most of the night. Without another voice to distract her she was forced to be alone with her own thoughts and her own fears and not for the first time in her life she was questioning the sanity of what she was doing. Was she really the "fly by the seat of her pants kind of girl" that she thought or was she just perpetually running away from life? If she was the "fly by" girl then she should feel exhilarated by her present life, but she felt anything but exhilarated – she just felt afraid, sick, lonely and miserable.

There was no flat back in her beloved Dublin any more, no job, no job prospects, no money, no savings and not much hope of things changing. Most bizarrely of all, in the midst of all this madness she also felt compelled to give birth to this growing life inside her. Once again she felt that her life was like watching an accident in slow motion and once again she had the best seats in the house for the impending disasters to come.

So in the midst of all this aloneness it came as a shock the next morning to hear a key turn in the front door and then hear the heavy door swing open and bang shut. The toast and peanut butter nearly gagged her when the kitchen door itself opened up and a tall and sinewy man in his sixties stood before her.

His clothes were all crumpled and he was wearing sandals and no socks even in winterish weather. His check jacket was well worn around the collar and elbows and a sagging trouser-hem was held together by two steel staples.

"Well?" he smiled at her.

Well what? she thought as she pulled the belt of her dressing-gown tighter around her waist. Thank God she was wearing pyjamas – if necessary she would be able to make a bolt for the back door faster than if she was wearing a nightie.

"Well – 'tis yourself so – himself told me you were here but to tell you the God's honest truth I forgot – just checking everything is in order," he said by way of explanation and suddenly she saw the resemblance as he smiled.

"You must be Michael, Karl's dad," she said, offering her hand for him to shake.

He was a queer sort of fella – this man who was the same flesh and blood as Karl. They were both fair-haired and there was a similarity in the shape of their eyes, but the resemblance wasn't too obvious until Michael smiled and when he did father and son were a certain match. Karl was slimmer – his father, although shrunken by the years, must have been a giant in his day. His hands were like spades while Karl's were long and slim. Even now she could see Karl's fingers caressing a guitar. This giant man had Karl's gentleness about him but he had a desperate shyness too and it seemed to Ali that if he could he would retreat into the very walls of the house to avoid her and yet he lingered like a hungry stray cat as if he wanted to find out more.

"You're a class of a writer, I hear," he continued.

"Well, I –"

"I suppose, if you had the time, you might be writing for John Joe Connor's paper as well."

"Have to admit I haven't met him yet," smiled Ali.

"Right so. If you don't want for anything I'll leave you. Sorry for tearing in – herself is waiting for me in the car. We're going to the shops."

Just like that he bolted as if he was some kind of untamed but curious animal.

"Herself" wasn't waiting for him in the car but she was leaning up against their filthy vehicle smoking a cigarette and looking decidedly agitated as she tipped ash on the ground in a frustrated manner. The wife had a mean pinched little face and looked twenty years older than "himself" as well. Her iron-grey hair was greasy and she wore it pulled back from her face with a plain elastic band.

All at once a vision of the beautifully groomed Julie entered Ali's head. Surely Karl's mother couldn't have been much older than her own and yet here was Julie's equivalent wearing an ill-fitting skirt and jumper, no make-up, snagged brown tights and the flattest, sturdiest and ugliest shoes that Ali had ever seen.

For a split second their eyes met and Ali began to quiver. Eyes like granite, eyes that said nobody took anything belonging to her, let alone a son, without a good fight. The woman put out the cigarette and got back into the car with a face on her like thunder. Ali wouldn't like to cross her; she felt if she did she would be the one crawling away to lick her wounds.

Later on Ali decided to watch some TV and by nearly dangling the aerial out of the window she managed to pick up a broadcast signal from the national airwaves. Karl had warned her that his house was in the middle of nowhere and that she would be lucky to get a picture on his dusty TV screen, but she did. She settled down in the tattered old leather armchair, feeling proud of herself, and all of a sudden there she was: the beautiful minx herself, Lucy!

My God but she did look gorgeous! In a scene with her new on-screen boss, bosoms heaving as she whacked him across the face for daring to kiss her, then threw him the eye as if to say she might be on for it tomorrow if he asked nicely first! Ali watched as Lucy flounced off the set with the familiar corn-coloured hair flaring after her.

It was hard not to feel nostalgic for the time she had spent in the office with her, with all the girls, having a laugh, but in an instant Ali felt her own destiny had changed. Though unfortunately she didn't know where she was going. *Good on you anyway, Luce, for being so brazen and so focused. You deserve everything you can get!*

After midnight, when there was nothing more on fuzzy four-channel TV-land, Ali called it a night and crawled into her bed under a heavy duvet wearing her fleecy cardigan and thick fisherman's socks and almost instantly fell into one of her heavy pregnancy slumbers where not even her worries had a chance in hell of keeping her awake for more than a minute.

So it was a wonder that in the early hours of the morning she managed to be woken up by a very loud scurrying underneath her bed.

It was an animal, no doubt about that. It sounded like an enormous demented cat, thumping, springing around and scratching. The noise was absolutely petrifying and, although it lasted no more than a few minutes, in Ali's ears it went on forever. Then there was nothing but Ali's own half-suffocated breathing and then the commotion under the bed started up again so that the hairs on the back of her neck stood on end. Minutes later, there was silence again for a while. And then there it was again.

As dawn broke she lay there too petrified to move and just

listened, ears straining like a dog, waiting for the scratching and scurrying and thumping to start up again, praying to God that whatever it was, was under the floorboards and couldn't take a notion to jump into her bed. Finally, when her pregnant bladder could take it no more, she was forced to bolt for the bathroom.

With an enormous scream, half out of her own terror and half as a bid to scare the bejaysus out of whatever was under her bed, Ali tore from the room, banging the door behind her to contain the awful beast.

When she recovered she rang Karl's mobile in Amsterdam, eight o'clock Irish time, and got straight through to his voicemail and left a message. But when the morning went by and she still couldn't get hold of him, she picked up her phone and rang the one contact she had close by: his father.

This time when Ali answered the door Michael was dressed half-respectably and she was the one who looked like a tramp. Too afraid to venture back into her own room to get her clothes, she had settled for a pair of Karl's tracksuit bottoms and his fleecy dressing-gown. She noticed Michael give her the once-over and politely say nothing.

"It's – it's – it's in my bedroom that there's the problem, that's why I'm dressed a bit peculiar," she explained.

"Right so," he said as he sprinted up the stairs with an iron poker swung over his shoulder like a young man of twenty.

From downstairs she heard the bedroom door open and Michael storm through it like a paratrooper. A few minutes later he was back downstairs, red in the face and breathless from effort and excitement.

"Nothing – nothing at all," he fumed. "That bastard, bastard rat!"

It was like the cold hand of death had just touched Ali's shoulder, then ran his fingers up and down her spine for best effect. Every cell in her body seemed to shut down for a split second as the gravity of what Michael had said hit her.

"Michael, did you just say what I think you said? Did you just say a . . . a rat?"

Of course the rat idea had occurred to Ali when she'd been alone in the bedroom with all that demonic scratching and thumping but she had by now convinced herself that it might not be so, that she had blown the whole thing out of proportion and that maybe it was something else she was hearing . . . a cat perhaps?

Ali's head was swimming as she watched Karl's father sit sadly on the rocking chair in the kitchen, laying the poker down on the floor and shaking his head with a sadness of a man who has been worn down by Nature. "Indeed and I did – I think it could be very possibly a rat all right."

Ali had to lean against the wall for a minute; she could feel her pulse quicken and her head about to spin. Every picture she had ever seen of a rat filled her head: from rats at tip heads, at docks, George Orwell's *1984*, pet-shop rats, laboratory rats, and she felt like she was going to throw up right there in the room.

"Clever bastards, rats, you know," Michael mused. "Awful hard to get the better of – *very* intelligent. Could take ten days or more to get them to be interested in any bait. And the snap traps," he made a sharp clapping sound with his hands, "they can drag them and shake them off, will bite through their very limbs to get them off if they have to – and as for poisoning them, well, now, that's a very dodgy business altogether – you could find them turning up dead just about anywhere and you'd *never* find the rotting corpse. I remember we had a dead mouse once rotting under the floorboards and we couldn't find the bugger, and the *smell* – three months of it we had – the sweet vile smell of decay from one little mouse. So you can imagine a fella as big as a rat – God knows how long you'd be smelling him and it's a smell you'd not easily get out of your nostrils I'm telling you . . . ."

It was maybe the talk of the smell of rotting corpses that did it, that and the lack of the breakfast and maybe the sleep deficiency as well. In seconds Ali was as close to the floorboards as the poor poisoned mouse which had been dead under them for three months. The lights went out. Ali fainted.

* * *

Karl's concern was urgent when he came through the door and found her curled up on the sofa in the front room hugging a hot-water bottle and wrapped in a duvet but Ali, smiling weakly, assured him that she was all right.

Karl rooted around his bag of duty free and tried to find a few things to put her in a better mood.

"Belgian chocolates, sweet wine and pâté with truffles in it," he smiled proudly but she waved them all away with a hand. "What about the pâté on toast even?" he asked.

"Not recommended in case of listeria," she explained.

He looked disappointed that all his presents had been rejected.

"Are you still in shock about the rat?" he asked.

"I'm not too delighted but your dad seems to think he'll catch him – eventually."

"I'll sleep in there tonight and see if I hear anything. I'm so sorry about not getting your message, Ali. My phone was dead and I left it in the room when I went to meetings."

His demeanour was so contrite that to humour him she said she'd try a small glass of dessert wine.

Karl laughed as he poured the honey-coloured liquid and on a whim he clinked their glasses together. "Here's to us!" he said with a smile.

"Yes, *us*," she said, tapping her abdomen. "We've kind of got this arse-ways, haven't we?"

"What?" he said, kicking off his shoes and massaging his shins.

"The *us* bit – I think we were meant to get to know each other a bit *before* we decided to shack up with each other and have a baby. You know, I've just realised I don't even know your middle name."

"It's David," he said, loosening his tie.

For a moment she felt a jolt as she started to think of her David, her Dave back in Dublin, but she recovered herself and continued her queries.

"There's so much about you I still don't know. Like your parents, for example. They're just so different from you, I never would have known they were your relatives – you don't even talk like them."

"Rough diamonds, the both of them," he said. "My father would have loved to have been a radio presenter, singer or an actor, something wordy or dramatic. He loves words but never got past fourteen in school. We don't talk about it much but I'd say he was probably dyslexic. The mother – well, she had a hard enough life too. Her mother died young and she basically reared three younger sisters, never had any luxuries. They put every penny they could into their three children, me especially. Niamh made her own way in Chicago and Cathy took off to Australia straight after college."

By this stage he had wormed out of his suit and shirt and was striding across the living room in his socks and jocks looking for some clothes to pull on from a pile of clean laundry stacked on an armchair. Something animal in her kicked in when he reached over his head to pull on his top and she saw his belly tense for a moment or two. She put down her drink and left the sofa, walked over to him and put her arms around his waist.

"I don't know where this is all going to end, Karl," she said simply.

"I don't know either," he said in sad resignation.

"Sometimes I feel as if I've torn up some rule book on how to live your life properly."

"Well, my life hasn't exactly been textbook either."

He took her hand from his waist and held it, then quietly turned his honest blue eyes on her face. Ali felt like a virgin before him, stripped down to her core, with no pretences or flirting or half innuendos or deception. They hadn't had sex since she'd come to live in his house but now for the first time since the conception of their baby she needed him as her lover and she wanted to put the baggage of the last few weeks behind her.

At first she felt as awkward as he, and their encounter was fumbled and shy. The earth didn't move. It was just plain, tender, wordless, lovemaking between two people, but at least it was honest. Afterwards, when they had clambered up the stairs and fell into bed, his hand reached to set his alarm clock and within minutes they both fell asleep on a long journey to God knows where.

23

"Karl is going away for a few days and leaving me in the house and the truth is I'm afraid," Ali heard herself say down the phone line.

"'Course you're afraid," gushed Karen, "stuck down there with nothing to do, nowhere to go, not knowing anybody, clearly off your rocker from hormones – anybody with half a brain would be afraid!"

"No, it's not that. I'm afraid because Karl will be away and there's a rat in the house."

After the ten-second silence Ali heard Karen's familiar bellyache laugh down the phone. "A rat? Pull the other leg! See you tomorrow afternoon."

The phone went dead.

* * *

The stupid bitch looked gorgeous – dripping in gold, highly made up and perfumed, with gorgeous shiny hair. It hardly seemed fair that someone like Karen who shovelled all kinds of nutrient-deficient fuels into her body could look this good – and she even smoked for God's sake.

The day was freezing cold but it still managed to be a bright Irish February day. Karen shoved her designer shades from her eyes and into her hair with her painted talons. Karen always said that she wore sunglasses when driving because a low wintery sun could be blinding but Ali knew this was only half the reason and that Karen would gladly wear her sunglasses to bed just to look cool. But today Ali could forgive her best friend any pretensions as she looked up and shot her a radiant smile.

"So seen any good willies lately? Oh I forgot, you *have* of course," said Karen as she made an exaggerated show of examining Ali's midriff with her big dark eyes.

"Show us around the castle then," she said, linking arms with Ali and marching her through the front door.

"Ooh, this is nice!" Ali's raven-haired friend stopped for a moment and surveyed the entrance hall.

"*Could* be nice," corrected Ali. "Could be nice, that is, if you had pots of money to rip bits out and slap new bits in."

"Potential, darling, potential – a nice little fixer-upper. A house is like a man – you just need a good base and after that, you know what they say, a woman's touch works wonders."

"Jesus, Karen, will you ever give over, you're beginning to sound like my mother. It's great that you're here though – we'll be able to snuggle up in bed together and talk all night, just like when we were little girls."

"Like a pair of lezzers? No, thank you! I'm expecting my own boudoir, sweetie, with an en-suite naturally."

"Oh yeah? And would Madame like the poor, pregnant serving girl to bring her breakfast in bed as well?"

"Not *likely*, you'd probably be puking in me Full Irish. Never met a pregnant woman yet who could stand the smell of cooking bacon."

In the cosy kitchen Karen kicked off her boots and curled up like a cat with her legs under her bum on a tattered old armchair. Like a child, she fidgeted when Ali handed her a cup of tea. "Quit the fags, again. This time I know I'll do it." She smiled, looking a bit uncertain. "Well, I'll give you the good news first. It seems the new man in your life isn't a serial killer. I made a few discreet enquiries, you know, got some of the girls to put out feelers, who he's snogged, fancied, shagged, anything like that, in the last couple of years, his bastard rating, quirks, bad habits, who his friends are, what they do – and it seems he's pretty normal really; a bit too normal maybe."

Looking like the cat that had devoured the cream, Karen sank back into the soft chair and smiled a very smug smile while Ali felt the nausea rise from the pit of her stomach. She shuddered to think what Karl might do or say if he knew that one of her closest friends was checking up on him.

"Janey, Karen, if you ever get fed up of being a nurse I reckon you might make a mighty fine policewoman. Have you ever thought seriously about joining the guards?"

"Well, now you've kind of led me to the bad news yourself. Dave was in casualty last week with a prisoner and I caught his eye. Naturally he didn't want to talk to me so I just went over to him myself."

Ali groaned. "Karen, do you ever think of *not* acting on impulse? I suppose he was pissed off?"

"Well, no, actually, he seemed quite indifferent, cold even. All he said was: 'Tell her, wherever she is, I want my CDs, stereo and black fleece back.' Then he turned and left."

With her head down, Ali scrutinised a nail with chipped varnish on it and then she found herself pushing back the loose paint with the thumbnail of her right hand. Karen's news of Dave's stony indifference left her feeling numb. There should be some feeling of sadness at the end of a relationship, but when Ali thought of Dave she felt like a cold hard rock was wedged in her stomach.

"I have his things here, brought them from Dublin for safe keeping," she said quietly. "Maybe you can meet with him sometime and give them back. I can't say I blame him, his coldness that is."

"Oh Ali, I know you mightn't want me to say it, but are you sure it's all over?"

"Of *course* it's over. I'm three months pregnant with another man's baby. I'd say that's pretty over, wouldn't you? Besides, he has his pride. I broke up with him once and threw him out of my apartment next. No, I'd say we're finished all right."

"And Karl? I know you're pregnant and everything, and I don't want to upset you, but you're not thinking that you're in love with him or anything, are you? I mean you've only just met him – well, you only just met him when you got pregnant and then with all those hormones kicking in – I mean, do you *really* know what you feel for him at all?"

Ali shrugged her shoulders and said nothing and Karen kept on talking.

"Ali, I don't mean to sound too mercenary but you do know if you continue living with Karl you won't get a Lone Parent's Allowance from social welfare – it's means-tested and, well, if things don't work out between you two, you have to be separated three months before you can make a claim and even then social welfare will be at you to get maintenance from him first for the baby . . ."

"And where would I go even with my Lone Parent's Allowance? I don't know anyone down here to move in with and I'd be lonely – and I'm not ready to move back to Dublin."

And Karen realised that, for now, the subject was definitely closed.

Outside it was sleeting. The weather forecast had promised proper snow for the next couple of days and the whole country was prepared to grind to a halt with the first few snowflakes. Karen was on her second cup of scalding hot tea and her third chocolate biscuit and her constant nattering managed to shatter the eerie silence of the house. For that Ali was grateful. It was not fun being alone in this big house without company, feeling cold most of the time, sick some of the time and confused all of the time.

With the passing of the hours, and with Karen telling her all the gossip, the old Ali began aching for the energy of the city where everything was within easy walking distance. In contrast the quietness of the country sometimes felt like death all around her, especially with Karen telling her all the gossip of all the "in" places she had been to, of cafés and pubs and late-night shopping and taxi rides home with friends and colleagues – and men, of course. Right now, right at this very moment perhaps she could have been with Dave, in the middle of all that noise and excitement, linking arms with him down the street, bantering with him in the car, curled up in his strong arms, having fun, laughing with him.

Now that she thought about it, she missed Dave's laughter, that and his complete irreverence for everything and his total love of life. For a moment it struck her that while Karl was considerate and caring, he was a bit too gentlemanly at times and while she thought Karl had a sense of humour she could hardly think of him as being a big, lovable child. Would he ever wrestle her to the ground like an overgrown toddler or tickle her till she screamed for mercy and had sex with him?

Granted, she was pregnant and maybe Karl was just handling her with extreme care, but sometimes Ali liked a bit of rough, a good fight and a passionate making up afterwards.

A bony finger, jammed in her ribcage, startled Ali from the lovely snooze she was having on the rocking chair and she saw Karen pretending to be outraged, standing hand on hip above her.

"Well, you're not much fun, missus – a fine thing to invite your best friend all the way down here only to fall asleep!"

"I'm sorry, Karen," yawned Ali. "It's this damn baby. All I seem to want to do is sleep."

Ali looked up from her stretch to find that Karen was already bounding up the stairs, suitcase bumping roughly behind her.

"I'll sort myself out so. I have a sleeping bag and pillows and all. The perfect guest, what?"

Her perfect guest disappeared behind the big white door of her chosen bedroom and Ali, following her, collapsed into bed without even brushing her teeth or taking off her clothes and fell into the drugged sleep which seemed to be symptomatic of her pregnancy.

All was well until about six in the morning when a pyjama'ed and screaming Karen tore into the room where Ali was sleeping and jumped onto Ali's bed.

"There's a fucking badger in that room – either that or a bloody loud poltergeist! The scratching and the – the thumping – good Jaysus, Ali, why didn't you warn me?"

For a minute a bleary-eyed Ali hadn't a clue what her best friend was rattling on about and then she smiled.

"I see you've met Ratzo and I did warn you! I told you on the phone and you fecked off tonight while I was half-asleep myself and I just forgot to remind you. Here, get under the duvet, would you?"

"Forget? How in God's name could you forget there's a big bleedin' rodent in the next room?"

"Because I've given up sleeping in there and have taken up sleeping in here now and I've managed to forget all about him – well, some of the time and anyway right now it's easy to forget – I'm forgetting my own name these days. Besides, we're not sure it *is* a rat and we haven't found any droppings and it mightn't actually be in the room, it could be in the walls or under the flooring. A while ago a few floorboards had to be ripped up to move a radiator and it's possible somewhere along the line something wasn't sealed up properly, and then there's the grate on that huge old fireplace, which is broken, and some of the bricks are loose there too and maybe something is even getting in from the roof, who knows! So, to answer your question," she looked at the alarm clock and checked the time, "at six twenty in the morning I can easily forget about Ratzo because thinking about him requires too much bloody brainpower! Besides, Karl's father has promised to *fix* him and although I'm still terrified of the bastard I trust Michael when he says that down the country these things aren't such a big deal."

Karen's eyes were huge with wonder and fear and Ali knew that her friend thought country living had made her totally mad in the head. She snuggled up to Ali like a little girl afraid of the bogeyman and in the darkness Ali smiled to herself. It was nice to be lying beside her childhood friend and to have her arms around her patting her tummy where the baby bump would soon be. It took her back to the times when they'd stay over in each other's homes as teenagers, gossiping about boys and wondering where their lives would lead them. The feeling of being with someone who knew her so completely and who expected nothing from her filled Ali with peace.

"Karen – do you think I'm mad in the head?"

"Undoubtedly, but then you always were."

"Why is it, do you think, that even though I was always brainier than you in school you were always smarter?"

"Why do you say that?"

"Because it's true. I know you're a mad bitch and all but you're street-smart, you're savvy – I wish I could be a bit more like that!"

Ali expected a typical funny reply but instead she felt Karen squeeze her arm tenderly. "You're just pregnant. Don't be too hard on yourself. Stick with me. I'll learn yeh eventually, Ali Hughes."

For a while there was just silence and then Karen started to rock with laughter.

"I bet you didn't tell me about the rat on purpose."

"I *did* tell you. I just forgot to *assure* you that it was true," Ali said, joining in with the laughter.

The giggling went on for ages until their sides were literally sore from their convulsions. Then Karen calmed down, made herself really comfy and began to chat contentedly about life back in Dublin.

"Oh, I forgot to tell you – I ran into your mother again a few days ago," she mused.

"Oh? Is she *terribly* concerned about my ulcer?"

"No, not really, but since her little trip down here she has decided that you live in a pretty part of the country, an area that is a 'safe investment, on account of the tourist appeal of the waterways', her words, and she says she intends to buy a nice little property right on your doorstep."

It was time for Ali to laugh. "I can tell you here and now, Karen, that she hasn't the money to buy *any* property which means you're spoofing."

"Oh Ali, your 'Old Ma' mightn't have had the money to buy a new property but your 'New Ma' is thinking outside of the box ever since she did her extravagant positive-thinking course. Turns out she's going in with a consortium and one of her business associates is none other than your ex-boss Simon!"

Like a scalded cat Ali sat bolt upright in the bed and turned on the bedside light to look Karen in the face. She wasn't joking.

"What's the big deal? It will be nice to have your mother on your doorstep, maybe in a nice little holiday home, an extra pair of hands once the baby arrives."

"You're talking my mother here! Remember she's not exactly motherly!"

"Ah yes, but you always said she made an excellent granny . . . night-night."

Ali turned out the light again and lay down. In the darkness she couldn't stop her brain churning. God damn it but her mother was like a filled tooth sitting on a dodgy nerve – trouble.

* * *

Within days of Karen leaving, Maggie appeared on the doorstep and Ali couldn't help thinking that her casual arrival had been part of a plan hatched up between her two best friends. Immediately she felt annoyed and embarrassed. Not that Maggie would ever voice her disapproval of Ali's life but Ali felt she'd be thinking it anyway.

"It's a nice spot here, isn't it?" said Maggie. "Couldn't have picked a more tranquil place if you needed to get your head together and think over a few things. Could be a lonely place too, though, girl – if you weren't careful."

In a few sentences Maggie had spelled out her concerns without criticism, just putting the facts before her without any fancy bows or ribbons.

"All right, Maggie – I hear what you're saying." Ali tried her best to smile but she knew her response was somewhat tetchy.

But Maggie, being Maggie, wasn't in the least bit offended. She had hardly her coat off when she started to look after Ali, putting the kettle on the boil, banging some cushions for her to ease her back into, finding her slippers.

"I'd never want to upset you, girl, you know that, it's just that we all have to face reality now and then. You are having this baby, you're living with the father but he's away a lot and it's a bit isolated here. Will you be living here when the baby is born? How will you get around to do the shopping or to bring the baby to the doctor considering you have *no car* and *no full driver's licence* and *it's a bit isolated here*?"

"I haven't got that far ahead in my thinking yet – sorting out the minor details, that is – and don't dare go on about social welfare entitlements when the baby is born – I've already had an earful from Karen!"

"That aside, you have to face *some* facts, Ali. We're all just a bit worried that you're undergoing some sort of Victorian confinement here."

"Janey, amn't I blessed to have such mammies for friends! So what do you suggest I do then, Maggie baby, 'cos it seems that between you and Karen, you have my life for the next few months mapped out for me."

"It's just that, when you're feeling a bit more like yourself, you'll need to plan – plan like you've *never* planned before, Ali, *and* carry your plans out."

There was no mistake it was a warning, as strong a warning as she was ever likely to get from Maggie and the last warning that Maggie was to issue during her stay. Every time Ali looked at her from then on she found her cleaning, sorting, scrubbing and acting like a general house servant.

"For Christ's sake," yelled Ali when she could stand it no more, "it's *me*, not *you* who's meant to have the nesting instinct!" And she pulled a duster from her friend's hand, replacing it with a glass of finest Irish whiskey.

24

Something wonderful happened. One day Ali woke up and felt normal, or at least nearly normal. The nausea lifted, her energy began to rise, the daffodils were out and the days were becoming sunnier. With a surge of happiness she threw open a big sash window, stretched out her head and shoulders and drank up the sunshine. Optimism, happiness and activity became the keywords, especially since Ratzo had apparently gone AWOL. Karl had been sleeping in the bedroom every few nights and had heard nothing – Ratzo had moved on – either that or he'd been poisoned but Ali didn't care.

Then Karen rang to report on the morning's post – Ali had decided to use Karen's address while she was temporarily of no fixed abode.

"There's a brown one here – it's either revenue or the other 'vroom vroom' one if you catch my drift. You did apply?"

"The driving test? Yeah, in a moment of madness I applied but I can't do it now, not now that I'm pregnant, I'll just have to cancel."

"Third time lucky?" cajoled Karen

"I don't even have a car any more and it's been months since I've driven."

"Hire one – same model – it's taken forever just to get a date for your driving test and you're letting the fact that you're preggers and carless stand in your way? You *know* how to drive, you *know* the route – for God's sake, you drove it every day for years! All you need is to chill. You know, you might even be able to use my car. If I can insure you for a week for under a hundred euro, I'll pay for it myself as a little pre-baby present to you, and there's a guy up here who gives lessons and he has the same car as me, so maybe it would make sense to book him. I'm off that week too . . . now you'll have to wear a sexy short skirt in case you get a male tester . . ."

There was no reasoning with her. Ali thought if she just let her rant on about it for a while it would eventually lose its appeal and she would let it lie, but she was determined. Two days later Ali received a *How to Pass your Driving Test* DVD through the post – along with a positive-thinking manual and a Good Luck card.

A week before the test Ali found herself in Dublin, staying in Karen's room on a blow-up mattress, booked in for intensive driving lessons and in Karen's car every chance she had doing manoeuvres in car parks and driving at a snail's pace through the city gridlock.

"I can't believe you insured me, you're the best friend ever," Ali gushed as she reversed around a bend in a housing estate and checked her position in the rear mirror.

"Less yackin' – more drivin'!" roared Karen. "Now don't forget to put your seatbelt back on after this manoeuvre or you'll fail." Ali's driving instructor was a lamb in comparison. He took her over the test route at every lesson and every day Karen and Ali did it again for practice. Karen made sure she was familiar with all the controls and got the feel of the gear stick, and her driving instructor made sure she knew how to prop up the bonnet and answer essential questions on the engine. Eventually she decided to do the test in Karen's car which happened to be identical to the driving school one. For some reason Ali's illogical brain had decided that red (Karen's car) was luckier than blue (the instructor's).

Ali was hyperventilating on the morning of the test.

"I can't do this," she told Karen right before her final pre-test lesson with her instructor – she'd decided not to go out with her instructor right before the test in case she got the heebie-jeebies – but here she was having them anyway. "People prepare *intensively* for this kind of thing for months. I can't expect to just turn up and pass!"

Out of her handbag Karen pulled a clear plastic bottle full of long brown tablets and she pressed one into her friend's hand. "Take this before your lesson and tell me how you get on. It's a natural supplement to calm your nerves, it's totally safe – won't hurt you or the baby one bit."

Ali took it – she'd trust Karen with her life – if Nurse Karen said it was safe and would help, then who was she to argue?

Ali nearly ran over Karen in excitement when she got back from her lesson.

"Good God, those supplement things really work! Can I have more?"

Karen shook her head and smiled. "Just one more – take it half an hour before the test and you'll be fine, especially since you're wearing a short black skirt and your little bump is nicely highlighted. Never heard of anyone yet who ever got a female tester and the combination of your sexiness and your mumsiness is bound to terrify the bejaysus out of any man, which might get him to overlook a few major errors."

"Karen, what if I do get a female tester? She might be pissed off about my skirt and what bump – I've no bump!"

"Well, if you do . . . no, trust me, you won't. I just have a feeling about this. I also thought I might make a personal appearance myself – at the pedestrian lights near the shopping centre, the one where you have to look out for idiots who put their foot on the crossing."

"What?"

"You drop me off there before the test and I'll watch out for the car, then I'll pop out of nowhere just to test your braking skills. He'll be *dead* impressed, especially since they say pregnant women have impaired coordination."

"My God, Karen!"

"Honey, if we are to pull this off, drama is everything! Just keep thinking of that baby inside you and how you're going to get around after it's born."

Half an hour before the test Ali knocked back her little brown tablet and almost instantly felt super-calm and floaty. She was cool and competent as he – it was a bloke after all – asked her to participate in the charade of opening the bonnet and pointing out engine parts that a woman might need to be familiar with should her vehicle ever break down. As if! If Ali was ever in mechanical trouble she knew she'd be calling a man – any man, an AA man, her boyfriend, a passerby or maybe even her father – to stick his nose under the bonnet and make an informed diagnosis.

Still, having gone through the engine ritual, Ali felt justified about forgetting about everything under the bonnet *forever*, and she sat unfazed as the instructor asked her every question Karen had predicted.

Without a bother she drove straight out of the test centre and took to the road. Chilled out, she hardly broke a sweat when the bin lorry pulled out in front of her, reducing her speed to a mere ten miles per hour, or when a driver, seeing how slow she was driving, decided to reverse his car at breakneck speed out of his driveway. The little brown pill just kept doing the trick, keeping her head feeling slightly fuzzy and perfectly relaxed.

As planned, Karen "unexpectedly" jumped out onto the pedestrian crossing with a slightly shocked face and Ali gently braked to let her cross, although for a moment she thought of leaving it to the very last minute and giving her a real scare.

There were only about fifteen more minutes in it and things were going so well she was almost afraid to breathe. Manoeuvres were as smooth as melted ice-cream and then they were on the home straight, the metal gates of the test centre were approaching and bar crashing into the damn things Ali hoped she'd done enough to be a fully-fledged driver on the nation's roads.

She passed. Perhaps she didn't deserve to pass. Perhaps she

hadn't done enough to pass, but she acted as though she should have passed and in the end she did.

Karen was beaming when Ali parked the car at the shopping centre, hauled her into the passenger seat and waved the precious piece of paper under her nose.

Then Ali kissed the paper that had eluded her in life for far too long and sighed contentedly. "Isn't it *amazing*!" she gasped.

"Yep, certainly is," smiled Karen.

"It was the tablet for sure. I have *never* felt so relaxed!"

Karen collapsed into laughter. "Oh Ali – do you think I'd drug you up with anything and you pregnant! It was nothing more than a Vitamin B tablet – supposed to calm the nervous system all right, but definitely nothing more, you sap! Talk about the placebo effect!"

Picking up her newly won piece of paper Ali began to wallop Karen around the head with it as viciously as if she was swatting a wasp. Then she broke into laughter. "I suppose you at least helped me achieve something important, you cow!"

They swapped places and Karen began the drive back to her house, eager to beat the evening traffic.

"Of course, now that you're in the capital you may as well take care of a bit more business. I wasn't going to say anything to you before your test but I had arranged to meet Dave in a bar and give him back some of his stuff, unless of course you'd like to do it yourself?"

Ali didn't answer. Reaching for the radio, she tuned in one of her favourite local stations and was overwhelmed with nostalgia.

"I'm not saying it would be a good thing or anything. It's just you kind of finished with him awfully abruptly. Maybe you should meet with him again just to be sure, you know?"

"All right, I'll meet him." The strength in her voice surprised her. "When is it?"

"Tonight."

"Tonight?"

"What's there to do except throw on a bit of make-up and wash your hair?"

"I'm not ready!" Ali protested.

"You'll never be ready and, besides, in a few more weeks baggy jumper or no baggy jumper you'll be showing."

"Yes, but I need time to prepare for seeing him again, to plan what to say. Tonight just seems so sudden!" Ali put her head on her hand. Oh, what the fuck, did it really matter?

* * *

Dave hadn't seen her yet; there was still time to do a runner. Inside, she saw him, leaning on the bar, pushing off the brass foot rail now and again, looking restless, drinking something that definitely wasn't a pint. He wasn't feeling in the mood for hanging around so. It was early, the place was quiet, but still his eyes were quietly taking in all the customers. She knew what he was doing. He was wondering which one of them might be criminals, might be armed for a gangland hit, what could be thrown down as an obstacle to impede a fleeing gouger. It drove Ali nuts the way he sussed everyone out, but he couldn't help it. It was just the training, you see.

Ali knew she looked gorgeous. It wasn't that Karen had just said it; for once the mirror did too. Ever since the nausea had stopped and her spots had gone to ground she had developed a shine about her skin and her hair was bordering on the luxuriant. As she drew closer she saw him slyly eye her svelte figure and she knew he didn't know it was her for she saw him jump as she came right up beside him.

They didn't even greet each other.

Dave drew himself up to his full height and stared at her with cold hard eyes.

"You were expecting Karen," she started.

"Just give me my stuff," he said, holding out his hand.

She did and she knew that part of him wanted to be indignant and leave right there but the dominant part of him, the bit that had to know the story, won out in the end. "I suppose you want me to tell you you're looking well? Living off the fat of the land is obviously agreeing with you."

His mouth was one tight line. He took two mouthfuls of his drink in quick succession and slammed down the glass, his movements telling anyone within a five-mile radius that he was one hell of an angry guy.

"Aren't you going to explain yourself, Alison? Fecking off like that . . . leaving me to wonder if you were coming back? Jesus, we've had arguments before. What the hell was so different this time?"

"I was fed up of you trying to control me, telling me what to do, how to behave."

"Controlling you? I was only trying to *help* you, especially since the accident."

"Sometimes the plot just moves on, I guess."

"That's some answer. Not that I really care any more." He spat out his answer with an intensity that shook the very air around her.

She could feel the heat of his anger, feel the very heat of him and felt the old defiance and sexual tension build up around them, just as it always did. Right there and then Ali knew that if they were to go home and have sex it would be charged, animal-like and truly amazing.

"I'm going. You can shag back off to wherever it is you've been holed up the last few months."

"Like you don't know – I'm sure you've got your sources keeping tabs on me," Ali said half-viciously.

"Get a grip! If you're fool enough not to be with me, well, that's your loss, what do I care? There's plenty, believe me *plenty* of women out there who'd die if I even gave them the time of day."

Coat slung over his shoulders, glass raised to his lips one more time – and he was leaving. Maybe this would be the last time she would ever see Dave O'Connor. He brushed against her, ready to leave, then spun on his heel and grabbed her face hard with his hand, crushing her jaw and lips to his mouth and kissing her so hard that she nearly stumbled.

"What you *never* realised was that you could have been the *one!*"

"Oh, the one to churn out the Dave O'Connor pups, is that it?"

she said sarcastically, wiping his spit away from her mouth and wondering at the intensity of her own anger.

"You would have been *damned* privileged to have any of *my* pups," he whispered hotly in her ear, "and now that I've told you that you could have been the one, you *never* will be. *Nobody* breaks up with me *twice* and gets back into my life!"

Watching him walk away she believed him too. Sure why would he wait for her? Great body, nice face, warm voice, funny, financially astute . . . and to think she could have been "the one". Great the way people never tell you these golden nuggets of information when they're relevant, but only when things are over, blasted to hell and torn to bits. Right at that moment there was no doubt in Ali Hughes' mind where she wanted to be. *God*, that man was sexy.

25

It happened in stages. First Karl did the decent thing and insured Ali on his car and then he virtually gave the damn thing to her and got a lift into work with a colleague. When he wasn't in the country it was hers anyway, and she loved the freedom it gave her whizzing around the bendy roads endangering the local bunny rabbits.

The April sunshine filled Ali with joy and on the way back from the doctor's one afternoon she parked her car at the lookout to the lake and sat there gazing at the view which was truly breathtaking. The surrounding mountains were like something out of a painting, blues and greys and whites melting into one another, the silvery splodges of the water mirroring the sky above.

In the water a powerboat zipped white through the blueness, passing out a lazy cruiser destined for the shore of Clare, or was it Limerick? Ali sighed as she watched. She never knew which county she was in exactly. It felt like such a spiritual place, such a spiritual moment and the freedom to get around and out of the house lifted her mood, made her feel that in some small way she was taking back control of her life.

Drumming her fingertips off the steering wheel, Ali thought

about the bump wedged beneath it. She was getting just a little bit fat but for the first time in her life she liked it – it felt wonderful to be getting heavy and not to give a toss. It felt powerful; she wished she were really showing so that she could put on a waddle just for effect.

Being pregnant was different to just being flabby fat; her belly was wonderfully hard and a bit mysterious. The thought of bringing new life into the world made her feel strangely optimistic about her own life even though logic dictated that her life would change forever and in ways beyond her imagination. Maybe it was the pregnancy itself that was making her optimistic, filling her with happy hormones.

Ever since the sickness lifted, things had been going right. Even getting her driving test without trying particularly hard was a good omen. Somehow that little event had struck a chord with Ali, had made her feel that maybe she had been trying too hard with life altogether, that maybe she could develop a happy-go-lucky mentality to get what she wanted without having to do things by the book or signing up for every approved course along the way. Starting the car, she said goodbye to the lake and headed home in search of lunch.

Feeling almost deliriously happy Ali pulled into the driveway only to notice with horror the set of wheels which were already parked outside her door.

"Hello, Alison."

The past had come back to haunt her. It was the blood-starved *Nosferatu* himself. As blond, weedy and creepy as ever but still surprisingly super-well dressed, although the expensive clothes didn't sit quite right on him yet.

Simon tried out a nice-guy smile that he had learned on his positive person's course. It made Ali feel uneasy to see the strangulated grin on his face.

"Darling!"

Alison almost swore that the baby inside her leapt in alarm at the sound of Julie's voice.

"Mother!"

"We'd almost given up hope on you, darling, but I told Simon that you'd probably popped out to get some milk or something. Isn't it a divine day?"

Good God, how did she always look so radiant, have so much energy and be so upbeat all the time? Maybe she really was a vampire, sucking the blood out of Simon and any other potential toy-boy types around. Ali wondered if Julie had become a total pain in the neck at the office yet. She could hardly fail to be, not with her intense personality. Give it a few more months and Simon would be sacking her and begging Ali to come and work for him once more. Then she'd take pleasure in saying no.

Julie's heels were already on the doormat, making it clear that she intended to at least stay for tea.

For a moment Ali hesitated behind the wheel. She didn't think her bump was obvious yet and she certainly wasn't rushing to show it off style-wise, preferring the old-fashioned method of covering it up rather than flaunting her fertility. Then she got out.

Once inside the door Ali made a quick excuse, then scuttled about hunting out any literature to do with pregnancy and throwing them into an upstairs cabinet. But she needn't have worried; she was in the company of two people who were so self-absorbed that they would have probably been oblivious to her if she had been suckling an infant at her breast. Her mother was especially hyper-ecstatic and it didn't take Ali long to realise that she was in danger of being subjected to an afternoon of Julie's long monologues.

The brochures tucked under Julie's arm indicated that Karen was right. Ali's mother was house-hunting down in the sticks for some little property to form part of her "portfolio" and Simon was obviously part of the "consortium". She was so excited that she just made herself at home, switching the kettle on and hunting out the teabags for some afternoon refreshment.

"Why, when I told Simon about the property situation down here and how with the development of the Shannon Waterways it was just ripe for investment, he was very interested in seeing prices for himself. We've just spent the morning with a few of the auctioneers and I must say I'm *very*, *very* pleased with the results."

Spellbound, Ali watched as her mother almost unconsciously rearranged little bits of furniture and ornaments around the house and banged a few cushions into more pleasing shapes. The woman just couldn't help herself; she just had to interfere in every little detail of her daughters' lives. The thought of having such a mother on her doorstep interfering in every aspect of her life was enough to get her heart racing.

"You wouldn't like it down here, Mum, it's far too parochial, nothing at all in the line of shopping that you would be used to and didn't you escape the country to marry Dad? You always said you'd never go back to it."

Julie smiled a small catlike smile and took a mouthful of her freshly made tea. "Why, darling, I wouldn't be *returning* to the country. In my mind it would be more like having a home in the city while having a country retreat. Maybe your father and I might even retire here, who knows?"

Even Simon thought Julie was losing the run of herself at this stage, either that or he was worried that she was suddenly diverging from the game plan. "It's not so much to *live* here. It's more that we're looking for some investment opportunities, national and international of course. I think we would be looking more at the luxury end of the market, maybe we might even acquire some nice little fixer-uppers that would serve as a weekend retreat for city slickers."

God, Ali detested this breezy, friendly but false side of Simon.

"So tell us about this part of the world that you've found yourself in," he said as he took off his jacket, spread it over the back of the chair and looked Ali in the eye. It was like he was interviewing her all over again. The nerve of the little git! Ali would have loved to have smacked him in the mouth with one of her matching set of coffee mugs.

"It's peaceful," she said firmly.

"A big change from Dublin," said Simon.

He was putting it up to her now. Something of the old sarcasm was seeping through his new friendly dude persona.

"*Huge* change – no traffic congestion for a start – then there's all the friendly country markets and accessible and cheap leisure and sports clubs. The pace of life is slower, your money goes further – sure what more could anyone ask for, Simon?"

Suddenly Ali bit her lip – his sarcasm had tricked her into boasting about the place instead of deterring him from investment. Then a flash of annoyance came over her as she saw him devour yet another of her chocolate biscuits.

"Speaking of money, what *are* you doing for cash, Ali?" he asked then. "Your mother says you're kind of taking a break. You know, if you're stuck I might be able to throw some freelance work your way."

The anger started from her feet and worked its way up to Ali's head in seconds. The tips of her ears were probably bright crimson. The cheek of him, as if she'd ever work for him again when he'd employed her mother to work for O'Grady's.

Then, out of the corner of her eye, she saw Karl's father's car stopped on the road, ready to make the turn into the driveway.

"No need for you to worry about me, Simon. I'm fine, thank you. I was taking a well-earned extended holiday but now I'm ready to start on my new career. I'm going to write for the local paper. It's all been arranged."

Picking up her mother's bag and coat, Ali escorted the duo out of the kitchen, and as she began her walk to the front door the lies came tumbling out at a furious rate.

"So as you can see, things are going very well and I'm house-sitting for a friend to boot so I don't even have to pay rent. All in all, I'd say the fact that I was forced to quit my job because you hired my mother has turned out extremely well."

"Alison, I . . ." blubbered her mother, stunned perhaps that she had been pulled away from her nice cup of tea.

"*Please*, don't just show up on my doorstep again uninvited, Mother. I don't like it."

"We won't trouble you the next time we're in the

neighbourhood," said Simon in his super-nice but snide manner.

"The *next* time?"

"Oh yes, I think we'll *definitely* be investing down here. From what you tell me, between the natural beauty, the cheap facilities and the fast drive from Dublin, this place can only go up in value in the years ahead."

Michael was hovering awkwardly between his car and the front door, obviously not knowing whether he should disappear altogether, and although Ali could see her mother was dying to know who this crumpled heap of clothes was, she managed to whoosh her firmly out the door with a quick peck to the cheek and a frosty smile.

"Good luck at getting the money out of the banks!" she said through gritted teeth as she waved her intruders goodbye. Then she realised that the whole time Simon was in the house he never mentioned her course. Why the hell didn't he mention the fact that she had only completed half the course? He might have known about her inability to produce a receipt for it too – a fellow like Simon missed nothing in the running of a small company.

"'Tis a bad time – you've had company. Maybe you need to go out or do some work?" Michael apologised.

"No, not at all, I've no plans – come in."

"Right, it was just about the rat I was calling."

"Oh he's left, didn't Karl tell you? We've had no trouble the last while."

Michael shook his head and smiled knowingly. "No, you might *think* he's left but he'll be back just like that other bastard – you know, what's his name, the shark – Jaws."

Like a shy dog Michael watched for any cues from Ali to tell him to come in and continue the conversation and soon found himself in the kitchen telling her all the latest news about rodents.

"There's a fella you can get from America, a contraption for fixing the feckers. It's a box with some bait in it and when the rat sniffs inside and has a feed, doesn't the fecker get electrocuted!" He slapped his hands together quickly and laughed. "Gas, isn't it?" The gentle giant went into hoots of laughter just contemplating the fate of the poor dumb rodent. "So will I order it so on the Internet?"

"Sure we might as well. It sounds like the business."

"Well, that's all I wanted to be asking you. I'll head off so."

"No, wait, Michael. Do you remember you were telling me about your friend with the paper? Jimmy John – Timmy John –"

"John Joe Connor, indeed and I do."

"Well, I think I'd like to meet him."

"No bother – can be arranged."

Ali felt triumphant. She got up on a chair to take down her old laptop from the cupboard in the kitchen and was in the rare position of looking down on the top of Michael's head.

"I suppose you'd have to have a very fertile imagination to be a writer," he said.

Ali looked down to see him blushing to his ears. He'd seen the little bump, she was sure of it.

26

Fumbling in her pockets Ali checked the address once more and stared up at the building in front of her. Outside the name-plate read *St Rita's* all right but she hadn't expected it to have net curtains and statues of the Virgin Mary and the Infant of Prague inside the windowsill.

The man on the phone had sounded very enthusiastic about interviewing her and she was wondering now if he was some kind of religious nut – maybe his paper was some kind of religious pamphlet or something. It couldn't be up to much if the office was in an ordinary-looking house. Part of her just wanted to turn on her heel and keep on walking but she decided to ring the doorbell anyhow – what had she to lose?

Taking another quick look at the Virgin Statue, Ali said a quick prayer. It was a bit rich really as she hadn't been to Mass for several years, but if you asked the Virgin to look out for you she was obliged to do it; that was part of the deal in being a Catholic, even a lapsed one, and Ali decided now was as good a time as ever to call in the favours.

Small and birdlike, with balding reddish hair and freckles on his polished egghead, the occupant of St Rita's greeted Ali with a huge smile and Ali quickly surmised that John Joe wasn't exactly stealing stories from under the noses of the national media every night of the week. Wearing a pair of granddad-type trousers and a grey sleeveless cardigan he welcomed Ali with friendly enthusiasm.

"Hello, hello! Won't you come in? Bridget the Deputy Editor is in the back office having tea."

The back office turned out to be the kitchen, complete with cooker, old newspapers, two desks, a cat and her kittens and an endless pile of stacked cardboard boxes while Bridget turned out to be a very dour-looking woman by the name of Brigitte Ní Mhurchú.

The lanky leather-booted one lost no time in telling Ali that she was German on her mother's side as she offered John Joe another piece of her home-made apple strudel.

"Take a seat, take a seat," said John Joe as he dumped a pile of newspapers on the floor and made room for Alison to sit beside the kitchen table.

"Alison is getting an actual qualification in journalism. We've never had that before," said John Joe with a smile to Brigitte.

"Ehm, well, I have another module to do first – I may even have to postpone it for a bit . . . it's in Dublin," Ali explained.

John Joe cleared his throat but made no comment while the sour-pussed one didn't bat an eyelid but crossed her arms defiantly as she sat in front of her cup of tea and home-made baking which was set out on the table like a prized possession. Pushing her waist-length dark and greasy hair away from her face with her unpainted fingers, she positively glared at Ali across the table.

Despite the dirty looks Ali was struck by how beautiful the wild half-German woman looked in her unkempt way. A bit of make-up, a decent haircut and a bit of colour to hide the grey could have made her look quite beautiful. Her figure, although perfect, was contained within some monstrously outdated dark and drab clothes. Probably she was in her mid-forties, although the unlined face could have been made to look years younger with a bit of effort.

Christ, Ali had heard that women started to behave like their mothers the older they got but she was now beginning to think like her mother as well and even do fashion makeovers in her head. Forcing her attention away from the Ayrian-Celtic beauty, Ali made a point of bringing all her concentration to bear on the strange little man in front of her, although she just wished she could down her cup of tea as fast as possible and bolt for the door.

"Now I may as well be up front from the beginning. I won't be able to offer you anything full time or pay you big money here but we *can* offer you experience," John Joe said as he read Ali's CV over his half-moon glasses.

Ali was flustered. Never before had she been to a job interview where it appeared the employers were offering her a job within the very first sentence.

"Well, I'm not sure I'd be what you're looking for," she said uncomfortably as she took in the surrounding room. The black and white mommy cat was now nursing her kittens in a corner behind a pile of newspapers with a look of total boredom on her face.

"Right, perhaps I can explain what we are hoping to do here and you can tell us if it might suit."

So on he went telling her about the knitting column that Brigitte was writing and how the gardening tips on the back were well thought of and widely read and how they did occasionally include some of the local court cases, but they were a bit dodgy about that in case anybody sued and so on and so on. It was clear John Joe's newspaper *The Voice* was not really a newspaper – it was more of a colour newsletter, maybe even a pamphlet – but they certainly got in a fair few ads she noticed, semi-impressed.

"I'm setting up a cine club as well, you see – it's a bit of a passion of mine –"

"Obsession," cut in Brigitte.

"Yes, well, a passion at any rate. There used to be a travelling cinema that came to the parochial hall every weekend till 1960 and I'm hoping to bring it back, the cinema that is, bring films right here from all around the world. We could badly do with a bit of

entertainment like that again. But there's so much to do – there's a
new projector to be bought – I need to see if I can apply for lottery
funding to get us off the ground – I'm hoping that maybe we can
even get a screen on a roller system, you know for easy set-up, then
there's sound equipment to be bought –"

"Obsession!" snapped Brigitte again.

"Ah, Brigitte, you won't say that when you see *Casablanca* on the
big screen – the most beautiful woman of all time – Ingrid Bergman!"
His eyes lit up and Brigitte rolled her own big eyes in irritation. "Well,
yes, as I was saying," droned on the little man, "I suppose we just need
a bit of general help here, you know, a bit of writing, a bit of proofing,
selling a few ads –"

Ali listened patiently and waved her hand when another cup of
tea was offered to her by John Joe, but all the while she was
thinking of how she could escape politely.

"Can you speak Irish?" the half-German snapped suddenly.

"Eh, well, is it required?" asked Ali, hoping desperately that it was
so that she could admit that she was far from fluent and make good
her escape.

"Yes, we have plans to become somewhat bi-lingual in the
future," said Brigitte.

"Now, Brigitte, you *know* we haven't exactly discussed that. No,
Alison, to answer your question, Irish is not a requirement to work on
this paper. But can you cook or at least write about cooking?"

For a moment Ali thought she was going to burst into laughter
and she found herself raising an eyebrow in disbelief.

"You see, we've a slot for a cookery column, effective
immediately."

The logical part of her was about to smile, say thank you but no
thank you and make moves for her departure, but then the light
bulb went on in her head that she was virtually penniless and that
any money at all would be welcome and that even if she couldn't
cook she knew someone who could write a million food columns for
her: her father. Besides, she thought she could see Brigitte about to
burst into flames. It was obvious she was something of an

accomplished cook herself and was probably indignant that John Joe hadn't sought her opinion on the matter.

"Actually, I'm a *very* accomplished cook and I think I would have some great recipes to include – maybe fast and sexy recipes for the time-pressed professional to whiz up – tips on how to impress that special someone in your life without lifting a finger. I've got *lots* of ideas."

John Joe was positively writhing in his seat with excitement and Brigitte fired Ali another dirty look to let her know that she was still the Deputy Editor and that she'd better watch it. But Ali didn't care – the she-devil inside her had been activated. In fact, she thought, it hadn't entirely left her since the day she had passed her driving test without even trying.

"Could you give us five hundred words by next week?"

Ali nodded and shook his hand. It was done and dusted. Feeling quite smug, she rubbed her little bump and smiled.

"Maybe it's you that's making me so goddamn sure of myself lately," she whispered to it as she left St Rita's with a spring in her step.

Of one thing she was certain, in a few months' time she would be expected to be a provider for a new, helpless life. There would be no choice but to get her act together and in the new world of Mommyhood cash was king.

Smiling as she made chat with Tom the cab driver on the way back to the house, Ali revelled in the optimism she was feeling. Maybe it was true that when one door closed on your life, no matter how scary things were, you should be happy because the door that opened might bring opportunity and contentment. Her newly happy self couldn't wait to tell Karl about how things were improving but from the moment she set foot in the house she could tell something was troubling him.

He didn't say much but she just knew. It was more what he didn't say than what he did. As always he made her a lovely dinner but when afterwards, on the couch, she tried to kiss him he pulled away, then rubbed her knee silently for a moment.

"Is it because my body's changing?" she asked him timidly.

He shook his head in exasperation. "Don't be silly – you're not *that* different – not yet"

"Well, what is it then?" she sighed.

He shifted uncomfortably in his seat and then abandoned the couch completely and began to pace around the room.

"Ali we can't hide things for much longer, not that we should or anything, it's just I don't really know what to say to people. What'll I say? This is my girlfriend, my friend, are we an item, what are my intentions . . . I guess the bottom line is I'm not sure if I'm ready to be a father."

Ali was quiet. She sympathised with him but at the same time she was angry. What was the point in all his wonderings? She was going to be a mother, she definitely didn't feel that ready but she wasn't going on about it and bemoaning her misfortune.

"Well, you're going to be a father whether you like it or not," she sighed, "and, besides, I think your own father knows already. He was talking the other day about writing and journalism and *fertile imaginations* while looking at my stomach and when I caught him staring he blushed red."

Karl groaned and poured himself another glass of red wine and then he started tapping his fingers against his teeth the way he was apt to do when he was puzzling over something that was troubling him. He got up to tidy away some of the dishes and midway through the clean-up he gave up and said he was on for an early night, that he had an important meeting in the morning and wanted to be fresh for it.

Meekly, Ali followed him up the stairs and was just about to hop into his bed when he asked her would she mind sleeping in the other room as there were things he wanted to think about alone.

"And it's an early meeting – it's better we sleep alone – I'd only wake you getting up," he tried to placate her but Ali suspected his desire to be alone had more to do with his confusion about their relationship than about her need to get a good night's sleep.

Hurt and angry, Ali bounded out of the room and plonked

herself in the windy front bedroom instead. There was no answer to his worries about their relationship. Neither of them knew what the future held for them as a couple or as a family, neither of them could know yet. The wind had an angry companion as she tossed and turned in the dark. Maybe it was only her imagination but it felt like she hardly slept more than ten minutes the whole night through.

* * *

It was like they lived the next few days in a kind of limbo, neither angry nor warm towards each other but just existing, wearily going through the motions and heading towards the inevitable – birth, parenthood and uncertainty. Since she was now "safe" from possible miscarriage, Karl told her, she might as well start announcing the impending birth to everyone, especially if it was likely that his father already knew. Still there was a lot that held her back from meeting his parents and telling them the news. Hesitatingly, she told him that really she should tell her own mother first; it was traditional after all. Then she watched as his eyebrows lifted and knew he wasn't buying that excuse.

No, the anxious feelings about meeting his parents came from something deep. Really the problem was with her, Mary, the mother. Deep down the woman gave Ali the creeps. She seemed hard, mean-mouthed. From the first glimpse, Ali knew that this was a mother who had invested a lot in her son and that she, Ali, would not be likely to be seen as a "suitable catch" for the golden-haired boy. Mary made Ali's knees knock and on the two or three occasions that she had been in the car when Michael called, that's where she stayed, in the car, with that frosty look chiselled on her face.

The day of reckoning was set for the weekend; Karl said he would do a roast lamb.

* * *

That Sunday Michael was all smiles, and the mother was too, but Mary's wasn't a real smile, it was a grimace and the eyes were hard as glass. Talk about meeting a crocodile. Ali felt this woman could have swallowed her whole.

Around her neck Mary wore a small gold cross on a fine gold chain and she didn't take a glass of wine or any other alcohol: she was a teetotaller, a Pioneer. It seemed nothing would warm her up and Ali felt like taking the wine bottle by the neck and throwing the drink down her own neck in record time.

The soup and rolls had hardly hit the table when the probing questions started.

"Do you like this place?" the older woman asked, holding the spoon to her lips and smiling the crocodile smile again.

Deciding to play dumb, Ali said that she found the countryside and the scenery delightful.

"No, *this* place, the house – isn't it a real jewel? Karl is great with his hands, he's making a great fist of it doing it up, but all this renovation business costs a fortune. I've heard you're a writer and researcher. It must offer great flexibility – Karl said you were doing some research for the government when you first came and now you're writing I hear. Do you do research *and* write for the national papers? Sure no matter, I'm sure there's great money in both."

Good God, the woman was brazen! To mention money so quickly was the height of rudeness. So much for the godly veneer – what she really wanted to know about was money, and did Ali have any or was she likely to fall into a pile of it any day soon.

The two men looked like they were about to die from embarrassment but Karl saved Ali from any more awkward questions by saying that she was taking it easy at the moment.

"I've just started to put a few feelers out," said Ali. "In fact, on Michael's recommendation, I've had a word with his friend John Joe and he wants me to start contributing to his paper from next week."

"John Joe? He used to be a priest, you know – terrible scandal when he left, his mother never forgave him."

Ali was startled at that but said nothing.

"Are you writing some snippets for him?" Mary asked a little too snidely.

"It's a column actually," Ali answered evenly.

"What on?" said Michael, trying to jolly the conversation on a bit as he stabbed a bit of lamb with a fork.

"Eh, cookery actually."

"Oh, you cook?" said Mary.

"No. Well, not very well."

"Karl was always a great man for the cooking. From a teenager we were able to rely on him to cook a meal. Such a *responsible* young fella, isn't that right, Michael?"

Somewhere after dinner and before dessert Ali cornered Karl and began hissing at him that there was no way the subject of pregnancy was coming up in conversation, that she couldn't just meet his parents for the first time and then spring the news on them that she was soon to become a "big fat momma".

"Maybe we can do this again next week," she pleaded, "maybe we can tell them then."

"Are you mad? Do you think I want to go through this whole rigmarole again next week? You're nearly five months pregnant – when do you suggest we tell people about your condition – when the placenta is delivered?"

But Ali persisted and put up with the dry conversation for another two hours before his parents decided to go home. Mary left, her eyes slowly moving over every detail, every item of furniture in the place. It was like she was stocktaking to make sure every family heirloom, no matter how worthless, was in its rightful place.

A rush of relief flooded through Ali as the door was banged shut, but Karl shot her a ferocious look as he headed up the stairs.

"What a waste of time!" he muttered angrily as he stomped off and banged his bedroom door.

Ali thought of Karen bear-hugging her tight, her own father making Sunday dinner, Maggie laughing and joking in the office and Dave grinning at her mischievously from under the bonnet of his car and every bit of her yearned for home, yearned for Dublin. How the hell did she end up here? There'd been more than a few times in her life when she'd found herself in daft situations but this time she had really surpassed herself.

27

Ruth rang at the beginning of the week to state in her best teacher's voice that she would be coming down to visit at the weekend, alone. Alarm bells went off in Ali's head as she thought about why her sister might be coming to visit. She tried everything to put her off, even telling her that she was starting her new career and had a terribly important piece of writing to put together and she would do better without any distractions.

"Sure I would be a help, not a hindrance," Ruth snorted down the phone.

"How's that?"

"Well, wouldn't I be able to correct it for you? Check your punctuation, that kind of thing."

"But you teach Geography, *not* English," said an exasperated Ali.

"That's beside the point. I *am* still a teacher. Punctuation and grammar are the tools of the trade. I'll see you early on Saturday morning, to avoid the traffic."

The phone went dead.

Then Ali rang her father, on the pretence of discussing her cookery column with him, but really she just wanted the comfort of hearing his voice again. She missed him. She wanted to tell him about her pregnancy but, on the other hand, she wanted to wait until she could tell him everything was going beautifully, that her life was in control, that she had a new job, a supportive partner, somewhere to stay, that kind of thing. She didn't want him to think that she had let him down, yet again, that she was some kind of serial failure.

"Hi, Dad."

"Alison, sweetheart – how are you? I was just thinking of phoning you. Will you hang on until I turn the soup down."

Soup! Wholesome, healthy soup! If her dad only knew she was pregnant he'd be mothering her and the baby with soup day and night.

"So how are you?"

"Great actually – I've just landed a new job writing a food column for a local paper, well, more of a pamphlet really."

He laughed. "Do you *actually* know how to cook more than boiled eggs, my dear?"

"No, Dad, and that's where you come in . . ."

He agreed to help her think up some snazzy recipes, not that there was much thinking involved, he was able to rattle several off straight away.

"Does it pay well then, this new job?"

Ali found herself hesitating, then she spat out the truth, that the money was shite for the time but wasn't it a start?

He agreed quietly and she knew that the problem was everything was "a start" with her but things never really progressed much past that.

"Do you want me to e-mail some recipes and ideas to you?"

E-mail, since when was her father a whiz at the e-mail?

"I'd get your mother to send it from her computer."

Since when was her mother a whiz at the e-mail?

Julie was obviously learning a lot on the job. Not for the first time recently, Ali found herself pining for her rotten job. It might have been irritating, but at least the measly money was there in her bank account once a month.

"No, don't bother Mum. I wouldn't want her to break a nail over me. Just give me a call tomorrow when you get the time."

True to his word, Liam rustled up some good recipes for her, some light and sexy starters and main courses involving fresh basil and cheese and cherry tomatoes which he rattled out over the phone the next day while she took it down in her almost redundant shorthand. "Now this one is a complete rip-off from that young trendy British cook, but we'll change the name and nobody will know the difference," he chuckled.

Ali edited what she got and banged it into the required number of words for her new editor who was delighted with her efforts. At least it would fill a hole in his newspaper, even if it didn't set the world alight.

By Saturday morning on the dot of ten Ruth was on her doorstep, smoking a cigarette. Karl had made himself scarce, having heard enough from Ali about her dragon sister to be "too busy" to hang around. Still in her nightdress with her eyes still glued to their lids, Ali greeted her sister, who was already fully powered-up. That's the way it was when you had kids, Ruth hissed. The little bastards always made sure your lie-in was scuppered so you might as well just get up early and battle the day. Ruth took another drag of her cigarette and looked like she would just love to bayonet the first person that crossed her path.

"Tea, Ruth?"

Her sister's face twitched in a manner that indicated she was receptive to refreshments being offered.

"Such a surprise to see you here – but I'm amazed you could get away from the kids and your corrections. Don't you have a *ton* of copies to correct for Monday?"

"Never mind *that* – I'm thinking of leaving Gerry."

"What?"

"You heard me. I'm thinking of leaving my husband and I might be looking for a bolthole for a while to get my head together for a few weeks. I understand the guy that owns this place is away a lot and you're house-sitting so I thought I might come and housesit with you."

"What in *God's* name are you talking about? Are you mad? You can't stay here, what about the boys?"

"I thought they might come too, at least for part of it – although I would also like some time on my own. I should really make that bastard take some parental leave to look after our two brats. Anyway, could I stay here for a while if I needed to?"

For fuck's sake! Ali screamed to herself. Her family really were like the Mafia – they were willing to track her down and harass her no matter what distance, no matter how long it took.

"No, Ruth, I don't think so and besides it's not really for me to say. It's not *my* house after all."

Then all of a sudden Ruth burst into tears and Ali watched as the end of her fag ash began to wobble and then caved in onto the table. "You just don't realise what's been going on. It's Gerry. He's been gambling. He's a total addict. We've no money left. He's made a massive hole in what savings we had and there's no reasoning with him. He thinks it's all justified, that he can make us rich."

"What do you mean gambling? Do you mean like Las Vegas gambling?"

"No, I did catch him on that online poker stuff once but he swears he's given that up – no, it's e-bay. He's addicted to e-bay. He's been buying all kinds of shite on it, advertised as antiques, things he *thinks* he can do up and auction on e-bay, but he never does *any* of it up or sells it on. He just buys more. Our entire garage is full of crap and the outside shed. The poor deluded idiot even thinks he'll be able to sell his rubbish at fairs around the country at the weekend. He's even shiting on that he might be able to set up an antiques shop as well. Can you imagine that? He just has this dream that if he could set up a shop he could give up teaching. It's all just horseshit really."

Fury welled up inside Ali. Here she was up the duff, by a guy she barely knew, holed up in the country without a decent job or a secure roof over her head, with scary news to tell Karl's scary mother and Ruth had to go and have her own crisis to rival that of her younger sister's.

"Do you have anything stronger than this?" asked Ruth as she held out the teacup.

Ali thought she was going to explode. She was the one who was pregnant. Ruth should be waiting on her. Overcome with irritation, she decided she'd shut Ruth up for five minutes, maybe even get a bit of sympathy out of her for a change.

"I'm pregnant."

"By that sexy policeman of yours?"

"No – by Karl, my new – friend."

Ruth burst into tears and for a minute Ali melted, thinking she'd given her too big a shock.

"You're not to worry about me, Ruth. I'll be fine. I'm coping."

"I'm not worried about *you*. I'm thinking what an exciting sex life you must have. Have you ever seen Gerry out of slippers?"

What a bitch!

"Well, if you really are pregnant, I *hope* you have a boy. I *hope* you have twins. You might have an idea then just how miserable my life is."

Ali stuck some whiskey in Ruth's tea and just let her get on with it. For several hours Ruth's jaw was stuck on wobble-gob and in between silent sighs Ali consoled herself by daydreaming out the window.

By late afternoon Ruth was more than a bit drunk and was beginning to enjoy herself. Not having the kids hanging out of her helped soften her mood and between that and chattering non-stop she even became vaguely sweet enough to tell Ali that motherhood wasn't all bad. Couldn't she take all her baby gear for a start because she was going to make Gerry go and have the snip or else tie a knot in his thingy or else she really would divorce the bastard.

"You've no bump at all," she said, making Ali lift her top. "That doesn't surprise me. They say babies of hidden pregnancies are always smaller."

"It's not a *hidden* pregnancy. I'm not supposed to be big now anyway, that's what all the books say."

"Of course it's a first pregnancy as well. Your muscles aren't slack.

Now if you were to have another you'd be as big as a house already. Don't you think it would be good if I came down a bit over the summer? I could be here to look after you when your back goes."

"When will that be?" asked a worried Ali.

"Oh, *definitely* by six months or a bit after, especially since you had that accident as well – you'll probably find you'll have a weakness in your back from that. You know Mum is thinking of buying property down here. Maybe we could all come down to help you out – baby-sit, that kind of thing – wouldn't it be great to have your family around?"

Great? Ali was getting the heebie-jeebies just thinking about her family moving in on her. She liked the thought of them being far enough away to avoid meddling in her life.

"What's his family like?"

Ali filled her in and told her about the scary mother.

"Do you want me to beat the crap out of her? Verbally, of course. I have *particular* experience in that line since I've often had to extract a confession out of a delinquent student?"

"No, I'll face her myself."

"When?"

"Soon."

Ruth was gone by Sunday morning. There wasn't a chance that she would hang about till the evening because no matter how much she talked about running away, changing her life, denouncing her husband, she was still a conservative at heart and she wouldn't leave late in case she ran into traffic.

Ali sighed with relief when she saw Ruth's car disappear around the bend and she closed the heavy wooden door and shuffled into the kitchen, pulling her light dressing-gown around her as she sat down to her tea and toast. God, Ruth was exhausting *and* such a drama queen. There really was more of Julie in her than Ruth would ever admit to. Still, it was nice to think that even outwardly sensible individuals could occasionally muck up their lives.

The kitchen door opened and Karl walked in, wearing a scruffy weekend fleece and an old tracksuit bottoms and sandals. He'd made himself scarce while Ruth was around and now that he had surfaced he hardly said a word as he poured some milk on his cornflakes and stirred them around a few times before pausing and looking her directly in the eye.

"I want to start telling people about the baby, I just can't hold it in any longer," he blurted out in a rush.

"Me too. I've told Ruth already and I haven't told her to keep her mouth shut, so that's my family sorted."

"Oh. Well, I suppose we might have another go at telling my parents then?"

Ali nodded and cupped her hands around her tea.

A look of relief passed over Karl's face and she saw his body relax into the chair. "That's settled then."

Just then they were both startled by Michael banging a fist against the kitchen window. Karl got up and let him into the back of the house.

"Well, now, sorry to be bothering you on a Sunday. It's just I got my hands on the Rat Gizmo and I couldn't wait to show you."

Michael was nearly looking over his shoulder as if checking for unwanted strangers and he spoke in a quiet voice as he extracted the rodent-frying device from a plastic shopping bag. "I've had a quick look myself and I think this will be the man for your rat. Do you see here, this is where you put the bait in and see here this light – this comes on when you've caught him. Do you want to try it out now?"

Excitedly, he was heading for the door when Karl caught a hold of his arm and told him to sit down again and have a cup of tea, that the last thing he wanted was for him to have a heart attack in pursuit of any rat, whether real or phantom.

Reluctantly, Michael sat down and had the tea although it was obvious he would have preferred to have been making rat-execution plans.

"How's the cookery column going for John Joe?" he asked.

"Fine. I have a secret weapon – my father – he's a cookery addict."

"Oh right, that would explain things. It's just I never would have thought you were a food person. I've never seen you eat much more than a slice of toast since you got here – except for Karl's dinner – very nice too – you can't beat lamb."

"I lost my appetite for a while and was feeling nauseous because . . . well, I think you already guessed, Michael . . . I'm pregnant."

A look of pure horror crossed Karl's face. So much for his saying he wanted to tell everybody.

"And there's no easy way of saying this but Karl is the father."

Ali could tell she had put Michael right off his Rich Tea biscuit. He was twiddling it between his fingers so much that it eventually snapped in two and startled him back to reality.

"Do you have any whiskey in the house?" Michael asked his son.

"Are you shocked, Dad?"

"Well, maybe a little but what matter – we might as well wet the child's head – amn't I going to be a grandfather?"

Karl tore into her as soon as Michael left.

"I'm sorry. I just saw the moment and went for it."

"But I meant to tell them *together* – now my father has to go home and tell that news to my mother. No wonder he was looking for the whiskey."

Ali shrugged. At least the news was out and she didn't have to face the witch yet, but the stress of keeping things quiet for so long suddenly started to get to her and she found her shoulders quivering and after that the big wet tears splashed on to her face and her sobs filled the kitchen.

"Oh for God's sake, please don't cry! Look, I'm sorry, okay?"

And after that they had the "I'm-angry-so-now-let's-make-up sexual experience" that made each feel contented and unafraid. Ali lay back on her pillow and thought it was true: pregnant sex was deeply satisfying and she was a randy old goat now that she was with child. She fell asleep and awoke to the sound of the phone ringing close to midnight.

It was her mother.

"Alison. Are you pregnant?"

"Yes," she said and hung up, immediately dis-connecting the phone at the socket so her mother couldn't call back. Then on the Monday morning, when Karl had left her and went to work, she looked in the mirror and swore she had developed an enormous bump. Of course, hidden pregnancy syndrome, Ruth was right after all.

28

June was starting out beautiful and so far Ruth hadn't carried out her threat and packed her bags to come and live down the country with Ali. The lake and mountains were at their most gorgeous. Yellow gorse turned the mountains to fire and the lake glistened between the dark green trees and hedgerows and every now and again it would open up into a huge expanse of water as she drove, taking Ali's breath away.

Her yearning for Dublin was decreasing by the day. She was beginning to feel an optimism for life and a joy in her bones. It started when Karl got up in the morning and kissed her forehead and whispered goodbye and it ended when he kissed her goodnight and laid his head on her tummy and talked to her bump.

Naturally, the logical part of Ali knew that this mister-and-missus behaviour was ridiculous, but her soul wouldn't let go of the joy of just being in the moment. Blissfully happy, isn't that what they called it, unshakeable happiness even? Half the time she felt like some kind of spiritual Buddha in a state of awareness that most people never attain, that kind of ridiculous thing, and even her occasional bouts of constipation couldn't change her overall feeling of peace.

So, it was all peace and calm in the hospital when the midwives took her blood pressure and examined her growing belly with knowing smiles and waved her off with next month's appointment. Feeling wonderful and sunny, Ali decided to take a jaunt into Limerick city centre, to treat herself to some decent coffee and a nice cake, maybe browse through some baby magazines, have a look at some trendy maternity clothes.

She had just finished looking at the cutest baby clothes – which she didn't buy, she was far too superstitious – and had headed into a coffee and sandwich shop for a frothy cappuccino and a trendy sandwich with crisps, when she caught sight of his reflection in the glass. It was Dave. For a moment her brain refused to accept the proof of her eyes. *What the hell would Dave be doing out of Dublin? It must be his doppelganger. Oh bloody hell! He must be giving evidence in a court case.*

Her next reaction was to do a runner, but her swollen feet wouldn't move and her bump was determined to stick around, loud and proud in front of him. He had seen her. From the pit of her stomach she could feel the sickness churn. She didn't want his inquisitive eyes on her, the Garda eyes that would go straight to her midriff and give her "the look" and his eyes maybe trying to guess how many pounds she now weighed or when her due date was or what the hell she was doing with her life.

Like a lamb to the slaughter she waited for the smart comment to be made but he said nothing. He was stunned. Never before in her life had Ali seen Dave O'Connor stuck for words but for once, here he was, completely speechless.

"You didn't know?" she said, finally to break the silence.

"*Fuck, no*, why would I?" The air hissed around his throat making the words sound strangled and rattley.

"I don't know. Maybe I half-thought you'd have me put under investigation to see what I was at."

"You're *pregnant*?" he asked in a stupid voice as he followed the queue while his eyes remained riveted to her bump.

"Thick or thin?" asked the bored girl at the cash register. "The bread?" she said in her bored voice as Dave looked at her like an idiot.

"Oh, thick."

"Thick for me too," Ali told the girl's fellow-worker. She might as well – she was eating for two now, no point skimping on calories.

They sat there awkwardly, facing each other with their sandwiches and it was clear that neither of them had any appetite. It wasn't possible to eat across from each other without bumping knees and clearly they didn't have that kind of body intimacy any more.

Pathetically she smiled and he took a bite of his sandwich. He looked sweaty and nervous as he downed a huge mouthful of coffee and then, in between the gulps and munches, there was an awful silence broken only by his sudden murmuring of, "God, you *really* are pregnant."

If he said that one more time she might even take a swipe at him.

"Want to walk?" he asked as he twisted his paper napkin for the last time and brushed the crumbs from his mouth.

A short waddle away was the Shannon and they walked along its banks, stopping at some iron railings overlooking the river. He was looking out, down past St John's Castle. The river was grey and dead-looking, but still he kept looking, saying nothing and breathing in a slightly laboured manner.

"I might as well say it because the thought is in there knocking around. Is it mine?"

"Basic Maths mustn't be a requirement to get in the guards these days if you even *think* it could be yours. You needn't worry. I won't be asking you to pay any child support," she said.

For a second Ali thought it was relief that flooded his face but then she wondered if it was actually disappointment.

"So it's this new fella then. I heard you were seeing someone. Well, I hope he treats you as good as I did."

"What are you on about? You were never round that much and after the sex was over you were like James Bond, international man of mystery and 'don't ask me no questions either'."

"Christ, you're some stupid bitch, do you know that?" In irritation he turned his back on the river and leaned on the railings. "So I work a lot, I *want* a decent future, so I'll have security for me and any family I might have, and yeah sure, maybe I was a bit cool with you sometimes, but it turns out I was right to be because yet again you went all flaky, taking off with someone you hardly knew, even getting yourself up the pole. How stupid was that, Alison?"

"I'll have you know I'm going to be fine. I'm going to be a great mother and I don't need help from anyone!"

"And this guy – is he going to be around for you?"

"I don't know. Maybe, maybe not. It doesn't matter. I can do this on my own if I have to."

"Please! Do you even have a job at the moment?"

That was it. She didn't have to take this kind of shit. She hated him though, detested the way he always could hold a mirror up to her life and say there were cracks as big as the Grand Canyon running right through it.

"Where are you going?" he asked in a panic.

"Home, back to where I live at any rate," Ali said, brushing away hot tears. *Oh, God damn these hormones – they were always letting her down.*

"Hold on, for fuck's sake! I can't let a pregnant, emotional woman run off like this. You might end up killed. I'll drive you home."

"No, thanks."

"Think of the baby – you need to rest," he said sternly.

So she rested her body in Dave's new car – of course he didn't let the motors grow under his feet – and she bristled every time his hand grasped the gear stick. It was only because she was pregnant. Everyone told her that pregnancy makes you frisky.

"Well, at least he can put a roof over your head," he said as he pulled up to the drive and eyed up Karl's comfortably sized home.

"Well, I suppose you're glad to be shot of me, especially as I am now the fattest you've ever seen me."

He laughed and drummed his fingers on the steering wheel before giving her a piercing look.

"I've never seen you look better and, to tell you the truth, I wish it *was* mine, this baby. I could have loved you, Alison – why would you never commit to us?"

Ali was shaken to hear the venom and the longing in his voice. At that moment she wanted to hug him and cry but too much had happened. Was it true that she was the one who hadn't committed to the relationship and not him? God, she had never seen it like that before. Then suddenly she felt a rage and snapped the nose off him.

"It's no good telling me about love *now*, you bastard! What good is that to me? Thanks for the lift home. You can feck off back to Dublin with a clear conscience!" She clambered out and banged the passenger door shut.

Immediately, Dave drove the car out of the driveway, then reversed, put down the window and shouted back at her.

"And I don't care what you would have me believe! There is *no* way you're having better sex with him than me. I hope you're happy, Alison!"

Happy, of course she wasn't happy and what did he mean by "*could* have loved" her? Did he love her or had he loved her or was he saying he might be able to love her in the future? No, Ali was definitely not happy. She was terribly, terribly unhappy and so agitated she couldn't get the lock on her door opened for a good four or five minutes.

29

Up until now Ali had managed to fire in her cookery recipes to "the paper" by e-mail. It was fast, impersonal and reliable and it meant she never had to set foot inside that strange building that called itself a newsroom. So far she'd also been able to wriggle out of the proofing and doing the ads and all the other stuff that required serious effort. Nonetheless the small part of her that had listened to Maggie knew she'd have to look for more work and yet she didn't have the confidence to knock on the doors of the big country newspapers, let alone tout for work with any of the nationals.

Even Ali knew that you couldn't really haggle for any kind of work over the phone. More work from John Joe's paper called for face-to-face communication and that meant having to tolerate that mad half-Irish/half-German fanatic, Brigitte. Still, even if she only got a crochet column out of it, wouldn't it be more money for buying baby essentials? Although Karl wasn't slow in putting his hand in his pocket for the bigger purchases – like the pram they had bought that she spent hours back in the house just walking round, thinking, "so this was what playing dollies was all about".

John Joe was in when she arrived but he made it quite clear that he was on the way out and in a terrible hurry.

"We've just heard that there are over a hundred cinema-style seats in a barn in East Galway and they're destined for the scrap heap if I don't head out now to give them the once over. Can you imagine it? If this works out the parochial hall will have a real honest-to-goodness cinema feel to it, Alison."

Like a demented tempest he was out the door, leaving the deputy editor/chief columnist and champion strudel-maker Brigitte at the helm. She was in the kitchen feeding cat food to the feline mommy and her growing brood. Ali noticed that this time the greasy hair was at least washed and that Brigitte didn't look as old as on her last visit.

"The little ones are growing big, *ja*?"

"*Ja*, oh yeah, I suppose they are," stumbled Ali.

"And your own little one is doing well too?"

"*Ja*, I mean yeah, fine thanks."

Ali then realised that although she'd never mentioned the baby to Brigitte and had hardly seen her, she nevertheless seemed to know all about her bump. Not for the first time she realised that while she must be the talk of the countryside, nobody actually talked to her personally about her impending arrival. They did sometimes gave her a sideways look but then quickly averted their eyes to make it look that they were looking at something else, anything else in fact: cows, clouds, neighbours.

"Tea?"

"If it's no trouble."

"No bother, no bother."

Ali was struck by the peculiarity of Brigitte's accent. Peppered with Irish idioms, her speech sometimes sounded quite rough and colloquial against her otherwise very proper and clipped voice. Now and again Brigitte even came out with the odd expression in Irish that completely took Ali's breath away.

It took an age for the kettle to boil and Brigitte was rooting around the room, moving piles of newsletters and parcels of printing paper in an effort to locate the cardboard box of tea. Every second seemed minutes long. Ali was only staying for tea out of politeness, she really had no great desire to shoot the breeze with this woman who at best seemed to detest her and at worst was openly hostile to her ever since she had usurped her for the cookery slot.

"Ah *ja* – I've found the feckin' things."

Ali smiled a smile of mock relief that the feckin' teabags had been located and she kept the same smile on her face as she wondered how fast she could drink her tea and leave without seeming impolite.

"John Joe out and about again – it must be hard to be on your own so much in the office?"

"Ah, John Joe – so much to do – he's nearly sixty you know but he won't slow down. He *ist fürchtbar* – terrible: terrible for taking on the big project and for letting nothing go. I tell him he must come painting with me sometime to see the lake and all her moods but he has none of the time for himself – and this cinema obsession, it has him taken over completely if he doesn't get sense." A look of sadness mixed with resignation crossed Brigitte's face as she brought the cup to her lips and shook her head sadly. "Enough of John Joe! This little one will be born when?"

"August."

"I see. I was saying to John Joe that maybe you would be needing more work and he says that too. I said yes, that we could definitely do with someone in the courts. John Joe does that now but he is no good because he won't name the feckers who do the crimes. You know, being a former priest he can't bring himself to name the boyos because he thinks everyone deserves one chance and that people are only interested in the stories anyway and not the details. Not true, I tell him. People already think we make up the whole shaggin' lot."

Another sad little sigh followed. Ali thought that in general there was probably very little that wasn't done if Brigitte thought it should be, but John Joe was obviously an exception to the rule.

"You want me to cover court cases?" *More feckin' guards!* That's all Ali needed.

Brigitte sighed and ran her long fingers through her straggly hair. "Well, I would like *anyone* to cover court cases but John Joe says the courts are still 'his baby' so maybe you would like to expand on your food ideas for the summer, maybe write some pieces on the markets, the festivals, the fairs, that kind of thing. You drive, don't you?"

"Er yes. What about the ads though? Don't you need help with them and getting the money in?"

Brigitte sighed and shrugged her shoulders with a weary acceptance. "Oh, don't worry. They always pay when I get on the phone."

Ali believed that right enough.

"Is it something in particular that you wanted to do, the ads?"

"No."

"That settles it then. You will stay with the food."

Ali desperately wanted to leave now. There was nothing else left to say and Brigitte being nice to her felt almost peculiar.

"You know, it's not for me to say perhaps," Brigitte went on, "but maybe you need to think of writing for someone else. There's not much money to be made here. I don't need *The Voice* to pay the bills, you see – I always have my homeopathy and my paintings and I can teach the art as well."

Yes, Ali knew. Karl had filled her in about how Brigitte had started by painting dramatic landscapes of the west coast and had given herself two months to paint scenes from the lake before working her way back to Dublin but she had never gone home. That was six years ago. In between there had been a fling with a surfer from Clare and the birth of a little boy with red curls and freckles, a child Brigitte had named Stefan Rua in honour of her own and the child's mixed blood.

Suddenly Brigitte leaned into Ali's tummy and patted it with what seemed like affection. The action nearly took Ali's breath away.

"Do you know yet if it is a boy or a girl?"

Ali shook her head. "I don't want to know."

Brigitte let out a long sigh. "Pity baby isn't due in February. If it was a girl you could call her Bridget for St Bridget's Day. Anyway I go get my own little man from the Gaelscoil now – we'll have a quick bite to eat before I take him to his drumming workshop." Brigitte rubbed the mommy cat's head with tenderness and the cat returned its affection by wrapping her flexible body round Brigitte's big black boots and purring with obvious pleasure.

* * *

In days the weather went from pleasantly warm to unbearably hot and every part of Ali's flesh felt damp, sweaty and irritated.

"That much – for a pregnancy swimsuit!" Karl gasped when he saw the price-tag.

Yes, it was daylight robbery, but she didn't care, she needed to get into a pool somewhere, she needed to take the weight off her swollen feet and to feel soothed and cool all over. At seven months pregnant she waddled into the Olympic-sized swimming pool in Limerick, smiled back at the older ladies who were smiling at her bump, lowered herself into the water and marvelled at the miracle of weightlessness.

Once or twice the baby inside her performed summersaults and Ali laughed at the thought of the baby swimming inside her while she attempted the breaststroke and battled with breathlessness. The gentle exercise and the release from any concerns made her feel incredibly happy; maybe it was just a little bit of serotonin feeding some happiness to her brain cells or maybe she just felt blessed.

New life, new fears and new possibilities. Sure what was life anyway only a chain of events, a chain of events which could be altered by one tiny action or reaction? To hell with it, she thought as she attempted a sit-down dive, every day in all sorts of ways we take the plunge. Brigitte's words of advice were ringing in her head: try somewhere else, get more work, get more money. Why not? If she didn't get any work she could always cry and if the editor was a bloke he'd likely do anything to get a crying, pregnant woman off the premises. *Do you think I'll succeed?* she asked the baby. *One kick, yes – two kicks, no.* There was one kick deep inside her belly and no more. That was it, she would be successful; her bump had said so!

* * *

Karl didn't want to. It was embarrassing he told her, especially since he was a local, but Ali said she was embarrassed too and he was to come and support her and hold her handbag if she needed him to or do anything she asked because it was required and that was that.

Somehow she had managed to convince her provincial paper to print a 1,000-word article on the food markets in the towns and villages around the Shannon.

The Dutch lady at the local Saturday market told her what you could do with exotic chutneys, sun-dried tomatoes and garlic olives and the Flemish cheese merchant bent over backwards to help her, slicing off small pieces of cheese for her to taste and delight in and suggesting ways to use different cheeses in cooking. Ali ate a few delicious crumbs, not really caring if the cheese was pasteurised or not – it was too nice and she was too hungry.

As she tasted a particularly yummy sheep's cheese she heard a voice announcing, "I'll try a bit of that," and was met by a vision of her mother wearing Jackie O oversized sunglasses, accompanied by an uncomfortable-looking Liam.

Ali's face must have said it all.

"What?" Julie shrugged. "It's the weekend! We did a bit of property viewing, we had a look at a few boats – we might buy a nice little cruiser as well, who knows? And we were looking for something to do to amuse ourselves when someone told us about this lovely farmers' market here, isn't that right, Liam?"

"So you didn't come all the way down here just hoping to run into me then?"

"Don't be ridiculous. I'm the future grandmother by the way." Julie extended her hand to Karl, waiting for him to announce his connection to Ali but he remained tight-lipped. Ali had warned him off her mother, the way you warn children to never ever accept sweets from strangers, especially if they seem nice.

"Alison, would you like me to buy you anything from any of the stalls, anything at all?" said Liam as he rooted for his wallet.

"Put your money away, Dad," Ali told him in embarrassment.

It was Karl who brought them back from their collective stupor and suggested that they go so somewhere quiet to talk, but the pub was jammed with revellers drinking pints, pretending they were on the Costa del Sol, and every picnic table was commandeered and the sound of a powerboat ripping through the water, pulling a jet skier was becoming more and more grating.

"Oh for heaven's sake, let's just sit in the car," Julie snapped as she waved away a particularly determined wasp.

The women sat in the car, both looking irritated. The men stood up outside, leant against the doors – Karl on Ali's side, Liam on Julie's – and tried to seem pleasant and relaxed. Nobody was in a rush to mention the bump, how the bump got there or what its future status was, but Ali knew her mother and knew that the friendly beating-about-the-bush talk would eventually cause her to explode.

"Oh for God's sake, I presume you're the father!" Julie snapped out the window to Karl at last, waving the wasp away in growing irritation.

"It's a presumptuous thing to presume, but yes I am," said Karl.

"We just want to know that you're all right, Alison – we don't mean to intrude or anything," Liam said apologetically.

"And that you have enough money to keep you going," Julie interrupted.

"I'm doing all right, I'm writing a bit, establishing myself for the future . . ."

It was too much really: if her mother hadn't muscled in on her workplace, Ali wouldn't have to establish herself, she'd still have a job – a crappy job maybe but a job nonetheless and valuable maternity benefits to boot.

"You needn't worry about Ali, she's not on her own here, you know." Karl stroked Ali's arm protectively.

Business concluded, there was a silence that seemed to last forever. The kind of silence that should be followed by lots of cigarette puffing, only none of them smoked.

"So what kind of mileage do you get from the car then?" Karl asked her father in an attempt to appear affable.

"Oh not so good these days, it needs to be serviced. Now on a good day on a good stretch of road . . ."

The conversation was killing Julie, it was killing Ali too, and it was just too damn hot in the car so almost simultaneously both mother and daughter got out and began to take a stroll towards the water, followed by the eager wasp.

"Nice enough fella," said Julie, motioning towards the car. "Decent – not bad-looking either."

Ali bit her lip and shook her head just a little.

"So what does he do anyway?"

The badness in Ali came to the fore; she couldn't resist it. Turning around, she looked her mother full in the face and said the words out loud enough for the whole car park to hear.

"He's a doctor!"

The gulping noise was followed by the opening fish mouth and then the piercing scream. Poor old Jules had hardly time to register her shock as the persistent little wasp finally dug in and stung her.

30

At 11.30 in the morning, she arrived two weeks early, all seven pounds five ounces of her, with little blue eyes wide open and searching around the room. Then the nurses brought the tea and toast with butter and jam and the portly midwife issued a stern warning to Karl that the food was strictly for the mother and was not to be scoffed by the new father. After the bossy midwife left, Ali told the sheepish Karl to take a slice anyhow. At first she was too overjoyed to care if he scoffed the whole lot, although the tea was gorgeous and on second thoughts she was ravenous.

"Sorry," she said, slapping Karl's hand away. "I'll leave you a bite."

Karen was the first on the phone for the news. She said she had been down on her knees saying novenas since she heard Ali had gone into labour – more likely hanging around corridors puffing on fags – but Ali assured her that she was fine, deliriously happy even. No doubt the happy hormones were kicking in big time.

"Aren't you ripped to bits from the baby?"

"No," munched Ali through toast.

"How many stitches?"

"None."

"Feck off! You're pulling my leg?"

Remarkably enough there was not a stitch, not a tear and it was all thanks to Brigitte, Brigitte who had turned out to be something of a friend in her last weeks of pregnancy. Once or twice Brigitte was a bit stuck collecting Stefan Rua from school and Ali had offered to meet him at the gates and even mind him in the office now and again while Brigitte ran out for a sandwich at the local deli. Somewhere along the line Ali had confided in the only woman she knew locally that she was more than a bit fearful of giving birth and it had turned out that Brigitte was more than just a homeopath but was virtually an all-round witch, knowing all about herbs and methods that kept your inner workings supple for childbirth. So Ali even found herself going to Brigitte's once a week to do some yoga with her, so that she could keep herself flexible for labour.

Between Brigitte and Pammy from O'Grady's recommending that she drink herbal teas, Ali had had a somewhat alternative pregnancy for her last trimester and it seemed to help her innards get a little bit more elastic.

After the first round of tea and toast the midwife came back with her junior member of staff and the two of them gave Ali one final look over like a pair of mechanics.

"Remarkable, isn't it?" the senior said to the junior.

"Were you doing anything to your perineum during your pregnancy, dear?" asked the nice midwife.

"A friend of mine told me to massage it, so I did, massaged it," munched Ali.

"Oh, *massaged* it, made a huge difference, fantastic condition," said the chief mechanic, then she left, but not before plugging the baby back into Ali's breast. "This one has a very strong suck."

That she did. Ali would have sworn there were teeth in those little gums from the ferocity of the suckling. Then the little thing fell asleep on Ali's shoulder and slept for a full seven hours in her cot giving Ali what she thought was a blissful glimpse of her harmonious new life with her baby.

* * *

Remarkably, Julie was one of the first visitors. As soon as she had heard from Ruth that delivery was imminent she had packed her bags and headed west in preparation for the birth of her first granddaughter.

"A bit cramped in here, isn't it, darling?" her mother hissed, taking in the public ward and its surroundings.

Everything in her mother's demeanour told Ali that the thought of communal germs and dirty bits was making her feel more than a bit uncomfortable. After all, your own dirt was one thing but exposure to other people's dirt was an entirely different matter.

"What a pity you weren't in Dublin – Daddy and I might have put you up in a really nice private hospital."

Naturally the glamorous Julie never even offered to change the new arrival but she was more than willing to clutch it for the customary photographs and smile at those who said she was far too young and lovely to be a granny.

Karen arrived the next day but even she wasn't too hot on doing much in the way of babies. Apologetically, she explained to Ali that just because she was a nurse that didn't mean she was familiar with the ins and outs of infants, especially the outs, and while she did offer to change a dirty nappy for Ali her first reaction when she looked inside was "Oh fuck, I don't think I can do this, Ali. I wouldn't know where to start."

So it was Brigitte who came to the rescue in a truly practical way. When all the fanfare had faded and Ali was checking out of the hospital, it was Brigitte who moved into the house for a week with Stefan Rua and helped Ali move about, Brigitte who rocked the little thing to sleep when Ali could stand the crying no longer and Brigitte who kept making Ali wholesome food to eat so she could "keep her strength up for the little one". Her genuine concern and help made Ali feel guilty for ever disliking her.

Karl wasn't much help at all. He professed to be interested in the little thing but he was like most men, she supposed, not exactly sure what to do with the floppy-necked, squawking 'little bundle of joy'.

There was very little joy in reality. After the first night in hospital the baby never slept, fed all the time and, despite Brigitte's best efforts, Ali's nipples cracked in pain every time the baby put her lips to the breast to suck.

"Any ideas about names?" Maggie asked over the phone one day.

Dracula, she thought, but didn't say it.

"It will come to me," she said instead as she held the for-once-sleeping baby and peered at the scrunched-up features, looking for any family resemblance. So far nobody knew whom the child took after.

In a fit of exhaustion, Ali laid the child down in the crib and tried to sleep but she couldn't and found herself beginning to cry. So exhausted was she that an hour slipped by and then another and she found herself too tense to slumber. Like a half-ghost Brigitte swept in and, assessing the situation, arrived back with herbal tea. "Sleep!" she said when Ali had drained the mug, and remarkably Ali did just that.

For weeks every day was like a dream, an exhausted dream, of waking and night-time traipsing around. An endless dream where night and day were pretty much the same and pretty much awful, and then remarkably somewhere around five weeks the baby slept a little better and when it did it looked quite sweet really, so sweet that Ali fell in love with it in a way that surpassed all feelings of love for any man that she had ever known.

Baby still remained nameless, much to everyone's irritation, and then one day Ali's baby names book fell open at E and she read that the name Elizabeth meant Gift from God and the name just felt right. For in Ali's heart she knew that this child was more than flesh and blood, she was truly a gift from somewhere and she felt nothing but thanks for Elizabeth who became her 'Baby Beth'.

* * *

Soon enough little Beth was four months old, adorable and clearly in need of something more than just mother's milk and Ali went to the nearest big town and stocked up on baby-food jars from the local supermarket. Brigitte was horrified.

"You can't let Baby's first mouthful be *this*!" she implored Ali as she checked the back of one jar. "It should be stewed apples, maybe with some cinnamon or pears and cardamom, vegetables and fennel – something from the ground, something nourishing for Baby not this *muck*!"

Grasping the "muck" in her hand, Ali felt awful and very tearful. Was it so bad that she wanted to feed the baby from jars now and again just for the convenience? They couldn't be that bad, could they? Besides, the bottom line was she just couldn't cook and she told Brigitte so.

"Stewed apples is cooking? No, no, no, I'll make the food for you, better still I'll teach you."

So baby-cooking started with stewing and blending and stirring and eventually Ali ended up with some fast and convenient recipes that were permanently in her head. Before long she was even experimenting herself, adding a bit of vanilla here, a bit of desiccated coconut there, adding fruits to rice and pureeing everything up with a handheld blender. Who would have thought it? It turned out she was her father's daughter after all.

Brigitte beamed with pride the day she arrived to see Ali with a whole batch full of dinners and desserts ready for freezing.

It was in the middle of all this new mommy mania that Ali received a phone call out of the blue from Ireland's latest hottie: Lucy alias Linda O'Dwyer from the national soap *Me Auld Flower*.

"This is still yer phone then?"

"Jaysus, Lucy, is it really you?" Ali gushed down the phone.

"Of course it bleedin' is. I'm still normal, you know, although the crowd I'm working with now are complete headbangers and you wouldn't believe who's shaggin who and who's cramming half a kilo of coke up their nose. Anyways we're filming here in your backyard in the next few days for, you know, the dirty-weekend-away scene, only because the bastards were too mean to go to West Cork, and I thought you might like to meet for a bevy. I don't suppose you'll be bringing that new baby of yours?"

Then Ali looked at the food smeared all over Beth's hair and face and tiny fingers and made an instant decision. Apple sauce and apricot puree were all very worthy but it didn't compare to complete escape from the happy lunatic asylum. "Probably not – that is, if I can get away."

A sigh of relief was breathed down the phone. Of course everyone professes to love babies but Ali knew in Lucy's mind boobs were for pulling fellas, not for feeding nippers. Ali couldn't imagine Lucy would be that taken by all the puking, burping and dirty nappies, never mind the wailing.

The wailing began almost immediately and Ali picked up her daughter and jostled her on her hip and made soothing mommy noises as if she had been at this mommy lark the whole of her life.

Then Ali looked down the front of her own top and found it covered with bits of goo and she wondered had she anything half-decent she could wear to meet the gorgeous Lucy. Turning sideways she caught her reflection in the downstairs mirror and noted with disgust that her tummy was still very fat and slack and her hair hadn't had a decent cut for months.

Sighing, Ali picked up the phone and dialled Brigitte to see if she would come and baby-sit for a few hours as Karl was working late, again. After three days of milking her breasts of any extra fluid, only a few frustrating mils, Ali was ready to attempt walking out the door.

"It's not very much, I'm afraid, you might have to give formula as well," Ali apologised to Brigitte.

Brigitte glared at the newly made-up cow's milk as if it were poison. Baby would have to be bawling before that stuff would be shoved into her, thought Ali as she put on her coat and bolted out the door straight into Tommy Moran's taxicab.

"She's getting big, isn't she?" Tommy said as he drove Ali towards one of the local pubs in the village where filming was taking place. "First time away from her?"

"Yes." Ali half-choked as the eyes held back the dam of tears. The mommy in her wanted to run back and hold the little bundle in her arms but the raver in her wanted to ride in Tommy's taxicab forever and that made her feel horrible.

It was the hair that Ali noticed first – she had forgotten how stunning that corn-coloured mane could look and of course it had been freshly styled by the on-set hairdresser. Lucy looked so amazing that Ali thought very seriously about turning on her heel and sneaking out before her old colleague laid eyes on her, her frumpish outfit and her new love-handles.

"Hey, Mammy, how's tricks?" the nymph said as she walked the floor to greet Ali with a kiss. "Come here till I introduce you to a few of me new workmates – they're a bit more flash than you lot in O'Grady's and they like their gargle a lot more too!" She laughed, tongue in cheek, but the truth was these people were in a different stratosphere to Lucy's previous work colleagues.

Dec the cameraman was funny and relaxed as he swung his lights in his hand to try and get them to cool down before he could return them to their case, and Renata was heavily pregnant and looked like something out of *Vogue*. No doubt she'd have the baby, get her nails done and be back to work within a week. They were a bit intimidating to say the least. And then there was Danny Sheridan, Lucy's on-screen lover who was still wearing his heavy make-up.

"Will you ever close your gob – you'll catch flies," Lucy said quietly in Ali's ear as she snuggled up to her at a table.

"Sorry, is it that obvious?"

Lucy poked her in her ribs and smiled her familiar catlike smile and Ali relaxed. The minx might now be a national celebrity but she was still the self-same Lucy at her core. Half-guiltily Ali downed a glass of Guinness and found that she was instantly drunk. It had been so long since she had drunk anything vaguely alcoholic at all that she got the giggles after just a few minutes of indulgence.

"So tell us about the new love in your life?" Lucy smiled as she downed her fifth straight vodka without a flicker of drunkenness in her face.

"Oh Beth – well, she's been life-changing, that's for sure. She's got blue eyes and the most beautiful blonde curls at the back of her neck and –"

"Not the baby – although I'm sure she's lovely and all – yer fella, tell us about your new fella."

Karl? What was there to say about Karl? He was out of the house as much as he could, working always working. It wasn't like he was abandoning her for the pub or the golf course or some time away with his mates, but he was gone nonetheless and it hurt to be alone for hours except for the odd phone call to her mates and maybe Brigitte calling in with some food or asking her did she need any dishes put away or the bed made up. Her fella was turning into another kind of Dave, always busy, always gone. The sudden realisation shook Ali to her core.

"He's intelligent, and he's away a lot – you know, working. And he speaks Spanish, speaks it fluently in fact."

"Ooh happy days, let me guess, you have him speaking to you in *tongues* every night of the week!" said Luce with a raise of her eyebrow.

"Still the same old Lucy!"

"Oh I am, all right – still the one-track mind – you know me!"

A young man in his thirties brushed by Lucy and she grabbed his sleeve and tugged it determinedly until he turned round in bemusement.

"Alan, this is a friend of mine from me pre-fame days. I used to work with Ali back in the days when I was underpaid and under-appreciated – some things never change! Alan is one of our producers, Ali."

He was dark with sallow skin and chestnut eyes and something about him reminded her of Dave. It wasn't just his face but the way he moved, the way he held his body with self-assurance. But he was smarter than Dave, wittier, and Ali laughed at all his jokes and life observations and after a while she found herself relaxed in his company and she didn't even mind when he discreetly glanced at her famous mammaries, which were even more massive now that she was breastfeeding.

After a flush of contentment, the way one feels when one knows one is being admired, Ali was seized with panic and when Alan beat a track to the bar she immediately stole a look at her boobs and noted that she wasn't leaking milk at least. Her breasts were feeling too full and a bit uncomfortable and she hoped to God the dams weren't going to burst at any minute. Guiltily she wondered how Brigitte was getting on with Baby Beth and then she remembered she had read somewhere that even thinking of your child was enough to start milk flowing. Christ, she didn't want that, not in front of this glitzy show biz and arty farty group!

Lucy went off to mingle just as Alan came back looking all sexy and intellectual and plonked himself down beside Ali.

"Will Lucy last another season, do you think?" asked Ali half-nervously as she raised her overpriced mineral water to her lips and tried to sound sophisticated.

"Oh, believe me, Lucy's character will run and run."

That's what Ali wanted to do – run and run – run home as fast as her legs could carry her – and then there was sudden death as Ali realised that she had just fallen off the conversation cliff and didn't have anything witty or fabulous to add to the communal chatter because she was now "a mammy". It had been weeks since she'd glimpsed Lucy on the box because she was permanently tired and even when Baby Beth did sleep Ali found she was cooking like Mrs Ingles in *Little House on the Prairie* or loading up the washing-machine with yet more babygrows while hoping that her baby-sensitive washing powder could deal with the latest explosions. Being a mommy was like being in a war zone but without the adrenaline rush and when the buzz of alcohol had worn off Ali knew it was time to ring Tommy to go home.

"Sure you had a great night," Tommy summed up when he saw her.

Had she? For Lucy the night was only beginning and Ali was

envious – she had never been one to leave a party early.

Ali didn't know who she was any more; all she knew was that she felt constantly uncertain. There was a time, not so long ago, when she would have been able to match the saucy Lucy word for word but Ali felt nine months of pregnancy and several months of mommyhood had dulled her brain and she wasn't fit for adult company any more.

Once upon a time she would have known instinctively what was hot and what was not but now she felt out of touch with everything – clothes, hair, news, fashion. If she could only have got rat-arsed drunk she would have lost her nerves in an instant. All night she had sat in the pub, wearing a mask, hoping that nobody would realise how disconnected she was and hoping that they wouldn't realise that she had turned into a machine, a big mommy-machine that cleaned bums, bathed limbs, placated wailings with milk and rocked and rocked and rocked until she sometimes felt she was turning into a lunatic.

When Ali came home Brigitte said nothing but she got the definite impression that she thought she had been out too long without any regard to the welfare of the baby.

"Baby is hungry," Brigitte said brusquely and handed the little bundle of squawks to Ali.

Ali settled down to feed in the rocking chair and yawned. Beth could take up to forty minutes of munching before she fell asleep and Ali had no idea if she could stay awake that long but it wouldn't have been the first time that she would have dozed off with her baby at her breast.

Clutching her handbag, Brigitte marched out of the house and Ali could hear the key turn in the ignition then the crunch on gravel as she turned her car out the driveway and zoomed away.

When Ali woke up in the early hours of the morning, the TV was still on and Karl still wasn't home.

31

Bloody tired and possibly hung-over from two glasses of Guinness and a couple of fizzy oranges – wow, she really was an old woman! Everybody told her that she'd feel great when she got a first night out after having the baby but Ali didn't. Her night out had done little for her self-esteem, and her body and even her baby was protesting. She swore the little tot was in the snots with her for abandoning her for a few hours – she was cranky all morning and pouted determinedly even when Ali tried to make her laugh.

Drudging around in thick socks, her nightie, and Karl's slippers and cardigan she reached to put on the kettle and was startled by a noise behind her.

She turned.

It couldn't be him. She must be hallucinating from sleep deprivation.

No, it was him, Dave, the bastard, there he was in front of the patio-door window, grinning frantically and making cup-of-tea motions with his hands. Well, she'd be damned if she'd let him in, ever, not after the last time.

"Ali – open the door!"

Determinedly she shook her head.

"Oh come on, Ali, I come in peace. Better still, I come in chocolate!" He held up a plastic bag through which she could clearly see the purple wrapping of chockie bickies.

It was impossible not to laugh; worse than that it was also impossible to hate the bastard.

"Don't say a word," Ali snarled as she opened the door. "Don't mention hairy legs, slippers, greasy hair or pukey clothes."

"God, I was only going to say that you look *fabulous*."

"And don't fucking *patronise* me either, especially not after the crap you said the last time we met!" she barked.

Her point was taken, she knew that he had seen the power of Scary Mommy and was backing off without any protest. Over the last few months Ali had learnt that Scary Mommy or, even better, Hysterical Sobbing Mommy could make men take off faster than Viagra.

In the bedroom Ali considered another attempt at squeezing herself into her pre-pregnancy jeans but she knew they wouldn't fit over the balloon that was her bum, tum and thighs, so she just wore the tracksuit and the wrinkled top, scraped her hair back in a pigtail and accepted that she looked crap and probably also smelt funny. When she returned she found Beth in Dave's arms and the little girl was all smiles.

"What? Didn't think I'd know which end is which? See a lot of kids on the job, you know!" he explained as he handed over the six-month-old outrageous flirt.

Yeah, Ali knew, she'd heard it all before: the babies of druggies crawling on floors when flats were raided, kids barely out of nappies nearly joyriding, ringing social services to take kids into care while they waited at the station. It's just she didn't think he knew how to *hold* a baby. After their two attempts at boyfriend and girlfriend she still didn't know lots about him, that was the problem.

"Want to go for a drive?"

"Why?"

"You look like you could do with some cheering up – sorry, I didn't mean to *patronise* you," he got in quickly.

Bloody guards, I suppose they got them to read body language at the Garda College as well. Too bloody right she needed some cheering up. The father of her baby hadn't come home last night, whatever the hell that was about.

"I don't know – she's in terrible form today," Ali fussed.

Beth disagreed with her mother in front of the lovely, friendly policeman and beamed from ear to ear in a way that made Ali feel quite cross.

"Don't be daft, she'll love the car!"

The little brat did too, and when they parked at the lakeside beauty spot in Dromineer she was snoring heavily in her car seat.

Ali wondered why he was here. Maybe he was going to talk some more about why he loved her or could have loved her, not that she was going to ask any questions first.

"Peaceful spot here," he said as he watched the swans drift by and said nothing else for an eternity.

"So which one then do you think is packing the UZI, the Mommy swan or the Daddy swan?" Ali snapped in irritation.

"What?"

"You're checking the bloody swans out – you're doing that thing again with your eyes."

"I am not, well, maybe I am – it's just when you have the power of arrest 24-7 . . ."

"You think even the wildlife is going to jump you, yeah, yeah."

"*Fucking hell,* this being a mammy is like having permanent PMT – you're vicious!"

The sniffling came from nowhere and then Ali's shoulders heaved and snots came out her nose and she knew she looked more than ever like a madwoman who has just crawled out of a bin and who probably smelled.

"I'm sorry, it's just, it's just . . . it's just everything!"

He pulled her close and let her sob all over him, he didn't even seem to care about the snots and then when she had reached maximum blotchiness and redness, he took a tissue and handed it to her as if it was his job to console out-of-control women every day of the week, which he probably did, in between extracting information from them.

"It's just I don't think I can do this being-a-mammy thing . . . I should have read more books about how to do it right. I needed more time and I'm – I'm confused about lots of things."

Dave laughed, but in a nice way, and Ali found herself laughing too, not because it was funny but because wailing was useless.

"She'll grow up before you know it."

"Become a strop of a teenager, causing me more worries, yeah, yeah, I know."

For a while they joked, but inevitably the conversation dried up until there was nothing but an uncomfortable silence which grated on Ali's nerves.

"Why'd you come, Dave?" she asked as she looked straight ahead out into the clear blue waters.

He shifted in his seat and suddenly she felt quite anxious.

"There's nobody in trouble or hurt back in Dublin, is there?"

"No, Ali, don't worry yourself – it's just I've had a bit of news, that's all, and I thought I should tell you myself rather than let you find out over the phone or by letter." Ali's white face must have unsettled him because he took her hand and gave it a small squeeze. "You know the auld fella who knocked you down on his moped, well, I've heard from the traffic cop that his solicitor has been making inquiries and it seems he's going to sue you."

"Sue *me*! But *he* knocked me down, the stupid dozy ole –"

"Yes, I know but he's claiming he had right of way and that you broke the lights and I understand he's claiming for injury and emotional trauma."

"Does he have a case?"

"Maybe."

Great! More bloody money problems! She'd probably have to get a solicitor, there would be fees, there might be a court case, she might lose, oh Jaysus, this could be a bad one!

"I didn't mean to upset you, but I know you're in that house alone a lot and I wouldn't want you to get bad news and be thinking about it all day. Are you okay, Ali?"

"Yes, of course." Then she burst into tears again and he awkwardly tried to console her.

He sighed and hugged her tightly. "It'll be all right, it'll probably not amount to anything. It's just I was going to Portlaoise anyway to check out buying a starter motor and a few other bits and pieces for my cars and you're just down the road here so I thought I should drop in and give you the news in person."

Oh great, so as usual he's just fitting you in with his other work commitments. I should have known. Dave Bloody Workaholic!

"Want me to check up on the old bastard and see if he has any outstanding parking fines?"

"You probably already have."

"Yeah – guilty as charged. Not a thing on him – a regular Joe Soap."

The feel of him, the comforting smell of him – Ali could have rested against Dave for an eternity. She felt him put a hand on her head and leave it there, uncertain what to do next, and then out of the corner of her eye she saw her.

It was the tight little smile that she saw first.

Mary!

What the hell was Karl's mother doing out here?

The mother-in-law threw her a queer little look, halfway between a smirk and a nod and she walked away.

"Take me back, will you, Dave?"

He had tea, out of politeness no doubt, and left soon after without much conversation out of Ali. Beth woke up not long after and screamed and Ali realised the baby had soiled herself and had been sitting in a dirty nappy for God knows how long and now had a red bum. The little mite was inconsolable and Ali felt like the worst mother in the world as she rubbed on the Sudocrem and plugged in to some mindless afternoon radio.

To think after all her degrees, courses and potential she had finally graduated to being a fully-fledged bum-wiper and a playmate to an adorable baby with just a few developing brain-cells! *Where do you see yourself in five years' time, Miss Hughes?* Oh, she used to know the answer – well, *think* she knew the answer at any rate – but when she thought about it now, planning at all for the future was one of the daftest things anyone could ever attempt to do.

32

It had been a weird day with Ali raiding cookery books looking for healthy baby recipes and Brigitte hovering around encouraging her as she played around with a few recipes of her own.

Brigitte was feeling optimistic. She had "secured" Ali a weekly cookery column with a big provincial on busy mommies and how to cook healthy food for their babies. Having decided that Ali would never get off her arse herself and get into a real paper, Brigitte had stormed the offices of the local paper and told the features editor that her friend was fantastic at writing on food and basically he would be lucky to have Ali's work published in their paper. The poor man agreed to give it a go, probably just to get rid of the dominant Brigitte who was even more assertive than normal as she had chopped off all her scraggly hair for a new, sexy, tousled style. "Too long with that boring old Brigitte – strong women need strong hair!" Ali wasn't about to argue.

Surprisingly, her first column with the provincial had been something of a local success, probably because something of Ali's naivety showed through. Someone in the village had stopped her and said that they found her column refreshing, especially since Ali wrote about cooking as if she was a total incompetent, which she was, and that was something her generation of women could identify with.

With mischief in his eyes, Karl's father had even asked if she would sign a copy of his paper. Michael was in great form lately having been roped into the latest village scheme. Everyone who had a trailer within a twenty-mile radius had been commandeered to make trips to Galway to bring back John Joe's precious cinema seats and the somewhat arty project had given Michael a great boost, probably because it reminded him of his old notions of becoming an actor or a DJ.

For the first time in a long time Ali felt vaguely important. The provincial paper had even sent a photographer to take snaps of her and Beth and remarkably Ali was wearing a clean top, had make-up on and her baby was in good enough form to be pictured eating some of the healthy produce instead of firing it at the nearest wall. Ali couldn't help thinking of Donal Dineen back in Dublin and his questions about sexy babes being present for photographers. Things were a bit different down the country, thank God.

But, once the excitement was over and this week's column written for the regional paper, the place seemed very lonely and Karl was working late and Ali ate alone, yet again.

It was after eleven that night when Karl parked the car outside. Ali was upstairs planning to traipse off to bed when she heard him shuffling into the kitchen. Hearing the microwave beeping she presumed he was making himself his latest nightcap – hot milk. Then she heard him climb the stairs and push open the bedroom door.

"I was hoping to see you – didn't know if you'd be in bed by now," he started cautiously.

Ali was too tired to talk and just nodded, not even making eye contact – she didn't want to. Karl put his cup to his lips and stared intently at Ali breastfeeding the child and his interest brought pleasure to Ali – maybe he could become an involved father after all.

"She doesn't look much like me. I don't even know if she looks like you," he announced sharply.

"Is this going anywhere in particular?" asked a weary Ali as she took the sleeping Beth and put her over one shoulder, patting her back from time to time and rubbing it in round circular motions.

"It's just, well, the mother told me she saw you the other day. She was at a poetry workshop –"

"Stop right there, Karl. I now know exactly where this is going."

"You see, she also told me a while back, before Beth was born, that she saw *him* at the house having a blazing row with you and I thought then it was none of my business . . . I tried to ignore it but now . . . now I just have to be sure . . . she *is* mine, isn't she, Ali? You're *absolutely* certain, aren't you, that Beth couldn't be his?"

"So that's why you've been so cold! You knew I met Dave before Beth was born and you said nothing? Why didn't you say something before now?" Ali glared at him as she rocked the little bundle back and forth in her arms.

"I was afraid to – you're so snappy these days – and as for being cold, I didn't mean to be, I was just quietly waiting for the right time to talk about things, but there never seems to be a right time, that's the problem," he sighed.

"I *know* finding time is impossible, and if I'm snappy it's because I'm tired – I've never been so tired in my life," she whispered angrily as she managed to settle the baby down in the cot.

In a huff she crept out the door and motioned for him to follow her. When he did she closed the door gently and then let rip – but in an undertone.

"Do you *honestly* think I'd come down here and bother you with all this if the baby *wasn't* yours? Do you honestly think I'd want to fuck up your world that much? I'm really upset that you'd think so little of me!" She was halfway between tears and anger. "And as for your mother seeing me with Dave, the first time I met him by chance in Limerick and he gave me a lift home and the second time he came to tell me some news about my accident, not the most pleasant news – I got upset and he put his arm round me – that's all, nothing more, okay?"

"Why didn't you tell me this?"

"Because I didn't want to burden you with any more of my problems and it seems I was right – you're burdened enough with me already."

"It's not that I'm burdened with you but I'm sorry it's just, well, like I said, I don't see any resemblance to my side in Beth and now you've confirmed that you have seen Dave since you left Dublin –"

"Do you know what I think, Karl? I think maybe this is just a bit more than you can handle. I think maybe I should move out, at least for a while, at least until you can figure out if you want anything more to do with me and *your* daughter, for believe me that's what she is, *your* daughter, not anybody else's, not the postman's, the greengrocer's, the local publican's and especially not Dave O'Connor's daughter, but until you can come to realise that all by yourself maybe I should just go!"

"Go, Ali? For God's sake, where would you go?"

It was a good question. Ali noted however that Karl didn't say something on the lines of: "Don't be mad, of course you can't go – you belong here with me."

Where would she go if not here, she asked herself as she busied herself in the kitchen in an attempt to work off her anger. If she left Karl's she'd surely be entitled to social welfare and rent allowance – eventually – but then she'd be in a house all alone, not knowing anyone and feeling lonely. Maybe she should head back to Dublin at least temporarily, back to her old family home, and just relax until she had more time to think about her future. Liam would only be delighted to wait on her and Beth hand and foot.

Hadn't he virtually reared herself and Ruth anyhow? Julie never did a tap, even when they were young, not if she could get away with it, not if the arthritis was in any way bad. Not that the arthritis was ever bad these days – from all appearances Julie was leppin' around like a young one whenever she got the chance.

No, despite any yearnings for the old homestead, Ali couldn't go home because her mother would have her so tormented that there would be no joy in any of her father's panderings.

Muttering to herself, Ali was just setting her face in frosty annoyance when close to midnight the phone rang and she heard Ruth panting down it.

"Are you sitting down, Alison? Is the baby somewhere safe?"

"In her cot – what's with the melodrama?"

"There's no easy way to say this. Mum's left Dad and you won't believe who she's thrown him over for – only your ex-boss!"

Sickly nausea welled up inside Ali. Good God, no! Not Simon! Surely Julie hadn't lost her senses altogether, surely even the new "Jules" would know that a naked Simon would be a pretty horrendous sight and that he was too self-absorbed to ever treat her as well as her husband Liam.

"Oh, how could she! Creepy Simon!"

"Good God, not him! No, the other boss, the top boss, that fella you sometimes called Charlie – like in *Charlie's Angels*."

"Joe? Joe O'Grady? She's shagging the Managing Director himself?"

For about ten seconds Ali was consumed with fury. First her mother had stolen her job and now she had shagged the ultimately shaggable Joe. Ali would have liked that chance herself. It took a few seconds for the blind anger to pass and for Ali to think of her father. Poor, poor Liam – what had he ever done to deserve such a wagon as her mother?

"So you'll have to come home."

"*Have* to come home. Why do I *have* to come home? Do you think I want to get caught in the crossfire, Ruth?" *What a bitch her mother was though, what an evil, cunning bitch.*

From the other end of telephone Ali heard the first sniffle and then the uncontrollable dramatic sobs. "I just can't believe it. I mean we've both known that she was as self-centred as they come but I always thought she would stay with Dad. He was always so good to her, let her away with murder."

"Yeah, but money and status were always big up there with

Mum and let me tell you, Ruth, my boss is *seriously* loaded. I'm pretty sure that's a big part of the attraction."

"Well, anyway, you have to come home. Dad is gutted and he could do with the distraction and sure you have nothing to do – you and the baby could entertain him for hours. Besides, as you're always saying yourself, you were always his favourite so it's *incumbent* upon you to help him over this."

Guilt got the better of Ali in the end. Bloody Ruth and her big words, and the way she could twist things so it seemed that Ali would be a cow if she didn't come to help her father over this tragedy. All right, she'd go, she told Ruth. Besides she didn't know if Karl would even miss her so she might as well go and when she came back, if she came back, she'd know what to do.

* * *

The receptionist where Karl worked asked a dozen questions about Baby Beth when Ali phoned. It was more than Ali cared to answer and besides it was awkward – she knew by other people's standards herself and Karl were a queer couple. They were probably gossiped about by the staff at lunchtime. When Karl's weary voice answered at the other end of the phone, he told her that he was "up to his tonsils" in paperwork.

Still, Ali didn't think twice about asking him to drive her to the train station for the next morning, even though she was still pissed off with him for asking about Beth's parentage. Of course she could have asked him the favour over dinner that night but they ate together so rarely these days – either he was working late, at a business dinner or she had fallen asleep with the baby in the early evening.

33

All the way to Dublin the following morning in the train, Beth was a little dream, sleeping, feeding and cooing at the middle-aged women who were trampling over each other to catch a glimpse of the adorable little baby with the gorgeous gummy smile. All the attention was a source of relief and Ali was glad that her little one was so easily distracted for her own thoughts were distraction enough.

How on earth could her mother be so heartless? Her dad had done everything over the years to keep her happy. "Whatever you want, darling" was his philosophy. He had spoiled Julie; she didn't know how good she had it, that was her problem.

The smell of baking was wafting through the air when Ali turned the key in her old family home. Loving with food was Liam's speciality and ever since he had heard that Ali was coming home he had gone into baking overdrive.

Brown bread, breakfast muffins, all healthy stuff for the three of them to munch over – even in the height of his distress Liam had the delicacy not to bake cakes and buns so that Ali wouldn't be tempted to load up on empty calories. He was always thinking of others: her mother, herself and Ruth, and now his granddaughter.

When Ali saw her father it was like seeing the old ghost again, that shell of a man she'd come across for the first time when her mother had headed for the Caribbean to "find herself". His clothes were crumpled and quite shockingly he hadn't shaved – he was a far cry from the neat man she was used to.

Once she had settled Beth down for the night Ali stayed up quite late and listened to his infuriating tale of how Julie was working more and more, had less time for him or even any of her old interests and how she had dropped the affair on him like a bomb one morning after breakfast.

Ali listened and nodded and tried her best to hide her own anger and shock and then, close to one o'clock she helped her own father into bed, fluffed the pillows around his ears, pulled the duvet up to his nose, kissed the top of his head and turned off the light. All in all, she was getting quite good at this mothering business.

* * *

Two days passed by and Karl still hadn't rung. The feeling that Karl was either a cold fish or a bit "other worldish" entered Ali's head on more than one occasion but she shrugged off the thought with determination; there were other matters to think of. For the second time in recent history Ali was thinking of heading out for a bit of adult social interaction and this time with Karen, although surprisingly her best friend seemed a bit reluctant to be tied down to an exact time and location to meet, even for the next week.

Puzzled, Ali lay down on her old bed in her old bedroom and surveyed the cracks on the ceiling. Much of her life had been spent in this same room with Karen – contemplating school, boys, future careers with enormous salaries, marrying sugar daddies, sabotaging teachers and just dreaming over cups of tea and chocolate biscuits while listening to music in the background.

Part of Ali was afraid that something in her relationship with her best friend was changing and she wondered was it the baby. There was less time to natter on the phone but there seemed to be fewer phone calls from Karen too and she wondered why. Karen had always been fun, outrageous and loyal, but she had always needed to be the centre of attention and it was hard to compete against a drooling, screaming, adorable bundle of joy.

Maybe Karen was even embarrassed by Ali's mumsiness. Perhaps she was even wondering how she was going to bring Ali anywhere remotely trendy, especially now that Ali's stomach had expanded both outwards and downwards in the last few months.

Finally Ali wore her old friend down and they agreed to meet up in a pub in the suburbs.

"You look fantastic!" Karen squealed a little too loudly when they met.

"Big knickers, hold everything in when the muscles have gone to hell, don't you know."

"And your boobs! Huge, ginormous – straight out of Hollywood! Would you like a drink, oh, can you drink what with feeding the baby?"

Ali nodded that a glass of Guinness would be okay. Liam was minding the baby tonight. He and Beth had bonded in an instant and he was of course, as ever, a dab hand with the bottle. He hadn't lost the touch, that was for sure and at least his fussing over Beth was taking him away from his own troubles.

When they were seated with their drinks, Karen coyly asked after Ali's parents and then she admitted that she knew the whole story about the affair. Apparently the whole neighbourhood was aware of Julie's departure as Joe was seen to pull up there in his Jaguar not long after the big departure speech was delivered.

"She's betrayed us all!" Ali hissed. "I don't think it would be too soon if I didn't see her another day in my life. Having an affair with my boss, of *all* people, *and* showing such disloyalty to my father who never denied her a thing!"

With every detail of the sordid affair Karen's body language seemed to become more uncomfortable and her reaction mystified Ali but she quickly dismissed it.

"And Karl, things are still going strong there?" Karen asked.

Fidgeting in her seat, Ali took her glass and gazed at it intently as if the bottom of the murky vessel might somehow have the answer to all her problems.

"We're both so tired, both so busy, both so . . . I don't know, thrown into the deep end," she said slowly, picking over every word, "that I guess our relationship has taken a bit of a backseat since the baby was born."

Karen raised an eyebrow at the convoluted explanation and then she shot Ali one of her knowing smiles.

"All right then, things are going shite and we're both freaked out at being parents to a baby when we don't know what the hell we're doing ourselves. In fact, I'll rephrase that, we're both freaked out at having a baby full stop and he even asked me recently was I *sure* that he was the father. Can you imagine that? He has me so rattled I'm thinking of moving out altogether. He's hardly there as it is. If I'm honest with you it's a bit like having an absentee boyfriend all over again but this time without *any* fun."

For a minute or two Karen sympathised with her friend over her plight and then she caught the eye of one of the bar staff and ordered another round of drinks because even though Ali had only taken a few mouthfuls out of her glass, Karen had drained every drop of hers. Half an hour later, while she was feeling a bit woozy, Ali had the nerve to ask Karen whether she or her nursey friends had seen Dave around town lately.

"I know there's no point in hankering about the past but he still looks great," Ali sighed.

"He said you looked good too."

"You've seen him then?"

Sighing, Karen tapped her long manicured fingernails off the side of her glass before meeting Ali's intense gaze. "In a club . . . not long ago."

"And you told him of course that I was over him, had a nice new life, right? I hope you did because the last time I saw him I kind of lost it a bit and cried all over him."

Karen was biting her bottom lip so hard that it was turning blue.

"Oh God, there is no easy way to say this. I shifted him, Ali. I didn't mean to, it just sort of happened. He was just opening up to me about you and it sort of happened. It was just a few kisses. I'm really, really sorry and I meant to tell you straight away only I didn't know how."

It was like someone had just snapped a large twig right in front of her nose; only Ali could have sworn she heard the noise in her brain instead. The whole room seemed to disappear, the noisy chatter became completely muffled and the people began to blur and the only thing remaining in focus was herself and an incomprehensible Karen, both trapped in a kind of bubble. It was suffocating and the urge to leave was immediate and overwhelming.

"Ali, did you hear what I said? Really, it was just a few kisses. I'm *sorry*."

"Don't call me, don't text me, don't knock on my door, *ever*." The spite in her voice was unmistakeable and then, just like that, Ali left, walking through the heavy wooden doors into the night air beyond.

Gasping for breath she raised her hand to her cheek and found her skin already moistened by tears. First her mother and now her best friend – was there any loyalty or decency left in the world when it came to men?

Like a reckless fool, Ali drove all the way home in her father's car in total disregard of any speed limits and when she turned the key in the front door all she could think of was Beth and of holding her tight and smelling her sweet innocent scent.

Hugging the little bundle to her, Ali climbed into the big double bed, held her daughter's tiny plump hand and listened to her contented breathing and after a while the need to cry subsided and Ali felt enough peace to sleep. For the time being all negativity could be ignored. Right now, she was like Scarlett O'Hara and all her problems could wait until tomorrow.

34

One day when Ali knew her daughter was due a long nap, she took her father's car and drove across the city to Maggie's. Beth fell asleep in her rock-a-tot seat and Ali was able to haul her, snoring, inside and park her in a corner of the sitting room.

Ali's bum was barely parked on the couch when Maggie told her Julie was turning into a nightmare at O'Grady's and "Jules" and Simon were no longer on lovey-dovey terms.

"Knew that wouldn't last." Ali rolled her eyeballs as she slurped a cup of tea and bit into one of her father's buns. Liam was in such a baking overdrive there was enough to feed a cast of five thousand so it made sense to offload a few buns on Maggie.

"Well, let's say your mother wasn't long in working out where the real power lay," said Maggie as she munched a slice of Liam's scrumptious apple tart.

"The real power being with Joe, of course. Poor Simon has now undoubtedly learned that with my mother, if you have served your purpose and are no longer useful you're disposed of and it's on to the next good thing."

"I mightn't have put it exactly like that, but yes, that's kind of what happened. And Simon is crushed that she no longer hangs on his every word. He's taken to drinking *real* tea again, with *sugar* in it and of late his suits have been known to show up to work looking crumpled," Maggie smirked.

Despite the gravity of the situation Ali began to laugh. In a weird sort of a way she actually had some respect for her mother for putting that little wimp Simon Webb in his place. Unaccustomed to his subordinates giving him the bum steer, it must be absolutely killing him that Jules was also getting the Big Boss's undivided attention. Munching on a second slice of pie, Maggie confessed that there'd been plenty of flirting between Jules and Joe in the pub over the last few weeks but there had been no hint until very recently that the flirting had progressed into a full-blown affair.

"Is she still coming to work?"

"Yes, loves the place, I don't think Joe is paying her big money or anything . . ."

"But he doesn't have to because my father is probably still supporting her. Work is just a hobby for Julie. Oh God, what an *horrendous* mother I have! I'm *truly* sorry that you have to work with her, Mags."

Putting a hand to her chin, Maggie smiled and looked at Ali from beneath her eyelashes. "Well, to tell you the truth I won't be in the job much longer. I've put in to become a researcher with one of the local authorities back home, and I'll be handing in my notice with O'Grady's next week. There's more money involved and the benefits and time off are good –"

"So there's nothing to hold you back," finished Ali. Clever Maggie! As usual the savvy country girl was moving on with her game plan, surely and slowly making progress with her life. Next up was probably the building of the house down home on her father's land and from there it was just a short stop to snaring a man. Why couldn't Ali have such a well-thought out and well-executed life plan? Why did her life have to have so many damn twists in it? Part of her would love to be as settled as her friend – not that she envied Maggie – you could never envy Maggie, she was too nice and was just taking what was rightly hers in the world.

"Will you be heading back to your *own* fields soon?" Maggie gently teased and that was when Ali poured out her problems, about Karl being remote these days and about Karen wearing the face off Dave recently in a Dublin nightclub.

"In fairness, Ali, you had two shots at Dave and you threw him aside both times – remember?"

Of course Ali remembered and sometimes she was sorry. Whatever Dave's flaws, he would have made a brilliant father to any baby, making funny faces for his little doll, rolling around with her on the floor to make her laugh, cradling her affectionately, introducing his 'Princess' to all the lads.

With her mouth stuffed Ali listened as Maggie pointed out to her that if she had been truly mad about Dave, she wouldn't have thrown him over even once and that maybe she was just raging with jealousy because he'd forgotten about her long enough to shift Karen.

"Is it worth breaking off contact with an old friend over a man that you yourself dumped twice, Ali? Can't you just forgive her?"

"No. In all my years I've never stuck my tongue down the throat of any mate's boyfriend, current or ex. Karen knew the rules as much as anybody and she's broken them."

"You know, Ali, thinking of Dave at all is not going to do your relationship with Karl any favours and after all it's *Karl* who is the father of your child, not Dave. And while we're at it – living in that big house away from the whole world when he's away so often is not good for you – neither is being so dependent on him. Just how much money are you making now from your food column and other features?"

When Ali told Maggie the piddling amount, the normally stoic friend couldn't keep from gasping. "That's just not enough, Ali, not with a baby to provide for. Do you know how much money you'll have to put aside just to send this child to school in the future? You've got to earn more money, you have no other choice, either that or you'll have to claim your social welfare benefits, rent allowance, you'll probably get a medical card too, but to do that you have to stop living with Karl – at least for a while."

"Living apart might not be such a bad thing for everyone – I like Karl, but we're not getting on the best at the moment and moving out and getting my allowances would make me less dependent on him, although in fairness he pays for everything without me even asking. But, Maggie, I don't want to be a social welfare recipient my whole life – I want more, I want to build a future – I want a career not just a cheque every month."

"Ever think of writing your articles for a national, maybe even a few magazines? Sure, we're all pining for the romance of the country, girl – the townies dream of it when they're stuck in their traffic jams and culchies like me pine for it until we can go home every weekend. Couldn't you be writing all about your country markets and festivals and beauty spots and be getting paid more for it into the bargain?"

It was a thought, a very exciting but very scary prospect. The logical part of her brain told her she wasn't ready but then, whenever she'd done anything on a whim in the last while, unexpected positive things had happened. In her head Ali could hear Karen's playful voice saying, "Ah, go on – would you risk it for a biscuit?" and then she felt sad.

It was going to be hard not having Karen in her life any more. Maggie might have been her gentle Buddha, her source of wisdom and solace when thing went wrong but Karen was Ali's adrenaline junkie, the woman who always jumpstarted her life and got her moving. Looking down at Beth yawning in her sleep Ali realised she had to be all kinds of woman now; she had to be her own woman.

* * *

For a while Ali thought she could find some refuge with her father in Dublin, but it was clear this bun-baking father – daughter binge couldn't continue indefinitely. Ever morning he got up, God love him, and baked – brown bread, scones, buns, muffins, apple tarts and whatever else took his fancy – but it was getting a bit crazy, the freezer was jammed, the neighbours were plied with the overspill and sometimes what he baked just ended up in the bin.

The only benefit to her father's sadness was that Ali actually learned to bake, learned to turn out a loaf and flour a tray for sultana scones and was even initiated into some of his secret recipes. In fact he seemed determined that she learn them; it was like passing on his legacy and there was a joy in their togetherness and a connection that was almost maternal.

Then, late at night when Ali sat down at her mother's computer and e-mailed her work to the paper, she always seethed with rage. Her mother was a woman with a stone heart, a perplexing automaton devoid of emotion. Her parents were such opposites in every way.

After a while Ali could take it no longer and decided that she had to return to the country because it was there she belonged, at least for the present, and there was no doubt in her head that she no longer belonged in the city. Where once she had longed for bagels and exotic coffee and hot fudge and high street shops, she now wouldn't care for any of that stuff, not if it came and bit her on the ass. Besides, everywhere she turned she saw reminders of her carefree single life and all her and Karen's favourite haunts and she was too hurt by Karen and by Dave to be looking for daily reminders of her pain.

Strangely, all the way from Dublin Ali felt confident and powerful. Things needed to be done and she would do them. With barely a nod of his head Karl met her at the station in Limerick and drove all the way back to the house in silence.

When she'd settled Beth down for the night and turned the bedside lamp down low so that she could just about see the little cherub features in the dark, Ali sighed and went to make herself a cup of decaf coffee in the kitchen.

It was then that she told Karl she would be moving out within the week. He nodded, as if he already knew. To be honest, she supposed she had long overstayed her welcome but he was too much of a gentleman to have suggested that she was in any way cramping his style – not while she was pregnant at any rate and not while she was vulnerable.

In the morning she had a big heart to heart with Brigitte who kindly insisted that Ali and Beth move into her renovated cottage in the village. It was the right thing to do, she insisted. She needed to be close to amenities, Beth knew her if there was any babysitting to be done and besides Ali and the baby would be company for herself and Stefan Rua.

Once again, life changed and Ali found herself sitting in the pretty period house amongst the china and the heavy wooden beams and looking out through the pretty cut-lace curtains to the side wall of Brigitte's yoga and meditation hall and into the small walled garden beyond.

"Will you tell me a story?" Stefan Rua asked her one night as she put him to bed for Brigitte so she could go to a jewellery-making class.

"How about one about the fairies?"

Stefan made a face and stuck his tongue out. "Fairies are girlie!"

"Oh not my fairies! They're called Bang Bang and Thump Thump and they are two boy fairies who play the drums!"

His smile told her to begin and he was asleep within five minutes of her finishing the fairytale. They grow up quick, these little children, Ali thought as she stroked Stefan's golden red locks. They grow up quick and the older they get, the more needs they have. Resolve strengthened inside her.

The very next day Ali made three phone calls that changed her life forever.

The first was to social welfare to check her Lone Parent entitlements and the second was to the Irish state agency which gave advice on pensions and the amount Ali should be saving every month to have a future as an old crone. When the woman on the other end of the phone finished her astute calculations Ali thanked her politely, put down the phone and burst into tears. Money, real money and lots of it would be required as soon as possible if she was to have any chance of a life as a crumbly.

Then she picked up the phone and asked to be put through to the features editor of a national broadsheet and in a confident and cocky voice told the man at the end of the phone a bunch of over-inflated lies about her journalistic triumphs to date and successfully managed to sell him two features on country living. Now all she had to do was write them. When Brigitte came home with Baby Beth from their morning walk, Ali was nearly hyperventilating from her success and Brigitte told her she could more than rise to the challenge.

"Think of Baby."

And Ali looked into those gorgeous big blue eyes, so trusting and sweet, and began to type.

35

Ali thought of both Dave and Karl a lot as she spent the next few weeks getting used to Brigitte's cosy cottage. Her hands would fly across the keyboard of her computer and the oddest images of the two of them would enter her head. She thought of the time when Dave had called round to the flat and her legs were unshaven and she thought of Beth's birth and how she was ashamed to give birth because the baby's early delivery had yet again caught her and her legs off guard.

One particularly tiring night, when she was responding to Beth's wails by sticking a boob into the roaring infant, Ali thought of how Karl had never really seen her at her best. Throughout the time she had gone out with Dave she had tried her best to maintain high standards but with Karl she'd gone to seed fast. Maybe she wasn't even fanciable any more. Her sex drive had gone through the floor too and all she ever thought about was sleep.

As she settled Beth to sleep and closed the door gently she met Stefan up out of bed and angling for a fairytale and Ali hushed him to sleep with one of her made-up stories, this time about a man called Mr Dirty Legs, who didn't like to wash and who kept tomato plants in his bath.

"Why are you so quiet tonight?" Brigitte asked her a short time later when the children were settled and the two of them were alone in the kitchen drinking peppermint tea and eating Brigitte's home-made cookies.

Ali sighed and then started to laugh out loud. "I was just wondering if men would ever be important to me again – they seem like alien beings right now. You know, right now, if I had to choose a week of great sex or a week of great sleep there'd be no contest. Isn't that sad, Brigitte? How have I become so numb to everything so fast?"

"Maybe you're better off – men hurt us so bad sometimes that it is better not to risk the getting hurt at all."

For a moment Brigitte hesitated and then her story tumbled out, about her romance with the red-haired surfer from Clare and how he broke her heart and made a fool of her till she felt she would never trust another man alive.

"He was ten years younger and I was flattered, I think, but he was only using me. When he had the drink on him he would nearly break down the door to get to me, saying 'Brigitte, you are my life' but he only wanted me for the sex. The only thing good to come of it was little Stefan."

"And now . . . now with John Joe . . . would you try again, do you think?" Ali asked gently

"*John Joe? A*re you *mad*? He's kind, I know, and clever and he needs a good woman, true, but he's *old*, Ali!"

"Depends on the way you look on it. You could say he's not old but mature – and kindness, kindness is so very underrated. We could all do with a little more kindness, Brigitte!"

"Yes, but *John Joe*!"

"You're saying you never ever thought about it? If I were a matchmaker I'd match you two for certain."

"Oh go away with you, Ali, you are becoming way too country, you with your match-making – making mischief more like, I think," laughed Brigitte as she played with a pretty coloured scarf that was a relief from her normal black and grey uniform.

Still, for the rest of the evening, Ali swore her German friend was lost in thought as she started to doodle some cartoons of Ali's made-up fairies Bang Bang and Thump Thump.

* * *

It was in the midst of all this man-pondering and miserable-mommy status, that Ruth decided to pay a visit and she would not be put off by Ali's gentle hints that Brigitte's pad was on the small side. Brigitte took off set-dancing to leave the two sisters alone, even though Ali begged her not to leave, and Ruth used the opportunity to kick off her shoes and pour herself a Baileys while listening to some of Ali's trendy CDs. Well, they used to be trendy – things could have moved on a lot in over a year.

"You're looking smug," said Ali as she poured Ruth a top-up, then adjusted the baby monitor so that the damn thing didn't sound possessed. "The last time you were here, you were on the verge of divorce, if I remember rightly."

Ruth snorted into her cream liqueur. "Thing of the past. I just worked out what needed to be done and did it – cracked the whip, that sort of thing." Seeing her sister's puzzlement, Ruth sat forward in her seat and started talking animatedly. "I wear the trousers now. I got fed up waiting for himself to shape up. I'd be waiting a long time, I'm telling you. So, I've redesigned Gerry, making him into the man *I* want. I might even get him out of those slippers into something sexier, maybe a furry thong or Tarzan pants or maybe a sexy policeman's outfit, you can get them for a steal on e-bay."

The thought of her brother-in-law as suburbia's slick new stud was enough to nearly make Ali choke on her hot buttered toast. Try as she might she just couldn't imagine the poor downtrodden teacher in any kind of macho role. His wife might be into buying him a new range of naughties but as far as Ali was concerned Gerry was not the kind of man one could easily "sex up". In her mind, Gerry would always remain the kind of fella who kept his socks on while doing the deed.

"Did you say e-bay? I thought e-bay was the source of all your problems? Was Gerry not buying all sorts of antique shite over the Internet? Isn't that what got you broke and put your marriage on the rocks in the first place, his so-called gambling?"

With a roll of her eyes Ruth leaned forward and grabbed a handful of salted cashews, stuffing them in her gob in one go. "You're not listening to what I'm saying. It's all about taking control. Sure he was effectively gambling but I just got in there and didn't I manage to sell all his old shite – or small collectibles as he calls them – back on e-bay, some of it even at a profit! In fact, you could even say that e-bay has saved my life and made me realise what a smart, confident, woman I am. I'm setting up my own shop on it and all!"

Yet again her sister's spell of bad luck was only fleeting. It was as Karen always said: "God help everyone when your sister has a plan, 'cos when your sister has a plan she'd move God himself out of the way to make it happen!" For a moment the corner of Ali's mouth curled into a laugh. She had been remembering a lot of things lately that Karen said. The thought made her feel quite depressed, so she rammed half a chocolate bar into her mouth and washed it down with a glass of red wine. Men might be gobshites, but she'd never want to redesign one, never ever. She didn't care what Ruth said, the trick, in Ali's book was to find a gobshite whom you'd love forever and who would love you back with all his heart.

Feeling a bit pissed and more than pissed off with the world, Ali pleaded with God to let there still be romance, because she'd hate it if the only way she could be destined for love was if she had a shopping list of manly qualities in one hand, and a sledgehammer in the other. Nostalgic for all imperfect men, Ali found comfort in the solid form of her pillow that night. Hugging it tightly she thought of the heavy arms of a man about her body, how his hand might rest on her stomach, his breath fall on the back of her neck, how he'd keep her warm or make her flinch with the slightest touch of his hand. Her longing for a man was so strong at the thought that she bit her lip and rolled over and groaned.

* * *

Mrs Gleeson in the shop-come-coffee-station down the road was watching Ali's every move. Being from Dublin made Ali a bit racy in Ma Gleeson's eyes. As she passed the change into Ali's hand along with the national broadsheet Ali knew she would want to know why she was buying a different newspaper today.

"That's a change from your usual, isn't it?"

"Yes."

If Ali had learnt one thing during her time down the sticks, it was: say nothing about your business. Let them think you were up to all sorts of debauchery but never answer questions fully and at all costs prevent the locals from ferreting out snippets about your life, however boring or banal. It's not that the details actually mattered to anyone, it was just finding out the details was a kind of game. So Ali flashed her usual parting smile at Ma Gleeson and departed, having frustrated all attempts to find out anything more.

Her hands trembled as she opened the paper, scouring for her name and then there it was: she saw it on page 5 – one thousand five hundred words on the benefits of country living and the joys of country markets where one could find anything from homemade cheeses to organic bags of spuds.

Brigitte hugged her when she walked through the door and Beth shot her a toothy smile. Her little baby was getting big and solid now and making quite a dent in her new high chair.

"A good start," laughed her friend, patting her hard on the back. "You are on your way now, Ali."

It was her first decent-sized article in a prominent newspaper. She'd written a few shorts to date and a few features for women's magazines but this was something different, something special. And although Brigitte's interest was lovely the truth was that Ali longed to get on to Karen, to scream down the phone and have a giggle, plan her future together the way they always did.

When Brigitte left the room for a minute Ali even traced her fingers over the familiar phone number but she placed the phone back in its cradle with a sigh. Karen had taken Ali's last command literally and there had been no contact between the two of them at all since that night in the pub.

Ali's contact with Karl was also sparse. He called to see Beth one or two evenings a week and for about two hours at the weekend and although he was hardly a hands-on dad, he was at least warming to the little girl and there was never again mention of paternity. Beth had Karl's nose and eyes and any fool could now see it, even his mother. Ali never had to ask him for maintenance money – he left more than enough, which didn't surprise her – Karl was always decent.

One Saturday morning when Ali had been trying on an old skirt over a new pair of funky tights to gauge how much – if at all – her figure was returning to normal – Karl called to see his daughter. Beth was grumpy and not in form to be played with and Brigitte took the tired infant away to be put down in her cot and when she returned the conversation was like lead.

"Why don't you two go for a drive?" she suggested. "I'll take care of Baby."

Ali flashed her a look to see what she was at, but Brigitte could be terribly impassive.

"Why not?" said Karl.

They drove for a while in silence and then he parked the car at the viewing point where the grassy banks almost plunged into the blueness of the lake and they made polite conversation about work, her recent successes and of course Beth. They drank in the beauty of the place and it couldn't but overwhelm them; it had that effect on everyone who ever came and took in the beautiful vision for more than a moment.

Gently, without much thought, he took her hand and squeezed it tight.

"What's that for?" she laughed but she didn't pull her hand away.

"I don't know. I suppose because you're a good person . . . and a good mother, well, trying to figure it out at any rate."

"There's not much choice about the mothering bit. Beth's left me in no doubt as to who the adult is now."

Karl turned to face her and his eyes were all earnestness. "And I *am* her father. I know I haven't been a great dad so far but I want to become more involved. If you weren't dead against it, I'd like to spend more time with you too . . . maybe you'd consider coming to dinner, maybe on a date?"

Ali laughed. "Oh Karl, are you sure you're not just trying to play happy families?"

"I don't know, that's the point. But we – we never really went on a date, Ali, I've just been thinking that. I mean I barely knew you and you were pregnant and sometimes I miss that, miss the fact that we never really had a falling-in-love period, that kind of thing."

"Had a 'romance' as my mother would say."

"Yeah, that's the word, a romance. There was something there in the beginning – there was a spark, wasn't there?"

For a moment Ali had a listen to the little voices inside her head, the one that usually told her to be wary, take it easy, harm could be around the corner, and to the one that sometimes told her to be reckless and got her into trouble, but for once the damn things were mute and she was forced to make her own decision. "All right, you can have your date, but I'm not promising anything."

"Will you promise me one thing?"

"It depends."

"Will you wear your hair up?"

"Why?"

"Because I love to see the back of your neck!" With that he lifted her hair and kissed the nape of her neck and then very cautiously her lips and she laughed and he laughed too and it was lovely to have some fun between them again and not tension, indifference or coldness.

Then their eyes met and suddenly they were all over each other like kids tearing apart selection boxes on Christmas Day. Ali knocked against the radio button in her haste to get at him and the

God-awful Kate Bush wailed into life at top decibel. Karl's right hand went charging up her top – but her bra clasp held out bravely against intruders. His other hand raced up her thigh but her thick funky tights prevented his attack from progressing on that front too. He was frustrated, she was frustrated, as they groped like hormone-obsessed teenagers on a time limit – which of course they were.

The sound of approaching tyres on gravel halted them in their fumblings and they peeled themselves off each other quickly – panting and complaining as blasted visitors came to the viewing point – just to fecking view!

"Hair up – you're *such* a gentleman!" she teased him as she checked her appearance in the passenger mirror and smeared on some lip-gloss.

"Oh, you'd better believe I'm not," he said, eyeing her up like a man on a starvation diet who has just had a glimpse of a nice juicy steak.

* * *

Ali was already planning what to wear, right down to the underwear, but when Brigitte saw what she was up to she stopped her with a frown.

"Absolutely not," she said when Ali started to go fishing in her lingerie drawer and pulled out her old friend, her black lacy suspender belt.

"Why ever not?" said Ali, a bit annoyed, as she ran a stocking over her hand and felt its softness.

"Because it will all end in sex. Didn't you hear him? He wants *romance*, so there is to be no sex for at least six dates."

"What?"

"Romance, Ali!" Brigitte wagged a finger, then smoothed her hand down the side of a beautiful pink skirt which she had bought in the trendy boutique in the nearest town. Then she caught Ali looking at her skirt and laughed. "So it's pink, not black. Maybe it's all the pink baby things I see around and maybe it's the new energy you and Beth bring to this place."

"'Pink, pink, to make the boys wink', my mother always said that. Be careful with your romantic ideas, Brigitte. Romance can be catching, you know!"

Still the thought of enforced celibacy and romantic dates nearly drove her wild – she supposed that was the point. Ali thought, not for the first time, that there wasn't really a romantic bone in her body. No, that wasn't true, she liked dates and surprises and spontaneity, all that was romantic. She just also liked sex.

Still maybe she'd play it Brigitte's way. It would have to be all big knickers and hairy legs so. The thought of it all pushed her almost forgotten sex drive out of neutral.

36

It was a wild and wet afternoon outside but inside Ali and Beth were having fun. Beth was rolling around the floor and gurgling and Ali was flicking through catalogues for Christmas presents. Every so often the baby would get in her way and try and eat the pages of one of the books, turning the paper into a big soggy mess, and Ali would laugh. All the young mother could feel was optimism. The date with Karl was looming and Ali was trying to not feel too excited.

Things were going well in the world of writing too – Ali had just finished a piece for a baby magazine on best baby car seats and buggies. It would hardly set the world on fire, but it was money and there would be enough money to buy some treats for Christmas – things could only get better in the New Year.

Brigitte had even started drawing pictures of Ali's funny kids' characters Bang Bang and Thump Thump. Maybe they could team up and be joint illustrator and author, the ambitious German had suggested. Ali had laughed at the idea, but even so she wondered. Brigitte had a way of doing that, getting you to push the boundaries till you felt excited with life's possibilities. Chase all the rainbows you can, she had told Ali; chase enough of them and you are bound to find a pot of gold.

It was the doorbell ringing that first startled Ali – around the village most people knew Ali and Brigitte well enough to rap on the window. When the bell rang again Ali cautiously peered through the cut-lace curtains to see the familiar shape of her mother. Something inside Ali froze and she scooped Beth up, shot past the hall door and bundled inside the kitchen.

But her mother was persistent. Before Ali knew it Julie was sticking her nose up to the kitchen window and pointing furiously at the back door with a gloved hand. For a while Ali thought about not letting her in. She hadn't heard from her mother in months and hadn't really missed her – besides, letting her in was in some ways betraying Dad.

Julie's gestures didn't stop however and with a sigh Ali went to open the door.

"Didn't you hear the bell?" her mother admonished her.

"It doesn't work," Ali lied.

Very quickly Julie worked out that she wasn't exactly flavour of the month but she hid it determinedly as she asked if she could make herself a cup of tea. Then her eye lighted on Beth on the kitchen floor and she crouched down to have a better look at her granddaughter.

"Isn't she gorgeous? But where does she get that nose from? Not from our side anyway!"

Irritation drove Ali to snap at her mother suddenly. "What do you want, Mum? And don't play the doting granny with me – you haven't seen her since the birth." She was shaking with anger as she rescued Beth from Julie's arms.

Suddenly, Julie's face crumpled and she fell in a heap in one of the chairs. Never had Ali seen her mother look so distressed before, but her lips were quivering and the flawless make-up was running like a chalk picture in the rain.

"He's left me, Joe's left me. His wife told him it was either me or her and the children."

"I thought he was separated!"

"So did I."

"Well, I can't say I'm sorry and I can't say I didn't see it coming and I suppose Dad, like the eternal gentleman he is, is taking you back. So why bother to tell me about it?"

For a long while Julie was silent or maybe it just seemed that way to Ali who had rarely seen her mother stuck for words. When she began to speak again Julie's voice was barely audible and was hoarse from emotion.

"Because there's no one else, just the old women I play bridge with – they're hardly my friends. And Ruth – Ruth won't speak to me but you've always been less judgmental, more open – I thought you at least might understand."

"Understand what?" said Ali as she tucked Beth underneath her shirt to let her suckle. It was going to be a long chat, she could see that, so she might as well try and get the baby off to sleep.

"Understand that my heart is breaking," and with that Jules broke down into deep sobs and the normally perfect face became a total mass of sludge and mascara.

As her mother sobbed harder and harder, Ali was truly shocked for it had never occurred to her that her mother ever had a heart to begin with.

"My life is a *mess* and I don't want to go back to your father. I met and married him when I was still a child and I know he is a good man but I wanted more. Is it a crime to have wanted more? Now look at me, I'm just somebody's wife and I have no means to live without him. I *have* to go back to him."

"Then why did you marry him?" said Ali, growing more and more irritated.

"Because I was pregnant!"

Ali felt her knees give way even though she was already safely sitting down.

"We always said Ruth was two months premature and she was a tiny baby, thank God, so people never said anything and I never liked to say when exactly I was married."

That was true, thought Ali – whenever anyone asked, Julie would just say she was a summer bride and the exact date never interested her daughters much anyway. Weddings were just distant photos of uncomfortable-looking people in daft clothes, nothing more.

"Your father, well, I was not much more than a teenager up in Dublin, with not much money and I was lonely and he seemed so – so sophisticated, I suppose, but he was never much to look at. I knew I would be the best he'd ever get and I suppose I never thought I deserved more. It was my fault too, that I got pregnant. I pushed him, I wanted to see what this sex thing was all about and I knew if anything happened he'd do the decent thing – he was always decent, your father."

Julie's long, manicured fingers grabbed a tissue and she blew her nose in a most unladylike fashion.

Beth was completely conked and, afraid that her mother's weeping would wake her up, Ali went and sneaked her into her cot and shut the bedroom door tight.

Then she made tea and took a mug in to Julie. "Do you want a drop of whiskey in that?" Ali gestured at her mother's tea.

Julie looked up surprised. "That's a country thing, a drop of the hard stuff in the tea."

"I am country now," sighed Ali as she poured the amber liquid.

It was a strange encounter and it was the most honest conversation that Ali had ever had with her mother in her entire life. Most of the time she had talked to her, she had felt she was talking to a robot and her mother told her that was because for most of her married life she felt she was living a lie, putting on a face to meet the world, burying all her own wishes and desires. It was hard to think of your own mother having desires, but now that Ali had a child of her own she could see how hard it was to parent and still go out and make something of your own.

"I admire you, Alison, so much. I admire you for all the chances you've taken in your life. I admire you for being here, being your own woman with your own child, doing your own thing. I admire you for not thinking you have to be a 'proper' family. I wish I could have been more like you."

"Different times, Mum."

Julie nodded and was lost in thought for a moment. Then, like a little child, she whispered her desire to spend one night with Ali before she rang Liam.

"He doesn't know yet. I need time to myself for a while before I prostitute myself again, you see."

Then Julie's mouth smiled wide while her eyes stayed frozen and for the first time Ali saw the real pain behind her mother's mask.

There was only one good side to the whole sorry mess and that was that Joe would hardly be chasing her after the money for her journalism course now – he wouldn't have the nerve.

* * *

Nothing was said. Julie just returned home to Liam's open arms and took to the bed for a while. At least that's the report Ali received from Ruth. Ali told her to be a bit more humane to Julie and relayed the story of the visit, the pregnancy bit and all.

"God, I never had an inkling – I feel a bit funny," gasped Ruth.

"So did I – I began to realise I had more in common with her than I thought, than I wanted even. The funny thing is, I not only felt sorry for her, I even began to like her – only a small bit mind. Underneath that facade there's a different woman, Ruth, a woman you and I know nothing about. Maybe we should just forgive her – she has her own pain to live with."

Ruth snorted. "It's a fine thing you talking about forgiveness. Have you forgiven Karen yet?"

There was a pause down the phone.

"See," Ruth continued with glee, "forgiveness isn't *that* easy. I've been living up in Dublin seeing Dad fall apart these last few months and I'm still boiling with our mother just like you're still raging with Karen."

* * *

327

Putting on her make-up in time for her big date that night, Ali couldn't help thinking about Karen and Dave. Had they met again since that night they had snogged in a nightclub? In some ways they had nothing to lose, neither of them was in contact with Ali and both were busting for a relationship. Or maybe Karen was playing the martyr and having nothing to do with him.

Wondering if it was even healthy to be thinking of her ex-lover as she was preparing to go on a date with the father of her child, Ali rummaged around in her underwear drawer and pulled out a standard pair of cotton passion-killers instead of some sexy briefs. With a half longing she eyed up her razor in the bathroom and with huge willpower left the house with stubbly legs intact. Romance! She'd give him romance, she thought as she ran her hand over the silky smoothness of her uplifted hair and plunged her legs straight into Tommy Moran's taxi.

* * *

The restaurant bar was fabulously expensive with leather suites and polished wood. Outside was bottom-of-the-ocean black but Ali could see the white globes of light reflected on the inky waters of the lake beyond. Later when they were shown to a table, he picked the wine, she scoffed the artisan breads smothered with butter, partly out of nervousness, and by the time the starter arrived she felt drunk and very giddy.

Remarkably, it really did feel like a first date. They chatted to each other politely, he complimented her outfit and especially her hair and when the waiter came to light their candle Ali felt like someone was doing cartwheels in her stomach. Buckets of red wine, chocolate everything and red beef, all the foods Ali loved and which always made her randy but, whenever lust entered her thoughts, Brigitte's stern face would float before her and she would sigh in disappointment.

On the doorstep he cupped her face and felt the soft curls and soft bits of hair which had defied gravity during the evening. He touched the back of her neck until she could feel the chills run up and down her spine. When their lips met the anticipation was so strong that she thought she would faint and that's exactly when Brigitte opened the door and stood over them, hands on hips like a veteran chaperone.

"Baby is awake and won't settle," she snorted.

Talk about killing the atmosphere in an instant.

It was all a plot really. Karl wasn't even allowed to cross the threshold – that pleasure was deferred until the second date at least, Brigitte had warned.

Ali sighed – it was going to be a long "romance".

37

It was Christmas Eve and Ali was feeling a bit ratty to say the least. Feeling like a Christmas present, perpetually wrapped up in fancy paper and trim, she was frustrated that so far she had remained unwrapped and had never got any further than being groped by her intended recipient. So far she had been on three dates with Karl and there was obviously not a romantic bone in her body as all she wanted to do was jump him every time.

In the village the air was charged with excitement and anticipation. After weeks of to-ing and fro-ing to Galway with trailers and with a last-minute hand from all the locals, especially Michael, John Joe's dream of a local cinema with real cinema seats had come to pass. The off-licence at the nearest petrol station had supplied the wine, the cheese had been bought specially in the snooty deli in the nearest town, Ma Gleeson had supplied the kids with boxes of popcorn and fizzy orange and for the first time since 1960 the Silver Screen was back with all its magic.

Under the safety of darkness Karl's mother Mary allowed herself a little smile as the film rolled and Ali saw her squeeze Michael's hand discreetly. The "Crocodile" must have a bit of warm blood in her

331

veins after all. Ali supposed that anyone who tried to write poetry couldn't be all bad. Maybe Mary would surprise her yet.

Brigitte stayed for the opening shorts, but disappeared home to mind the children before the promised *Casablanca* lit up the room with its romance. Before she left Ali could clearly hear her say "Bergman" and "obsession" under her breath.

* * *

The whole parish was signed up by Michael as cine-club members and all were out in time to sprint to the local church. After going to Midnight Mass, and not being struck down by the Almighty for her long years of absence, Ali walked hand in gloved hand with Karl down the street to his waiting car. Before he opened the car door he turned and smiled at her and asked would she come home to his place instead, just for a celebratory drink of cream liqueur or mulled wine and maybe some chocolate.

Chocolate; she didn't need to be asked twice.

As the car pulled up to the familiar gravel path Ali saw the light streaming from the fanlight in the hall and she was filled with nostalgia. Inside, Karl had really made an effort to make the place picturesque for Christmas. With Ali's help he had chosen warm and vibrant colours to brighten up the north-facing reception room and the long dark hall. There was the Christmas tree that Ali and Beth had helped dress and she noticed that behind pictures and clocks Karl had placed red-berried holly cut from his father's bushes.

In the kitchen the stove was burning bright and he reached in, took a light and lit the scarlet candles on the table. He had salmon and brown bread waiting and wine and little treats bought from one of the trendy supermarket chains in the city. All so casual but intentional, of that Ali was certain.

Later in the living room they curled up on the sofa, clinking crystal glasses and talking about their plans for the New Year. He thought he might be in line for a promotion already, she thought she might be cocky enough to raise her asking prices for her articles. They felt young, hopeful, excited about life, never mentioning the past, or the confusion, anger and upset they had felt over the last year.

He played with her hair and told her she looked beautiful. She flirted outrageously and looked at him from behind mascara-plumped lashes. Then she kissed him warmly and moulded herself into his arms. Suddenly he pulled away and said he wanted to give her something, that it couldn't wait until the morning, and he flew out the door and came back with a little box wrapped in gold paper and ribbon.

Please don't let it be a ring, not yet!

When she opened the box she found it contained the most beautiful pendant hanging from a fine gold chain. In the light of the fire she could see the stone burn with flames of gold and red, then with a flick of her wrist it turned again to green and yellow. It was the most beautiful opal she had ever seen, a rainbow of colour on a chain, and it must have cost a small fortune. He was right; it was a gift that couldn't wait till morning, especially since it looked its best in the darkness with only the firelight to play with its beauty.

"See how it changes," he said, taking it from her for a moment. "I wanted to give you something that was truly you and its fire, its colour remind me of you, Ali, your vibrancy, your energy. I liked it because it changes, because it reminds me that everything changes in life, nothing stands still, not you, not me, not us. Do you like it?"

Of course she bloody liked it, it was the most beautiful, well-thought-out present that she had ever received from anybody and she couldn't wait for him to slip it round her throat and to caress the smooth, cold gemstone with her thumb. Again and again she kissed him in the shadows and the light and she knew she wouldn't be finding her way back to Brigitte's any time soon.

Four dates was enough and even Brigitte couldn't expect her to play the role of the romantic virgin for much longer. It was Christmas Eve and Ali had known she would be spending the night with Karl even before he had asked her to his house, even before he mentioned chocolate. She had known because she was wearing a completely new set of sexy underwear and of course, most dangerously of all – she had shaved her legs!

* * *

It was the best Christmas of her entire life. Sure, she'd thought she'd had fantastic Christmases in the past but nothing compared to this season of festivities. Karl couldn't keep his hands off her and was practically tripping her up to get her under every sprig of mistletoe in every house he could find. As always Brigitte was a friend to them, taking care of Beth when they needed time alone, making sure there were pots of tea on the go.

It was the one Christmas where Ali didn't feel stuffed to the gills. She was mostly too excited to eat and even when she did her nervous energy had the calories burned off her in an instant. She was so happy she felt like a helium balloon, in danger of floating off into the clouds. So much had happened in a year and inside she felt strong and terribly assured. It was a feeling she had been chasing her whole life, the feeling of being happy and comfortable in her own skin.

All over Christmas she felt content and optimistic but somewhat sad too – it had been the first Christmas since she was a very little girl without Karen in her life and she wondered what was going on in her best friend's life.

Karl's parents took Beth for the night on New Year's Eve and Stefan Rua insisted on going too. Little Stefan had struck up quite a relationship with Karl's father Michael, even asking in a childish way if the crumpled granddad was the real Mr Dirty Legs from Ali's stories.

On New Year's Eve Ali watched again as the fireworks exploded over Karl's house and she thought for the hundredth time: what a difference a year makes.

One year on, she still didn't know all his guests, but at least this time she wasn't a total stranger in the corner. That New Year's Karl introduced her to everyone as his girlfriend and nothing more and she felt that his description of her was just right.

For now she was happy. Time would tell how things would be and

Ali vowed that never again would she rush time. Sometimes one had to just live, to just be, without a thought or care for the past or the future or for what might or should or could have been.

When all the excitement was over and the champagne popped and poured and the good wishes exchanged, Ali reached into her bag to check her phone for New Year messages and she returned a few instantly. But even though she wished it, there was none from Karen. In her most honest moments Ali knew she didn't want to go through a lifetime without Karen. She wanted to share her current happiness with her. She wanted her daughter to grow up knowing all about mad Auntie Karen, she wanted to forgive and to be forgiven.

When Ali had a quiet moment on New Year's Day she drew a deep breath, picked up the phone and dialled Karen's mother's house. Of course she could have called her friend's mobile but that would have given Karen the chance to dodge her, but Ali knew Karen and Ali knew that she would spend New Year's with her mother until the end of time and that Karen's mother would never ever say that Karen wasn't home if she was. Karen's Mammy didn't "do" lying, she never had.

After an exchange of pleasantries Ali heard Karen's mother roar out her daughter's name, then in the background she heard Karen's familiar cackly laugh and some urgent whispering. The anticipation was enough to cause Ali's throat to nearly close over with nerves.

Then came Karen's voice on the phone: "Hello?"

The silence was heavy and frightening and when Ali found her voice she realised that everything she had practised had left her head.

"Hello?"

"Karen. It's me."

"Yes?"

The frost in her friend's voice was unmistakable.

"I'm sorry and I miss you."

"It was only a few kisses, Ali, a few fucking kisses."

"I know."

"And it's not as if I've seen him since either."

"Although you're perfectly entitled to if you want – you're both free agents after all."

"Too bloody right!"

"So are you then, still a free agent?"

"You mean have I seen any good willies lately?" Karen's filthy laugh reverberated down the phone. "Sure if you behave yourself I might come and visit you soon and tell you *all* my sordid deeds."

"That would be lovely, Karen. I'll have the kettle ready."

In an instant they were back in their own familiar routine, the words bounced off each other as if they were playing ping-pong. Both of them knew they would be friends for life, for life was always better when the two of them were in it.

When Ali hung up she heard her phone beep-beep and when she scrolled down she discovered a message from Dave: "*Old fella not goin head wth case agnst U. Nokd down nd kilt by bus aftr leavn sex shop ovr Xmas.*"

Well, Ali couldn't say she was delighted by the news, but she was somewhat relieved. She'd hardly read one message when the mobile beeped again with a message from Brigitte. "*Snoggd john joe undr mistletoe watching Casablanca. JJ put on film in hall just for him and me! Understand obsession now!*"

Ali laughed. It was shaping up to be an interesting year.

38

This year was going to be her year. Ali could feel it. All the years before she felt a longing, a hope that the coming year would be good, would bring rewards, excitement and knowledge, but this year she just knew good things would be coming her way. All those times she had been travelling around the world she had never felt content, just more and more agitated, more and more restless. It was like she could never get enough and would never find happiness.

Then there were all the crappy little jobs and career ideas she'd had that never seemed to bring her any sense of calm or peace, the perfect men she had chased, the perfect weight she thought she wanted to be. It was all baloney and it was only now that she was beginning to realise that you had to look inside yourself to find real contentment. All those years she had been chasing around trying to find contentment and happiness and as it turned out it was inside her all the while. What a waste of time!

To celebrate her newly found optimism and sense of spirituality, in the middle of January, just before her 30th birthday, Ali decided to have a big girlie detox-style party in Karl's big old house.

Naturally it took Karen to bring Ali back down to earth with a bang.

"Don't talk shite. I'm bringing booze, fags and bags of chocolate and before you ask, yes, I *am* on them again, and no, I'm not giving them up yet. I mean, it's so clichéd to quit in January of all months."

So that was the end of the spa-like makeover session Ali had planned. The new positive Ali thought they could meet for the weekend and do facials and wax each other's legs but all everyone wanted was to do was load themselves up with toxins.

A week and a bit later Ruth, Mags, Karen, Brigitte (minus children – Karl was doing the parenting thing with Beth and Stefan Rua) and Julie all turned up at various times for the 'toxic weekend special'. Lucy sent her regrets as she was making a live TV appearance for the festive season. Ali felt obliged to send an invite to Pammy too, knowing that she wouldn't accept anyway. The Mammy sent her an e-mail back declining the offer, she had something on with Tom, but she and the angels wished Ali nothing but good vibes and would Ali ever send her e-mail to at least seven of her friends so that the angels could continue their good work on earth.

There was no doubt that Ali was looking forward to seeing all of her guests but she was a bit hesitant about seeing her mother again, although the hand of forgiveness had to be extended some time, at least that's what Ali had told the still indignant Ruth. Besides, Ali was sure Julie was very sorry and embarrassed for all the upset she had caused over the last year. Hadn't she as much said so, the last time she called to see her?

As always, Ruth looked relieved to be anywhere without her children. Brigitte was glowing following her success in snaring the romantic John Joe. And Julie, Julie was different to say the least. Ali nearly died when she opened the door to see her mother booted up with skinny denims, a floaty hippy top, beads and a scarf in her hair. Trust Julie, or Jules as she still preferred to be called, to rapidly get over her broken heart and any guilt or shame to reinvent herself again.

"Mum!" Ali gasped. For the first time she realised her mother's hair was streaked with grey. Good God, she was even braless, she noticed as her mother's boobs bounded around like two excitable ferrets.

"Oh don't start, Ali! I've had to deal with a lunatic pubescent who tried to play chicken with me on the road all the way down. For God's sake, give us a cigarette, Ruth, will you, and don't look at me like that – I just want to try one again." With a practised air Jules lit up a fag and disappeared into a cloud of smoke without even a cough. "These really are crap," she announced loudly after a few puffs. "I remember now why I gave them up when I was twenty."

A look of horror spread over Ali's face. God, she hoped her mother wasn't going to start smoking dope or doing acid!

"Got any Coke?" her mother asked in a semi-irritated fashion.

Ali felt her feet freeze to the floor.

"I fancy a vodka. Do you have any Coke?"

When Karen entered the hallway Ali found herself pulling her long-lost friend by the elbow, asking her to give her professional assessment as to whether her mother was on the slippery slope to depression or breakdown or had she just plainly lost it. For nights on end Ali had imagined that when Karen came through the door they would hug, maybe wipe away a quiet tear; then later be deep in conversation in corners, crying into their drinks – but yet again her mother had to go and steal the show.

"Mrs Hughes!" exclaimed Karen when she saw her. "You're looking very, very . . . I mean you usually looked so groomed and now you look very . . ."

"Very casual?" piped up Jules

"Er, yes, that would cover it all right."

"I'm rediscovering my lost youth, Karen, and am doing all the things I never did when I was a girl. I totally missed the late sixties, the booze, the drugs, the travel, the free love . . ."

"So what do you think?" hissed Ali to Karen as they popped out to the kitchen to get glasses.

"No idea yet. Let's get some booze into her and see if she talks?"

"And that's your professional assessment, is it?"

"No, it's just I fancy some booze myself and if you want my perfectly honest view, Ali, I think your mother looks great. She's a bit like Madonna, your mother, always reinventing herself, keeping us guessing."

On entering the living room they found Ruth looking like she had swallowed a lemon and Brigitte talking animatedly and matter-of-factly to anyone who would listen about g-spots and multiple orgasms.

"My current boyfriend, John Joe, has led a very sheltered existence. It is my opinion that he has never actually *been* with a woman, although he has never said this, and I have hopes that his first experience of the lovemaking and orgasm will be very enjoyable," said Brigitte as she played with a beautiful silver and bloodstone pendant that she had made in her jewellery class.

"Well, I have only *recently* had a proper orgasm myself but I would definitely like to have a multiple before I turn fifty-five," Julie announced loudly.

"Why, shame on you, Mother," said Ruth, "flaunting your recent little victories while Dad sits at home –"

"In his slippers. My orgasm wasn't with a *man*, Ruth, it was with a little gizmo I have picked up called the Randy Rabbit. Maybe you should get one – it might relax you – you always seem so stressed, darling, and unfortunately for us married women our men all start wearing slippers . . . eventually."

"Good Jaysus!" Karen nearly choked on a peanut.

"Oh, Karen, be careful, you're probably the only one here who could perform the Heimlich manoeuvre in an emergency," laughed Julie as she poured herself another stiff vodka. "And now that I still remember, tell me, Karen, who was that fine thing I saw you talking to last week outside Murphy's pub, a dark-haired chap, very nice car too if I remember!"

Karen shot Ali a quick look and she made a face. From the pit of her stomach Ali could feel the rage building. So she had been seeing Dave after all! What a cow and to think she had extended her the hand of friendship, opening her home, well, Karl's home, plying her with alcohol and luxury chocolates!

"Well?" Ali's arched eyebrows asked silently.

Squirming in her seat Karen looked up, gulped half a glass of vodka and made for the kitchen with Ali following afterwards, her arms tightly crossed and her face scowling.

"All right, I met him but not by arrangement. We just bumped into each other and we had a chat, mainly about you, he apologised for the night we snogged, that sort of thing."

"But there's something there, isn't there?" snapped Ali.

"Oh for God's sake, what do you want? You asked me to stay away from him – I'm staying away from him."

"But I'm right that there is something there, isn't there?"

Leaning back against the counter top, Ali held her friend's gaze tightly and wouldn't avert her eyes until Karen answered the question, truthfully.

"All right, I fancy him. I haven't had a boyfriend in well over a year and I'm a bag of raging hormones and I fancy the pants off him. But I'll get over it all right – you're my mate and you obviously still have a thing for him – so you don't have to worry, Ali – I'll start saying the rosary every time I see him to distract myself. Satisfied?"

For a moment Ali said nothing and Karen didn't know if she was about to blow up but then a smile started in the corners of Ali's lips and soon it cracked into a beaming grin.

"You know what? I *don't* fancy him any more. I just did a quick mental check and I'm not in the least bit jealous so he's fair game if you want him."

"Not a chance, not now, you might change your mind."

"Pity – Dave could do a lot with a bag of raging hormones."

"Oh yeah, he's probably terrific in the sack, indoors, outdoors, on the floor –"

"On the floor! You fucking bitch! I knew you were awake that night, the night of his party when you nicked our bed. You were, weren't you? And Dave was sure you were dead to the world."

"Well, let's say I've probably seen a few more corpses than Dave O'Connor."

"Jesus, you're a real psycho which makes you just Dave's type. He likes a bit of mad cow, you know."

"You're a mad cow yourself, Ali."

Slowly Ali shook her head and felt the rim of her glass with her finger. "No, I'm just happy, happier than I've ever been, Karen. I have a new life now and I feel so, so powerful, so content. I'm my own woman and I know where I'm headed. If I find the right man to journey with me, that's a bonus, but I'll be okay on my own too."

For a moment Ali fingered the opal at her neck and the stone caught the light and Karen's attention.

"A present from the new love then?"

Was he a new love? Yes, she supposed he was. Karl connected with her head, her heart, her emotions and her body. Dave had been her companion in lust but Karl was a soul mate. But even Dave deserved a chance to find a soul connection – maybe it would be Karen, or maybe he'd just drive Karen crazy too. Still there was no reason why her friend shouldn't have a fling. Hell, Ali almost felt like being the matchmaker.

"I'll think about your matchmaking suggestions," said the slightly suspicious Karen. "This weekend is just about the girls though, right?"

Nodding, Ali clinked Karen's glass and wished her the best for the New Year. Then the two of them hugged tightly. It was great to have Karen home in her heart again and to know that her best friend would always be part of her future.

So they sat down, becoming more and more raucous, then mellow, and the whole affair began to resemble a hen night more than anything else.

True to form, pervy Karen had arrived down with a sack-full of really old "suggestive" videos and they all had a good laugh as the Chippendales got their kit off and they nearly stood on their heads trying to work out what was going on in the *Lover's Guide*. Jules in particular was intrigued and eventually mother and daughters were in convulsions of laughter at the thought of trying to make their men more "sensitive".

In the evening Ali tuned in to see Lucy give an interview about her life and her character to the country's top TV broadcaster. Her character was making news this week as the middle-aged Lothario she was having an affair with had died of a heart attack while she was in the throes of passion with him.

"Could happen," agreed Jules nodding wisely.

"Isn't she great though? She always knew what she wanted and went out and got it? Things in the office went downhill after she left," sighed Maggie.

"You too, you're great too, Mags," rallied Ali. "Aren't you doing well down the country in your new job, with your new bungalow being approved and all."

"I'm hardly a trailblazer though, girl."

"Who says we have to be? I've had the happiest times of my life just being me, with no make-up on and my legs –"

"Unshaven," piped up Karen.

"That's right and –"

"Being braless and grey," added their mother. "Do you know, I think you're right, Ali – all the years I was at you and Ruth to wear make-up I didn't want to give a damn myself. I think I was just worried what others would think if they saw me without my face on."

They drank and laughed with the TV flickering in the corner with the sound turned down. The bottles, glasses, cigarette butts in saucers littered the room; as did the greasy plates.

After midnight Ali found her mother in the hallway crying down the phone and talking softly. Embarrassed that she had stumbled upon her Ali tried to creep away but then her mother hung up abruptly and gave a surprising and joyous laugh. Julie spotted her, laughed a bit more and brushed away the tears.

"Alison, would you believe it? Daddy's only gone and said he'll go to India with me. I can't believe it – I'm on cloud nine! And him saying he'll go, it means a lot to me, you know, especially since my confidence hasn't been the best, what with the banks knocking me back on my property developing schemes. Well, to hell with them now, the bastards – I'm going to India!"

"That's great, Mum. I'm happy for you, really I am!"

"It's just you know after our little trouble with . . . with Joe it's good to set things right again."

Ali chewed her lip in half-embarrassment and just nodded, not that her mother seemed to notice.

"And, Ali, I hope you don't mind but I found out about your marketing course from Joe because . . . well, when you didn't send them up their receipt they contacted the college directly and found out you were really doing journalism instead. I didn't want you upset when you were pregnant so I just sort of fixed the problem for you, I had some money saved from working and . . . well, I hope you don't mind."

Ali thought she was going to cry right there and then. "Fixing" her course problem was probably one of the nicest things Julie had ever done for her and it restored her faith that somewhere along the line all mothers had good motherly intentions.

*   *   *

In the early hours of the morning, with all her guests safely tucked up in bed, sofas and in sleeping bags, Ali walked the rooms shutting off the lights and closing over doors and caught her reflection in the huge gilt mirror over the fireplace. She smiled; for the first time in a long time, maybe as long as childhood, Ali felt truly happy to just be.

Upstairs she flung herself backwards into the bed only to discover a lumpen shape that quickly revealed itself as Karen. Of course, as always her old friend was quick to sniff out the best bed in the house, no sofa for Karen. Snores from the dead-to-the-world Karen indicated that she wasn't likely to budge and exasperated Ali took off and blew up an inflatable mattress Karl had stashed under the stairs.

Within minutes she was transferred to another world – that is, until an unearthly scream shattered the silence at about six in the morning.

"Jesus, Mary and Joseph – Ali, Ali!" a breathless pyjama'ed Karen raced down the landing at top speed and almost jumped into her friend's arms. "It's back! The rat – it's back!"

"Oh yeah, Karl said it had come back. I'd totally forgotten about it and we haven't got round to zapping it yet."

"Forgotten about it? How could you just forget about it?"

A smile began on Ali's lips and then a big grin broke out and before she knew it she was doubled up laughing while all the while Karen got crosser and crosser.

"It scared the living daylights out of me."

"Well, it serves you right for nicking my room and for nicking my boyfriend!"

There was a deadly silence and the two locked eyes for what seemed like an eternity, then Karen's familiar cackle began and before long she was shaking from her shoulders to her toes.

"You're a mad bitch, Ali Hughes."

"Takes one to know one."

"Well, if you think I'm going back into that room again you can feck off, move your arse over and let me into your waterbed or whatever you call it."

In seconds Karen was out like a light – snoring and hogging all the duvet. Ali looked at her and smiled. It was great to have her back.

* * *

An hour later Ali woke up really refreshed without a trace of a hangover and just had to get up. It was remarkable, but all night, in a kind of pre-birthday present to herself, she had drunk nothing but dead expensive wine and champagne. God knows what they made the cheap crap with, antifreeze probably. Feeling happy she switched on the shower and let the water run over her closed eyes for minutes on end. As always, she nearly scalded the skin from her bones.

For another hour she did nothing but clean and tidy and dream and sing to herself, while her guests snoozed their hangovers away.

Close to nine Karl arrived with Baby Beth looking gorgeous and Ali put on her slap and greeted the photographer who arrived at the door.

"What's all this?" hissed Julie who was first down the stairs, still looking a bit hippy but not nearly so trendy.

"Oh, it's nothing to worry about, Mum. It's just I'm doing a piece for *Irish Woman* on swapping the city for country living."

"You *might* have told me," berated her mother as she zoomed back up the stairs, nervously feeling her newly greyed hair.

"Mother of God," Ali heard Karen scream upstairs. "It's on the bleedin' curtains now!"

And her mother's reply, loud and clear: "It's a squirrel, Karen."

"Are you sure, Mrs Hughes?"

"Of course, Karen, wasn't I brought up in the country?"

"But I thought they slept the winter, Mrs Hughes."

"Oh, not the whole time, Karen – why would they store all those nuts if they were going to actually hibernate?"

"Well, if you ask me this one is so pissed off I'd say someone definitely pinched his nuts!"

So the mystery of Ratzo had been solved. Ali would have to ring her local animal protection crowd to see if they could catch him.

Never had Ali seen guests depart so fast. It seemed none of them wanted even the threat of being photographed hanging over them while they were in their dishevelled state.

When the last shots were taken Ali stood at the door with Baby Beth in her arms and waved goodbye to Alan the photographer as he disappeared down the now familiar drive. Suddenly Karl scooped Ali and Beth up into his arms and smiled at them with warmth and affection.

"What *are* you doing?" she laughed.

"I just want to carry the two women in my life over the threshold."

He must have been crippled by the weight but he gallantly struggled on, holding her and Beth together and carrying them just over the threshold before his knees gave way.

"We'll have to do something more exciting than this for your birthday," he laughed as he put her down and put his arms round her and his baby daughter.

"Why bother, I've got all the excitement I need right here at this moment."

"Do you really mean that?"

"Yes, Karl, I do."

"I want to celebrate *all* your special birthdays with you, Ali – your fortieth, your half century, all of them. I love you, Ali Hughes. Will you move back in with me, you and Beth, all of us together?"

Her brain didn't have to give it a second thought. "I will."

"And maybe one day, who knows, maybe you and I will be more than just boyfriend and girlfriend?"

Their eyes connected and she kissed him tenderly. There'd be many days together with Karl, she knew it in her heart, and he did too. It was just too early to speak it yet, and for once Ali Hughes did a wise thing: she kept her mouth shut and just nodded. Together they closed the big wooden door and held hands as Baby Beth nestled into Ali's shoulder and yawned sleepily.

Life was full of wonderful possibilities and Ali had never felt them so keenly as when she stared into the eyes of her lover and then at those same eyes in her baby daughter, who was snuggling down for an afternoon nap. In her short life Ali Hughes had chased down many a rainbow and when she finally struck gold it was as part of an ordinary, happy family. Who would have thought!

THE END

LIMERICK CITY AND COUNTY LIBRARY

In conversation with
Nuala Woulfe

Congratulations on the publication on your first book,
Chasing Rainbows!

Have you always written or is it a new discovery?

When I was very little I wrote rhyme and when I was at
secondary school my English teacher, Mrs Small, would read
my essays out every week. It was brilliant, because I could see
that my target audience liked when I wrote funny.

At fifteen I won my first creative writing competition
and the prize was a trip to New York. After my Leaving
Cert I studied journalism for two years and worked as a
reporter until I was about twenty-four, when I went back to
university to do an Arts degree. When I became a mother I
had very little time and even less brainpower but I was
itching to express myself so I started to write short comic

verse and then one day I had an idea to write a novel and I started the first chapter of *Chasing Rainbows*.

Tell us about your writing process; where do you write? When? Are you a planner or "ride-the-wave" writer?

I roughly plan the plot and characters in my head and when I reach the point where I need to get things down on paper I just start to write and trust that I'll get there in the end. I write until I get to the stage where I am forced to do the first edit and that edit usually clarifies things so I can start writing again. An outsider looking at my work at this stage would probably find it very disorganised. For me writing is an organic process. I am always influenced by something I hear on the radio, TV, in a film or in a conversation. The writing process is like sculpting but at the same time it involves constant layering. I try to write every day but I give myself the weekend off, although I find even then I am running information through my head and clarifying things. I try to write for about two hours a day, night time is often most convenient, but I often write stuff while my youngest is taking a nap and her two older siblings are playing together. If I hit a point where I get a bit of a block I read a book maybe for a day or two, take a break, go swimming, dancing or look at nature and de-stress. It always works – creativity needs fun.

As a former journalist did you find the creative challenge of writing an easy one to master?

There are definite benefits to having had a journalistic background. When you are a reporter you learn to write despite distractions – newsrooms can be very loud and you must learn to block out noise. I often write around my kids now – I can block out their voices or TV and write because of my journalistic training. Also, because I learned to type properly I can write as fast as I think which is very helpful and at college they teach you to write snappy and look for angles – that's useful when you're trying to hold the reader's attention. Overall I think writing is writing – you just have to learn to switch modes, and any writing experience is valuable.

What has the experience of getting your first book published been like for you?

To be honest it's been a bit daunting because it's something new and there was a lot to find out. I also have a slight fear that people will never be truthful with me ever again; that they will tell me, "oh I loved your book" when secretly they thought it was rubbish. But there's no turning back, the book's out there now and I just have to get used to it.

Do you have a favourite character in Chasing Rainbows?

I'm fond of a few of them, "Karen the crazy live for now Nurse" and "Brigitte the half German-half Irish artist" are two of them. "Sexy Dave" the policemen is another – I didn't plan writing him in at all but he kept turning up and annoying me until I finally said okay, "I'll give you a few scenes and you can buzz off." Little did I know that once in the book he'd start doing his own thing! However, the one that stands out most is "Lucy the hard as nails receptionist/actress" because she "owns" the office and no one would dare cross her. I love her

Dublin accent and wit – I think I created her when I left Dublin because I missed my capital city so much.

Ali moves away from the hustle and bustle of Dublin and Celtic Tiger Ireland, and by doing so she finds herself and becomes happy and satisfied – do you think that location played a key part in Ali's journey?

Absolutely. All cities are by their nature fast, so fast that you can distract yourself from your troubles but things are slower in the country and there are fewer distractions and maybe more time to think. Over the last decade Dublin has become something of a concrete jungle, but when Ali moves to the country I think nature
and the beautiful scenery help her spirit soar and maybe help her put some of her problems into perspective.

What character and scene were most difficult to write?

Ali's sex scenes were the most difficult to write because sex scenes have the potential to be embarrassing. However, I was determined that I wasn't going to close the door on the sex scenes, that I was going to write about exciting sex, shy and awkward sex, loving and vulnerable sex, and ridiculous sex. I think I'm descriptive without being too graphic because I want to give the reader the opportunity to step into those scenes themselves and let their own imagination take over.

Titles can be critical when deciding what to call a beloved manuscript – where did Chasing Rainbows come from?

In my early thirties migraine hit me and I started to keep a food diary. The symptoms got so bad that I booked myself in with a kinesiologist for allergy testing. She told me what my food sensitivities were and suggested colour therapy. After the therapy she said I might have strange dreams for a few days and might see flashing colours whenever I shut my eyes. The next morning I woke up and announced to my husband with absolute certainty, "I'm going to write a book" and this was something I had never considered before.

Not long afterwards the title *Chasing Rainbows* came to me. It seemed to accurately sum up Ali's quest – to chase something elusive, and I liked it because the book was literally born in colour and what can be more colourful than a rainbow?

Who are your favourite authors and favourite novels and why?

Where to start – there are so many authors that I've never even read! So of the authors I know and like the obvious ones are Marian Keyes – many have been compared to her but she's a one off and very special because she holds nothing back. I'm returning to Ms Jilly Cooper again because she writes sexy, funny and smart. Irish author Maureen Martello is a must read if you like laugh out loud humour, and at the moment I'm a bit hooked on bodice-rippers, Philippa Gregory author of the *Other Boleyn Girl* is a current favourite. My all time favourite novels are *Rebecca*, *Wuthering Heights*, *Dracula* and *East of Eden*. I've only recently realised that all of these novels have very strong verging on seriously mad female characters in them, so crazy is obviously something I like.

Tell us a bit about your next book – have you started writing it yet?

I'm a good way into it. It's about two sisters: one married to a high-flying executive – they've a young family and are comfortable but not rich, the other sister is beautiful, young, spoiled, bored and married to a rich and self-made man. Things change for the two of them until they are both up against a deadline. The idea is what would you do if you were up against unforeseen circumstances or an ultimatum, would you run scared or would you start looking deep inside for what will make you happy? I hope I can succeed in making the story funny and quirky. So far, as well as ladies' rugby, there is pole-dancing, shopping, fast cars, lingerie parties with the girls, and a smattering of nappies!

POOLBEG WISHES TO
THANK YOU

for buying a Poolbeg book and will give you
20% OFF (and free postage*)
on any book bought on our website
www.poolbeg.com

Select the book(s) you wish to buy
and click to checkout.

Then click on the 'Add a Coupon' button
(located under 'Checkout') and enter
this coupon code

POOLBEG

CAUEA15165

(Not valid with any other offer!)

POOLBEG

WHY NOT JOIN OUR MAILING LIST
@ www.poolbeg.com and get some
fantastic offers on Poolbeg books

*See website for details

Poolbeg Press and
colour**me**beautiful

www.colourmebeautiful.ie

want to bring a rainbow
of colours into your life!

Award Winning Image Consultants with over 200 image consultants in the UK and Ireland and a further 600 in Europe, Colour Me Beautiful are Europe's leading image consultants. We can give you the confidence to make the most of your personal and professional image with our range of services, including Style Consultations, Colour Analysis, Make-up Lessons and much more.

Just enter the competition to be in with a chance to win an amazing life changing experience.

✩✩✩ *Prize: Platinum Gift Package* ✩✩✩

The premier pampering and image makeover package! This package consists of a Colour Analysis with a personalised colour wallet containing 42 fabric swatches, **a Make-up Lesson** with hints, tips & a customised Beauty Workbook. Then a **Style Consultation** with a 20-page Style Workbook with detailed notes and guidelines for your bodylines. This package is the perfect 3 step solution for a stunning, new and confident you! Duration: 3 hours

To win answer the question below, fill in your contact details and send your entry to: *Chasing Rainbows* Competition, Poolbeg Press, 123 Grange Hill, Baldoyle, Dublin 13.

According to legend, a crock of gold is found at the end of what?

Answer: _____

Name: _____

Contact number: _____

Address: _____

Email: _____

Entrants must be over 18 years of age. Terms and conditions apply. The first correct entry drawn will be the winner. Competition closing date is 31st August 2010. Employees and families of employees of *Poolbeg* and *Colour Me Beautiful* are not eligible to enter. Competition valid in Republic of Ireland only! No cash alternative will be given and prize is non transferable. Winner to be notified by phone. If you do not wish to receive special offers from *poolbeg.com* or *Colour Me Beautiful* please tick box ☐

✂

p.o'e.